WYOMING COWBOY BODYGUARD

NICOLE HELM

KILLER INVESTIGATION

AMANDA STEVENS

MILLS & BOON

First Published in Great Britain 2019
by Mills & Boon, an imprint of HarperCollins*Publishers*
1 London Bridge Street, London, SE1 9GF

Wyoming Cowboy Bodyguard © 2019 Nicole Helm
Killer Investigation © 2019 Marilyn Medlock Amann

ISBN: 978-0-263-27426-4

0719

MIX
Paper from
responsible sources
FSC™ C007454

This book is produced from independently certified FSC™ paper to ensure responsible forest management.

For more information visit: www.harpercollins.co.uk/green

Printed and bound in Spain
by CPI, Barcelona

Nicole Helm grew up with her nose in a book and the dream of one day becoming a writer. Luckily, after a few failed career choices, she gets to follow that dream—writing down-to-earth contemporary romance and romantic suspense. From farmers to cowboys, Midwest to *the* West, Nicole writes stories about people finding themselves and finding love in the process. She lives in Missouri with her husband and two sons and dreams of someday owning a barn.

Amanda Stevens is an award-winning author of over fifty novels, including the modern gothic series The Graveyard Queen. Her books have been described as eerie and atmospheric, "a new take on the classic ghost story." Born and raised in the rural South, she now resides in Houston, Texas, where she enjoys binge-watching, bike riding and the occasional margarita.

Also by Nicole Helm

Wyoming Cowboy Marine
Wyoming Cowboy Sniper
Wyoming Cowboy Ranger
Wyoming Cowboy Justice
Wyoming Cowboy Protection
Wyoming Christmas Ransom
Stone Cold Texas Ranger
Stone Cold Undercover Agent
Stone Cold Christmas Ranger
All I Have

Also by Amanda Stevens

Criminal Behaviour
Incriminating Evidence
Pine Lake
Whispering Springs
Bishop's Rock (ebook novella)
The Restorer
The Kingdom
The Prophet
The Visitor
The Sinner

Discover more at millsandboon.co.uk

WYOMING COWBOY BODYGUARD

NICOLE HELM

For the female songwriters in country music whose songs make up the bulk of my book soundtracks, thank you for the inspiration.

Chapter One

Tom was dead. She'd been ushered away from his lifeless body and open, empty brown eyes thirty minutes ago and still, that was all she saw. Tom sprawled on the floor, limbs at an unnatural angle, eyes open and unseeing.

Blood.

She was in the back of a police cruiser, moving through Austin at a steady clip. Daisy Delaney. America's favorite country bad girl. Until she'd filed for divorce from country's golden child, Jordan Jones. Now everyone hated her, and someone wanted her dead.

But they'd killed Tom first.

She wanted to close her eyes, but she was afraid the vision of Tom would only intensify if she did. So she focused on the world out the window. Pearly dawn. Green suburban lawns.

She was holding it together. Even though Tom's lifeless eyes haunted her. And all that blood. The smell of it. She was queasy and desperately wanted to cry, but she was holding on. *Gotta save face, Daisy girl. No matter what. Never let them see they got to you.*

It didn't matter the name her mother had given her was Lucy Cooper. Daddy had always used her stage name—the name *he'd* given her. Daisy Delaney, after his dearly departed grandmother, who'd given him his first guitar.

She'd relished that once upon a time, no matter how much her mother and brother had disapproved. Today, for the first time in her life, she wondered where she might be if she hadn't followed in her famous father's footsteps.

She couldn't change the past so she held it together. Didn't let anyone see she was devastated, shaken or scared.

Until the car pulled up in front of her brother's house. He was standing outside. She'd expected to see him in his Texas Rangers uniform of pressed khakis, a button-up shirt and that shiny star she knew he took such pride in.

Instead, he was in sweats, a baby cradled in his arms.

"You shouldn't have brought me here," she whispered to the police officer as he shifted into Park.

"Ranger Cooper asked me to, ma'am."

She let out a breath. Asked. While her brother was a Texas Ranger and this man was Austin PD, Daisy was under no illusions her brother hadn't interfered enough to make sure it was an order, not a request.

When the officer opened the door for her, she managed a smile and a thank-you. The officer shook hands with Vaughn, then gave her a sympathetic look. "We'll have more questions for you, Ms. Delaney, but the ones you answered at the scene will do for now."

She smiled thinly. "Thank you. And if there's any break in the case—"

"We'll let you and your brother know."

The officer nodded and left. Daisy turned to Vaughn.

"You shouldn't have brought me here," she said, peeking into the bundle of blankets. She brushed her fingers over her niece's cheek. "It isn't safe having me around you guys."

"Safety's my middle name," Vaughn said, and there wasn't an ounce of concern or fear in his voice, but she could feel it nonetheless. Her straitlaced brother had never understood her need to follow their father's spotlight, but he'd always been her protector. "You didn't tell me you'd come back to Austin."

She'd thought she could keep it from him. Keep him and Nat from worrying when they had this gorgeous little family they were building.

Daisy had been stupid and foolish to think she'd be able to keep anything from Vaughn. She couldn't afford to be stupid and foolish anymore. Though she'd lived in fear for almost a year now, she'd believed it would remain a nonviolent threat. Her stalker had never hurt her or anyone she'd been connected to.

Now he'd killed Tom. The man Vaughn had hired to protect her. It wasn't her own failure. Rationally, she knew that, but kind, funny Tom, who'd done everything in his power to protect her, was dead.

"Come inside, Lucy." Vaughn slid his free arm around her shoulders and the first tear fell over onto her cheek. She couldn't let more fall, and yet her brother's steadiness, and the name only he and Mom called her, was one of the few things that could undo her.

Well, that and murder, she supposed. "Tom…"

"We'll handle the arrangements," Vaughn said, squeezing her shoulders as baby Nora gurgled happily in her daddy's arms. "He was a good man."

"He shouldn't have died protecting me."

"But he did. He signed up for that job. You'll have time to mourn that. We all will, but right now we need to focus on getting you somewhere safe."

She wanted to say something snotty. Vaughn could be so cold, and though she knew it was his law-enforcement training, it grated. Except he held his baby like the precious gift she was, and Daisy had watched years ago as his voice had broken when he'd made his vows to his wife.

Vaughn wasn't cold or heartless. He just had control down to an art form. And his concern was her. Daisy felt like such a burden to him, and yet there was no way to convince him this wasn't his problem.

"Nat's got coffee on and Jaime is on his way over," Vaughn said, locking the door behind her then leading her up the stairs of his split-level ranch.

"What's Jaime got to do with this?" Daisy asked warily. "You can't get the FBI involved. I—"

"I'm not getting the FBI involved. I'm using my FBI connections to find a safe place for you while we let the professionals investigate."

"And by professionals you mean you."

"I mean anyone and everyone I can get on this case. With our connection, I'm not legally allowed to be part of the official investigation."

Which meant he'd launch his own unofficial one. No matter how by-the-book Vaughn was, he'd always break rules for his loved ones.

Nat came out of the kitchen as they crested the stairs. She pulled Daisy into a hard hug. "How are you?" she asked, brown eyes full of compassion.

Daisy had no questions about how Vaughn had

fallen for Natalie, but she did have some questions about the reverse.

"Unscathed."

Natalie pursed her lips. "Physically. Which wasn't all I meant." She eyed her husband. "Coopers," she muttered with some disgust, though Daisy knew—for as little time as she managed to spend with her family here due to her crazy touring schedule—Nat spoke with love.

The doorbell rang, Nora fussed and Nat and Vaughn exchanged the baby and words with the choreographed practice of marriage. It caused a multitude of pangs in Daisy.

Her divorce had started the press's character assassination—thanks to Jordan's team, who were desperate to keep his star on the rise.

Then the stalking had started, and everything had become a numb kind of blank.

But she could still remember marrying Jordan with the hope she'd have something like Nat and Vaughn had. That had been a joke.

"Sit down. You want to hold Nora for me? I've got to go check on Miranda." Nat was maneuvering her onto the couch, placing tiny Nora into her arms and hurrying off to check on their other daughter as Vaughn and his brother-in-law ascended the stairs.

"Ah, the cavalry," Daisy said with a wry twist of her lips.

"Good to see you again, Daisy," Jaime Alessandro greeted. An FBI agent, married to Natalie's sister, Daisy had met him on a few occasions. He was more personable than Vaughn, but the whole FBI thing made Daisy uneasy.

"Let's get straight to it, then," Vaughn said, taking a

seat next to Daisy on the couch. Jaime settled himself on an armchair across from them.

"I'm sure you know how concerned Vaughn's been even before the murder."

Daisy eyed her brother. "No. You don't say."

Jaime smiled. Vaughn didn't.

"We've been looking into some options, along with the investigation. As long as the stalker continues to evade police, the prime goal is keeping you safe. To that end, I have an idea."

"That sounds ominous coming from an FBI agent."

"How do you feel about Wyoming?"

"Cold," Daisy replied dryly.

"I have a friend I was in Quantico with. He has a security business. I talked to him about your situation and he came up with a plan. It involves isolating you."

"I was isolated before. The cabin—"

"Is isolated, but not completely off the grid," Vaughn said of their old family cabin that had been vandalized during her last hiding stint. "It was traceable, and you've been easy to follow. We're going to take extra precautions to make sure you aren't followed to Wyoming."

Daisy wanted to close her eyes, but she shifted Nora in her arms and looked down at the baby instead. "So you want me to secretly jet off to Wyoming and then what?"

"And then you're safe while we find this guy. This is murder now. Things are escalating, which means everyone else's investigation is going to escalate."

"We can have you there by tomorrow afternoon," Jaime said. "They'll be ready for you."

Part of her wanted to argue, but Tom's lifeless body flashed into her mind. She didn't want to die. Not like that. And more, so much more, she didn't want Vaughn or his precious family in the crosshairs.

"Just tell me what I need to do."

ZACH SIMMONS SURVEYED the town. It looked like every picture of a ghost town he'd ever seen. Empty, window-less buildings. Dusty dirt road that would have once been a bustling Main Street. You could feel the history, and the utter emptiness.

It was perfect.

He grinned over at his soon-to-be brother-in-law and business partner. "Still worried about the investment?"

Cam Delaney eyed him. "Hell yes, I'm still worried." He scanned the dilapidated buildings and the way the mountains jutted out in the distance, like sentries, in Zach's mind. This would be a place of protection. Of safety.

"This job's a big one for your first."

Zach nodded. He was under no illusions this wasn't a giant challenge. Tricky and messy and complicated. He couldn't explain to Cam, or anyone really, how thrill-ing it was to be out of the confines of the FBI's rules and regulations. He wouldn't take his time back as an agent for anything, but it had been stifling in the end.

So stifling he'd ended up getting himself kicked out.

This was better. Even if the first job was with some spoiled country singer star who'd gotten herself in a mess of trouble. Probably her own doing. But she was in trouble, and Zach and Cam's security company was getting paid, seriously paid, to keep her safe.

"Laurel come up with any connection to you guys?" Zach asked, hoping Daisy Delaney's last name was a coincidence. Not that he'd tell anyone, but all the Carson and Delaney coupling worried him a little.

He was technically a Carson, though his mother had run away from her family at eighteen and only started reconnecting this year. He told himself he didn't believe in curses or the Carson-Delaney feud the town of Bent, Wyoming, was so invested in.

So invested, Main Street was practically split down the middle—Carson businesses on one side, Delaney businesses on the other. Then there was the curse talk, which said if a Carson and Delaney were ever friendly, or God forbid, romantic, only bad things would befall Bent.

But over the course of the past year Carsons and Delaneys had been falling for each other left and right, and while there'd been a certain uptick in trouble in Bent, everything and everyone was fine.

Which his cousins and their significant others had turned into believing it was all meant to be, and went on and on about love solving things.

Zach didn't buy an inch of either belief—but still, the idea of a Delaney under his protection gave him a bit of a worried itch.

"She's still researching. It's giving her something to do now that she's on maternity leave. Baby should come any day, though, so I'm not sure she'll come up with any answers one way or another. You can always ask the woman."

Zach shrugged. "Doesn't matter either way."

Cam chuckled. "Sure. You're not worried about what might happen if she's some long-lost cousin of mine?"

"No, I'm not. I'm worried about keeping Daisy Delaney safe from her stalker, assuming there really is one." Because the Daisy Delaney case would set the tone for what he wanted to offer here. On the surface it would look like a ghost town. But below the surface it could be a place for people to find safety, security and hope while the slow wheels of justice handled things legally.

If he believed in life callings, and these days he was starting to, his was this. He'd been a part of the slow wheels of justice. He'd failed at protecting because of it. Now he'd do all he could to keep those entrusted to him safe.

"I should head off to the airport. You'll do the double check?"

Cam nodded. "Is turndown service offered as part of the package?"

"Up to you, boss," Zach said with a grin, slapping Cam on the back.

Cam eyed him, but Zach ignored the perceptive look and headed for his car. He didn't need Cam giving him another lecture about taking things slow, having reasonable expectations for a fledgling business.

Zach had endured a bad year. Really bad. His brother had been admitted to a psychiatric ward, and his long-lost sister had forgiven the man who'd murdered their father and kidnapped her. He'd been kicked out of the FBI—which meant no hope of ever getting back into legitimate law enforcement. And then he'd tried to help one of his cousins outwit a stalker-murderer and been hurt in the process.

In some ways all that hardship had brought him everything he'd ever wanted—his long-lost sister back in his life, a job that didn't seem to choke the very life out of him and some closure over the murder of his father.

Then there was this project. Ghost Town. He couldn't tamp down his enthusiasm, his excitement. He had to grab on to the rightness he finally felt and hold on to it with everything he had.

He didn't want to go back. He wanted to move forward.

Daisy Delaney was going to be the way to do that. He drove down deserted Wyoming roads to the highway, then to the regional airport in Dubois where his first client would be landing any minute.

Zach parked and entered the small airport, all the excitement of a new job still buzzing inside him.

He'd facilitated crisscrossing flights with his former FBI buddy, and only Zach knew the disguise she'd be wearing. Though he wondered how much a wig and sunglasses would do for a famous singer.

Zach liked country music as much as the next guy, so it was impossible not to know Daisy Delaney's music. She'd somehow eclipsed even her father's outlaw country reputation with wild songs about drinking, cheating and revenge. Country fans either loved her or loved to complain about her.

Of course, since her divorce from all-American sweetheart Jordan Jones, the complainers had gotten more vocal. Zach hadn't followed it all, but he'd read up on it once this assignment had come along. She'd been eviscerated in the press, even when the stalking started. Many thought it was a publicity ploy to get people to feel sorry for her.

It had *not* worked.

Zach couldn't deny it was a possibility, even if a man was dead—the security guard. A shame. But that didn't mean it wasn't a ploy. You never knew with the rich and famous.

Still, Zach was determined to make his own conclusions about Daisy Delaney and what might be going on with her stalker, or fictional stalker as the case may be.

The small crowd walked through the security gates. He'd been told to look for black hair and clothes, a red bag and purple cowboy boots. He spotted her immediately.

In person, she was surprisingly petite. She didn't exactly look like a woman who'd burn your house down if you looked at another woman the wrong way, but looks could be deceiving.

He'd done enough undercover work to know that well.

He adjusted his hat, gave the signal he'd told her people to expect and she nodded and walked over to him.

"You must be Mr. Hughes." She used the fake name Jaime had chosen and held out a hand. The sunglasses she wore hid her eyes, and the mass of black hair hid most of her face. Whatever her emotions were, they were well hidden. Which was good. It wouldn't do to have nerves radiating off her.

He took her outstretched hand and shook it. "And you must be Ms. Bravo." Fake names, but soon enough they wouldn't need to bother with that. "Any more bags?" he asked, nodding to the lone duffel bag she carried.

She shook her head.

"Follow me."

She eyed everyone in the airport as they walked outside, but her shoulders and stride were relaxed as she kept up with him. She didn't fidget or dart. If she was fearing her life, she knew how to hide it.

He opened the passenger-side door to his car. She slid inside. Still no sign of concern over getting into a car with a stranger. Zach frowned as he skirted the car to the driver's side.

But he wiped the frown into a placid expression as he slid into his seat. "We have about a thirty-minute drive ahead of us." He pushed the car into Drive and pulled out of the airport parking lot. "You could take your wig off," he offered. "Get comfortable."

"I'd prefer to wait."

He nodded as he drove. Tough case. A hint of nerves here and there, but overall a very cool customer. Cautious, though, so she clearly took the threat of danger seriously.

He drove in silence through the middle of nowhere Wyoming. He flicked a few glances her way, though it was hard to discern anything. He didn't get the impression she was impressed, but he hadn't expected her to be. He imagined she preferred, if not the glitz and glam of the city, the slow ease of wealthy Southern life she was probably used to.

Wyoming wouldn't offer that, but it would offer her security. He drove down the main street that was now his domain, this ghost town he and Cam had bought outright.

At some point they'd all be safe houses. Or maybe even a functioning town behind the facade of desertion and decay.

For right now, though, it was just the main house. He pulled up in front of the giant showpiece.

It had been built over a century ago by some railroad executive. From the outside the windows were all knocked out, the wood was faded and peeling paint hung off. Everything sagged, and it had the faint air of haunted house.

It made him grin every time. "Well, here we are."

For the first time he could read her expression. Pure, unadulterated horror. He'd be lying if he said he didn't get a little kick out of that. "I promise it's not as bad as it looks."

She wrenched her gaze away from the large house, then stared at him through the dark sunglasses. "Can I see your ID or something?" she demanded.

He shifted and pulled his wallet out of his pocket and handed it to her. "Have at it." He pushed open the door and got out of the car. "When you're ready, I'll show you where you'll be staying."

Chapter Two

What Daisy really wanted to do was call her brother and ask him if he'd lost his mind. Call Jaime and ask if she was sure this guy was sane. Call anyone to take her home.

But inside the wallet the man had so casually handed her was a driver's license with the name Jaime had given her. The picture matched the man currently standing in front of the horror-movie house outside the car. There were also all sorts of security licenses and weapon certifications.

Vaughn had said this place was isolated, even more isolated than their old family cabin in the Guadalupe Mountains. But she hadn't been able to picture how that was possible.

Oh, was it possible. Possible and horrifying.

She flipped the wallet closed and then looked at the giant, falling-apart building. If she didn't die because a stalker was after her, she'd die because this building was going to fall in on her.

It had to be infested with rats. And probably all other manner of vermin.

She couldn't get her body to move from the safety of this car, and still, the man whom she'd been assured would keep her safe stood outside, grinning at the dilapidated building in front of him.

He wasn't sane. He couldn't be. She was stuck in the middle of nowhere Wyoming with an insane person.

But Vaughn would never let that happen. So she forced herself to get out of the car and slung the duffel bag over her shoulder. She tried not to mourn that she hadn't been able to bring her guitar. This wasn't a musical writing escape. It was literally running for her life.

She stepped next to Zach. She still didn't trust him, but she trusted her brother. She looked up at the building like Zach Simmons did, though not with nearly the amount of reverence he had in his expression.

"I know it looks intimidating from the outside, but that's kind of the point."

"The point?" Daisy asked, studying a board that hung haphazardly from a bent nail.

"From the outside, no one would guess anyone's been here for decades."

"Try centuries," she muttered.

He motioned her forward and she followed him up a cracked and sunken rock pathway to the front door.

"Watch the hole," he announced cheerfully, pointing at the gaping hole in the floorboards of the porch. He shoved a key into the front door and pushed open the creaky, uneven entry. "Even if someone started poking around, all they'd see is decay."

Yes, that is all I see. She looked around. She had to admit that although everything appeared to be in a state of decay, there were some important things missing. She didn't see any dust or spiderwebs. Debris, sure. Peeling wallpaper and warped floorboards, check, but it didn't smell like she'd expected it to. There was the faint hint of paint on the air.

He led her over the uneven flooring, then pushed a key into another lock. When this door opened she actually gasped.

The room on the other side was beautiful. Clean and furnished, and though there were no windows, somehow the light he switched on bounced off the colors of the walls and filled the room enough that it didn't feel dank and interior.

"This is the common area," Zach said. And maybe he wasn't totally insane. "Then over there past the sitting area is the kitchen. You're free to use it and anything inside as much as you like. Once we ascertain that you weren't followed on any leg of your trip, you'll be able to venture out more freely, but for now you'll have to stay put."

Daisy could only nod dumbly. Was this real? Maybe *she'd* gone insane. A break with reality following a stressful tragedy.

He locked the door behind them, which was enough to jolt Daisy back to the reality of being in a strange ghost town with a man she didn't know.

But he simply moved forward to a set of two doors. "Your bedroom and bathroom are through here." He unlocked the one on the right.

"What's that one?" she asked, pointing to the door on the left as he pushed the unlocked door open.

"That's where I'll stay."

"You'll… Right." He'd be right next door. This stranger. Hired to protect her, and yet she didn't know him. Even Vaughn didn't know him, and Jaime hadn't known him since they'd trained together in the FBI. Why were they all so trusting?

He handed her the key he'd just used to unlock the door. "This is yours. I don't have a copy. The outside doors are always locked up in multiple places, so how and when you want to lock your room is up to you."

She knew he was trying to set her at ease, but she could only think of a million ways he could get into the room even without a key. Or anyone could.

People could always get to you if they wanted to badly enough.

He studied her for a moment, then gestured her inside. "You can settle in. Make yourself at home however you need to. Rest, if you'd like."

"Is it that obvious?"

"You've been through an ordeal. Take your time to get acquainted with the place. I'm going to do a routine double check to make sure you weren't followed from Austin. If you need me…" He moved over to the wall, motioned her over.

Hesitantly, she stepped closer, still clutching her bag on her shoulder. He tapped a spot on the wallpaper. "See how this flower has a green bloom and a green stem instead of a blue flower like the rest?"

She nodded wearily.

He pushed on the green flower and a little panel popped out of the wall. Inside was a speaker with a button below it. "Simple speaker to speaker. You need something, you can just buzz me through here. I can either answer, or come over, depending."

He closed the panel and it snapped shut, seamless with the wallpaper once again. How on earth had her life become some kind of…spy movie? "You've thought of everything, haven't you?"

He smiled briefly—something like pride and affection lighting up the blank, bland expression. Just a little flash of personality, and for one surprising moment all she could really think was *gee, he's hot.*

"That's what they pay me for." Then the blankness was back and whatever had sparkled in his blue eyes was gone. Everything about him screamed *cop* again, or, she supposed in his case, *FBI.* It was all the same to her. Law and order didn't suit her the way it had her brother, but she'd be grateful for it in the midst of her current situation.

She studied the room around her. Gleaming hardwood with pretty blue rugs here and there. Floral wallpaper and shabby-chic fixtures. The furniture looked antique—old and a little scarred but well polished. The quilt over the bed looked like it belonged in a pretty farmhouse with billowing lace curtains.

It was calming and comforting, and in a better state of mind she might even be able to ignore all the facades and locks and intercoms and the lack of windows. But she wasn't in the state of mind to forget that Tom, who'd been paid to protect her, was dead.

"Settle in, Ms. Delaney. You're safe here. I promise you that."

She carefully placed her duffel bag on the shiny hardwood floor. Exhaustion made her body feel as heavy as lead, and she went ahead and lowered herself onto the bed with its pretty quilt. "I'm not safe anywhere, Mr. Simmons."

He opened his mouth to argue, but she wasn't in the

mood, so she waved him toward the door. "But I feel safe enough to take a nice long nap, if you'll excuse me."

He raised an eyebrow, presumably at her regal tone and the way she waved him off, but she was too tired to care.

He moved to the door, twisted the lock on the interior knob, then closed the door behind him as he exited.

Daisy took off the wig and then let herself fall into sleep.

ZACH SPENT THE afternoon going over the information he'd been given about Daisy's stalking, and the information he'd gathered himself in anticipation of her arrival.

The murder of her bodyguard while she'd been on stage was certainly the tipping point. The formal investigation had been lax up to that point. Except for the private one her brother had launched.

Zach appreciated the detail of Ranger Cooper's intel, and since he knew too well the stress and helplessness of trying to keep a sibling safe, Zach was grateful for his willingness to share.

Still, there were things that had been missed—well, maybe not missed. Overlooked. Probably still not fair. One of the things that had allowed Zach to do so well in the FBI was his ability to work out patterns, to find threads and connect them in ways other people couldn't.

The stellar way he'd handled himself as an agent prior to his brother's involvement in a case and Zach going rogue was what had kept him from having a splashier, more painful termination from the FBI.

He shrugged away the tension in his shoulders. He hated that it still bothered him, because even if he could rewind time, he'd do most things the same.

Daisy's doorknob turned, and she took one tentative step out. She'd finally ditched the heavy black wig, and her straight blond hair was pulled back into a ponytail. She'd done something to her face—it'd take him a little more time to get to know her face well enough to know exactly what. If he had to guess, though, he'd say she'd freshened her makeup.

She'd changed out of the sleek black outfit into a long baggy shirt the color of a midsummer sky and black leggings. On her feet she wore thick bright purple socks.

She'd been in there for five hours, and from the looks of it, she'd spent most of the time sleeping—unless her makeup magically fixed the pallor of her skin and the dark circles under her eyes.

"Got any food in this joint?"

He stood and walked over to the side of the common area that acted as a kitchen. "Fully stocked kitchen, which of course you're welcome to. Tell me what you want to make and I'll show you where everything is and how to work everything."

"Coffee. Scratch that. Coffee hasn't been settling lately." She sighed, some of that weary exhaustion in her voice even if it didn't show in her face.

"My suggestion? Hot chocolate and a doughnut."

A smile twitched at the corner of her mouth. "That's enough sugar to fell a horse."

He scoffed. "Amateur hour."

She sighed. "It sounds good. I guess if I'm stuck with a crazed psychopath ready to kill those who protect me, I shouldn't worry about a few extra calories."

"I think you'll live."

She rolled her eyes. "You've never read the comments on photos of women online, have you? Still." She waved a hand to encompass the kitchen. "Lead the way."

"You sit. I'll make it. We'll go over where everything is in the kitchen tomorrow. You get a pass today."

"Gee, thanks." But she didn't argue. She sat and poked at his stacks of notes. "That's a lot of paperwork for keeping me out of trouble."

"Investigating things takes some paperwork," he returned, collecting ingredients for hot chocolate.

"I thought you were just supposed to keep me safe while Vaughn and the police figured it all out."

He slid the mug into the microwave hidden in a cabinet and put a doughnut onto a plate. "I could, but that's not what CD Corp is all about."

"CD Corp sounds like the lamest comic villain organization ever."

"It's meant to be bland, boring and inconspicuous." He walked over and set the plate in front of her.

She smiled up at him. "Mission accomplished."

"And this mission," he said, tapping the papers, "is keeping you safe by understanding the threat against you." Not noticing the little dimple that winked in her cheek or the way her blue eyes reminded him of summer. "Anything I can do to profile or find a pattern allows me to better keep you secure."

"Can I help?"

He turned away, back to hot chocolate prep and to shake off that weird and unfortunate bolt of attraction. Still, his voice was easy and bland when he spoke. "I'm counting on it." He stirred the hot chocolate and then set that next to her before taking his seat in front of his computer.

"Have you noticed the pattern of incidents?" he asked, studying her reaction to the question.

With a nap under her belt, she didn't seem as cold and detached as she had on the ride over. But she also didn't seem as ready to break as she had when he'd shown her her room hours ago. As they'd walked through the safe house earlier, he'd finally seen some signs of exhaustion, suspicion and fear.

Now all those things were still evident, but she seemed to have better control over them. He supposed singers, being performers, had to have a little actor in them, as well. She was good at it, but it had frayed at the edges when he'd told her she was safe.

She'd shored up those edges, but there was a wariness and an exhaustion, not sleep related, haunting her eyes.

"The pattern that they always happen when I'm on stage? Yes, my brother pointed that out, but as I pointed out to him, that's just means and opportunity or whatever phrase you guys use. They know exactly where I'll be and for how long."

"Sure, but I'm talking about the connection to your songs."

She frowned, taking a sip of the hot chocolate.

"The incidents, including the murder of your security guard, always crop up in the few weeks after one of your singles drops on the radio. Not all of them, but I compiled a list of titles."

"Let me guess. The drinking, cheating and swearing songs?"

"No. There's not a thematic connection that I can find." Though he'd look, and would keep considering that angle. "But the connection right now seems to be that things escalate when the songs you wrote your-self do well."

She put down the doughnut she'd lifted to her lips without taking a bite. "That doesn't make any sense."

"Not yet. I figure if we pull on it, it will."

"How did you…"

He shrugged. "I'm good with patterns."

"Good with or genius with?"

He smiled at her, couldn't help it. He'd been trained as an undercover FBI agent. Took on whatever role he had to. He'd learned to hide himself underneath a mil-lion masks, but his personal attachment to this job and the safe world he'd created made it hard to do here. "Hate to bandy a word like *genius* around."

She laughed and for a brief second her eyes lit with humor instead of worry. He wanted to be able to give that to her permanently, so she could laugh and relax and feel *safe* here.

Because that was his job, his duty, what he was good at. Completely irrelevant to the specific woman he was helping.

He looked down at his computer, frowning at the uncomfortable and unreasonable pull of emotion in-side him. Emotions were what had gotten him booted from the FBI in the first place. He didn't regret it—couldn't—but it was a dangerous line to walk when your emotions got involved.

"So, I think we can rule out crazed fan. It's more personal than that."

"Fans create a personal connection to you, though. They think they know you through your music—whether it was written by me or someone else doesn't matter to them."

"It matters to someone," Zach returned. "Or the incidents wouldn't align so perfectly with the songs you wrote."

She pushed out of her chair, doughnut untouched, only a few sips of the hot chocolate taken. She paced. He waited. When she seemed to accept he wasn't going to say anything, she whirled toward him.

"Look, I don't know how to do this."

"Do what?"

"Hide and cower and…" She gave the chair she'd popped out of a violent shove, then raked shaking hands through her hair. "A good man is dead because of me. I can't stand it."

The naked emotion, brief though it was, hit him a little hard, so he kept his tone brusque. "A good man is dead because good men die in the pursuit of doing good and because there are forces and people out there who aren't so good. Guilt's normal, but you'll need to work it out."

"Oh, will I?"

"I'd recommend therapy, once this is sorted."

"Therapy," she echoed, like he was speaking a foreign language.

"Stalking is basically a personal form of terrorism. You don't generally get through it unscathed. Right now the concern is your physical safety, but when it's over you can't overlook your emotional well-being."

"You spend a lot of time evaluating your emotional well-being, Zach?"

"Believe it or not, they don't let you in or out of the FBI without a psych eval. Same goes for in and out of undercover work—and a few of those messed me up enough to require some therapy. Talking to someone doesn't scare me, and it shouldn't scare you."

"That hardly scares me."

But the way she scoffed, he wasn't so sure. Still, it was none of his business. Her recovery was not part of keeping her safe, and the latter was all he was supposed to care about.

"Let's talk about the people on this list," Zach said, pushing the computer screen toward her. On the screen was a list of people she'd told her brother she thought might want to hurt her.

Daisy rubbed her temples. "Vaughn gave you this?"

He rose, retrieved some aspirin from the cabinet above the sink and set it next to her elbow. "Your brother gave me copies of everything pertaining to the stalking."

Daisy frowned at the aspirin bottle, then up at him. "Am I supposed to tip you?"

"Full service security and investigation, Ms. Delaney. Speaking of that, Delaney's a stage name, isn't it?"

"What? You don't have a full dossier on my real name and everything else?" She smirked at him.

He shook his head. The Delaney connection wasn't important. As unimportant as the way that smirk made his gut tighten with a desire he would never, *ever* act on.

What was important was her take on the list and what kind of patterns and conclusions he could draw. So he turned the conversation back to the case and made sure it stayed there.

Chapter Three

Sleep was a welcome relief from worry, except when the dreams came. They didn't always make sense, but Tom's lifeless body always appeared.

Even hiking up the mountains at sunset. It was peaceful, and Zach was with her, smiling. She liked his smile, and she liked the riot of sunset colors in the sky. She wanted to write a song, itched to.

Suddenly, she had a notebook and a pen, but when she started to write it became a picture of Tom, and then she tripped and it was Tom's body. She reached out for Zach's help, but it was only Tom's lifeless eyes staring back from Zach's face.

She didn't know whether she was screaming or crying, maybe it was both, and then she fell with a jolt. Her eyes flew open, face wet and breath coming so fast it hurt her lungs.

Somehow, she knew Zach was standing there. It didn't even give her a start. It seemed right and steadying that he was standing in her doorway in nothing but a pair of sweatpants, a dim glow from the room behind him.

Later, she'd give some considerable thought to just how

cut Zach was, all strong arms and abs. Something else he hid quite well, and she was sure quite purposefully.

"You screamed and you didn't lock your door," he offered, slowly lowering the gun to his side. He looked up at the ceiling, and gestured toward her. "You might want to…"

He trailed off and in her jumble of emotions and dream confusion, it took her a good minute to realize the strap of her tank top had fallen off her arm and she was all but flashing him.

She wasn't embarrassed so much as tired. Bone-deep tired of how this whole thing was ruining her life. "Sorry," she grumbled, fixing the shirt and pulling the sheet up around her.

"No. That's not…" He cleared his throat. "You should lock that door."

She wished she could find amusement in his obvious discomfort over being flashed a little breast, but she was too tired. "Lock the door to shield myself from lunatics with guns?" she asked, nodding at the pistol he carried.

"To take precautions," he said firmly.

"Are you telling me if I'd screamed and the door had been locked you wouldn't have busted in here, guns blazing?"

"They were hardly blazing," he returned, ignoring the question.

But she knew the answer. She might not know or understand Zach Simmons, but he had that same thing her brother did. A dedication to whatever he saw as his mission.

Currently, she was Zach Simmons's mission. She wished it gave her any comfort, but with Tom's dead face flashing in her mind, she didn't think anything could.

"You want a drink?" he asked, and despite that bland tone he used with such effectiveness, the offer was kind.

"Yes. Yes, I do."

He nodded. "I'll see what I can scrounge up. You can meet me out there."

She took that as a clear hint to put on some decent clothes. On a sigh, she got out of bed and rifled through her duffel bag. She pulled out her big, fluffy robe in bright yellow. It made her feel a little like Big Bird, which always made her smile.

Tonight was an exception, but it at least gave her something sunny to hold on to as she stepped out of the room. Zach was pouring whiskey into a shot glass. He'd pulled on a T-shirt, but it wasn't the kind of shirt he'd worn yesterday that hid all that surprisingly solid muscle. No, it fit him well, and allowed her another bolt of surprisingly intense attraction.

He set the shot glass on the table and gestured her into the seat. She slid into it, staring at the amber liquid somewhat dubiously. "Thanks." But she didn't shoot it. She just stared at it. "Got anything to put it in? I may love a song about shooting whiskey, but honestly shots make me gag."

His mouth quirked, but he nodded, pulling a can of pop out of the fridge.

"No diet?"

"I'll put it on the grocery list."

"And where does one get groceries in the middle of nowhere Wyoming?"

"Believe it or not, even Wyomingites need to eat. I've got an assistant who'll take care of errands. If you make a list, we'll supply."

She sipped the drink he put in front of her. The mix

of sugar and whiskey was a comforting familiarity in the midst of all this…upheaval.

"You don't shoot whiskey."

She quirked a smile at him. "Not all my songs are autobiographical, friend. Truth be told, I'd prefer a beer, but it doesn't give you quite the same buzz, does it?"

"No, but I'd think more things would rhyme with beer than whiskey."

"Songs also don't have to rhyme. Fancy yourself a country music expert? Or just a Daisy Delaney expert?"

"No expertise claimed. I studied up on your work, not that I hadn't heard it before. Some of your songs make a decent showing on the radio."

"Decent. Don't get that Jordan Jones airtime, but who does? Certainly no one with breasts." This time she didn't sip. She took a good, long pull. Silly thing to be peeved about Jordan's career taking off while hers seemed to level. Bigger things at hand. Nightmares, dead bodyguards, empty Wyoming towns.

"The police don't suspect him."

She took another long drink. "No, they don't."

"Do you?"

She stared at the bubbles popping at the surface of her soda. Did she think the man she'd married with vows of faith and love and certainty was now stalking her? That he killed the person in charge of keeping her safe?

"I don't want to."

"But you think he could be responsible?" Zach pressed. Clearly, he didn't care if he was pressing on an open, gaping wound.

"I doubt it. But I wouldn't put it past one of his people. After I filed for divorce they did a number on me.

Fake stories about cheating and drinking and unstable behavior, and before you point it out, no, my songs did not help me in that regard. Funny how my daddy was *revered* for those types of songs, even when he left Mama high and dry, but me? I'm a crazy floozy who deserves what she gets."

Zach's gaze was placid and blank, lacking all judgment. She didn't have a clue why that pissed her off, but it did. So she drank deeply, waiting for that warm tingle to spread. Hopefully slow down the whirring in her brain a little bit. "I don't want to have a debate about feminism or gender equality. I want to be safe home in my own bed. And I want Tom to be alive."

"I'm working on one of those. I'm sorry I can't fix the rest."

He said it so blankly. No emotion behind it at all, and yet this time it soothed her. Because she believed those words so much more without someone trying to *act* sincere.

"What did you dream about?" he asked as casual and devoid of emotion as he'd been this whole time.

Except when he'd been uncomfortable about her wandering breast. She held on to the fact that Mr. Ex-FBI man could be a little thrown off.

"Hiking. You. Tom. It's a jumble of nonsense, and not all that uncommon for me. I've always had vivid dreams, bad ones when I'm…well, bad. They've just never been so connected or relentless."

"I imagine your life has never been so relentless and threatening."

"Fair."

"The dreams aren't fun, but they'll be there. Meditation works for some. Alcohol for others, though I wouldn't make that one a habit. Exercise and wearing yourself out works, too."

"Let me guess, that's your trick?"

He shrugged. "I've done all three."

"Your job gave you dreams?"

"Yeah. Dreams are your subconscious, the things you often can't or don't deal with awake. It's your brain trying to work through it all when you can't outthink it."

"You've given brains a *lot* more thought than I ever have."

"There's a psychology to undercover work. Your work deals with the heart more than the brain."

Because he cut to the quick of her entire life's vocation a little too easily, and it smoothed over jagged edges in a way she didn't understand, she chose to focus on the other part of the sentence.

"You went undercover? Yeah, I can see that. Bring down any big guns?"

He shrugged. "Here and there."

"What's the point if you're not going to brag about it?"

He pondered that, then gave his answer with utter conviction. "Justice. Satisfaction."

She wrinkled her nose. "I'd prefer a little limelight."

"I suppose that's why I'm in security, and you're in entertainment."

"I suppose." She finished the drink. She wasn't really sure what had mellowed her mood more—the buzz or Zach's conversation. She had a sinking suspicion it was both, and that he was aware of that. "I guess I'll try to sleep now. I appreciate the…" She didn't know what to call it—from responding to her distress to a simple drink and conversation—it was more than she'd been given in…a long time.

Well, if she was fair, more than she'd allowed herself. And that had started a heck of a lot longer ago than the stalking.

She stood, never finishing her sentence. Zach stood, as well, cleaning up her mess. For some reason that didn't sit right, but she didn't do anything to remedy it. She opened the door to her bedroom, took one last glance back at him.

He was heading for his own door. A strange mystery of a man with a very good heart under all that blankness.

He paused at his door. He didn't look at her, but she had no doubt he knew she was looking at him.

"Daisy." It might have been the first time he'd said her name, or maybe it was just the first time he'd said her name where it sounded human to human. So she waited, breath held for who knew what reason.

"You've been through a lot. It isn't just losing someone you feel responsible for losing. You've uprooted your life, changed everything around you. You might be used to life on the road, but this is different. You don't have your singing outlet. So give yourself a break."

With that, he stepped into his room, the door closing and locking behind him.

ZACH DIDN'T NEED much sleep on a normal day, but even with the usual four hours under his belt, he felt a little rough around the edges the next morning. He supposed it had to do with them being interrupted by Daisy's screaming.

It had damn near scared a year off his life.

Any questions or doubts he'd had were gone, though. Someone or something was terrorizing her. Didn't mean he wouldn't look at cold, hard facts. Hadn't he learned what getting too emotionally involved in a case got you?

Yeah, he was susceptible to vulnerability. He could admit that now. Being plagued by dreams, by guilt over the man who'd died only for taking a job protecting her, it all added up to vulnerable.

And he was *not* thinking about the slip of her top because that had nothing to do with anything.

He grunted his way through push-ups, sit-ups, lunges and squats. He'd need to bring a few more things from home. Maybe just move it all. He wasn't planning on spending much time back in Cheyenne with his business here.

His room still needed a lot of work, and he'd get to it once this case was shored up—as long as he didn't immediately have another one. Still, he had a floor, a rudimentary bathroom and a bed. What more did a guy need?

He knew his mother worried about him throwing too much into his job, whether because she feared he'd suffer the same fate as his father—murdered in revenge for the work he'd done as an ATF agent—or because she just worried about him having more of a life than work, it didn't matter.

He liked his work. It fulfilled him. Besides, he had friends. Cousins, actually. Finding his long-lost sister meant finding his mother's family, and he might get along more with the people they'd married, but it was still camaraderie.

He had a full life.

But he sat there on the floor of a ramshackle room,

sweating from the brief workout, and wondered at the odd pang of longing for something he couldn't name. Something he'd never had until he'd met his sister—of course that had coincided with being officially fired from the FBI, so maybe it was more that than the other.

It didn't matter. Because not only was he *fine*, he also had a job to do.

He could hear Daisy stirring out in the common room. Coffee or breakfast or both, if he had to guess.

He'd hoped she'd sleep longer because there were some areas he wanted to press on today, and he'd likely back off if she looked tired.

Or he could suck it up and be a hard-ass, which was what this job called for, wasn't it? He knew what being soft got him, so he needed to steel his determination to be hard.

He ran through a cold shower, got dressed, grabbed his computer and stepped out to find Daisy in the kitchen.

She was dressed in tight jeans and a neon-pink T-shirt that read *Straight Shooter* in sparkly sequins on the back. On the sleeve of each arm was a revolver outline in more sequins. When she turned from the oven where she was scrambling some eggs, she flashed a smile.

Her hair was pulled back to reveal bright green cactus earrings, and she'd put on makeup. Dark eyes, bright lips.

The fact she'd made herself up, looked like she could step on stage in the snap of her fingers, he assumed she was hiding a rough night under all that polish.

But the polish helped him pretend, too.

"Want some?" she asked, tipping the pan toward him.

"Sure, if you've got enough." He dropped the laptop off on the table and then moved toward her to get plates, but she waved him away.

"You waited on me yesterday. My turn. Besides, I familiarized myself this morning. Thanks for making coffee, by the way. Good stuff."

"Programmable machine," he returned, not sure what to do with himself while she took care of breakfast. He opted for getting himself a cup of coffee.

He didn't want to loom behind her, so he took a seat at the table and opened his laptop. He booted up his email to see if there were any more reports from Ranger Cooper, but nothing.

She slid a plate in front of him, then took the seat opposite him with her own plate.

"So, what's the deal? Play house in here until they figure out who did it?" she asked with just a tad too much cheer in her voice—clearly trying to compensate for the edge she felt.

"Partially. We're working on a protected outdoor area, but staying inside for now is best." He tapped his computer. "It gives us time to work through who might be after you."

She wrinkled her nose. "Believe it or not, sifting through who might hate me enough to hurt me isn't high on my want-to-do list."

"But I assume going home, getting back to your family and your career is. Lesser of two evils."

She ate, frowning. But she didn't try to argue, and he was going to do his job today. Nightmares and vulnerability couldn't stop the job.

"I want to talk about your ex."

"So does everyone," she muttered.

"Your divorce was news?" he asked, even though he'd known it was. Much as he didn't keep up with pop culture, he'd seen enough magazines at the checkout counter with her face and her ex's.

"Yeah. I mean, maybe not if you don't pay attention to country music, but Jordan had really started to make a name for himself with crossovers. So the story got big. And I got crucified."

"Why didn't he?" Zach asked casually, taking a bite of the eggs, which were perfectly cooked.

"Because he's perfect?"

"You wanted to divorce him," he pointed out. "He can't be perfect. No one is."

"Or that's exactly why I wanted to divorce him."

He studied her. The lifted chin, the challenge in her eyes. "Yeah, I don't buy that."

Her shoulders slumped. "Yeah, our families didn't, either. Neither did he, for that matter. I don't know how to explain… Do we really have to discuss my very public divorce?"

"Yeah. We really do. The more I understand, the better I can find the pattern."

"And if it's not him?"

"Then the pattern won't say it is."

"People aren't patterns, Zach. They're not always rational, or sane."

"Yeah, I'm well aware, but routine stalkers are methodical. It's not a moment of rage. It's not knee-jerk or impulse. It's planned terrorizing. Murder of your bodyguard? There was no struggle. It was planned. This person is methodical, which means if I can figure out their methodology, I can figure this out."

She heaved out a sigh. "You believe that."

"I know that."

"Fine. Fine. Why did I file for divorce against Jordan? I don't know. It's complicated. It's all emotions and… Did your parents love each other?"

Unconcerned with the abrupt change, because every thread led him somewhere, he nodded. "Very much."

"Mine didn't. Or maybe they did, but it was warped. It hurt."

He thought about his brother, alone in a psych ward, still lost to whatever had taken a hold of his mind. "Love often does."

"You got someone?"

"Not romantically."

"Family, then?"

He nodded.

"I used to think loving my brother didn't hurt, not even a little—not the way loving my father did, or even my mom. Vaughn was perfect, and always did the right thing. He protected me and loved me unconditionally. But this hurts, thinking he could be in danger because of me."

"He's a Texas Ranger."

"That doesn't make him invincible. He also has a wife and two little girls and…" She swallowed, looking away from him. "I can't…"

"The best thing for 'I can't' is figuring this out. Looking at the patterns, and finding who's at the center."

"You really think you can do that?"

"I do. With your help."

She nodded. "Okay. Okay. Well, sit back and relax,

cowboy. The story of Daisy Delaney and Jordan Jones is a long one."

He lifted the coffee mug to his lips to try and hide his smile. "We've got nothing but time, Daisy."

Chapter Four

"We met at a party." It was still so clear in Daisy's head.
She'd stepped outside for air, and he'd followed. He'd
complimented her on her music—never once mention-
ing her daddy.

She'd been a little too desperate for that kind of com-
pliment at the time. She'd made a name for herself, but
only when that name directly followed her father's.

"And this was before any of Jordan's success?"

Zach sat there, poised over his computer like he'd
type it all out. Jot down her entire marriage in a few
pithy lines and then find some magical *pattern* that either found Jordan culpable or…not.

"My brother looked into Jordan, you know."

"Yes, I know. I have all the information he gathered in regards to the…let's call it *external stuff*. But
there's a lot of internal stuff I doubt you shared with
your brother."

She laughed. "But you think I'll share it with a complete stranger?"

Zach blew out a breath, and though he had to be irritated with her, it didn't really show in the ways she
was *used* to people being irritated with her.

"I know this is personal," Zach said, all calm and

even and perfectly civil. "It hurts to mine through all these old things you thought were normal parts of a normal life. I'm not trivializing what you might feel, Daisy. I'm trying to understand someone's motivation for stalking and terrorizing you, and murdering your bodyguard."

"So you can find your precious pattern?" she asked, her throat too tight to sound as callous as she wanted to sound.

"Yeah, the precious pattern that might save your life."

She wanted to lean her head against the table and weep. Somehow, she had no doubt Zach would be kind and discreet about it, and it made her perversely more determined to keep it together. "He was sweet, and attentive. We had a lot in common, though he'd grown up on some hoity-toity, well-to-do Georgia farm and I'd grown up on the road. Still, the way he talked about music and his career made sense to me. He made sense to me. He asked me to marry him assuring me that it didn't have to change my career—because he knew where my priorities were."

"So you married for love?"

"Isn't that why people get married?"

"People get married for all sorts of reasons, I think. In your case, you've got fame and money on your side."

"Are you suggesting Jordan married me for my fame and money?"

"No, I'm asking if he did."

"I didn't think so." Even after she'd asked for a divorce, she hadn't thought Jordan could be that cold and manipulative, but after everything that had happened since the divorce… "He was so careful about any work we did together. Had to make sure it was the right project. He didn't insinuate himself into my career. So it didn't seem that way…"

"But?"

She didn't like the way he seemed to understand where her thoughts were going. She was clearly telegraphing all her feelings, and Zach was too observant. She needed to pull her masks together.

"He didn't fight me on the divorce. We'd grown apart. He'd thrown everything into his tour, his album, and I was touring and… We were both sort of bitter with each other but couldn't talk about it. I said we should end it and he agreed. He agreed. So simple, so smooth. Everything that came after was…calculated. Careful. He wanted us to split award shows."

"Huh?"

"Like choose which award shows we'd attend. If he was going to be at one, I wouldn't be. Like they were holidays you split the kids between. I don't know. I remember when my parents got divorced, it was screaming matches and throwing things and drunkenness. Not…paperwork."

"So it was amicable?"

Daisy hesitated. She'd dug her own grave, so to speak, with some of her behavior after she'd asked for the divorce. Because when he'd politely accepted her request and immediately obtained the necessary paperwork, she'd been…

Sometimes she tried to convince herself her pride had been injured, but the truth was she'd been devastated. She'd thrown out divorce as an option to get some kind of reaction out of him, to ignite a spark like they'd had before they'd gotten married.

But he'd gone along. Agreed. Wanted custody agreements over *award shows*.

So she hadn't handled herself well. At all. She'd never imagined *this*. She'd only acted out her hurt and anger and betrayal the best way she knew how.

Breaking stuff and getting drunk.

"*He* was amicable, I guess you could say. I was… less so."

"But you were the one who asked for the divorce."

"Yes." As much as she didn't want to get into this with Zach, she supposed she'd end up giving him whatever information he thought might help with his precious patterns. What else was there to do? How else did she survive this?

"Yes, because I wanted him to fight for me, or be mad at me or react to me in some way. But he didn't. I started thinking he'd never loved me, because he was so calm. If there'd been love, it would have gone bitter. Mine did. I think he just used me for as long as I'd let him, then was happy to move on." As if it had been his plan all along.

Even now, a year later, the stab of pain that went along with that was hard to swallow down or rationalize away.

There were bigger tragedies in the world than a failed marriage, including her dead bodyguard.

"So maybe it could be Jordan, but if it is him, it's not because I divorced him. Trust me, he got everything he wanted and *more* out of that situation. I don't think he'd sully his precious reputation by slapping back at me, when the press did all the work eviscerating me for him."

"Okay. What about other exes?"

"Because only a jilted lover could be after me?"

"Because we're going through the rational options first. We'll move to the irrational crazed fan angle after—" The sound of a phone trilling cut him off.

He pulled his cell out of his pocket, glanced at the display, then answered. "Yeah?" His face changed. She couldn't have described how. A tensing, maybe? Suddenly, there was more of an edge to him. The blandness sharpened into something that made her stomach tighten with a little bit of fear, and just a touch of very inappropriate lust.

If only she knew how to be appropriate.

He fired off questions like *when?* and *description?* jotting down what she assumed were the answers on the back of one of the many pieces of paper in the file.

"Get what you can for me," he said tersely and hung up.

He jotted a few more things down then got to his feet like he was going to walk off to his room without saying anything.

"What was that?" Daisy demanded, hating the hint of hysteria in her voice.

"Just some updates. Nothing to worry about."

She fairly leaped out of her chair and grabbed his arm before he could disappear into his room.

He clearly didn't know her very well because he raised a condescending eyebrow, like that would have her moving her hand. But she'd be damned if she was letting go until she said what she had to say. "You want me safe? I have to know what's going on."

"That isn't necessarily true," he replied in that bland tone of his. "Knowing doesn't do much. All you have to do is stay put. I'll be back."

"You'll be back? You don't honestly expect me to—"

"I expect you to listen to the man currently keeping you safe. Do me a favor? Don't be cliché or stupid. Which means stay put. I'll be back." And then he walked out the front door.

And locked it from the outside.

ZACH HAD NO doubt he'd made all the wrong moves in there, but he didn't have time to make the right ones. He pocketed his keys, double-checked the gun holstered to his side and stepped out into daylight.

He took a deep breath of the fresh air, trying not to feel the prick of guilt at Daisy being locked inside for close to twenty-four hours. But it was for her safety, and Cam's phone call proved to him that he had to keep being excessively vigilant.

Which was why he scowled when Cam pulled up to the shack that disguised a garage behind the big house. Hilly was in the passenger seat so Zach tried to fix his expression into something neutral, but his sister being here complicated things.

Hilly was acting as their assistant. She ran the errands for groceries and the like, and she was helping with some of the paperwork while she went through nursing school.

Cam pulled his truck into the garage, then he and Hilly exited. Zach pushed the button himself to close the door so it went back to looking like a falling-down shack.

Cam's expression grave and Hilly's suspicious. "I still can't believe this place," she said with a little shudder. "It's so *creepy* from the outside."

Zach smiled thinly. "And, as you well know, perfectly livable from the inside. So what's the deal?"

"Is she in there?" Hilly asked with a frown.

"Yeah."

"Well, let's go inside."

Zach rocked back on his heels. "Not a great idea right now. Besides, she doesn't need to know about this."

Hilly's frown deepened. Zach wanted to scowl at Cam for bringing her, but that would only make Hilly angrier.

Truth be told, he didn't understand the way Hilly got angry at all. It was sneaky, and came at you in new and confusing ways. Like guilt. He didn't care for it.

She glanced back at Cam. "I thought I was here to see what Daisy needed."

"You are," Cam agreed. "I just have some things I need to discuss with Zach about the case privately. I thought maybe I could do that while you talk to Daisy about anything she might need."

She looked back at Zach, her lips pursed, surveying him. An expression he never knew how to fully read. Judgment? Disappointment?

"I still think we can go inside and talk. There are rooms. Or you can let me go inside while you two pow-wow out here."

"Aren't you going to demand to know what's going on?"

"No. Cam and I agreed that there were certain cases that required his confidentiality. I'm okay with that. So why don't you let me in?"

Zach nodded. He didn't particularly want to introduce anyone to Daisy, but she was likely tired of just *him* and walls for company. Hilly could talk to her about anything she needed, maybe make her feel a little more at home, and Cam could fill him in on the details in the privacy of his room.

They walked to the front of the house and Zach unlocked and relocked doors as they entered, and when he stepped into the common area he frowned at the absence of Daisy.

Then at the fact the door to his room was open. He stepped toward it, hand moving to his gun without fully thinking the move through.

He stopped short in the doorway, shock and irritation clawing through him at equal measure. "What the hell do you think you're doing?" Zach demanded from the doorway.

Daisy didn't even have the decency to jump as she sat there on his bed, rifling through his things.

"I can't say your room holds any deep, dark surprises, Zach. Bland guy. Bland… Oh, hello." Daisy leaned her head to the side to look around him.

"Get your hands off my stuff."

She blinked up at him oh so innocently. "Won't you be doing the same for me? Or have you already?" She got to her feet in a fluid movement and crossed to Hilly and Cam and held out her hand.

"Daisy Delaney," she offered with a sassy grin that likely served her well on stage.

"Hi, I'm Hilly," Hilly said eagerly, shaking Daisy's hand. "I'm Zach's sister."

"Zach's sister." Daisy looked at him and raised an eyebrow before her smile sharpened. "Well, Hilly, you might be my new best friend."

"Sorry, if you're looking for dirt we only kind of found out about each other last year."

"Okay, so you can't give me the Zach dirt. How about you tell me what the hell is going on? I'm presuming you know." She moved her gaze to Cam. "Or you do."

"I, uh…" Cam cleared his throat, looking shockingly ruffled and uncomfortable.

"He's a big fan," Hilly stage-whispered.

"I am not," Cam retorted, sounding downright strangled. "I mean, I *am*, but not… Oh, hell."

Hilly laughed, leaning into Cam. They were more of a unit than Zach would ever be with his own sister, and he was never quite sure what to do with that sick wave of jealousy that swamped him sometimes.

Hilly had been kidnapped and raised as someone else. What would he envy of her life?

But when she linked hands with Cam and talked excitedly to Daisy, he knew exactly what.

"Hilly, why don't you take Daisy out to the kitchen and get her list. Hilly's our assistant. She can run any errands you need."

"Oh, he's dismissing the womenfolk," Daisy said with a sweetness that went bitter at the edges.

Zach could tell Hilly was trying to suppress a smile. But she didn't fight him. "I'm sure there are some things you'd like to have, Ms. Delaney. I can get you whatever you need."

"Call me Daisy," she replied, heading for the door with Hilly.

Zach *knew* he should keep his mouth shut, let it go. But she downright needled him. "We'll talk about you going through my stuff later," he muttered as she passed.

"Ooh, shaking in my boots, baby cakes."

He sneered, as irritated with himself for letting her get to him as he was at her for being obnoxious as hell.

"Things are going well, then," Cam offered once Daisy and Hilly disappeared into the common room.

"Things are going fine. I want the full report."

"We didn't catch him at the airport, but a man was quizzing Jen at the General Store. Get many strangers, etc. She gave me a call and I ran him. Came in on a flight from Texas, but after Daisy's. No connections yet, but probably more than a coincidence. Someone's following her."

"I want to know *how*."

"Don't you want to know *who*?"

"Maybe. But if this is the stalker, they suddenly got so dumb they're sniffing around a small town thinking they won't make waves. My money's on a plant, or a hired hand. The *how* is more relevant than the *who*."

"He's rented a room in Fairmont, but I have some suspicions that's to throw us off."

"Does he know about *us*?"

"Unclear. As far as I can tell, he only has a vague idea of where she is. I assume he knows she's under some kind of protection, but he didn't make Hilly or me, and nobody followed us out here."

"We took every precaution." But something hadn't worked. Something had gotten through.

"It happens, Zach. Now we focus on protecting her. Jen's getting together her security footage and I'll work on an ID and any connections to Daisy. I'm sure you'll obsess over a pattern. Bottom line, we'll keep her safe."

Except hadn't he already failed at that? Maybe she was safe *now*, but the threat was at her door just like it had been back in Texas.

"Hey," Cam said. "Nothing's ever going to go according to plan. You know that."

Zach nodded at Cam. But a mistake had been made—plans or no plans—and that mistake had to be figured out before the consequences of his mistake started knocking.

Chapter Five

Daisy liked Hilly. She hadn't thought she would when the young woman had ushered her out of Zach's room with only a mild display of amusement.

But Hilly was sweet, a little heavy on the earnestness, which Daisy could only find endearing. The fact she'd ask for Daisy's autograph to give to the man huddled in Zach's room appealed to both Daisy's ego and the idea that love didn't always have to be messy. Hilly clearly loved her boyfriend and wasn't miffed that he'd gone a little tongue-tied over Daisy.

"So you don't know what's going on with the caveman clutch in there?" Daisy asked, scowling at Zach's door as Hilly finished up the list. It would be nice to have some *real* food in this place.

Hilly smiled. "They aren't really. Cavemen, that is. They're just…serious."

Which didn't answer the question. "No offense, Hilly, but one's your brother and one's your…" She trailed off, glanced at the rock on Hilly's hand. Not bad taste for a caveman, but Hilly could have picked it out herself. "Fiancé. You're not an unbiased observer."

"I suppose not, but they're good men. They both helped save me from people who wanted to hurt me."

"Really?"

"Zach's saved a lot of people, and gotten himself hurt in the process more than once. He's a good man. That I can promise you."

Hilly smiled as Cam and Zach stepped out of Zach's room, looking just as Hilly had described them: serious.

"I'll tell you about it sometime. Or ask Zach."

"Ask me what?"

Hilly shook her head and stood, slipping the list into her pocket. "I should head out to get the supplies so I can get them back to you before dinner."

"I'll keep in touch," Cam said to Zach.

"Aren't you going to say goodbye to Daisy, Cam?" Hilly asked sweetly.

He glared at her but then offered Daisy a smile and a nod. "It was nice to meet you, Ms. Delaney," he offered stiffly.

"Call me Daisy, sweetheart."

Cam made a little noise that might have been a squeak if he wasn't so tall and broad. Hilly ushered him out and that left her with Zach.

She scowled at him. Truth be told, she should be used to overly serious men worrying a little too much about her safety, but she'd always managed to keep Vaughn on the fringe of all that. Travel and no real trouble had helped until the past year.

But regardless of Vaughn's interference in her life, she wasn't used to someone being all up in her business. She wasn't used to someone getting under her skin in such a short amount of time.

And none of it mattered, because at the end of the day, her irritation with Zach didn't matter. Getting through this mattered. "I want to know what's going on."

"And I want to know why you were rifling through my stuff," he retorted, a slash of temper barely leashed.

Was it wrong she liked temper on him? That he wasn't all Mr. Bland Stoic? Because *this* was a lot more enjoyable than his pat, crap answers. So she grinned at him, since it seemed to make him grind his teeth together. "Show me yours, I'll show you mine."

"Someone followed you."

It took any and all enjoyment out of the moment. She sank into the chair when her legs went a little wobbly. "What?"

"Someone followed you here," Zach said, his voice flat but his eyes flashing with anger.

Was it at her or whoever was here? She wasn't sure she wanted to know.

"So I need a list of everyone who knew you were coming."

"You know the list," she replied, trying to keep the tremor out of her voice. "You, Jaime and my brother. Hate to break it to you, but they're not high on my suspect list. Well, I don't know you. It could be you."

"You didn't tell anyone that you were going out of town, or post a picture from the airport or—"

Injured pride reignited her irritation. "Oh, screw you."

"Hey, someone is *here*, and now I have to keep you safe under an even bigger threat, so a little truthfulness would be nice."

"Because I'm such a liar?"

"Get it through your thick, obnoxious skull that your pride doesn't matter right now. One person, any person, who might have known you were leaving town, heading to the airport, anything. Because it matters. Clearly, if someone is here looking for you, it matters."

It was on the tip of her tongue to immediately dismiss him. But…it wouldn't be true, and she wanted to be safe more than she wanted to be righteous.

Just barely.

"I… I told my manager I was going to Wyoming, but—"

"Of all the idiotic bull—"

"I trust Stacy with my *life*," she shot back before he could finish. "I trust her with everything. It isn't her."

"Okay, great. So the three people who knew you were coming to Wyoming were your brother, an FBI agent and your manager. Who spilled the beans?"

"Maybe *you* did, jerk."

"Sure. I'm a security professional, but I bragged about bagging a big star client to someone who has a connection to you."

"I don't know you! You could have."

"But I know me, and I didn't. Stacy… Stacy Vine. That's your manager, right?"

"You cannot look into her."

"Can. Will."

She would not be so weak as to cry. She'd save that for when he couldn't see and lord it over her later. But her voice wasn't nearly strong enough. "You're asking me which of these people I *love* wants me dead."

He softened. She saw it all over his face and wanted to hate him for it. It would be easier if he was just the overbearing jerk, but he offered empathy far too often for it to be that simple.

God, she wanted something, anything, to be simple.

He took one of the chairs and moved it across from

her. He sat, facing her, so that their knees were almost touching. He leaned forward, and she found herself wanting to lean forward, too. Wanting to be touched, comforted.

Wasn't that a joke? She knew better on a good day, with a man who actually liked her. This was neither of those things.

"It doesn't have to be that cut-and-dried. She could have mentioned it to an assistant. Written it down and someone read it. This is why the *who* is important, Daisy. If it's someone who's got a personal tie to you, they might be stalking people you know and love, too."

"How many ways do you want to hurt me, Zach?" She held up a hand before he could answer. He wasn't trying to hurt her. He had a job to do, protection to see to. Anything that hurt was all hers. "Sorry. That wasn't fair."

"You don't have to be fair. I'm going to do my job no matter what you are. Be mad, be unfair, but I need the truth. Always. It's the only way we get you out of this."

We. Like they were some kind of team. Which was too much the story of her life. Thinking some man was in it for her—Dad, Jordan—only to find all they cared about was their own bottom line. She didn't know how to weather that again.

What other option was there? She could lie to him, not trust him, and where did it get her? Nowhere. She was in the hardest lose-lose situation of her entire life, and boy, was that saying something.

"She's the only one aside from Vaughn and Jaime that knows. Nat—that's Vaughn's wife—might know, but Vaughn's pretty by-the-book. Even if he told her, he'd swear her to secrecy, and Nat would listen. You could always ask them, but I doubt they'd be careless."

"So we'll look into your manager."

"Yeah, sure. Fantastic."

Zach sighed, then rested his hand over hers. Warm, strong, capable. She really wanted to hate him, and he made it so dang hard.

"One thing at a time, okay? And eventually, we'll get there."

It was a cliché, and stupid, and worst of all, it made her feel better.

ZACH SPENT MOST of his day looking into the manager, her connections and trying to figure out how anyone had followed Daisy here.

It couldn't be cut-and-dried because the person didn't know *exactly* where Daisy was, so that made any patterns sketchy at best. A frustrating point of fact Zach was having trouble accepting.

He also spent considerable time checking his security measures and watching the footage of the security cameras he had positioned on different places outside the house. When he was half convinced he saw a tumbleweed pass across his deserted Main Street he knew it was time to do something else.

Still, no matter what he did or how little he interacted with Daisy, he could practically feel the stir-crazy coming off her.

When Hilly returned with the groceries, and some updates on the tasks he'd asked her to accomplish, Zach thanked her and sent her away, though it was clear she wanted to stay and chat.

Much as Zach trusted Hilly and Cam to be aware of

anyone following them, he didn't want to take too many chances on comings and goings being noticed—whether by the wrong people or even by locals who might talk.

Armed with the special item he'd tasked Hilly to find, Zach went to Daisy's room. She'd been inside with the door closed for about an hour. He knew she wasn't sleeping because he could hear her moving around.

He knocked, feeling stupid and determined in equal measure. It wasn't his job to set Daisy at ease or make her comfortable, but it wasn't *not* his job, either.

She opened the door with that haughty, bad-girl smirk, though it couldn't hide the wariness in her gaze. Still, both smirk and wariness softened as she noticed what he held in his hands.

"A guitar," she breathed, like he was holding a leprechaun's pot of gold.

"I don't know much about music, but there's a music shop in Fairmont and Hilly stopped in and picked one up. Probably not the quality you're used to, but—"

"Hilly stopped in and picked one up or you asked her to?"

"Does it matter?"

She tilted her head, studying him. In the end, she didn't say anything. She took the offered guitar and slid her fingers over the wood, the strings, the body and the arm.

There was something a little too erotic about watching her do that so he moved into the kitchen. It wasn't quite dinnertime yet, but they could certainly eat. If only to keep him from embarrassing himself.

But he couldn't quite seem to keep his gaze off the way she stroked the instrument, which meant he had to say something. *Do* something. Anything to keep his mind out of places he couldn't let it wander.

"I get a free concert, right?"

She grinned, turning the guitar over in her hands. She slid the strap over her shoulder, picked at the strings, fiddled with the knobs and whatever else.

"Ain't nothing free in this life, sugar." She said it, and then she sang it, noodling into one of her father's songs. The relaxation in her was nearly immediate. She softened, eased and lost herself in the song.

It was…enchanting, which wasn't a word he'd ever used or probably even thought, but she was mesmerizing. Like a fairy. With a dark, mischievous side. She moved seamlessly from one of her father's raucous drinking songs to one of her newer ones—the one she'd had some success with right before her bodyguard had been killed.

Sadness crept into her features, but not fear. She moved into a song it took him a few chords to recognize as one of the few duets she'd ever recorded with her father.

She stopped abruptly halfway through the song. "Hell, I miss that old bastard," she muttered.

That was a sadness he understood, and it made it impossible not to try and soothe. "My father wasn't a bastard, but I know the feeling."

"Not around?"

"He was murdered."

"Well. Hell, Zach, ease me into it, why don't you. Murdered?"

Zach raised a shoulder, no idea what prompted him to share that information. Soothing was one thing, but volunteering details was another. Yet, they piled up and fell out of him at a rapid rate. "Risks of the job. He was in the ATF, investigating a dangerous group. A long time ago. It happens."

"It shouldn't."

Why that simple phrase touched him was more than beyond him. He'd had a lot of time to deal with his father's death, accepting it and the unfairness of life. He'd investigated his father's murder, made sure it didn't consume him like it had his brother. He'd come to terms. He'd dealt.

But it shouldn't happen. No. It shouldn't.

"Is that why you do this?" she asked, still fiddling with the guitar.

"No, but it's why I went into the FBI. I'm assuming your father is why you went into music."

"Yes and no." She played a few more chords, humming with them. "He pushed me into it, and I did it partly for him, because of him, but I did it partly because it's in me. The chords, the stories." She pinned him with a look. "I'd say the same is true for you. Your father's life pushed you into law enforcement, but there's something in you that fits it."

"You'd be surprised," he muttered. "What sounds good for dinner?"

"Whatever," she said, taking a seat at the table and still playing random chords on the guitar like they were a link to safety or comfort. "I guess you didn't find anything with Stacy."

"No. Cam's working on the identity of who's here, and I'll have a report tonight, along with some video I'll want you to take a look at."

"Who's here. Why do you say it like that?"

"Like what?"

"Like who's behind this and who's here might be two separate people."

Her worry was back. She gripped the guitar hard enough her knuckles went white.

Part of him wanted to lie to her, but that wouldn't do. That was letting himself get too emotionally invested. "It's certainly a possibility."

"So there could be two of them?"

"No, I'd say it's more likely someone hired."

"Like…a hit man?"

"Or just someone sent to find you. A lot of shady things are for hire out there. It'd be a way to ferret out your exact location without getting caught themselves."

"So even if you catch *this* guy, it won't mean you can connect them to the stalker?"

"Doesn't mean we can't, either. We don't know yet."

She rubbed at her chest. "I thought I knew how to deal with the unknown. You never know what's going to succeed or fail in music. I thought I would always just go with the flow, but if I hear you say we don't know one more time I might have a mental breakdown."

"Hey, this is the place for mental breakdowns. Creepy ghost town facade and all the modern comforts of home."

She laughed, but it faded quickly. "Home. Do you have a home?"

"I assume you mean home in the symbolic sense, not just four walls and a roof?"

"Bingo, cowboy."

Zach thought it over. Home to him was his grandparents' ranch they'd moved to after Dad had died. He'd never made one for himself. This place he was standing in meant something to him—bigger than just a building or a job—but it still wasn't...*home*.

"I guess not. I haven't really had anything permanent as an adult."

"I never had anything permanent."

"Do you ever wonder how you ended up the nomadic singer and your brother the stay-in-one-place Texas Ranger?"

"Are you just like your siblings?" she asked with one of her haughty raised eyebrows.

He sobered at the thought of his brother in a mental hospital, working through all the things that had twisted inside him since their father's death.

"You and Hilly seem similar," she offered as if *she* was trying to comfort *him*.

"Hilly and I only met just this year. I mean, I remember her when she was a baby, but—"

"She said the same thing. Add that to the murdered father and I'd say you've got quite the story, Zach."

"She was kidnapped by the men who murdered my father and raised under a different name."

Daisy blinked and opened her eyes wide. "I'm sorry, *what?*"

He shrugged, uncomfortable both with the subject and his idiocy for discussing it. "It's complicated, but... Well, it's all figured out now."

"Does the calm, bland, bored facade ever get exhausting?"

He didn't care for how easily she saw through him, so he did his best to raise his eyebrow condescendingly like she did. "Who says it's a facade?"

Her mouth quirked up at one side. "You weren't so bland or bored when I was rifling through your stuff."

Even now the reminder made his jaw clench, even more so when she full-on grinned and pointed at him. "See? Underneath all that robot exterior, there is a man with a living, breathing heart." She looked down at the guitar in her lap and frowned. "Believe it or not, Zach, I'd rather have a man with a heart on this case over a robot. That's why I was going through your things. I wanted to see if I could get to that heart."

"Believe it or not, Daisy, I do what I have to do to keep you safe. Robot exterior included."

She pursed her lips together as if she didn't quite believe him. As if she took it as some kind of challenge.

Lucky for him, he was not a man to back down from a challenge any more than he was a man to lose one.

Chapter Six

Zach was dead. Lifeless blue eyes. Blood everywhere. Just like Tom.

She turned to run, to save herself, but she tripped over another body and gasped out a sob.

Vaughn. *No.*

But even as she wanted to reach out, grab her brother, breathe some life into him, she ran. She didn't know how, because her brain was telling her running into the dark was all wrong.

But she kept running into the black. Into the danger.

"Daisy. Come on. Daisy." Zach's voice. But he was dead.

Still, she ran.

"Daisy. Stop."

She tried to speak, but she couldn't. She could only run and Zach swore viciously, the words echoing in the dark around her.

"Let's try this."

Why was Zach's voice haunting her? He was dead. She was alone. No, not alone. Running from…from who?

"Lucy?"

It wasn't immediate, but slowly she realized it wasn't

totally pitch-black. A light glowed in the corner of the room. She smelled paint, not blood. And she could feel Zach there. Somehow she knew it was him, touching her shoulders.

"Lucy, wake up now."

Zach. Calling her by her real name. He was sitting on her bed. Twisted so that his hands gripped her shoulders, strong but gentle. He was using her real name and she was in Wyoming.

Dreaming.

"A dream," she muttered out loud.

"There now," he said, relief evident in his tone as he ran a hand down her spine. Weird to be comforted in a strange room with a man she barely knew touching her through the thin cotton of her pajamas.

But she *was* comforted. Enough that when he began to pull away she only leaned into him, ignoring the way his body stiffened. "You were dead. Vaughn was dead. And all I did was run."

His body softened against hers, and though his arms were more hesitant than take-control, he wrapped them around her.

A comfort hug. Maybe even a pity hug.

She didn't even care. She'd take comfort from pity if she had to. The images of that dream stuck with her, flashed in her head every time she closed her eyes. She focused on Zach instead.

He was warm with all that surprisingly hard muscle. He smelled like soap. She closed her eyes and breathed in deeply. She soaked in the warmth and rested her cheek against his chest, listening to his heartbeat.

A steady thump. As comforting as the rest of him. She could feel his breath flutter the hair against her cheek. When he breathed, her body moved with the movement of his. Underneath her hands, splayed against his broad, strong back, she could feel his warmth seep into her.

What would all that muscle feel like without the Henley between her palms and his skin? To have her cheek pressed against his naked chest instead of soft cotton? She'd seen him with his shirt off. She could almost picture it.

So much better than the other pictures in her head.

It took her a minute to realize the buzz along her skin was pure, unadulterated *want*. And another minute to roll her eyes at herself for being so stupid and simple. She straightened, pulling away from him. His arms easily fell off her and he got to his feet quickly.

It amused her, soothed her a little, to think he might feel that bolt of attraction, too. What would be going on in that regimented brain of his?

"How about some ice cream?" he asked.

It made her smile. "Is sugar your answer to all of life's crises?"

"I wouldn't say sugar is the answer. Sugar is the… comfort. Besides, you had Hilly buy you some low-cal fruit atrocity kind. I figured you might be up for it."

"I'll take it." She slid out of bed. She'd learned her lesson that first night and had worn something acceptable to be seen in to bed.

Though, if she was honest with herself, she now regretted it. Thinking about an attraction to Zach, and what could be done about it when they were stuck in a weird safe house together, was far better than thinking about her dream or even her reality.

So she tried to decide what kind of come-on Zach

Simmons, part robot, would respond to as she followed him out into the kitchen area. Nothing subtle. Being attracted to her was probably *very* against his personal code.

What would it take to make him break his personal code? She remembered the way he'd uncomfortably stared at the ceiling when her pajama top had been too revealing the other night. It made her laugh, which felt immeasurably good after the terror of that dream.

"Something funny?" he asked, looking at her with some concern—like maybe she'd lost it a little bit.

Maybe she had, but she figured she had a right to. "Just trying to think of things that make me laugh instead of cry or scream."

He frowned at that as he pulled out the carton of the frozen yogurt she'd requested. "I've been thinking about someone being here, and about what we can do."

"Thinking? Don't you sleep?"

He shrugged as he scooped the yogurt into the bowl. None for him, she noted. "When necessary."

When necessary. She had no idea why this man was such an endearing piece of work. Maybe it was because most of the men she knew pretended to have feelings when they really didn't, and Zach was the exact opposite.

"I think the leak is through your manager. It's what makes the most sense anyway. So we pull on that." He set the bowl in front of her, then went back to the freezer and pulled out a different carton.

She stared at the sad bowl of low-fat fro-yo that sometimes tasted good enough to make her forget about ice cream. Less so when someone wanted her dead or traumatized or whatever.

"What does *pull on that* mean in cop speak?"

Zach slid into the chair next to her. The bowl of dark chocolate, full-fat ice cream he set in front of him made Daisy's mouth water.

"Send a few fake messages, see which ones get followed. I haven't worked it all out yet, but that's my thought, and I'll need you to do it."

"You want me to lie to Stacy?" Daisy asked, her stomach turning at the thought. She was a decent enough liar, what with being a performer and storyteller and all, but the idea of lying to Stacy to prove someone she loved and trusted was part of this nightmare...

Yeah, fro-yo wasn't going to cut it.

"They don't have to be lies. They just have to be leads. Something we can follow and see who picks it up."

It still sounded like lying to her, and it sounded complicated. So she reached over and scooped a lump of his ice cream onto her spoon. Their eyes met as she slid the ice cream into her mouth.

It might have been funny if he didn't watch her so intently. If that direct eye contact didn't make her entire body simply *ignite*.

Under that stuffy exterior, Zach was proving to be a very, *very* dangerous variable in this whole mess. Because along with stalkers she didn't know what to do with, murder that scared her to her bones, and guilt that nearly ate her alive, she was still herself. Daisy Delaney. Lucy Cooper.

And she'd never been very good at pulling her hand out of the fire.

ZACH NEEDED MORE SLEEP. Clearly, a lack of it was the cause of his current lack of control.

Not that he'd done anything aside from watch her steal a scoop of his ice cream. And open her mouth around the spoon. And swallow the bite.

Then nearly spontaneously combust.

He looked down at his ice cream and tried to remember anything about what they were talking about. Anything that wasn't her mouth, or the way she'd leaned against him in the bedroom earlier.

He should cut himself a little slack. He was only human after all, and she was beautiful and engaging. She had that *thing* that made people want to watch her, get wrapped up in her orbit.

Maybe he'd like to be immune, but he was hardly a failure just because he wasn't.

But the one and only time he'd let his emotions get the best of him people had almost died. People he cared about. People he loved.

He couldn't—wouldn't—make that mistake again. No matter how tempting Daisy Delaney proved herself to be.

All his paperwork was in his room, as was his laptop. He had no shields to wield against her, and he had to think of this as its own version of war, even if it was only a war within himself.

"You could reach out and say you're willing to do a few shows," he said. He might not have his papers, but that didn't mean they couldn't talk through some options. When in doubt, focus on the task at hand. When tempted beyond reason, focus on what needed to be done.

"That'd go through my agent—the actual booking."

"Does your agent know you're here?"

"No. Not unless Stacy told him. I doubt she would have. She would have just told him I'm unavailable."

Maybe. The problem was, you never really knew what people told other people, and who those other people knew. There were so many fraying threads and he felt frayed himself. By her, by all this close proximity and by this damn dogged frustration that the case wasn't as simple as he might have thought.

"What about Jordan?"

She slumped, toying with her spoon. It amazed him the way she'd been mostly blamed and decimated in the press for being the instigator, the uncaring party, while Jordan poured his brokenhearted soul into his next album.

But every time Zach mentioned her ex-husband, she had a visceral reaction—in ways she didn't with other topics.

It twisted something inside him he refused to investigate, because emotions had to stay out of this. No more guitars. No more going into her room if she was having a nightmare. No more...

She took another bite of his ice cream.

Zach kept his gaze on his bowl. No more ice cream sharing, that was for sure.

"What *about* Jordan?" she asked, giving up on his ice cream and her own frozen yogurt.

"Would anyone have told him where you are? Does he have any connections to your manager or your agent?"

"He got a new agent when we got divorced. We never shared managers, though I guess Stacy was friends with

Doug. In the way two people who sometimes have to work together are friends. She knows... Look, she was there through the divorce. She wouldn't give Jordan any information, and I don't think my agent is a fan of Jordan's after the way he was treated."

Or maybe he's not a fan of yours. Zach made a mental note to look deeper into the agent. "I don't really understand the ins and outs of your...what would you call it, staff?"

"Team," she replied emphatically.

"Let's go over the hierarchy there."

She shook her head. "I think I'd rather go back to bed and take my chances with nightmares."

"That's fine."

She eyed him. "It's fine, but be prepared to do it in the morning?"

Zach shrugged. "I have to dig, Daisy."

"No, you actually don't. You just have to keep me alive."

It was true. He hadn't been hired to investigate. He'd been hired to protect. But that didn't mean he couldn't or wouldn't do both. He needed her cooperation, though, which meant he had to go about getting the information a little more...strategically.

"You're right," he said, doing his best to sound like he agreed with her. "I don't have to poke into this or you. It's not my job." He stood, taking both bowls and walking them to the sink. "I'll butt out."

He turned, ready to head to his room. If temper flared a little unsteadily inside him, he snuffed it out. Emotions weren't his job, either.

Not investigating wasn't an option for him. But if she didn't want him digging into it, he'd do it without her.

She stood and stepped very deliberately into his path to his door. She cocked her head, studying him in a way that reminded him of being back in the FBI Academy—constantly being sized up for his effectiveness and usefulness.

He hadn't minded it then. He'd been full of the utter certainty that he belonged there, and that he was more than fit to be an agent.

Now, here, it scraped along his skin, unearthing too many insecurities he'd much rather pretend didn't exist.

"You did one hell of a job undercover, didn't you?" she murmured.

He was surprised at the change in topic, but he didn't let any of his unaffected poise loosen. "I suppose."

"The problem now is that you aren't undercover, so when you put on the act it doesn't add up."

"I don't follow."

"You don't care if investigating isn't your job. You're going to do it anyway. You don't let things go, and one way or another, you'll keep poking at me. There's something under this…" She waved her fingers in front of his face. "I'd say I don't understand it, but I do. I may not have grown up with my brother, but I recognize that cop thing—truth and justice above all else."

"So I remind you of your brother," he said flatly.

Her mouth curved, slowly, and with way too much enjoyment. The move so slow and fluid and mesmerizing he watched it the entire time—from mouth quirk to full-on sultry smile.

"No, I can't say you do, Zach."

He wanted to shift, to clear his throat, to do *anything* that might loosen all this tightening inside him. But it would be a giveaway.

Would it matter if you gave it away to her? She isn't your enemy.

"But what I will say is that if it wasn't for my brother, I wouldn't believe in the existence of good men with an inner sense of right and wrong and a deep-seated need to protect."

He held still. He met her gaze with all the blankness he'd honed in his time undercover. You made eye contact, but you didn't fall into it. You didn't get conned into believing you could act so well that someone saw what you wanted them to see.

So you gave nothing. You counted eyelashes or recited the Gettysburg Address. You didn't think over your plan, and you didn't give in to trying to analyze their thoughts or feelings—because thoughts and feelings couldn't be analyzed or predicted. They couldn't be patterned out.

Which, unfortunately for Daisy, was why he thought this whole thing was *personal*. Someone who wanted to hurt her for something more than her music or her reputation.

"So you can keep poking at me, and I'll keep poking back, but that doesn't mean I don't understand what you're trying to do. It doesn't mean I don't want you to do it. It means I'm frustrated and you're an easy target. All that rational, factual thought is the rock I can toss my irrational emotion against. And isn't that nice?" She patted his chest. "Maybe we'll even get to the point where we enjoy all the...poking."

He might have risen to the bait. Laughed or coughed or fidgeted at her overt sexual innuendo, but he knew that no matter how smart or worried she was, she was hoping whoever was terrorizing her was a random stranger and his investigation was pointless.

He couldn't let her think that by getting distracted over her purposeful baiting. Because it didn't fit, in Zach's mind. Whoever was doing this *knew* her, and it was very possible Daisy trusted them.

He didn't have to tell her that. He didn't have to poke at her—in any way, shape or form—though he might have wanted to rest his hand over hers…*just* to offer a little comfort.

Instead, he held still. Unearthly still. He kept her gaze, until that easy, flirtatious grin of hers faded.

"Your safety is my primary concern. However, it isn't my job or my aim to cause you undue emotional distress. Therefore, if my method of questioning is problematic, I can easily engage in other avenues of investigation that don't require any…" He desperately wanted to say *poking.* Wanted to smile and make a joke and ease all of that sudden tension out of her.

But maybe it would be better for everyone if there was a little tension that kept them from being too friendly.

"That don't require any avenues of questioning that might feel problematic on either of our ends."

She blinked. "Primary concern," she echoed. "Emotional distress." She shook her head and took a few steps back. The look she gave him was one of suspicion.

Since it wasn't his job to have her *trust* him, such a look couldn't bother him at all.

At all.

"Yeah, I bet you were a *hell* of an undercover agent, Zach," she muttered, but she was gathering herself. She was sharpening all those tools she so effectively used against him—an insightfulness, a confidence that she lashed against him like a weapon. "But news flash. You aren't anymore. Keeping me safe, investigating this thing, you can be regular old Zach Simmons, and it'll be more than enough."

How would that ever be enough?

But he couldn't say that to anyone, could he? So he merely nodded. "Noted."

Then, with absolutely no warning, she stepped forward again. She reached out and touched his face—a gentle caress one might bestow upon a loved one. She held his gaze with a softness he couldn't possibly understand.

Then she did the most incomprehensible thing he had ever in his entire life witnessed or been on the receiving end of.

She lifted onto her toes and pressed her mouth to his.

Chapter Seven

It was wrong. Daisy had been well aware of that when she'd done it. Maybe she'd even done it because it was wrong.

But he'd laid down a challenge—whether he'd known it or not. He'd tried to turn off his personality, his entire essence. He'd tried to use the robot on her and that had only spurred her on to try to short-circuit the robot.

She would never again be told she didn't really mean anything, that she could be easily moved aside and closed off in a room without a second thought. No. Not for a man she'd been married to and not for a man who'd been tasked to keep her safe.

She would show *him*. She would get to him. And what better way to do that than to use her mouth?

His initial stiffness was shock, obviously, but when she didn't move away, changing the angle of the kiss instead, something shuddered through him.

Or maybe something broke inside him. *She'd* broken something inside him, because he didn't just return the kiss—he started one of his own.

Not a challenge or some kind of attempt at one-up-manship. This was…just a kiss, except *just* didn't fit.

It was real. It was Zach. As if a few days under the

same roof could make you feel things for one another. But his mouth crushed against hers like they were long-time lovers, used to the act of kissing enough to have it practiced, but not so much that it didn't *melt*. A warmth that soaked into her bloodstream like alcohol, and a sudden weakness she knew she'd regret at some point.

But there was nothing to regret now with Zach's mouth on hers, his arms drawing her closer so that she was pressed against all that muscle and restraint.

Except there was nothing *restrained* about how he kissed her. It wasn't the explosion of lust she might have expected or understood. It was deeper, stronger. The kind of thing that didn't rock you for a moment, but forever. A kiss she'd remember *forever*.

Maybe because that thought horrified her enough to startle, Zach broke the kiss. He pulled his mouth from hers and nudged her back and away from him. Her knees might have been weak, but she saw a flicker of *something* in his gaze. Some kind of complicated emotion that disappeared before she could get a handle on what he might be feeling.

He fixed her with a gaze, and spoke with utter certainty. "This will never happen again."

She absolutely *hated* the way he said *never*, as if he were God himself and got to decree the way the world worked, the way *she* worked. So she smiled, all razor-edged sweetness. "Zach, don't you know better than to challenge me by now?"

"Do you want to *die*?" he asked with such a bald-faced certainty her insides turned to ice. Immediately.

"I don't know how a kiss is going to kill me," she managed, though she sounded shaken. She *was* shaken.

Even with the ice of fear shifting everything inside her, her limbs felt like jelly.

She could still feel Zach's mouth on hers. He'd wanted her, or was it all another act? A mask?

No, he might be blank now but there was a kind of anger radiating off him. One she didn't understand because it didn't show up in any of the ways anger usually did. No yelling, no fisted hands, no threats or furious gazes. Not even the condescending sigh Jordan had perfected during their short marriage.

"You are in a dangerous situation," Zach said, and his robot voice was back but it frayed along the edges. "Potentially a life-or-death situation, and you're adding…" He sucked in a breath and then slowly let it out. His next words were no more inflected, but they were softer. "Listen to me, as someone who's been in a few life-or-death situations myself. The only thing that happens when you tangle emotion into dangerous situations is catastrophe."

"It was just a kiss," she managed, wincing at how petulant she sounded.

"It was a complication. One you can't afford."

That stoked some of her irritation back to high. She lifted her chin. "Don't presume to tell me what I can afford."

"Are you always so damn difficult?" he demanded, the slightest hint of a snap to his tone.

"If you have to ask that, you haven't been paying attention."

He rolled his eyes, and she had no doubt she was about to be dismissed. Part of her wanted to throw a fit, make herself into more of a nuisance, but her surroundings were too much of a reminder of where her fits and anger and *feelings* had gotten her.

A failed marriage *everyone* got to have a say about. Isolation and loneliness that went deep because so many people were willing to believe the worst about her and think she deserved whatever she got.

Kissing Zach had been a mistake. She felt suddenly sick to her stomach at how much of one. Thoughtless reaction, plain and simple. When would she ever learn?

Mr. Control kissed you, too.

And since when did someone else's culpability matter to her end result?

His phone chimed in his pocket and he pulled it out, clicking a few things. His expression never changed.

But it was something like four in the morning. Who would be contacting him at four in the morning? Only someone with bad news, and since she was his current bad news...

"What is it? Is someone hurt? Is Vaughn—"

He shook his head sharply. "My cousin's wife had her baby."

Zach didn't exactly strike her as the type to receive middle of the night texts about a cousin's baby. "Don't lie to me about—"

He held out the phone and on the screen there was a picture of a red-faced baby wrapped in pink. Underneath the picture the text read:

Amelia Delaney Carson, 6 lbs 11 oz, 20 inches. Batten down the hatches.

It was *odd* that a pang could wallop her out of no-where, when she'd convinced herself that she wasn't even sure she ever wanted babies. That she and Jordan had come to the conclusion they wouldn't rush bringing *children* into the world when they had careers to build.

But her career had already been built, and what she hadn't admitted to herself was that she'd been hoping marriage would be a transition of sorts.

What she'd really wanted out of marrying Jordan had been a home. Full of music and joy and no tours or constant travel. Stability. She'd dreamed of a peaceful life. Not one devoid of performing, of being *Daisy Delaney*, but one where she got to choose when and where to play the role.

Daisy *was* her, and she loved that persona. But it had been her whole childhood and adolescence, and the older she got the more she felt like she'd earned a little time for Lucy Cooper.

Why she thought she'd be able to build that with Jordan, in that distant future he always talked about, was beyond her.

She handed the phone back to Zach. "Cute," she managed to offer. "I like the middle name."

He made an odd face. "It's the mother's last name," he offered, studying her warily.

"A Wyoming Delaney?"

He very nearly *winced*, which she couldn't quite figure though she decided to enjoy his discomfort anyhow.

"Do you know… Wyoming Delaneys?" he asked, failing at the odd casual tone he was clearly trying to maintain. "I mean, Daisy Delaney is a stage name, though."

He seemed a little too desperate to believe it was true. "Yes and no. Why does this weird you out? Worried we're related or something?"

"Carsons and Delaneys aren't related."

"I thought you were a Simmons."

He shook his head. "Anyway. We should try to get some sleep. We'll come up with some things to tell your manager and see if we can't get a lead."

She studied him. There was something weird about his discomfort over the shared name. Since she was more than a little irritated with him, she wanted to poke at it. "My legal name might be Cooper, but my stage name was my grandmother's name before she got married. Daisy Delaney. She was born in some little town in Wyoming. Something with a B? I'd have to text Vaughn. He'd remember. Oh, wait, it was Bent. That's why Daddy always used to wear his hell bound and whiskey *bent* shirt."

"Jesus," Zach muttered, looking so downright horrified she nearly laughed.

"What?"

"Nothing," he said far too quickly.

"Are we close to there?"

"Kind of. Anyway. Bed."

"Maybe I'm related to your cousin's wife. Wouldn't that be a trip?"

"Yeah, a real trip. Goodnight, Daisy."

ZACH WAS TIRED of women. Particularly opinionated ones. Pretty ones. Infuriating ones.

He really didn't need his sister to add to it, but here she was, trying to tell him what to do.

"You have to come," she said, her tone something closer to a demand than he was used to hearing from her. Still, it seemed every day Hilly got a little more

confident, a little more situated to life outside the isolated cabin she'd been raised in.

He stood on the dilapidated porch of the building
that usually gave him such satisfaction. After last night,
not much did.

"I'm in the middle of a job. I can't just leave Daisy
here locked up."

"You could bring her with you."

"Yes, that's genius. She has some kind of stalker
snooping around Bent, so why don't I bring her to the
hospital and potentially endanger every member of our
family." *And hers, apparently.* Because Daisy Delaney's
grandmother was from Bent, Wyoming.

He didn't believe in all the metaphysical nonsense
spouted by his cousins—that the old Carson and Delaney feud had morphed into Carson and Delaney unions
that were meant to be.

He didn't believe in meant-to-be.

"Are you okay?" Hilly asked.

The fact she even suspected he wasn't caused him
to straighten, to remind himself he didn't have *time* for
stupid worries over stupid nonsense.

"Of course I am. But this job is important. And we
haven't found any solid leads. I can't leave her here, and
I can't risk taking her somewhere else."

"She can't possibly still want to be cooped up in
there."

"Hilly."

"I know. I know. Safety. Precautions. But…" She
looked up at the dilapidated building. "How long can
you feasibly keep her in this place? It's going to start
to feel like a prison."

"Better a prison than a coffin, Hilly."

"Why do you have to be so *practical*?" she muttered.

"I believe it's in the job description."

"But your life isn't a job description, Zach. And neither is Daisy's."

Zach didn't know what other string of words would get her to stop this incessant merry-go-round. The flash of something far off in the distance put him on instant alert—enough so he no longer cared about words. Only getting her away.

"We're going to walk to your car. Once you're inside, I want you to call…" He racked his brain for someone who'd be able to help. Cam needed to watch the other guy. Most of his family was at the hospital with Laurel and Grady. Getting the cops involved would be tricky.

"What is it?" Hilly asked, her voice perfectly even, her expression still mildly bemused. But she understood.

He took her by the arm and they strolled back to her car. "Someone's out there."

He needed to make it look like he wasn't living here. He needed to lead the man somewhere else. And somehow, he had to get in contact with Daisy so she knew to stay the hell put.

"I couldn't have been followed. Cam's sitting on the guy." Hilly smiled brightly up at him as if he'd just said something hilarious.

"Well, then we have a second guy."

"All right. I'll call Cam and head his way. We'll come up with something. Don't worry about me. Keep Daisy safe."

"I don't want him following you."

"You can't want him staying here."

It was too close. Too dangerous. Unless he played all his cards right. "Go. Call Cam."

For the first time her cheerful, just-talking-to-my-brother facade faded. "I don't trust that tone, Zach."

"Trust the man who used to be the FBI agent, Hilly."

She hesitated, which cut like a knife even though she had every reason to doubt him. Hadn't Cam almost died because Zach had been too concerned about his brother's welfare to take care of business?

"I don't want you doing something on your own."

"I won't be on my own. I'll have you calling Cam for backup. But I need you to go on the chance he does follow you." Zach was counting on the former, but if it was the latter…

Well, he had a plan for that, too.

Eliminate the threat.

"Drive to Cam. Okay?"

"All right. Only because I can't think of a better plan. Do not do anything on your own, do you hear me?"

"I hear you."

She sighed disgustedly, presumably because she knew *I hear you* didn't mean he agreed to anything she'd said.

She reached out and took his hand, giving it a squeeze. She forced a smile for the sake of whoever might be watching them. "Just be careful. Because if you get hurt, I will have to end you." Her smile was a little more genuine at the end, and she turned and got in her car.

Zach couldn't spare a glance for the house, for Daisy. He stood exactly where he was and watched Hilly's car disappear.

Whoever was out there didn't follow.

Zach didn't head back into the house, and he didn't check on his sidearm or his phone, though he wanted to grab for both.

He didn't know who or what was out there. Someone could be watching, it could be a vehicle left behind as someone approached town on foot. It could be his eyes playing tricks on him, but the back of his neck prickled with foreboding.

Which meant taking every precaution necessary.

He walked down the dusty side of the road as if he didn't have a care in the world. He even forced himself to whistle. He turned down the alley, keeping up the act of unhurried unflappability.

Once he was around the corner, he sprang into action. He'd been keeping his car hidden since that first day, just so no one happened upon it. He popped open the hidden keypad on the garage hidden in the building. He entered his code and moved as quickly as he could, watching for anyone who might pop into view. There was the possibility whoever had been watching was trying to break in the house, but that would take time.

He'd use it.

He drove the car out and closed up the hidden garage. When he pulled out of the alley, there was no sign of anyone trying to get into the house. So he took the opposite way out of his town at a slow pace.

He caught the flash again. This time he could tell it was a small compact car half hidden behind one of the far buildings in town. He couldn't make out the license plate—number or state—only the black fender glinting in the sun.

He kept his breathing in check and drove on, remaining slow and unhurried and looking around, pretending to smile as he enjoyed the beautiful Wyoming landscape.

When the car didn't follow after several minutes, he swore.

They suspected someone besides him was in town, and that was absolutely no good. So he swerved off the road and ditched the car. Since he wasn't being followed, he didn't worry about hiding it. Time was more important.

He ran back the way he'd driven, darting behind buildings on the opposite side of the car and mostly tried to keep out of sight of the car.

He stopped for a second on the opposite side of the road as the house Daisy was in. He stilled and listened.

No motor running, so they wouldn't have a head start on him. But he didn't like their proximity to Daisy. Because he couldn't even be sure someone was in the car. Whoever was watching could have gotten out to start snooping around the house.

He wished he knew how long they'd been there and that he could be sure the car had followed Hilly. Because if they hadn't followed Hilly, they had more information than Zach liked to consider.

Either way, Daisy had a leak and now she was in the direct line of fire.

Which meant Zach had to move. And fast.

Chapter Eight

Daisy impatiently tapped her fingers against the countertop. Where the hell was Zach? It wasn't like him to stay holed up in his room with the door closed, though she supposed he might have had a break in the case or was making phone calls he didn't want her to hear.

Since *she'd* been holed up in her room strumming on the guitar he'd gifted her, it was more than possible he'd left. She couldn't fathom him doing that without telling her, no matter how irritated he was about the kiss.

She smiled to herself. Oh, the moments after hadn't been any fun, but the in-the-moment had been something she'd willingly relive over and over again.

It was the first time in a while where she'd felt…normal. Like Lucy Cooper, or even the Daisy Delaney from years ago when she hadn't had anything normal outside the music. There had been a simplicity in that time.

Of course, there was nothing simple about being either version of herself now, and certainly nothing simple about the aftermath of kissing Zach.

Still, she gave herself permission, here alone, to enjoy the memory of something she could pretend was simple.

The slight creaking sound brought Daisy out of the

memory. She tried to shake away the wiggle of alarm. It was an old house—no matter what improvements Zach had made—of course it creaked.

But in the silence that ensued after, her heart beat harder until it became such a loud thud she knew she wouldn't hear the sound again even if it came from one of the walls.

She looked around, trying to remind herself she was safe. Locked and hidden away.

But someone knows you're nearby.

She marched over to Zach's door. She wouldn't tell him about the noise. She'd just insist he give her some information. Maybe she'd come on to him. Whatever it took so that he was around and making her feel safe.

She knocked. Harder than she should have.

He didn't answer.

Alarm went from a wiggle to a flop. She grabbed the knob and tried to turn it.

Locked.

The wiggles and flops turned into chains that restricted her breathing. "Zach," she croaked. She cursed herself for the nerves, the fear, the total ineffectuality of her voice. She breathed in and out, tried to use some of her old tricks for the occasional bout of stage fright.

"Zach," she repeated, louder this time but more firm. Surely, he'd hear it through the door.

Nothing happened.

She wouldn't panic. Couldn't. She pounded against the door for a while, but then she heard something else—a creak, a moan. Something definitely from the outside. Which meant if there was someone other than Zach outside, they could definitely hear the banging.

But he had to be in there. He was probably trying

to teach her a lesson or something. Scare her so she'd stop hitting on him. Yes, that had to be what this was.

Well, wouldn't he be sorry? She marched to the kitchen, ignoring the way her hands shook and her heart beat a painful, panicked cadence. She grabbed a butter knife and marched back to the door and got to work.

It took longer than she would have preferred as she had to wiggle the knife in the slot, then between the door and the frame. She was shaking at this point. Where *was* he? She thought for sure he'd pop out if she started trying to break into his room. Surely, he'd only locked it to keep her out.

The door finally gave and she swung it open. "Aha!" she yelled, pointing the knife into the room.

But it was empty. She moved around, searching every corner and under the bed, even the closet.

No one. Not a soul.

"Oh, God. God. Zach, if this is some kind of joke or test, I'm over it."

But he didn't appear, and those *noises* kept coming from outside this hellhole disguised as a safe place.

Panic bubbled through her, paralyzing her limbs and squeezing her throat. Her heart beat too hard in her ears and she desperately wanted to scream.

But she'd been through worse than being left alone. Seeing Tom dead was the worst. No one had a right to make it worse than that.

Then something rustled in the closet. Something big. But she'd just been in that closet. How could—

A figure stepped out and she screamed before her brain could accept that it was Zach *miraculously* showing up out of nowhere.

"How did you do that?" she whispered. He wasn't *magic*. There had to be an explanation.

"Tunnel. Shoes."

"Tunnel shoes? What does that—"

"Get some damn shoes, Daisy. Purse if it's handy. Ten seconds." Without further explanation he strode out of the room and into the kitchen. She scurried after him but stopped short when he pulled two guns out of the top cabinet above the refrigerator while she only stared.

Until he gave her a sharp look.

"Move," he ordered, snapping her out of her shock.

She had to move. Questions were clearly for later when he wasn't grabbing extra guns. She hurried into her room, shoved her feet into tennis shoes and looked around for her purse. Ten seconds. She had way less than ten seconds now and she was not the neatest person on the planet.

But she caught a glimpse of the strap under her duffel bag and lunged for it, tugged it from the haphazardly spilled-out bag and ran back to Zach. He held a laptop across one arm while he typed with the other, a huge backpack strapped over his back.

When she peered over his shoulder at the screen of the laptop—which had been full of pictures of the ghost town they were in—he snapped it shut. "The front is the best option. Follow me. *Stick* to me. Do whatever I say without question and everything will be fine. If something happens to me, no matter what, you run. You understand me?"

"Zach. I don't understand *anything*."

"We'll figure it out when we're safe." He took her by the hand and pulled her to the door.

Even as a million questions assaulted her, she understood Zach Simmons was not a man to overreact. If he wanted them to run, she'd run.

He pulled her out into the first room that looked as dilapidated as the outside. "Lock the locks," he said, handing her a key chain with three keys on it. They weren't labeled, but she didn't ask which one was for which—she just kept trying till she had all three locks locked.

He was peering at something through the wall. "See that picture frame on the ground?"

She looked down. There was an old, battered picture frame with a ripped piece of paper inside. "Uh, yeah."

"Hang it up on that rusty nail."

She did so, and blinked as it perfectly hid the key holes from view.

"Now, come hold my hand again."

She wanted to make a joke about hitting on her, but the words stuck in her throat. They were running, and that couldn't be good.

So she slid her hand into his and let him pull her along. He slid out the door, and she followed suit. He didn't lock this door, instead left a rusty-looking padlock hanging off the handle.

His gaze swept everywhere, and then he gave her hand a squeeze. "Now we run. I'm not going to be able to hold your hand without whacking you with the bag, so you'll just have to follow me. If you can't keep up—"

"I'll keep up." No matter what.

He nodded firmly. "Good. All right. Let's go."

He moved across the dusty road, and it was only then she realized he held the closed laptop in one hand and a gun in another. Still, she followed him, behind one building, and then through the alley between two even worse-off ones. Caved-in roofs, fire-scorched walls.

He reached the small ramshackle building at the end of the road and handed off his laptop to her while hanging on to his gun. With his free hand, he reached through a jagged break in the glass window of the back door, fiddling around until the door popped open.

He slowly pulled his arm out, and then opened the door just as slowly. It took her a minute to realize he was trying to mitigate the squeaking noise that echoed through the air as he opened it. When the opening was big enough, he gestured her inside.

Trying not to balk at the dark, or the spiderwebs, she stepped into the dank, smelly interior. Zach followed suit, pulling the door closed behind him before fishing a flashlight out of his pack.

He led her farther inside and she kept waiting for the nice part—the part that had been redone inside all the dilapidation.

But this one had no new pretty interior. No working kitchen. It was abandoned and untouched for years. "We're going to stay…here?"

Zach had put his pack on the floor and took his laptop back without a word. She was sure he wasn't paying any attention to her at all as he worked furiously.

When he finally spoke, she fairly jumped with adrenaline.

"*You're* going to stay here. I'm going to figure out what the hell is going on. You know how to shoot a gun?"

She blinked at the weapon he held out to her. Thanks to her brother, she'd had a few shooting lessons. She was even somewhat familiar with the kind Zach held out to her.

She nodded, and he handed the gun over.

"Anyone comes in here that isn't me or Cam, or doesn't say the code word *feud*, you shoot. Understood?"

She swallowed, and managed another nod.

With that, he got to his feet, strapped multiple guns to his person and strode for the door.

ZACH SLID OUT of the building, making sure no one was around to see him. It was painful to leave Daisy wide-eyed, scared and alone, but he couldn't hole up with her and hope the guys went away.

He'd learned, over and over again, that waiting in safety often caused more problems than it solved. Sometimes you had to act to keep people safe.

He hurried behind the buildings, keeping his body out of sight from as many angles as possible.

From what he'd been able to tell with his video surveillance, there were two men. One who'd been poking around the house, and the one who'd stayed in the car—presumably ready to drive off.

It turned his stomach to think he was ready to drive off with Daisy. Even more so that *two* men were here.

It had to be the manager leaking information to someone, whether maliciously or with an accidental slip to someone. He didn't have time to figure out the pattern, though. He had to stop those men before they had a chance to hurt Daisy.

He moved into a position where he knew he'd be able to see the driver of the car with minimal chance of being detected. He angled his body and his head, and managed to make out the car.

The driver was no longer in it, so Zach moved forward—until he saw both of them standing in front of the car, discussing something.

They had their backs to him, so descriptions would be hard, but it wouldn't matter. These weren't the masterminds trying to get to Daisy. Everything about them screamed hired muscle.

Which, again, in Zach's mind meant not a crazed fan, but someone with a personal connection. And someone with money.

Like Jordan Jones.

And if it *was* Jordan, he'd have endless funds to keep sending people just like this.

Zach moved back behind the building. Taking them out was only a temporary solution. More would come in their place. But if he could question them, he might be able to glean enough information to make the connection.

The only question was how to immobilize the threat of two men with guns who wanted the woman he was trying to protect.

He needed them to separate, and even then it would be risky. But it would be a risk he'd have to take. He examined the building he was hiding in. He needed somewhere he could isolate one man, without getting trapped by both.

He needed to get one headed in the other direction. He pulled the phone out of his pocket and pulled up the app he used to control security in the safe house. He poked around until he came up with an idea.

Have the back door alarm on the house go off. Once they started heading over, he'd make enough noise they'd feel like one of them had to come his way.

It took a few minutes—first the men headed toward the siren, alert and with hands on their weapons. Zach kicked at a board next to him, the hard crack of impact then splitting wood loud enough to hopefully get one's attention.

He couldn't watch for their approach. Instead, he had to stay hidden and hope he was about to fight only one man.

He saw the gun first and immediately moved. He kicked the gun out of the man's hand. The man leaped forward, but Zach had better vision and grabbed him from behind. Zach managed to get an arm around the other man's throat. Zach was taller, though the man was thicker.

"Who are you?" Zach demanded in a whisper as the man struggled against him.

The man didn't answer, and no one came to his rescue. Elsewhere, the alarm continued to beep, which was a good sound cover for the fight Zach was about to have here.

"Who sent you?" Zach asked, tightening his grip and dodging the man's attempt at backward blows.

The response was only a raspy laugh as he twisted and nearly got free before Zach strengthened the choke hold.

They grappled, but Zach kept the choke hold. He asked a few more questions, knowing he wouldn't get an answer but hoping he might get *something* that would ID the man or give him a hint.

Over the sound of his alarm, he heard something else. Something just as shrill. Sirens in the distance. It was unlikely to be coincidence that sirens were closing in on the empty ghost town. Cam and Hilly must have decided to call the cops. Hell. Zach sure hoped they'd sent more than one because he had no doubt that the other guy was now on his way back.

"You think the cops will help you? Or her, for that matter?" the man rasped.

"Guess we'll find out." Zach managed to jerk one of the man's arms behind his back, but it left him open to an elbow to the gut. His grip loosened just enough to have the man slip out of his grasp.

The man tried to take off on a run, but Zach lunged, tackling him to the ground. They tussled, landing blows. The other man was bigger but Zach figured he could hold his own until the cop car actually got here.

The next blow rattled his cage pretty good, so much so that he thought he heard a dog bark and growl.

But then there really was a dog, growling and leaping. Zach had a moment of fear before he recognized the dog, and it jumped at his attacker. The man screamed, and Zach managed to wrangle himself free of his grasp.

A cop appeared, gun held and trained on the man on the ground—the man who was clearly scared to death as the dog growled and snapped right next to his face.

"Free. Sit," Hilly's voice called.

The dog stopped growling, planted its butt on the ground and wagged its tail before turning his head toward Zach.

"Thanks for the assist." He gave the dog a rubdown, wincing only a little as his face throbbed. He glanced up as Hilly, who'd given her dog the command, came running. He was a little surprised when she kneeled next to him instead of her dog, Free.

"You're bleeding." She ran her hands over him as if checking for breaks or injuries, but he held her off.

"It's just a split lip. Please tell me Cam is here and you didn't try to white knight this yourself."

"It wasn't just me. I had Free. Plus the cops."

Zach swore, but he couldn't muster up much heat behind it. "I've got to get to Daisy." He glanced at the Bent County Sheriff's Deputy who was handcuffing the man who'd attacked him. Deputy Keenland efficiently did the job and read the man his rights.

"There's another one," Zach offered.

"We've already got him," the cop replied.

"I want to talk to them."

Keenland gave him a raised eyebrow. "We'll be transporting them to the station, where *we'll* question them. We'll take your report, as well."

He didn't have time for this. He glanced at Hilly. He didn't even have to ask. She nodded.

"Far building on this side," he said quietly so Keenland, busy pulling the arrested man to his feet, wouldn't hear.

He'd have to entrust Daisy to Hilly while he took care of this. It bugged him, but it had to be done. He pulled out his phone and turned off the security so Hilly could get into his apps, and then handed her his phone and his keys to the building.

"Be careful." They all needed to be a hell of a lot more careful.

Chapter Nine

Back in the fake nice house inside an outside dilapidated old house, Daisy couldn't find any of the calm or resignation she'd had in the days leading up to this.

Someone had found her here. Maybe they hadn't gotten to her, but they'd tried. In this place that was supposed to be a secret from everyone.

Which meant someone she loved and trusted was either out to hurt her, or close enough to someone who did to slip the information to them.

God, her head hurt. Almost as much as her heart as she went back over so many interactions.

Could Jaime be the bad link? She didn't know him that well, even if he was Vaughn's brother-in-law. He could have told anyone, couldn't he? But Zach trusted him. Surely, Zach would know…

Except Zach wanted her to believe Stacy was responsible. Could her manager harbor some secret hatred of her? Was it as simple, and heartbreaking, as that?

Or was it deeper, messier, more complicated?

Worse than the riot of emotions and fear and questions pulsing inside her, Cam and Hilly were being obnoxiously and carefully tight-lipped about what exactly had gone down after Zach had left her in the abandoned house.

Only that he'd be back soon to explain everything. But time kept ticking by as she sat at the table, watching Cam and Hilly.

Which was actually the worst part of all. Hilly and Cam moved around the kitchen and common area acting like the perfect unit. A team. A partnership.

She felt so completely alone. The separation of the past few years echoing inside her like she'd been emptied out—of love and companionship and hope. There was only fear left.

She rested her forehead on the table and did everything she could to keep from crying. No one was going to see her cry. Nope. She would brazen through this like she'd brazened through everything else in her life.

Maybe she was tired. Maybe she wanted *normal* for a little bit. Maybe she wanted a little house in the country and a nice man she could trust to build a family with.

And maybe Daisy Delaney and Lucy Cooper weren't made for those things.

Her phone chimed and she nearly fell over lunging for it on the table. Surely, it would have to be Zach. Everyone else had stopped calling and texting and surely—

She stared at the text message from Jordan. The first sentence made her uneasy, so she clicked it to read the whole thing.

I just heard you're out of town for a few days. Someone told me it might be rehab. I really hope you get the help you need. Peace to you.

Peace. Peace? Anger surged through her, and while some of it was prompted by all the fear and things out of her control right now, most of it was prompted by that *ridiculous* send-off.

Peace to you.

Peace.

She'd like to give him some peace. Right up his—

"Is everything okay?" Hilly asked gently, but with concern.

Daisy smiled up at Hilly, though she knew it came out too sharp when Hilly took a step back. "Yes. Just a text from an annoying…acquaintance. Apparently, the rumor is I'm in rehab." She wanted to bash the phone into little bits. "How do I respond to a text like that?"

"You don't," Cam said in a voice that reminded Daisy of Zach.

Where *was* he?

"You'll have to excuse me if I don't want the world thinking I'm in rehab. My reputation is in enough tatters."

"But if people think you're in rehab, they won't think you're *here*," Cam replied reasonably. Apparently, whatever trouble had happened had cured him of his slight starstruck nature. Or he was just getting used to her.

Daisy couldn't say she cared for it. "Whoever is after me already knows I'm here."

"But the fewer people who know, the fewer people your stalker can use to get to you."

It was so reasonable, really unarguable, and now she wanted to bash her phone against Cam. She was tired of being reasonable in all these impossible situations. She wanted to act out. She wanted to *fight*.

She wanted to tell Jordan to go jump off a cliff. Or

write a song about lighting all his prized possessions on fire.

One by one.

But Cam was right and Daisy's only choice was sitting here, not responding, not reacting. Just waiting for someone to succeed in hurting her.

"Did Zach okay the cell phone use?" Cam asked, his attempt at casual almost fooling her into thinking it was a generic question.

"Yes, thank you very much. He did something to my phone to block traces or something. But he wanted me to be able to email my agent from my phone and a few other things. I don't know. Techie stuff. But it's perfectly Zach-approved." Because everything in her life now suddenly was Zach-approved.

Except herself. She could still rile him up to the best of her ability. Assuming he came back and didn't abandon her here.

She closed her eyes, nearly giving in to tears again. Oh, God. That was what she was *really* afraid of. Not that someone had found her, but now that they had, Zach would leave her.

Hilly pushed a mug and plate at her.

"Drink some tea. And eat some cookies."

"You Simmonses and your ungodly sugar addiction." An unexpected lump formed in her throat. "Where *is* he?" she asked, hating that the emotion leaked out in her scratchy voice.

Hilly patted her hand. "He's safe, and he'll be back soon."

She didn't need him to come back. She didn't *need* Zach Simmons. At *all*. He was a bodyguard, more or less.

But God, she wanted him here pushing cookies on

her, telling her what the next step would be, and reassuring her he'd take care of everything.

"FIVE MINUTES."

The deputy didn't move, didn't even spare him another condescending look. "We've taken your statement, Mr. Simmons. You're free to leave."

"I need five minutes. Hell, I'll settle for two questions."

"Simmons."

Zach turned around and sighed. Detective Thomas Hart stood, plain-clothed, in the doorway, and Zach knew he was officially done.

He followed Hart out of the building and into the parking lot. It was dark now, and Zach wasn't all that sure he knew how much time had passed. But he hadn't gotten what he wanted yet.

"There has to be something you can tell me."

"There isn't. Sincerely. He's not giving us answers."

"I want a name, Hart. A last known address."

Hart turned, crossed his arms over his chest. "You won't get one. Stop harassing the deputies. Go home. Deal with whatever business you've got going down on your own."

"I can hack into your system in five seconds flat," Zach returned disgustedly.

Hart held up a finger. "First, I didn't hear you say that. Second, be my guest. Because I can't give you that information. Zach, you know as well as I do, whatever they're after—however it connects to your mysterious business—these guys are hired muscle. They're not going to tell you or me anything you really need to know."

"But you'll investigate who's paying them."

"If it's pertinent."

Zach swore. "You're killing me."

"Hey, it's my day off. You're killing *me*. The only reason McCarthy called me is because he knows we're friends. You better know you'd have been arrested for disturbing the peace and interfering with an ongoing investigation if not for your connection to Laurel."

"I'm a Carson. Doesn't that mean your kind is always tossing mine in jail for no reason?"

"No real Carson was ever an FBI agent, that I can tell you." At Zach's scowl, Hart grinned. "Want to go play darts? Take your mind off it so you can work out the knots?"

Part of him did. It was something he and Hart did often when Hart was stuck on a difficult case and needed something mindless to do. Maybe it was exactly what Zach needed. Maybe he could get somewhere on this whole mess if he just separated himself from it for an hour or so.

But Daisy was back there and something had to be done. She couldn't spend the night there. Even with these two guys locked up, more would be coming. More might be on their way, and while Zach could lock them up in that building pretty tightly—anything could happen.

Damn, but he needed some answers. "Can't. Got work."

Hart nodded. "I'll leave you to it. Just leave the deputies alone."

"You going to pass along whatever information you find out?"

"Night, Simmons," Hart said, opening his car door and sliding inside.

Zach sighed but he dug his keys out of his pocket and walked to his car. He *could* keep pounding at the deputies, but they wouldn't budge. And the more he did, the less chance he had of sneaking some information out of Hart later.

He didn't have time for either, though. Action was required. Cam wouldn't approve of the idea forming, which meant Zach would need to be especially sneaky.

He drove back to the house, watching for tails, taking the long, winding way and missing the turn off the highway twice and doubling back before he was satisfied no one had followed him.

He parked his car back in the hidden garage, though he wondered if it should be easier to access.

Well, not if he could get his plan wheels turning ASAP. He'd need to get rid of Cam and Hilly first.

He texted Cam that he was disengaging the security from the outside and coming in. Then set about to do just that. When he finally stepped into the common room, Daisy jumped to her feet from where she'd been seated at the table.

"Oh, my God. You're hurt."

It startled him, the gentleness mixed with horror in her tone. Like she cared. She even rushed over to him and touched the corner of his mouth, which was a little swollen from the elbow he'd gotten there.

"I'm all right," he managed, his voice rusty. "Just a tussle." He ste/pped away from her too soft and too comforting hand. "I need to get the security systems—"

"I'll get them running," Cam said, holding up Zach's phone. He went to work and Zach turned back to Daisy.

She looked pale. Exhausted.

"Thanks for your help, guys, but you should head home," he said to Cam and Hilly, keeping his voice neutral. "We'll all sleep and reassess in the morning."

Cam studied him, and Zach did his best to look blank. Cam couldn't know what he was planning. Not yet.

Cam handed the phone back and looked at Hilly. Something passed between them because Hilly nodded.

He'd never been able to communicate with anyone like that, and he wasn't sure if that was just the nature of never having been in a serious, committed relationship the way Cam and Hilly were, or some fundamental lack inside him.

Right now was certainly not the time to wonder about it.

"Show him the text message," Hilly said, laying a comforting arm on Daisy's shoulder before she passed by.

"What text message?" Zach demanded.

Daisy glared at Hilly, but Hilly and Cam slid out the door, clearly leaving Zach to handle it.

"Daisy. Show me the text message."

"It's nothing," she replied, but she picked up her phone, tapped a few things, then slid it his way. "Just Jordan being oh so very concerned."

Zach read the text message, scowled at the screen. "Where did he hear you're out of town?"

"Zach. I'm sure any number of people are saying that about me since I'm not home or touring or anything else."

But Zach didn't like it. For a wide variety of reasons he'd parse later, once he got his plan off the ground.

"Does Jordan often contact you?" If this was out of the blue, it would give some credence to Jordan being involved.

"Not often. But a text message isn't out of the norm. Things like 'I'll be at x place on y date. I'd appreciate a lack of a scene.'"

Zach's mouth quirked, though he knew it shouldn't amuse him. "Let me guess. You caused three scenes."

She grinned at him, eyes sparkling. "How'd you know?" But she sighed. "I don't let anyone tell me what to do, most especially some *man* who thinks he has a right when he gave that up. And trust me, I want nothing more right now than to show up at his door drunk as a skunk. But I've learned not to give in to the impulse *every* time—because half the time it's a publicity stunt. He wants a scene from me so he can play the injured, horrified party."

A publicity stunt. "He wants to ruin you," Zach said flatly.

"He wants to make me look bad. I think there's a difference." She shrugged jerkily, pretending it didn't bother her. But he could see the bother written all over her tense posture and the way she gripped the phone. "The more I think about it, the more I can't pin him for this. He's too much of a narcissist. Nothing he does to me is trying to ruin me—he's just trying to help himself."

But a dead ex-wife could be helping himself, making him a sympathetic figure once again. And being a narcissist didn't make a person less likely to exact revenge if they felt they'd been wronged.

But he didn't need to argue with her or convince her of anything. Jordan was as high on his suspect list as her manager. He'd find out the truth and she'd deal with that one truth, instead of all the possible ones.

Weary, aching body, Zach lowered himself into one of the kitchen chairs. "Then your response should really stick it to him."

She looked at him sideways. "Go on."

"Verbal judo."

"What's verbal judo?"

"I won't give you the whole spiel, but basically it's a way of talking to people that neutralizes a confrontation."

"I don't want to neutralize it. I want to explode it."

"I know you do, sweetheart, but we're trying to give you a low profile."

"He expects me to explode. Shouldn't I give him what he expects? Just to keep him from looking too deeply into things? Or maybe even salvage some piece of my reputation."

Since Zach didn't believe Jordan was all that ignorant of what was going on, he merely shrugged. "You could, but he knows *something* is up. This is his version of fishing. So instead of giving him the reaction he wants, drive him crazy. Just say thank you for your concern. It gives away nothing. It harbors no ill will, and it admits no guilt. It'll probably eat him alive since he was clearly fishing for a reaction. It's *that* part I don't trust." Or the timing—reaching out just as two people trying to get to Daisy were taken into custody by police. Pretending he thought she was in rehab. Zach wasn't going to trust any coincidences.

Daisy stared at her phone, contemplating. "You really think a response like that will eat him alive?"

"He knows you, right? Understands that you'll do

the opposite of what he says, understands that any attempt at peace offerings will end with fiery explosions. So you don't give him what he wants."

"You make me sound like a shrew."

"No, I'm trying to make him sound like a jerk. Because he could just not. He doesn't need to reach out, doesn't need to poke at you. He could leave you be. But he's trying to piss you off, and so much worse than that, he's doing it under the guise of concern. Don't give him the satisfaction, because trust me, he's getting some satisfaction over that or he wouldn't be reaching out."

She contemplated her phone, then she picked it up and began to type.

Thanks for your concern!

She angled the screen toward him. "Is the exclamation point too much?"

"I think it works."

"Send," she said, tapping the screen with a flourish. Then she sighed and stared at him, her eyes lingering on the split lip and the bruising along his jaw. "I thought you were convinced Stacy was the culprit."

"I'm not convinced anyone is the culprit. We're looking into any possibility." And they needed to find them sooner or later.

He opened his mouth to tell her the rest of his plan, but she moved over to him and touched the part of his cheek that throbbed. Everything inside him tangled tight. She studied him, her fingers gently tracing over the line of his bruised jaw.

If he'd known what to expect, he might have been able to ward it off, but her gentleness undid him. Mag-

netized him. He couldn't remember anyone… His life
was taking care of people, finding out the truth, saving
people when he could.

No one ever asked if it was a burden. He'd never
wanted or needed anyone to comfort that burden. It
was his.

But Daisy's touching him was being given a gift
so perfect, he wouldn't have ever thought to ask for it.

She slid into his lap. He held himself still, even if
with all that stillness a desperate desire rioted inside
him. It wasn't like the other night, her trying to prove
something, defuse something, or just forget her circumstances.

There was a sweetness to this, even as close as their
bodies were. Even though she made him want her in
totally unsweet ways. She was gentle. She was…caring.

"Daisy." It was a croak, but he didn't have the wherewithal to feel self-conscious over it.

"Shh." She pressed her mouth to the side of his, just
the gentlest, featherlight brush. "Someone's got to kiss
the hurts."

A breath shuddered out of him, and even though it
was the absolute last thing he should do, he closed his
eyes as she gently kissed all along the bruised portion
of his jaw. It was comfort and it was relief, and he had
no business taking it from her when he was supposed
to be keeping her safe.

Safe. Not hiding in abandoned buildings while someone prowled *this close* to being able to touch her.

No, today he'd failed. There could be no more failure. Only action.

"We don't have time for this." Which wasn't precisely true, but it was a hell of an excuse because his willpower was fading.

"I think we have all the time in the world," she replied, pressing her mouth to his neck.

His vision nearly grayed before he had a chance to slide her off his lap. Dear *Lord*, was that hard to do. Harder to let her go after he nudged her back a pace.

But he did it. "Pack your bags, Daisy. We're headed to Nashville."

Chapter Ten

Daisy felt…strange leaving Zach's little ghost town. Like she'd miss it. Which was crazy since she'd been cooped up in that odd little house, not out enjoying the blue sky or mountains in the distance or in this very early morning's case, the stars out in their full and utter splendor.

Nothing had been good here, and yet she didn't want to leave. Didn't want to face Nashville or the people she knew, even with Zach at her side.

Because facing meant accepting that someone she loved and trusted might be behind this.

But she didn't argue. She'd packed her bags like Zach had said. She'd enjoyed maybe thirty seconds of looking up at the vast universe before Zach had whisked her into his car and started the drive.

He'd said nothing about the kisses, but for a few moments he'd relaxed under her.

She smiled a little to herself. Well, not *all* of him had relaxed.

She gave him a sideways glance. He was driving to some tiny independent airport in some other part of middle of nowhere Wyoming, where they'd fly in some tiny little plane to a few airports all the way to Nashville.

Nashville. It wasn't home, because she didn't particularly feel like she *had* a home. She'd been touring since she could remember, only ever staying with Mom and Vaughn for bits of time. As an adult she'd bought a house in Nashville, but she'd sold it when she'd married Jordan.

Then they'd sold the house they'd bought together. The house she'd thought she'd start a family in, have a life in.

"You know, I don't have a place in Nashville," she said after a while.

"I do."

"You have a place in Nashville?" she asked incredulously. She'd believed he knew enough people to take a small plane halfway across the country, but this seemed far-fetched. And yet, she trusted him implicitly, regardless of what seemed believable.

"I know people, Daisy. I found us a safe place to stay."

She kept staring at him, because something about the split lip and the bruising on his face—even with the dark five-o'clock shadow over it, made her feel safe even when she knew she wasn't.

But Zach would protect her, no matter the circumstances. Even though she knew Zach was human and that anyone could reach her if they wanted to badly enough, someone would fight to keep her safe.

Take blows. Give blows. For her.

He could push her away or insist they didn't have time for more than a kiss, but one thing Daisy knew was that Zach wasn't stoic or unaffected. He was worried about getting emotionally invested because he was already on his way to getting emotionally invested.

The thought cheered her enough that she dozed off, until Zack was waking her up with her real name again.

"Sleepy you doesn't seem to answer to the name Daisy," he offered, his voice rough with exhaustion and yet his lips curved.

"That's because Daisy Delaney doesn't sleep."

"All right, Lucy Cooper. You should really talk to that alter ego of yours, because you could both use some sleep." He gave her head a little pat and then slid out of the car.

She could only stare after him. There was something about the way he said her given name. It slithered through her, a not totally comfortable sensation—because it was too big for her skin. It made her heart swell and her eyes sting.

Jordan had never called her Lucy, even after she'd asked him to. Because she didn't want to be Daisy Delaney to her *family*. She'd wanted to separate it all out.

He hadn't understood.

Zack probably didn't, either, but he still used her name as though it didn't matter what he called her— she was the same. Not two identities fighting for space.

He opened the passenger door and looked at her expectantly. Right. She was supposed to get out of the car, not get teary over something so stupid.

"You haven't told me what the plan is," she said as she got out of the car. He grabbed their bags out of the trunk and headed for a squat little building.

The sun had risen, but it was still pearly morning light. And they had a long way to go to reach Nashville.

"Well, first we'll go see your manager."

"Together?"

He shrugged. "I don't see why not. You'll just tell people I'm your bodyguard." He walked to the building and knocked on the door, waiting for an answer.

When a scrawny young man answered he greeted Zach by name. They conversed for a while and then the young man led them through the office and out a back door.

Daisy felt like she was in a dream, complete with a tiny plane that made her breath catch in her lungs.

It didn't look safe, and if she'd been with anyone else she would have brought that up. But Zach would never take risks with her—that she knew. It had to be safe.

For a tin can hurtling through the air.

Zach helped her up the stairs and gave her hand a squeeze. "Afraid of flying?" he asked empathetically.

"I never have been before." She looked around the tiny cabin. "This plane changes things a bit."

"We'll be fine," Zach assured, and she was sure he thought so. She wasn't sure he was *right*, but she knew he believed he was. He gestured her into a seat and she took it.

"Why are we going to Nashville now?" Because if he talked maybe she wouldn't feel like running screaming in the opposite direction.

"Waiting isn't working. We're not getting closer—the trouble is only getting closer to you, and without warning. So we go straight to the potential leaks. We ferret them out. Besides, this way the rehab rumor can't really get anywhere."

He fastened her seat belt for her as she only stared, that same feeling from before—heart too big, skin too small.

She swallowed, trying to sound normal or just *feel* normal. "What does my reputation matter?"

"Jordan's taken enough from you, and whoever is behind this has taken even more. You don't need to give them pieces of yourself, too. We'll nip any rumors in the bud, and we'll find out the leak in one fell swoop."

No one had ever cared how many pieces she gave of herself as long as they got the pieces they wanted. Even Vaughn, for all his wonderful qualities, didn't understand her enough to do more than worry about her safety.

So she did the only thing she could think to do. She leaned over and pressed her mouth to his. She smiled against his mouth when he kissed her back for a brief second, then stiffened and eased her away.

Oh, he wanted her. She thought he might even *like* her.

"You have to stop doing that," he said sternly.

She did it again, a loud smack of a kiss, though this time he was tight-lipped and less than amused. Still, she flashed him a grin. "Stop kissing me back and maybe I will."

He didn't say anything to that, which made her settle back into her seat with a smile.

SHUTTLING ON AND off planes was exhausting. Add to that, Zach hadn't slept—not since the night before. But he drove the rental car through Nashville to the little farmhouse on the outskirts that one of his law-enforcement friends used as a safe house sometimes.

Daisy would like it. Somehow, he knew that. But he hadn't been prepared for the way her delight wound through him.

"Oh, my God! A chicken coop!" She jumped out of the car and practically ran over to it, leaning over the fence around the fancy little coop. He didn't see any chickens, but the gray, cloudy skies were spitting out a drizzle that probably kept the animals safe in shelter.

"My friend says there's a list of chores to do, if you're into that kind of thing."

She turned to look at him, eyes bright and smile wide. "Are you kidding? Why didn't you bring me *here* in the first place?"

He didn't mention it had been because he didn't trust most of the people in Nashville who had any connection to her. Her brother had wanted to isolate her to keep her safe.

It had been a failure of a plan—Zach's own fault for not seeing the holes in it.

He shook that failure off—had to until the job was done—and focused on the new plan. "I do want you to give your manager a call and tell her you're planning to come into town tomorrow. Tell her you want a meeting, morning or afternoon doesn't matter, but I want her to believe you're leaving in the evening."

"And are we keeping this meeting?"

"Of course."

Some of her simple joy over the chicken coop had faded, but she didn't argue with him. Didn't try to tell him for the hundredth time she trusted her manager. "And…"

She trailed off, turning her gaze back to the chickens. He couldn't read her feelings from just looking at her back, but he thought the fact she was hiding her face told him enough to gather she wasn't happy.

"You'll be with me, right?"

"You aren't going any damn where without me, sweetheart."

She turned to face him again, lifting an eyebrow. "Oh, is that so?"

"You're not going to be contrary over that. Not right now. This isn't about telling you what to do. It's about keeping you safe. You and me are stuck like glue."

She smiled sweetly—which should have been his first clue something was off, but he was dead on his feet. She sauntered over to him, chickens forgotten. She reached out, and he stiffened against the touch.

Not that it didn't shudder through him as she playfully walked her fingers up his chest. He tried to ward it off, but then she looked up at him under her lashes.

"Like glue? What kind of sleeping arrangements were you planning?"

Lust jolted through him so painfully it was a wonder he didn't simply keel over. Or give up...and in to her.

But he wouldn't. He couldn't. "We'll figure it out inside."

"Don't tease, Zach." She sighed heavily, lifting her palm to his cheek.

It was becoming too common, too much of a want to have her hands on him. Still, he couldn't move away, could barely hold himself back from leaning in.

"You need to sleep."

"Safety first."

She looked around the picturesque yard. Even with the drizzle falling, it had a cheerful quality to it. Green grass and trees, red chicken coop and barn bright and clean in the rain. It was the complete opposite to the desolate, decaying place he'd originally taken her to.

It felt weirdly symbolic, only he was so exhausted he didn't know if it was good or bad. He ushered her inside with the security information his friend had given him. He dropped the bags and followed the email instructions on how to set all the security measures for the house.

"What's the best way for you to contact your manager?"

She eyed him and he had to stifle a yawn, had to work to keep his eyes open.

"In this case I think I need to call her. She'll have to rearrange her schedule to see me, I'm sure. She'll do it, she'll want to, but we'll have to work out the when and where."

"Okay. So, you'll call and set up a meeting." There'd be security to worry about—if the leak was through her manager's office someone would know she was there and accessible. "Make sure she doesn't think you're getting in until tomorrow, and thinks you're leaving in the evening."

"Okay. Can I make the call in private or do you need to listen in and make sure I'm a good girl who follows instructions?"

He wasn't sure what that edge in her tone meant, so he decided to ignore it. He made sure he held her gaze and didn't yawn, though one was threatening. "I trust you. There are three bedrooms. Take your pick. Just give me the time when you're done."

She stared back at him for a few humming seconds. He thought about the plane, when she'd kissed him and he'd been stupid enough to kiss her back.

Even though intellectually he knew it was a failure

to get emotionally tangled with her, that it would put her in danger—put them both in danger. Though he never forgot how emotional entanglements had almost caused so much loss last year, he couldn't seem to help it. He was emotionally tangled.

There had to be a way to block it off. He knew better now. His brother was in a psych ward, and Cam had almost died. There were *costs* to an emotional connection—and if he couldn't control the connection, he had to find a way to keep it separate and make sure it didn't affect the case.

He knew better now, didn't he?

"You don't want a play-by-play of the phone conversation?" she asked after a while.

"The time will be enough." Because he had to focus on the facts of the case. The facts of what it would take to protect her. Enough with his precious patterns and trying to understand her and her life. He had to focus on the *facts*.

If he'd pulled her into more danger by bringing her closer to her stalker, he didn't have room for anything else.

Eventually, she nodded, picked her bag up off the floor and went in search of a room.

Zach picked up his own bag and pulled out his laptop. Before he could fall into blissful sleep, he had some work to do.

He'd been ignoring his phone for most of their travel, so he turned that on while he booted up his computer.

He winced a little at the ping of voice mails and text messages that sounded a few times. Yeah, a couple of people weren't too happy with him or his disappearing act.

He didn't bother to read all the text messages, and he deleted all the voice mails from Cam and Hilly without listening. But he did read the most recent text from Cam.

I hope you know what you're doing, because your client—you know, the guy paying us—isn't too thrilled.

So Zach would tell Daisy to contact her brother. Except, Texas Ranger or not, couldn't the leak just as easily be on his side?

Better to play this out as secretly as possible even if it meant everyone was angry with him. He'd suffer some ire to keep Daisy as safe as possible, and the best way to keep her safe was to test every possible leak in isolation.

So he didn't respond to Cam's text and went ahead and turned his phone back off. He needed to outline a plan for tomorrow.

He'd just close his eyes for a second, recalibrate the plan in his head, then formalize his hazy plan into something more specific. More…something.

The next thing he knew, someone was taking his hand. "Come on, sleeping beauty," an amused voice said.

He couldn't manage to open his eyes, but he was being pulled to his feet. Everything seemed kind of dim and ethereal. It was probably a dream.

Yes, he was dreaming Daisy was taking him somewhere, nudging him onto a bed, slipping the shoes off his feet.

He really was dreaming that after a while she curled up next to him, rested her hand on his heart and brushed a kiss across his cheek.

And since it was a dream, he let himself relax into it. Place his hand over hers, pull her curled-up body closer to his and settle into sleep.

Chapter Eleven

Daisy wasn't sure what had compelled her to climb into bed next to Zach. He wouldn't appreciate it when he woke up. But she felt safer here, nuzzled against him, than anywhere else.

Talking to Stacy had been an exercise in torture. Daisy had wanted to tell her friend what was really going on, but all she'd been able to do was vaguely apologize for disappearing and ask for a private meeting, trying to evade Stacy's questions.

Daisy had read into every pause, every question. Was Stacy the one who wished her harm? Would this meeting end up being dangerous?

She swallowed against the lump in her throat and focused on Zach. The room was dark, but the glow from a bedside alarm clock was enough to illuminate his profile. His big hand over hers.

She felt safe with Zach. Not just the whole "in danger with a security expert and former FBI watching out for her" thing, but she felt…emotionally safe with him. Which was weird. She didn't even feel that with Vaughn or Mom. She felt she had to be careful around them, because she'd followed Dad's footsteps and they hadn't approved—even if they loved her, they didn't *understand* her.

She wasn't certain Zach did, but so far it sure felt that way.

And are you really stupid enough to think Zach is different than all the other men who've let you down?

Except she'd watched Vaughn fall in love with Nat, the way it had changed him, opened him up. Because good men existed. She just hadn't known very many. Could she really trust her own judgment that Zach was one?

Except here she was, curled up next to him, with none of those doubts that had plagued her with Jordan. She didn't doubt Zach. He didn't make her doubt.

She let that thought lull her to sleep. She awoke to the jerk of his body, and male cursing. She smiled before she opened her eyes.

"I fell asleep?" Zach demanded, practically leaping out of bed. Outrage and sleep roughened his voice. She tried to press her lips together so she didn't smile, but she failed.

"Yeah, you were kind of dead on your feet, cowboy," she offered, stretching lazily out across the bed. "I tried to wake you up, but the best I could do was half drag you to bed. I didn't take advantage, though."

He gave her a sidelong look. Then he scrubbed his hands over his face and through his hair. Her fingers itched to do the same to him, but she knew Zach would want to right himself and get to work.

And quite frankly her heart felt a little soft, waking up next to him—even with the jolting wake-up. She wanted to wake up next to someone, which was not a new dream or fantasy, but it was certainly even more compelling with Zach as that someone.

"The meeting with Stacy is at eleven."

"Eleven?" He swore again. "That only gives us about two hours to plan."

"Why don't you take a shower, and I'll make coffee. Then we can plan." She didn't wait for him to agree before she slid out of bed and started heading for the door. She needed…coffee. A little coffee would steady the fluttering feeling in her chest.

But Zach stopped her on her way out of the room— a hand to her shoulder—and the flutters only intensified. He stared at her for the longest time, his big, warm hand resting on her shoulder.

"Whoever is behind this is to blame for all of this, no matter how much you trusted them. You can worry about a lot of things, but I don't want you worrying that you should have seen through someone."

Was that the fear inside her? Maybe. Whether it was Jordan or Stacy, part of her didn't want to know because then it would mean she was wrong.

At least she already knew she'd been wrong about Jordan. Maybe she'd root for him to be the person who wanted to hurt her. Except… She'd still feel stupid. Stupid and guilty that Tom's life was lost over something so…

Zach pushed a strand of hair behind her ear, sending a shiver of delight down her spine. Easing some of that band around her lungs. "We're going to figure this out, and then you're going to go back to your life. I promise you that." He smiled, a small smile meant to reassure. "And now that I've actually slept, no one's about to stop me. Trust that."

"I do," she whispered with far too much emotion. More than the situation warranted. But he made her feel all of these things she'd yearned to feel her whole life. Only music had ever soothed her this way. Only music had ever given her a sense she deserved anything good.

Here was Zach. Good, through and through, standing there close enough to lean in to. To kiss. To believe in.

She cleared her throat and took a step away. It was one thing to kiss him when she was trying to get under his skin, or forget about all the things wrong with her life right now. It was another thing to kiss him when she felt this…vulnerable.

She turned and walked carefully to the kitchen. She poked around until she found the coffee. It was percolating when Zach came out of the room they'd slept in, showered and dressed. He'd shaved, and the ends of his hair glistened.

It wasn't just lust that slammed through her. It was something so much bigger than that. Which kept her from acting on the lust.

She cleared her throat and placed a full mug on the table. "Here. I already put way too much sugar in it."

"Thanks." He placed his laptop on the table, slid into the seat, drank a careful sip. "Perfect."

And this was far, far too domestic for her poor heart right now. "So what's the plan?" she asked, sliding into her own chair. She was in danger. *That* was a far more important, and in weird, emotional ways, safer, topic.

"We'll go into the meeting together. You can introduce me as your bodyguard. No names, that way we don't have to remember a fake one. You'll say you're worried about your safety, but you really think your reputation needs a few shows to prove you're not in rehab."

"Like I said before, that'd go through my booking agent."

"Right. We'll stick with a version of the truth. You don't trust anyone else right now. You want to work everything out through her. Maybe it's not her normal job, but she could do it with extenuating circumstances."

"I guess so."

"As casually as you can, mention how you're heading home tonight."

"I don't have a home," she returned, too soft to make a joke out of it.

But Zach didn't even blink. "Who knows that?"

"What do you mean?" she asked, trying to drink enough coffee to chase away her dogged exhaustion.

"I mean, who of our suspects would say you don't have a home? Would Jordan?"

"He'd probably say Nashville. Home is where the career is, after all."

"And Stacy?"

"She'd probably say Texas, since my brother is there and she knows how much he and his family mean to me."

"Okay, there's a flight to Austin at ten. So you mention you're heading home tonight. If Stacy or someone on her staff heads to Texas, we know it's her. If Jordan starts poking around Nashville, we have reason to suspect him."

"How will you know all that stuff?"

Zach shrugged, tapping away at his computer. "It's not a perfect plan, but I've got eyes and I've got ears." He took another sip of his coffee then looked over the table at her. "All you have to do is talk to her like you normally would."

"But I don't feel normal. The phone was bad enough. In person?"

"In person, I'll be there. I can talk for you if need be. Just pretend to be overwrought."

"I'm never overwrought," she replied, but she kind of wished she could be. Wished she could hand it all over to Zach and let him take care of it. But no matter what he'd said about it not being her fault, this was her doing. Some choice in her life had made this happen.

She had to stand on her own two feet to fight it.

ZACH KNEW DAISY was nervous. It radiated off her as they slid out of the rental car, three blocks away from Stacy's office building.

Still, Daisy had that chin-in-the-air determination pushing her forward, and she didn't hesitate to walk with him. She didn't let those nerves overcome her.

Zach scanned the sidewalks, the buildings, the people who walked in front of them, as they zigzagged their way to the office building. He kept close to Daisy, hand always ready to grab his concealed weapon if need be.

But he didn't see or sense a tail. He'd expected to. It was a relief, though, and sadly not just for Daisy's safety. If he could scratch her manager off the suspect list he knew it would take a weight off her shoulders.

Zach opened the front door to the office building and gestured Daisy inside. For the remainder of the time he didn't walk by her side, but at her back, as most bodyguards would.

They rode the elevator in silence and walked down another hall without a word. Daisy's demeanor changed from vibrating nerves to cool determination, and that struck him as sadder somehow. How hard she was trying.

He noted every name on every door or sign, would write them all down after. Investigate any possible connections. Even though he shouldn't hope for any particular outcome because it would cloud his judgment, he hoped he could prove Stacy had nothing to do with anything.

As they entered the office labeled *Starshine Management*, a young woman behind a big desk immediately jumped to her feet with a bright smile. "Ms. Delaney! It's been so long."

"Hi, Cory. I've got a meeting with Stacy."

"Of course. Of course. Oh, my gosh, though, Ms. Delaney. I have to tell you, 'Put a Hex on My Ex' is getting me through a really tough breakup. I swear. I don't know what I'd do without your music."

Daisy smiled tightly. "You'd muscle through, but isn't it great we can have music to ease our hurts?"

"That's *exactly* right. I'll get Ms. Vine now." She grinned and bopped down the hallway before disappearing into an office with the blinds of the big glass front windows closed.

Daisy's expression melted into sadness. Worry.

"I'm not familiar with 'Put a Hex on My Ex.'"

Daisy's mouth quirked as he'd hoped it might. "Not many people are. It was on my first album after I stepped away from my dad's label and people didn't quite jump on the bandwagon right away. Not my most popular hour, though I love that song. Even more now."

He'd meant to change the subject, but it brought up

an interesting point he'd overlooked. "Did you write your own music with your dad's record label?"

Daisy rubbed a hand to her temple and closed her eyes. "A few songs, I guess. Though I had cowriters with all of them, I think."

It was an angle he hadn't looked into enough—that someone who might want to hurt her might have a connection not just to her, but to her father. "Did Stacy have any connection to your dad's label?"

"Yes. She was an assistant. I convinced her to leave and take me on as her first client."

Could that be the connection? But he didn't have time to press her for more details because a woman who didn't appear much older than Daisy stepped out with the perky secretary.

"Daisy! *God.* I've been worried sick." She engulfed Daisy in a hard hug before giving Zach a lifted eyebrow perusal.

"This is my bodyguard," Daisy said with a dismissive wave. "You know how my brother worries."

Stacy slipped her arm around Daisy's waist and started leading her down the hall. "Well, as he should. I'm so sorry this is happening to you, Daisy. What can I do?"

"I was hoping you'd ask that."

They were led back to Stacy's office, big and spacious, with a large window letting in a lot of light. Stacy didn't settle in behind the giant desk, instead taking an armchair that faced the one Daisy slid into.

They opened with small talk about mutual acquaintances, and Zach didn't notice anything odd about Stacy's demeanor. She acted like a friend, a concerned one, and a businesswoman invested in her client's career.

Daisy, to her credit, seemed perfectly relaxed, but there was just *something* about the way she held her purse in her lap that kept him from believing the act.

Daisy went through everything he'd tasked her with bringing up. The potential of a small, intimate concert with lots of security to promote her next single, the fact she was going to go home to relax for a few days. Asking Stacy to keep that last part secret.

"Daisy. Are you sure everything is okay? You don't seem like yourself."

"Would you seem like yourself if you'd found your bodyguard dead?"

Stacy winced. "I'm sorry. I'm just worried." Stacy gave Zach a cursory glance. "Not just for your safety, but for *you*. Are you sure you want to do any kind of performance with this going on? We can't exactly background check fans. I know you want to promote the album, but—"

"Wait. Why do you assume the person who killed Tom is a fan?" Daisy asked, and there was dismay clear as a bell in her voice.

Stacy blinked, all wide-eyed innocence Zach didn't know whether or not to believe. "Who else would it be?"

A loud siren interrupted the conversation, making all three of them jump at the jarring blast of sound.

Stacy frowned, glancing around the office. "What terrible timing for a fire drill," she called over the blaring noise.

Stacy looked uneasy, Daisy even more so. As for Zach himself, he didn't trust the timing at all.

"We should evacuate," he offered, holding out his hand for Daisy to take. "What route would you normally take for a fire drill?"

Stacy shrugged helplessly, getting to her feet. "I... I don't remember. The stairs, obviously. Outside the doors. Then out the front? Or is it the back? Cory would know."

Zach nodded grimly, keeping his grasp on Daisy firm as he led her to the door.

Cory was standing in the middle of the office's waiting area, a bunch of things in her hands. She glanced back at them, worry and confusion replacing her previously cheerful expression. "I don't know what to grab and what to leave and—"

"I'm sure it's just a drill..." But Stacy's words trailed off as Cory pointed to the hallway outside the glass doors of the office. Smoke snaked across the floor.

"Come on," Zach ordered, pulling Daisy for the door. "Keep low. Evacuate the building in the most efficient way possible."

"Someone should call 911," Cory said, her voice trembling as Zach opened the door and pointed Stacy and Cory out, keeping Daisy next to him.

"We'll call when we're out. The most important thing is getting outside right now."

Stacy and Cory seemed totally helpless in the hallway, staring at each other as smoke continued to snake around them.

"Follow us. Form a chain," Zach ordered, keeping Daisy's hand in his as he led them toward the staircase he remembered seeing.

The stairs were worse when it came to the smoke, but there was no heat—no flame that he could see. There weren't sprinklers going off, and Zach had a bad feeling it wasn't a fire so much as a distraction. Or a diversion.

Once they made it down the stairs, the lobby was filled with even more smoke, thick and acrid.

Daisy was tugging against his grip. He looked over his shoulder, but the smoke was thick enough he could only barely make her form out behind him. He didn't want to speak, trying to avoid inhaling as much as possible. But she kept pulling, harder and jerkier.

He nearly lost his grip on her, squeezing it tighter at the last moment and giving her a jerk toward him. "Stay with me," he ordered, and began pulling her through the smoke.

"Wait," she croaked.

But they were wading through smoke in a dangerous situation and he would most assuredly not wait.

He got them out of the building, milling crowds pushing at them the minute they stepped outside. Still, he kept pulling her, weaving through the crowd and away from the building.

"Zach! I lost my hold on Stacy. We have to go back," Daisy said desperately, her voice raspy from smoke.

Zach didn't stop moving or pulling her along. "They're fine. I don't think it's a fire. Now, what the hell was that stunt? Pulling on me that way? If I'd lost my grip on you—" He glanced back when she hacked out a cough.

Tears were streaming down her face, and his heart twisted painfully in his chest at her misery.

"It was Stacy," she offered weakly. "She kept grabbing and pulling at me in the opposite direction. I think she knew a better way out."

Zach nearly stopped cold, but the smoke and chaos reminded him to keep moving—with Daisy firmly in his grasp. "She did what now?" he demanded. It was easier to move faster out here where there was less of a crowd, so he hurried.

"I'm sure it was an accident. She was panicking and thought we needed to go in the other direction. But when you pulled on me, she lost her grip. She and Cory went out the back way, I think."

Zach shook his head, pulling her toward where they'd parked the car blocks away. He wanted to protect her from the truth, but he couldn't. It wasn't his job. "That doesn't look good for Stacy, Daisy. That wasn't a fire. It was smoke bombs, or something similar. Someone was trying to create a diversion. Someone knew you were coming and wanted to get to you, and it looks like Stacy was trying to help someone do just that."

Chapter Twelve

Daisy didn't talk on the drive home. The pretty little farmhouse didn't cheer her up at all. She went straight to the bathroom and got into a steaming-hot shower and cried herself empty.

She'd trusted Stacy with her *life*. Everything Daisy had built for herself had been done with Stacy at her side.

She wanted to believe it was panic that had made Stacy try to pull her in the opposite direction of Zach. Maybe there was some explanation, but they hadn't stuck around to get it. Maybe she could still believe Stacy only *looked* guilty accidentally. Nothing was proven. Nothing was sure.

Except Zach, who was most definitely sure Stacy was involved.

Daisy half wished someone would just *do* something to her. At least it would be over then.

But that thought made her feel sick to her stomach. She didn't want to be harmed or worse, even if it ended this waiting game. Upset and alive was better than at peace and dead.

She got dressed in comfortable pajamas even though

it was only late afternoon. Part of her wanted to sleep until this whole thing was over. It wasn't possible, but maybe for tonight while she came to grips with how bad this looked for Stacy's connection to everything.

She stepped out of the bathroom, tempted to head into the room she'd put her stuff in yesterday. Which was not the room she'd spent the night in with Zach.

Zach. She couldn't shut him out even though she wanted to. He was trying to keep her safe, determined to. It wasn't his fault she apparently had terrible judgment when it came to people. It wasn't his fault the people she thought were trustworthy and honest were potentially wishing her harm.

So she forced herself to walk back out to the pretty little living room. It reminded her of something out of *Little House on the Prairie*, but there was a sheen of cleanliness and chicness to it. It was its own little fantasy world, and boy, could she use a fantasy world.

Complete with hot protector guy standing in the kitchen cooking. No doubt making her dinner. No doubt he'd watch like a hawk to make sure she ate.

When he turned to glance at her, there was sympathy there. It made her throat close up all over again. She didn't want to cry in front of him, though, much as she knew he'd comfort her and be perfectly sweet about it.

She wanted to be strong, not to prove something to him, but to herself. That a fleeting thought about wishing someone would just end things didn't mean she particularly wanted to be ended.

"So that was more eventful than I thought it would be." She settled herself onto a stool at the counter that separated the kitchen from the dining area.

"That it was. I know it's hard for you to think Stacy could be a part of this, but we have to accept that possibility."

Daisy nodded, spinning her phone in a little circle on the counter. "Yeah. I get that."

"If it helps, I don't think she's acting alone. The hired muscle back in Wyoming, smoke bombs. She doesn't strike me as someone who could run a demanding business and plan all this. I think she might be a pawn."

"Oh, gee, more people out to get me."

"She might be an unwitting one."

"Whatever she is, she's connected." Even saying the words made Daisy's stomach twist. She kept thinking she'd accepted it, and if she accepted it she could move forward.

Except she couldn't accept it. Even when Zach was calm and reasonable.

"All evidence points to yes." Zach drained pasta in the sink with a deft hand.

"Where'd you learn to cook?" she asked, wanting to talk about anything other than Stacy.

"My mother. She believed in raising boys who could take care of themselves." Something on his face changed.

"Boys. You have brothers?"

"A brother."

"You've only mentioned Hilly and your murdered father. I didn't know there was a brother."

He shrugged. "Did you want my life history?"

Because the honest question hurt her more than it should, she smiled sharply at him. "Well, we did sleep together, sugar."

His mouth quirked as if he almost found her funny. "Uh-huh. Well, I have a brother."

"Is he Mr. Protector guy, too? Or are you more like me and my brother?"

"What's you and your brother?"

"Opposites, through and through."

"But you love him."

"Of course I do. Vaughn was one of the very few uncomplicated relationships in my life. Well, mostly uncomplicated. I always knew he didn't really approve of me, but he supported me anyway." She hadn't always appreciated that support the way she should have, and she'd never thanked him for it.

Although he'd be horrified by a display of emotion, even if it was gratitude. The thought made her smile a little bit. But she realized, as Zach placed a bowl full of spaghetti in front of her, he'd very efficiently avoided the question.

"So what does your brother do?"

"He's done a lot of things."

She raised an eyebrow. "You know, when someone touches a sore subject with me I tell them to jump off a cliff."

"And I doubt it dims their curiosity regarding the sore subject," Zach replied.

"Avoiding the question doesn't dim my curiosity."

"Ethan's in a psych ward. He, in fact, nearly murdered Cam."

"Cam, your business partner, Cam? The man marrying your sister?"

"The very same."

He really, *really* never failed to surprise her. She might have thought him cold at the way he delivered that so emotionlessly, but his eyes didn't lie as well as the rest of him. The less sympathy she offered, though, the more he seemed to reveal to her. "Well. I can see why it's a sore subject."

"Dad's murder hit him particularly hard. He tried his hand at a lot of things, but the unsolved case was an obsession, one that became unhealthy and dangerous. I love my brother, even knowing his... I hesitate to call them faults. He's mentally ill. He's... Well, my attempts to protect him, to care for him, not only put the entire undercover FBI investigation I was a part of in jeopardy, but nearly got Cam killed, too. You learn from experiences like that. And, in my case, you get kicked out of the FBI."

"Which is why you shouldn't get emotionally involved," she said, remembering how seriously he'd asked her if she wanted to die after she'd kissed him that first time.

He tapped his nose, then focused on eating.

"It isn't the same," she said softly.

He raised an eyebrow, and somehow she'd known he'd give her that condescending look he thought hid all the turmoil inside him. Maybe he managed to hide it from other people, but not from her.

"You knew your brother had issues, and you kept protecting him until you didn't have a choice. That isn't the same as feeling something for me. Emotion didn't cause those mistakes. Underestimating your brother's illness and your power over it would have been the issue. It doesn't mean you'll make the same mistakes with me."

"Who says I won't?"

She blinked at that, more than a little irritated when

her phone trilled. Downright furious when it was Jordan's number calling her.

"Why can't that bastard leave well enough alone?" she grumbled, reaching for the phone to hit Ignore.

"Take it," Zach said in that leader-ordering-a-subordinate tone that would have angered her more if she wasn't so confused.

"Huh?"

"Take it. See what he wants. On speaker."

She didn't want to talk to Jordan, not when she was getting somewhere with Zach. Not when today was already in the toilet. But she did as Zach ordered her to do because she didn't know what else to do in the moment besides stomp her feet and throw a tantrum like a child.

"Jordan," she greeted as coolly as she could muster.

"Daisy. Thank God you're all right."

Fear snaked through her. While Zach had told her the smoke bombs at Stacy's office had made the news, people had been distracted enough not to notice she'd been in the building. So far. "Why wouldn't I be all right?" she asked, trying to keep her voice devoid of emotion.

"The attack on Stacy's office! They're claiming it was an innocent prank, but this is all too close for comfort. I'm worried about you, Daisy. What kind of trouble have you been getting yourself into?"

She glanced up at Zach, who had that icy law-enforcement scowl on his face. But again, in his eyes she could see the truth. Heat and fury.

"You know I'm in town?" she asked carefully.

"I keep tabs, Daisy. I've told you that before." He sounded so disdainful she wanted to punch him. "I have to know if you're going to show up and make one of your scenes."

"But you said you thought I was in rehab."

"No, I said that's what people were saying, and that I hoped you were getting help. You need help."

And you need a knee to the balls.

"We need to talk, Daisy. In private. No staff. No bodyguards. I have some important news for you and I need to make sure you're going to handle it the correct way."

She opened her mouth to say she'd show him the correct way to handle something, but Zach reached across the counter and tapped her hand. He scribbled something onto a piece of paper then angled it toward her.

Take the meeting.

She jerked the pen from his hand and wrote her own note back.

Without you?

"Daisy? Listen. Meet me at our old lunch place. What do you say, eight o'clock before your flight?"

Daisy stared at Zach, who nodded emphatically. She let out a sigh. "Fine, Jordan. I'll be there at eight. Goodbye." She hit End on the call before he could say any more.

"Stacy had to have told him you were here. She's the only one who knew about that flight," Zach said, scribbling more things onto a new piece of paper. "There has to be a connection there."

"Between Stacy and Jordan? They didn't like each other. Trust me. Cory could have told him, too."

"Cory didn't know about your flight unless she was eavesdropping. Besides, Jordan and Stacy disliking each other isn't valid enough to disregard the potential connection. Because it doesn't have to be a connection of friendship, does it? The enemy of my enemy is my friend and all that—and before you say anything, I know Stacy isn't your enemy, but sometimes people harbor resentments we don't know about. You said she was at your father's label with you."

"No, she was my father's manager's assistant. We used to sit around and complain about what a smarmy old codger he was, so when I finally got the guts to go out on my own, I asked if she wanted to come with. We'd been friends, dreaming about futures where we didn't have to answer to anyone. Might have been tough work those first few years, but I'm pretty sure Stacy has been amply rewarded."

Zach paced. "None of this adds up," he muttered. "We're missing something." He tilted his head, clearly working something out in that overactive brain of his. "Or someone. What about someone who would know both Jordan and Stacy separately. Someone who who knows you well enough to use them both against you? Who in your life would know both Jordan and Stacy enough to understand their relationship to you?"

"My agent. Jordan's staff—his manager, his assistant—basically anyone on his payroll who would have worked with Stacy during one of our joint ventures before the divorce."

"I looked into Jordan's staff before, but we'll go through them again. See if we can find a specific connection to Stacy. And then triangulate it to your father."

"And while you're doing all that?"

"You better get ready. Because you're going to have to hide some of your fury toward Jordan. Just long enough to get us through this meeting and get what we want out of it."

THE PATTERNS DIDN'T add up, but Zach was beginning to think he'd been looking at them all wrong. There were a lot of players, but no clear leader. No clear link.

If he could find the link, the pattern would fall into place.

Daisy didn't think anyone would have something against her writing her own songs, but Zach had to believe it was industry related. Jordan, the rising star. Stacy, the star's manager—who came from her father's record label.

"What about this manager? The one Stacy worked for."

"What about him?" Daisy asked, staring out the window as Zach drove through drizzly downtown traffic to the restaurant Jordan had picked out.

"Could he have been angry at you for stealing Stacy away?"

Daisy snorted. "He didn't care about Stacy. He cared about power."

"What does that mean?"

"Look, he'd be like…eighty now. I doubt he overpowered Tom and killed him. I doubt he'd have the wherewithal to follow me around the country."

"*He* isn't. Whoever is behind this is sending people, Daisy. What would this guy be angry about?" He didn't add *and why the hell didn't you tell me*, which he considered a great feat of control.

Daisy shifted in her seat. "Nothing. He got away with it all. There'd be nothing to be angry about."

"Got away with what exactly?"

She sighed heavily. "He just said some kind of inappropriate things and I told my dad about it. But it's not like… There was nothing to be angry about. Nothing happened to him."

Zach parked in the lot in front of the restaurant, then looked over at her. "*Said* some inappropriate things, or *did* some inappropriate things?"

She waved a hand and pushed the passenger door open. "Doesn't matter."

"It *does* matter," he insisted, but she got out of the car and started walking toward the door—which was not the plan they'd agreed on. He hopped out of the car, stopping her forward progress. "Follow the plan, Daisy. And tell me about it."

"It doesn't *matter*. Trust me. Nothing bad ever happened to him. If he's angry with me, it's not enough to want me hurt. Why would he be angry? He's old and rich and retired, I believe. Hell, he might even be dead. Whatever he is—he's fine, and not out to get me."

"Name."

"Oh, for God's sake, Zach. Can't you trust me?"

"I trust you implicitly. I don't trust anyone who would say or *do* inappropriate things to you when you were a teenager."

They couldn't keep having this conversation in public, even with her big sunglasses and baggy clothes.

"He grabbed me. I told him no. He grabbed me again. I said I was going to go tell my dad. He laughed and said Dad wouldn't do anything. And guess what? He was right. *Oh, Don's just old guard, Daisy girl. Don't be alone with him.* Problem solved, right?"

"The hell it is."

She shook her head, wrapping her arms around herself. "It was forever ago. It's ancient history."

It wasn't. He could tell it wasn't, but she didn't

want to discuss it and here wasn't the place. "What about Stacy?"

"What *about* Stacy?"

"Did he assault Stacy, too?"

"He didn't *assault* me, Zach."

"Grabbing is assault, Daisy," he returned forcefully. But he softened because even for all the difficult situations he'd been in, he'd never had to mine through his past. Never had to wonder who was against him. He placed his hands on her shoulders. "I know it hurts. I can't imagine how much it hurts to wonder about everyone you trust, or everyone you don't want to have to think about. I wish there was some other way, but we're missing a link and the sooner I can find it, the sooner whoever is torturing you can be brought to justice."

"I just want this to be over. I'm not even sure I care about justice," she said, looking teary.

He let her lean into him. Rubbed his hand up and down her back. "I know. I know. One link. I just need one link and then I can connect it all. I can make it over for you. Let me follow this lead. A name, and all you have to do is—"

She lifted her head off his shoulder, and nodded behind him. "Have dinner with my ex-husband?"

Zach didn't turn. Instead, he kept his arm around Daisy, kept looking down at her. "We're going to play this a little differently than we planned."

"Oh, really?"

He dropped his head and brushed his mouth against hers, inappropriately enjoying that for once he'd been the one to surprise her with a kiss. "Not your body-guard this time."

Her mouth quirked up. "Well, this should be interesting."

He slid his arm around her waist and turned to face Jordan Jones, who did *not* look happy to see them.

Zach grinned. "Indeed it will."

Chapter Thirteen

Daisy's whole life, she'd prided herself on standing on her own two feet. Even when her father had been taking her from show to show as a little girl, she'd understood that it was necessary to prove a certain amount of independence so she didn't turn into her father's toy or trophy. If she hadn't inherently understood that, her mother had made sure to remind her.

Daisy had wanted to be a singer, and she'd become one. On her own terms. But there had been things that had undermined that independence, that certainty. Her father ignoring the fact his manager had—as much as she hated it, she'd use Zach's word—*assaulted* her. Jordan being…well, self-serving, she supposed.

Could she hate him for that?

"I thought we were going to have dinner, Daisy. I don't appreciate—" he trailed off, looking Zach up and down "—whatever stunt this is."

Turned out, she could hate Jordan for a lot of things. "No stunt. My boyfriend refused to let me out of his sight with everything going on." She patted Zach's chest. "He's very concerned about my well-being."

Jordan sighed, all long-suffering martyrdom. "If

that's supposed to be a dig against me, perhaps I should apologize for treating you like an independent woman?"

Perhaps you should apologize for being an emotionally abusive jerk wad. But she smiled sweetly. "Jordan Jones, this is my boyfriend..." She tried to come up with a fake name, but Zach intervened.

"Zach Simmons," he offered, holding out a hand for Jordan to shake. "I'm in law enforcement, so I understand just how dangerous this threat against Lucy is. Her going anywhere alone wasn't a great idea. I'm sure you understand her safety is paramount."

It...warmed her somehow that he was using her real name, and his. Jordan probably wouldn't notice or care, but it was...a gesture.

"Well." Jordan straightened his shoulders. "Of course. That's what I wanted to talk to Daisy about. Her safety."

"Great!" Zach said so genially Daisy wanted to laugh. "Let's head in." Zach kept his arm around her waist as he led them inside and told the hostess they had three in their party.

It was something to watch, how easily he could switch into someone else. A role. She understood that a little. After all, there was a certain amount of *role* she stepped into when she got on stage. Daisy Delaney was parts of Lucy Cooper carefully arranged into a different package.

But she'd really never expected too many other people to understand that. It had been part of the attraction of Jordan—that he understood the complications of being someone else at the same time you were yourself.

But she supposed there were all kinds of ways people put on masks every day, not just to go on stage.

The hostess led them to a dimly lit booth and Daisy had to fight the need to laugh hysterically. She was sitting in a restaurant with her ex-husband and her security expert slash fake boyfriend slash man she really wouldn't mind seeing naked.

While apparently, said man suspected both her manager and her ex-husband of stalking and murder.

Zach draped his arm over her shoulders easily, chatted with Jordan about the music industry. Daisy could hardly pay attention to Jordan's pretentious rambling about his career. Had she really been this *fooled*?

But she had been. Fooled or desperate or something. It made her feel sick and ashamed she hadn't seen through him—but he hadn't talked about himself back then. He'd talked about her. Flattered her—in just the ways she'd been desperate to be flattered.

A strange thought hit her sideways as Jordan nattered on. Could he have been coached? Told what would hit all her vulnerabilities, and then used them against her?

Oh, that was insane. Whatever was happening to her hadn't been going on for *years*. Her failed marriage was hardly some kind of convoluted plot to…hurt her or whatever. She was getting paranoid. Insane maybe.

"Which brings me to why I called," Jordan was saying, his gaze moving from Zach to Daisy. Pretty blue eyes the color of summer skies. She'd thought she'd seen love in them once, and she didn't know if she was just that delusional or if he had actually felt something for her and it had disappeared.

It made her unbearably sad. And then Jordan continued.

"The rumor *was* you'd disappeared to go into rehab,

and it got me thinking how great it would be if you just did that."

"What?" she replied, because surely he didn't mean what she *thought* he meant.

"You might want to work on your comedy, buddy. Because that isn't funny," Zach said, steel laced through his fake genial tone.

"Can I get y'all something to drink?" a perky waitress asked, clearly not reading the mood of the table.

They all ordered robotically, except Jordan, who smiled and flirted when the waitress recognized him and expressed her undying love for his music.

If she recognized Daisy, she didn't mention it.

When she disappeared to get the drinks, Jordan looked at them both with that patented *Jordan Jones* smile. It was charming, and he was handsome. She wanted to punch him in the nose, but Zach's arm around her shoulders had tightened as if keeping her seated.

"It seems to me a rehab facility would be safer than going around disappearing with—" he looked at Zach "—boyfriends. Especially the way your last one ended up."

"Tom was my bodyguard and he died trying to protect me, you inconsiderate—"

Jordan held up his hands, looking at Zach with a sigh as if to say, *What do you do with a problem like Daisy?* "I'm only suggesting a safe place for you, Daisy."

"You want me to fake going into rehab so I can be *safe*?"

The waitress put glasses in front of them, and this time she gave Daisy a much longer look. Though she was smart enough not to say anything.

Jordan sipped from his glass. "I mean, you could actually go."

"I'm not an alcoholic, Jordan. Contrary to your staff's attempts to make me out to be."

"Of course. Of course." He opened his mouth to speak, but the phone he held in his hand trilled. He glanced at the screen, a slight frown pulling at the corner of his lips. "I have to take this," he said, sliding out of the booth. "If you'll excuse me." He moved away from the table and Daisy couldn't hear what he was saying.

"I can't believe you married this joker," Zach muttered when Jordan was out of earshot.

"*That* is not the joker I married." No, Jordan knew how to slip into a role, too. Was she forever falling for men who acted one way, then turned out to be another? "You know a little bit about pretending to be someone else to get what you want, don't you?"

He looked at her, something like sympathy in his gaze that made her want to punch him, too. Or lean into his chest. She really wasn't sure.

He reached out and pushed a stray strand of hair behind her ear. "All I want right now is to keep you safe."

Which softened her up considerably.

"Which means I'm going to get my hands on his phone."

"Huh?"

"I don't trust this rehab thing."

"He's just trying to make me look bad, Zach. Ever since I asked for a divorce, that's his number one goal. Because if he can make *me* look bad, he can make himself look better."

"Maybe. Maybe that's all it is, but he doesn't strike

me as particularly smart. Manipulative, yes. A good actor? Sure. But someone is pulling his strings, Daisy. I'm going to find out who."

"It's got to be someone on his staff."

"I agree. His manager, maybe? Was there anyone he was particularly...deferential to?"

Daisy tried to think back over her time with Jordan. "I think he's been through something like three managers. He used to talk about some uncle who was in the industry, but I never met him. If he mentioned him by name, I don't remember him."

"I need his phone. So when I give you the signal, you're going to spill your drink on him. I'm going to palm his phone and head off to the bathroom to wash up."

"You're going to palm his phone? How?"

"Trust me." He smiled, tapping her nose. "If you do, maybe I'll teach you a few things about going undercover."

It amused her, even though all she really wanted was to have her life back. "You better be quick, though. His phone is like an arm. He'll notice it's missing."

"You just spill his drink. I'll handle the rest."

SHE DID SO, and beautifully. Perhaps with a little too much enjoyment as the dark soda splashed across Jordan's white shirt, but hell, Zach enjoyed Jordan's outrage a little too much himself.

Zach immediately jumped to his feet, calling for the waitress and shoving napkins at Jordan. It gave him ample time to slip the phone out of the sticky soda and pretend like he was going to run to the bathroom for more paper towels even though the waitress was hurrying over with a rag.

Zach moved quickly to the bathroom, locked himself into a stall and went to work on Jordan's phone.

Zach didn't have time to try and figure out Jordan's passcode, so he used a quick hack to bypass the code and get into Jordan's home screen.

He pulled up the contacts list. The first fishy thing was the lack of names. Everyone was labeled with letters and numbers rather than anything that helped Zach identify who they were. Pretty confusing for a guy who had tons of contacts in his phone.

And pretty damn suspicious. Zach pulled up the recent calls. With his own phone, Zach took a picture of the screen. Of the eight calls on top, two were repeated three times each. It might be nothing. It might mean everything. Now that he had the numbers, he'd go from there.

Text messages didn't reveal anything of importance, and his apps were as run of the mill as any. Zach didn't have time to dig further. Hopefully, the phone numbers would be something to go on.

He stepped out of the stall, wiped off the phone with a paper towel and turned it off, ready to head back to the table. If Jordan had noticed his phone missing, Zach would just explain he'd gone to wipe it down and Jordan would be none the wiser.

But when he stepped back into the restaurant, the few patrons had their noses and phones pressed to every available window, and Daisy stood next to an empty table, hand to her mouth.

"What's going on?"

She gestured faintly at the window, but there were so many people crowded around it he couldn't see anything.

"The cops came and arrested him." Daisy looked up at him, searching for some kind of answer, but he was as confused as she was.

"The cops came in and arrested Jordan?"

She nodded. "A-at first it was just… They asked if they could speak with him outside. He looked so confused, but wholly unconcerned. I think he even thought maybe they were going to ask for his autograph or something, but instead… I looked out the window and he was being handcuffed. *Handcuffed.* Zach, it doesn't make any sense, and it's already being uploaded onto the internet in three million ways."

Zach looked down at the phone in his hand. "I guess I should give the cops his phone."

"Did you find anything?"

"I took some pictures of his recent call numbers, but if he's being arrested for something, the police should have it." He led Daisy outside through the small crowds of people, pushing his way through to the female cop holding the curious onlookers as far back as she could.

"Excuse me, Officer? I have Jordan Jones's phone right here."

The officer looked at him with a raised eyebrow as he held out the phone, but she didn't say anything.

"We had a little drink spill," Zach explained. "I cleaned off his phone for him. But figured you might want it."

"And you are?" the cop asked with no small amount of distrust.

Zach explained who he was, and the cop managed to escort him and Daisy to a slightly private corner. Zach showed the police officer all his identification and permits to prove he was Daisy's security, and gave an account of the drink spill.

The cop took and bagged the phone. "I imagine our detectives will be in contact with you, Ms. Delaney."

"Can you tell me what he's being arrested for?"

The cop looked at Daisy, then him. "The murder of Tom Perelli."

Daisy audibly gasped, and Zach might have, too. *Jordan* as murderer? Even though he'd suspected Jordan was involved, it was hard to believe the man he'd just had dinner with was capable of murder.

But he didn't have time to dwell on that. Some people were beginning to look at Daisy and murmur among themselves. Phones began to move from the cop car where Jordan was now loaded up, to the dim corner where he and Daisy stood.

He moved his body to shield her from the prying eyes and phones, then discussed the best way to get out of the parking lot undetected. As the cop began to instruct the crowd to leave so she could back up the patrol car, Daisy and Zach slipped around the crowd and into Zach's car.

Daisy didn't say anything as they drove back. Zach couldn't read her mood, but he couldn't concentrate on it, either. He paid attention to every car on the road with them.

Quite frankly, he expected to be followed. He expected…something. Surely, this wasn't *it*. It was too easy, too neat. Something else had to be at work here.

But in the end they made it back to the farmhouse without any tail Zach could see. Once inside, he made as many calls as he could to weasel some information out of a few overly talkative individuals.

Daisy sat on the couch, staring at nothing. During one of his calls he'd fixed her some tea. She hadn't touched it.

After he'd gotten the answers he'd wanted, or at least *some* of the answers, he sat down next to Daisy. She didn't move. Didn't say anything. He supposed she was in shock.

"The police received an anonymous tip, which allowed them to obtain a search warrant for Jordan's place. They found the gun used to kill Tom in a hidden safe in his bedroom closet."

"Anonymous tip," Daisy echoed. "Someone else knew he… He couldn't have…" She swallowed. "Zach, I don't understand. I really don't. Maybe I could believe he stalked me, or even threatened me all those months, but to kill Tom? I can't…" She shook her head. "But it's over, isn't it? If Jordan is the murderer, and he's in jail, this is over."

Zach didn't know how to tell her he didn't think it was over, that this was all too easy. And maybe it *was* over. Maybe it wasn't his gut telling him things were too neat. Maybe it was his desperate desire to be with her.

"Zach?"

She looked up at him, and in all that confusion and despair there was hope. Hope that this meant she got to go back to her real life and feel safe again. Hope that this could all be put away as some ugly part of her past.

For her, he wished he could believe it. Even if it meant their time together was up. She deserved to go back to normal, instead of living in fear.

"It's possible it's over," he said carefully, not wanting to burden her with his doubts. "Obviously, we'll want to see if they give him a bond. I'd hope not, but we want to make sure he's going to stay in jail before it's...fully over."

Daisy nodded, wringing her hands together. "I can't... I didn't know him. I thought I did. I loved the version of himself he showed me, but it wasn't him. I can't imagine him *killing* someone, but I certainly can imagine him wanting to hurt me."

She popped to her feet, began to pace. "He wanted me to go to rehab. He wanted me swept away so I wouldn't be credible. That's why he wanted to meet."

It was possible, Zach supposed. But the timing struck him as odd, even more so with the arrest in front of Daisy. Zach had some research to do on those numbers from Jordan's phone before he fully accepted this version of events. And he'd want to read the police report and—

"What about you?"

He looked up at Daisy, his mind going over all the things he still needed to do to be *sure*. "What about me?"

"You'll have to go home, then, won't you?"

It felt like a slap, even as she watched him with wide, sad eyes. He cleared his throat. She might have kissed him a few times, he might have grown to like her quite a bit, but their odd relationship was a temporary one.

He pushed away all those conflicting emotions that were no doubt clouding his judgment about Jordan's guilt. "My job is to keep you safe. Until we're assured Jordan stays in jail, that means I'm still here."

She nodded, gave him a tremulous smile that just about cracked his heart in two. "Good." When she sat, she didn't sit next to him. Instead, she slid onto his lap, much like she had way back in Wyoming.

She cupped his face with her hands, looked right at him. "Then be with me. Really."

Chapter Fourteen

Daisy poured everything inside her into the kiss. The pain, the uncertainty, the horrible sadness that swept through her at the idea Zach wouldn't be in her life anymore.

She wasn't sure if it was the kiss that finally broke through Zach's whole "emotions are distractions" thing—because it was one hell of a soul-searing kiss—or if it was as simple as he believed this was over.

She wished she could, but everything felt wrong and off. Maybe she couldn't believe Jordan was a murderer because it made her look like a fool, but there were all these wiggles of uncertainty inside her she couldn't quash—even with Jordan in jail.

Zach's kiss could eradicate it, and all the other painful things inside her. She could focus on pleasure and the absolute safety she found in him and leave everything else behind, even if only for a little bit.

She thought she'd have to convince him, but his arms banded around her and his mouth devoured hers as if he hadn't rejected her attempts at this *routinely*.

He maneuvered her onto her back on the couch, sprawling himself over her so that she sank into the cushions. She reveled in that feeling of being covered completely, safe and complete somehow—like being in Zach Simmons's arms was exactly where she needed to be.

He kissed her like she was the same to him—the place *he* needed to be.

There were so many ways she'd been made to feel small and insignificant in her life by the men who were supposed to love her. Zach had never mentioned love, but he made her feel cherished and important more so than anyone else. He believed her, he trusted her, and time and time again he'd put her above his own interests.

She pulled his shirt off quickly and efficiently. She sighed reverently, tracing her fingers down his abdomen. "I've been waiting for this since I saw you shirtless that first night."

He muttered a curse and then kissed her again, a fervency and an urgency she appreciated because it seared away everything else—all those awful things in the real world out there. It was only him and her, perfectly safe.

His hands streaked under her shirt and then pulled her up into a sitting position, his body straddling hers.

"If this is a curse, I'll damn well take it," he said, his eyes bright and lethal.

"Curse?"

"Carsons, Delaneys, long story." He closed his eyes and shook his head as if he couldn't believe he'd brought it up. "I'll tell you later." Then he lifted her shirt over her head and let it fall to the ground. His mouth streaked down her neck as his hands made quick work of her bra and she forgot her questions as he kissed her everywhere.

His groan of appreciation as he tugged the button

and zipper of her jeans made her feel like a goddess. "One favor. Don't call me Daisy."

He paused briefly, then met her gaze as he pulled her pants down her legs. "All right, Lucy."

It squirmed through her—somehow beautiful and uncomfortable at the same time. But she didn't want to be Daisy to him, not because she was ashamed of that part of her, but because Daisy had to keep people at arm's length from all the demands inside her—from her music, from her drive to succeed, from the chaos that sometimes existed in her head.

But if she was Lucy, just herself without the mantle of fame or curse of being a storyteller, then she could feel like she really belonged to *him*. Not something bigger than them. Just them.

Zach stopped suddenly, keeping his body ridiculously tense. "Wait. Condoms. We don't—"

She patted his cheek. "Never fear, sweetheart, condoms and booze are two things I never leave home without."

"Do I even want to know why?"

"Sometimes a girl has a rep to protect. Or destroy, as the case may be. I like to be prepared."

"Well, I won't look a gift bad girl in the mouth. Wow, that sounds wrong."

She laughed, and was surprised to find it made the moment that much more special. That she could want him and laugh with him and feel safe with him. She brushed her mouth against his as she slid off the couch. "Come to bed, Zach."

He followed her and she rummaged through her bag, in only her underwear and socks. She might have felt a little silly if Zach wasn't watching her as though he'd like to devour her from top to bottom, then bottom to top.

That made her feel powerful no matter what she had on. She found the old crumpled box of condoms, discreetly checked the expiration date and then pulled one out, holding it between her fingers. "Aren't you lucky?"

"Yes," he said reverently, so reverently her eyes actually stung. She tried to saunter over to him, keep it light—focused on the attraction and the laughter, not... not the way her heart felt squeezed so hard she could barely catch a breath.

But when she reached him, she didn't know how to keep it all together. All she could do was lean against the warmth of his chest. Try to find some strength of spirit against that strong, dependable frame.

"I don't want this part to be over. The us part," she whispered, listening to the steady beating of his heart. She'd never, ever revealed herself like that before, laid her emotions that bare.

But she'd never let herself be Lucy with anyone outside her brother and her mother, and even they still saw her as part Daisy. Why she thought Zach understood the dichotomy inside her, she wasn't sure. Maybe she was stupid—the kind of stupid who married a murderer and—

He swallowed and ran a hand over her hair. Sweet and full of care. "Lucy," he said raggedly.

She shook her head against that despair in his voice. "I know. It's impossible. And God knows I shouldn't trust my own instincts when it comes to men. Maybe you're a secret murderer, too. How would I know?"

She wanted to run away, but Zach pulled her back and took her face in his hands.

"Lucy," he repeated, quieting her. She still felt wound up and stupid, but his hands on her face were a balm.

She wanted to stay here—right here—forever. Safe with Zach, who was good, and understood her somehow. A man who cared, and not just for show. She kept trying to convince herself it was just her dumb brain fooling herself again, but looking at that steady gaze she knew. She *knew* Zach was different.

And she was head over heels in love with a man she couldn't have.

But she kissed him anyway, fell to bed with him anyway, and let the sensations overwhelm her so she didn't think about anything except pleasure. Except finding release with this man who meant everything.

This man she'd have to say goodbye to, and soon.

But he kissed her, filled her, and for sparkling minutes of ecstasy she forgot everything except them.

ZACH WASN'T SURE he'd ever slept so soundly, or so long. He woke up feeling like a new man.

Of course, that might have been the sex.

Which really shouldn't have relaxed him considering it added quite a few complications to his nagging worry that Jordan's arrest was too easy. How could he tell the difference between what was true, and what his feelings for Lucy made him *want* to be true?

But facts were facts, right? There was evidence Jordan had done it. Why was he letting emotion sway the facts again? Didn't he know how that ended up?

He was almost grateful for the pounding on the door. If it didn't worry him. He slid out of bed as Lucy grumbled complaints.

Lucy. It was funny how easy it was to vacillate between the names. She seemed like both women to him, but somehow it seemed more…meaningful that he'd gone to bed with Lucy.

Possibly he was losing his mind.

He pulled on his pants and grabbed his gun that he'd left in the nightstand. With the pounding continuing at increasing levels, he didn't have time to strap his holster on, so he simply held it behind his back as he made his way through the living room to the door.

He checked the security camera on his phone, but the man on the stoop wasn't familiar. He was about Zach's height, wearing jeans, an impeccably unwrinkled button-up shirt and a rather large cowboy hat.

Still, he was knocking. It could be information about Jordan. Zach eased the door open, weapon at the ready.

The man's cool blue eyes took in Zach's shirtless form and those eyes hardened.

"Can I help you?" Zach asked as he flipped the safety off behind his back.

"Vaughn!"

Zach glanced back at Lucy, who pulled the bright yellow robe she was wearing a little closer around her as she stepped forward.

Zach was glad he recognized the name as her brother's or the hot burn of jealousy at the pure delight in her tone might have had him acting stupidly and rashly.

"What are you doing here?" she asked, approaching them. She looked like she was about to lean in to hug her brother, but instead gripped her robe tighter. "I told you everything was fine."

Yeah, it wouldn't exactly be rocket science to figure out what they'd been doing together last night. And she certainly hadn't told him she'd contacted her brother.

"I came to take you home," Vaughn said, his voice cool and detached. But the words made Zach's blood run cold even as he set the gun back down on the counter.

"You didn't have to come collect me like I'm a sheep to be herded," Lucy countered. She glanced at Zach, but he couldn't read whatever was in her expression when she quickly looked away again.

"Maybe not," Vaughn countered. "But I thought Jordan being the suspect might hit you a little hard and you'd want—" he looked Zach up and down "—a friendly face."

"Uh, right. Well. Vaughn, this is Zach. I don't suppose you two have met, though you know of each other."

"Of each other, yes. Jaime spoke highly of you." After another moment of cold perusal, Vaughn offered his hand. "I was impressed by the detail in your reports."

Zach shook it. "Same goes. It's good to meet you," Zach offered, trying to sound businesslike despite the general lack of shirt, socks and shoes.

Vaughn did not return the sentiment, though it was hard to blame him. Zach hadn't had a normal brother-sister relationship with Hilly since they'd grown up apart, and she'd come into his life already connected to Cam, so there'd been no big-brother suspicion to be had.

But that didn't mean he couldn't understand Vaughn's. Especially considering Vaughn had arranged for Lucy's protection.

"Why don't you go get dressed?" Vaughn said to Lucy. He gave Zach a sharp smile. "Zach and I will chat."

Lucy rolled her eyes. "Yeah, you're a real chatter-box. But I'll go get dressed since I'll be more comfortable, and since I have no doubt Zach can stand up to the likes of you." She gave her brother a little poke, and then drifted her hand down Zach's arm as she sauntered away.

Zach thought he could probably handle her brother—Texas Ranger or not—but he didn't quite need her stirring the pot on the subject.

Especially when it gave him a quick few minutes alone with her brother, which meant, even though he still had his doubts, he had to tell Vaughn he didn't think this was over. Somehow, he had to convince her brother that it wasn't Zach's heart doing the talking.

"I don't think she should go back home with you," he said when Lucy disappeared into the room, firmly and sure, but with absolutely no transition or finesse. He *could* have eased into it, but Lucy could also only take a few seconds to change. Time was of the essence.

Vaughn merely raised an eyebrow, reminding Zach a little uncomfortably of Lucy.

"I'm not saying Jordan isn't involved, but..." Zach knew he'd be shot down, but the incessant worry in his gut meant he had to say it. "There was evidence he's the murderer—I can't refute that. What concerns me are the loose ends. I'm not convinced this is it, or that Jordan's arrest means the danger to Lucy is over."

Vaughn studied him, and Zach braced himself for some kind of condescending lecture about being stupid.

It didn't come.

"I'm not, either," Vaughn said. When Zach could only stare at him, openmouthed, Vaughn continued. "Which is why I came out here. I didn't want her alone thinking she was safe, any more than I wanted to have to tell her she wasn't."

"Join the club," Zach muttered. He had to tell her. *Had to*. And yet, she was just accepting her ex-husband was a murderer. How could he add the fact it didn't make Stacy or anyone else less potentially involved?

"Should I ask your intentions when it comes to my sister?" Vaughn asked with a wry twist of his lips.

"Why? Did we fall back in time a century? I'm pretty sure Lucy can handle my intentions." Not that he knew what they were, or why he suddenly wanted the curse to be true.

Vaughn didn't smile, but Zach didn't get the impression Vaughn was a particularly smiley guy. Still, his mouth loosened in what Zach would term *amusement*. Maybe.

"Lucy," Vaughn repeated as if surprised Zach was using her given name. "Well, that's new."

"Is it?"

Vaughn shrugged. "I don't make it a habit to poke into my sister's personal life, but she isn't keen on letting too many people call her by her real name."

It was funny how Vaughn said *real* and it didn't sit well with Zach. They were both real enough—Daisy and Lucy—they were both her. He shook his head. "So how do we break it to her?"

"I'd like to not. To protect her on the sly until we figure out the whole picture."

Zach snorted his derision, unable to stop himself.

"I said I'd *like* to, not that it would work." Vaughn sighed heavily and scrubbed a hand over his face. He didn't appear mussed by travel or beset by fatigue or worry, but that simple gesture told Zach he was all of those things. Sick to death worried about his sister's safety.

Vaughn gestured Zach to sit down on the couch, so Zach did so, Vaughn taking a seat next to him. "Quickest version you've got of the loose ends you think still exist?"

"Two main ones," Zach returned, keeping one eye on Lucy's bedroom door. "One, how Jordan had enough information to know Daisy was going to be with Stacy—which to me points to a potential connection with Stacy."

"What about other people in the office?"

"I laid a little bit of a trap. We gave information to Stacy and only Stacy—of course she might have slipped and told someone, but I'm willing to bet Stacy told Jordan, or someone who knows Jordan."

Vaughn shook his head. "That's going to hurt—worse than Jordan—if Stacy's involved."

"Yeah. And I'll be honest—the second thread? I think there's someone else. Someone from her past, or maybe your father's. Someone who is using Jordan and Stacy and whoever else to exact some kind of... revenge."

"Why do you think that?"

"Patterns. Hunches. The way it's all played out."

Vaughn sighed. "You got notes?"

"You wouldn't believe the notes I have."

"I'll want some time to go over them." He glanced back at Lucy's still-closed door. "We don't have time."

"No. We don't. Look, why don't you let me tell her? That way she can be mad at me instead of her brother. We don't have to go into details. We can just say we're taking precautions until we're sure Jordan worked alone."

"How good of a liar are you, Zach?"

Zach's mouth quirked. "I've worked any number of undercover jobs for the FBI. How good of a liar do you think I am?"

"To her," Vaughn replied simply, which made Zach's stomach lurch. "Believe it or not, I've...been where you're standing. At least, if my assumptions are correct—and they usually are. Protecting someone can lead to a lot of strong feelings."

"I don't think we're going to appreciate you warning me off. Grown adults. More important things at hand."

"The most important thing at hand is my sister's safety. Which you've been in charge of. Feelings—"

"Can complicate that. I'm well aware."

Vaughn gave him a look Zach couldn't read, then shifted uncomfortably in his seat. "Believe it or not, emotions aren't always the enemy when it comes to keeping the people you...care about safe."

"Not my experience, no offense."

"And yet in *mine*, I kept the woman safe, married her and have two amazing kids with her. So...you know. I guess it just depends."

Before Zach could say *anything* to that, because *marriage* and *kids* made his tongue stick to the roof of his mouth, Vaughn switched gears.

"Number one thing we should focus on?"

Zach forced himself to change gears, too. "Jordan was arrested over an anonymous tip, so someone out there knows something."

"It could be Stacy."

"It could be. No doubt."

But Zach was sure there was more, and that he was running out of time to find it.

Chapter Fifteen

That was how Lucy found her brother and her lover, heads bent together going over the details of her case. She couldn't hear what they were saying in their low tones, but it made her realize Jordan had never really mingled with her family or her friends.

He'd never sat next to Vaughn on a couch and discussed anything with this kind of serious back and forth.

Of course, Zach and Vaughn weren't exactly arguing the finer points of the Cowboys' defense or the Astros' pitching staff. They were discussing Jordan or the case or something about her. Keeping her safe, while she wandered around wondering how many people in her life had betrayed her.

The second they noticed her there, Vaughn loudly mentioned something about the home value of a place like this. Lucy shook her head. "All right. Let's cut the crap."

Zach looked back at her, picture-perfect innocence. She couldn't understand why his ability to put on and take off masks with such ease didn't scare her, but it didn't. It was a part of who he was, and so far he hadn't used it for any negative reasons against her.

"Crap?" he asked cheerfully. But he watched her, steady and concerned, and maybe that was why she couldn't get uneasy about him. He never pretended about his emotions toward her. Oh, he might bottle them up, but he didn't try to fake any.

She moved into the living room, fidgety and desperately trying to hide it by perusing the books laid out on the coffee table. She wanted to be steady and calm like them, but she never could really get there.

"Did they give Jordan a bond?" she asked, hoping to sound casual and unaffected. Last night Zach had explained to her that when it came to murder most judges denied bond, but in cities like Nashville it wasn't unheard of to simply set the bond high.

And she knew no matter how high a bond, Jordan wouldn't just be able to pay it, he'd be certain to.

"No bond. He'll stay put in jail until the trial," Zach returned, watching her in that eagle-eye way of his. She might not have minded that too much, but her brother was doing the same thing.

It brought home how much she'd kept Vaughn at arm's length over the years, and how much he would have been there for her if she'd let him. She couldn't blame his stoicism or disapproval, because it had been she who hadn't wanted to give anyone that piece of her.

She hadn't even given Jordan any pieces of herself. She'd weaved dreams and fantasies about their future, but she'd never let Jordan in on any of them. He'd been more like a statue to build her fantasies around than a person to build a life with.

He might have manipulated her and taken advantage of her vulnerabilities, but he wasn't exactly the whole reason their marriage had fallen apart. Any more than she could really truly believe he was the full reason Tom was dead, no matter how much she desperately wanted it to be that easy.

"He's going to have himself a hell of a lawyer," Lucy replied, trying not to sound grim or resigned, but perfectly reasonable instead. "Money buys a lot. He could be out in no time."

"I imagine you're right," Vaughn agreed, devoid of emotion one way or another.

She wanted to scowl at the both of them, demand they *react* in some way, but they both looked at her. Concern and... Oh, she was stupid to think Zach was looking at her with love, but she'd already determined she was stupid, so why not just ride the wave?

"So when are we going to talk about the fact Jordan couldn't have known about the smoke bombs or to call to meet me without Stacy telling him?"

Vaughn sighed. "I'm sorry, Luce."

She tried to smile at Vaughn, though she knew it was weak at best. She perched herself on the arm of the couch on Zach's side. "I'm sorry, too, but...well, Jordan had a reason to hate me, I guess. Stacy didn't." No matter how many ways Lucy went back through the past few years, she couldn't even make up a reason.

Daisy Delaney could be prickly and difficult, but she'd always been those things with Stacy. Since those first days of stepping out of her father's shadow. Nothing about her behavior had changed. Except the addition of Jordan into her life and, in some ways, career. If this had happened while she was still married to Jordan, she might have been able to blame that, but she'd divorced him.

What reason did Stacy have to hate her now that she'd dropped the demanding weight around both their shoulders?

"I just can't understand why she'd want to hurt me. I know, I *know* there aren't other explanations for how Jordan got the info, but I can't understand it. That weighs on me."

"I've been pondering another angle," Zach said in that gentle way of his, which meant it would not be a gentle angle *at all*.

She saw the warning look Vaughn gave Zach and shook her head. She couldn't bury her head in the sand and let these two men handle things, though they would have gladly done it and it might be easier on her emotional well-being.

This whole time she'd been holding back, hoping things would right themselves. Hoping it would be taken care of by someone else, and it hadn't been. Oh, she'd thought about her past, who might hate her, but she hadn't tugged on old hurts or scars, because she'd thought surely all the people paid to keep her safe would figure it out.

But that just wasn't going to work. She needed to be present. She needed to revisit those scars so they could end this completely. Vaughn and Zach could only do so much—she was the real center of this problem—which meant she had to center herself in the solution.

Tom was dead. Jordan was in jail. She suspected one of her oldest, closest friends of being part of it.

Now was not the time to hide. It was time to be the woman in her songs—not just in name but in deed. The kind of woman who went after what she wanted and got it no matter the consequences, no matter what she had to sacrifice or lose.

She leveled Zach with an even stare. "What's the angle?"

"Your father."

She hadn't braced herself for that. The flinch that went through her had to be visible, and if only Zach had seen, that might have been okay, but Vaughn being here for this...

Vaughn hadn't had much of a relationship with Dad, and she knew that Dad's dying with no reconciliation weighed on him.

She stood back up and headed to the kitchen. She started the process of making coffee in the hopes that having something to do would ease her tightly wound insides. "Well, Stacy has a connection to Dad, sort of, as an assistant to Don. It's an awful long game for her to want to hurt me over something a dead guy did. Especially now after so many years of opportunity."

"I want to go back to the conversation we had before the whole Jordan debacle. Your father's manager— Stacy's boss."

She stiffened again. She should have known Zach would come back to this, no matter how it didn't connect. "I don't see how this connects to Don."

"I don't, either, but we have the fact that he hurt you, which caused you to leave your father's fledgling label. After which, that label fell apart—if my research is correct."

"Don hurt you?" Vaughn demanded.

Lucy gave Zach a warning look not to say more. "It fell apart because Dad didn't know what he was doing.

Excellent entertainer. Not so great on the business front. Everyone knew *he* was the reason for the failure, not me leaving."

"How did Don hurt you?" Vaughn demanded again.

"It was nothing," Lucy insisted. It bothered her to realize so many years later Vaughn would have supported her and protected her no matter what if she'd told him about the incident. But she'd known it would have come at the cost of the career she wanted…so she'd just kept quiet. Better to keep what she wanted and ignore the hurts, right?

"Lucy, you will tell me—"

"I don't need a big brother!" she shouted, slamming the can of coffee against the counter. So much for being calm and collected—but who said calm ever got a woman anywhere? Maybe she needed to be *angry* and let it out. Maybe she needed to rage and act.

"I need this to be over," she said a little more evenly but with just as much emotion. "So look into Don Levinson, who is probably *dead*." She flung a hand toward Zach. "Look into anyone who might have hated my father. I'll give you every name I can think of. I just need this to *end*."

Zach stood, moving over to the kitchen. He didn't touch her, though she desperately wanted him to. Wanted that anchor to something solid and true, because no matter how she told herself to be strong, all her foundations were shifting under her. Zach seemed to be the one thing left that wouldn't.

"We all want it over, because we all want you safe," he said gravely.

She wanted to tell him she didn't know how to *deal* with that. Who had ever protected her? But that wasn't fair to Vaughn, who would have if she'd have let him. Because the real issue was, who had she ever *let* protect her?

Zach.

She didn't even have the good sense to question that because he stood there, handsome and sweet, and she'd never been so certain of Jordan. She'd convinced herself she was in love with Jordan, convinced herself to love him because of his act. But she'd never *felt* it wash over her as some irrefutable fact.

She'd had to work at loving Jordan and believing in that love. This thing inside her that waved over her whenever she looked at Zach was different, and it was real—no matter how little she understood that.

Zach wasn't an act. She'd *seen* him act. The real him was the man who'd made love to her last night.

She wished she could rewind time—stay right back there—where she didn't have to deal with loose ends or her brother.

But both had to be dealt with. Standing in this kitchen, looking at Zach, wishing this could be normal life without her safety in question—she realized for the first time in this whole nightmare year that at some point her life would be hers again.

She'd lived in the scary *now* for a year, most especially this past awful week. But it would have to end at some point and once it was over she'd have her life back. Completely. She'd be able to visit Vaughn and his family without worry. She'd be able to settle down somewhere and build whatever kind of life she wanted—including one with a partner, a real partner.

Maybe even in Wyoming. Maybe even with Zach.

Why not? It was her fantasy life right now, so why not indulge in all those impossibilities?

"What about trying to ferret out the anonymous tip?" Vaughn asked, singularly focused on the task at hand. "Surely, the cops have some way of tracking it."

Zach turned back to his conversation with Vaughn, so Lucy focused on the coffee and the nice little fantasy of settling down in a ghost town where no one could find her if she didn't want them to. Zach could protect people and she could write music.

She was brought out of the reverie that eased some of that tension inside her by the vibrating of her phone in her pocket.

Lucy slipped the phone out and looked at the message. From Stacy.

She glanced at Vaughn and Zach, but they were deep in computers and papers and theories, so she opened the message.

911. Call back. No ears.

The *no ears* made her uneasy, but what could Stacy do over the phone? Maybe she was calling to warn her about something. Explain something. Hell, maybe she was calling to confess all.

She looked at the two men in her life again. They certainly didn't need her for whatever it was they were doing, and she wasn't so sure she needed them for this.

Part of her knew she should tell them about Stacy's text *before* she made the call, but they were handling everything else. Why couldn't she handle a simple phone call?

She opened her mouth to make her excuses, then

realized neither one of them would come up for air for hours if she left them alone.

She eased her way into the hall. Then toward the back door. Slowly and as quietly as possible, she undid all three locks. She hadn't been out here, but Zach had mentioned a back porch she could use. She just hadn't had a reason to yet.

She stepped out onto it. It was less of a porch and more of a sunroom. The walls were made out of glass, glass she suspected was reinforced with whatever special security measures someone protecting people might use—if the giant keypad lock on the door to the outside was anything to go by.

Still, the day was sunny, and everything outside the glass was a vibrant, enticing green. God, she was tired of being cooped up, of feeling like she had to be in someone else's presence for every second. She hadn't realized how much she missed just stepping outside and lifting her face to the sun.

Which meant this had to end and she had to talk to Stacy. She dialed Stacy's number, staring at the green outside, trying to breathe in the sunshine to offset the nausea roiling around inside her.

"Oh, thank God, Lucy. I don't know what's going on. Everything is so messed up. Jordan's in jail? What is happening?"

Stacy only ever called her Lucy outside work, those occasions they interacted as friends. Stacy had never had any trouble keeping both names straight. Was it because she was a two-faced backstabber?

"I don't know what's happening," Lucy replied flatly.

"Jordan's team is trying to lay the seeds that you've framed him."

Lucy snorted, lowering herself into a cushioned wicker chair and pulling her legs up under her. "The police didn't seem to think that was a possibility." She closed her eyes, trying to ignore the seed of fear and worry that Stacy had planted. God, would he succeed at that, too?

No one could prove she was trying to frame Jordan. Of course that didn't mean the tide of public opinion couldn't turn even further against her. That was what Jordan's team would try to do. Not just a wild, alcoholic cheater, but a murderer, too.

"I mean, Jordan's stupid enough to be set up," Stacy continued. "I'd certainly commend you for your creativity and for getting his big mouth out of the way."

"Are you accusing me of something, Stacy?" Lucy asked coldly, because an unforgiving chill had swept through her. Any conflict she had over not trusting Stacy was fading away with each statement. If Stacy was really worried about *her*, wouldn't this conversation go differently?

"No, God, of course not." Stacy sighed heavily into the receiver. "Everything is so messed up. So confusing. Can we meet for lunch?"

"Not without two bodyguards," Lucy retorted sharply.

"Two?" Stacy asked—the question one of confusion, or was it calculating the odds? Was it filing away information to use later?

It broke Lucy's heart to think Stacy was fishing. Broke Lucy's heart that she had to lie. "To start. You know how overprotective Vaughn is. I swear he's hired half the country to look out for my well-being and investigate what on earth is really going on." She tried to make herself laugh casually, but couldn't muster the sound.

"You don't think Jordan did it?"

"All evidence points to yes, based on what I've heard, but you know, some people are more concerned for my safety than how much information I've got."

"You know, don't you?" Stacy said, her voice hushed and pained.

Lucy had to swallow at the lump in her throat. She waited for the confession, but Stacy didn't speak.

"What do I know, Stacy? Why don't you go ahead and tell it to me straight for once."

"God." Stacy's voice broke. "Don't hate me, Luce. It was an honest mistake. They all were."

An honest mistake. Tom was dead and Stacy had made an *honest mistake*. Lucy couldn't speak past the lump in her throat.

"Okay, okay. Just hear me out, okay? I know I'm the reason Jordan knew you were in town. I would have told you, but I didn't even realize it until someone told me you'd been at dinner together when he got arrested. Then I pieced it all together and—I'm sorry, okay?"

Lucy frowned. That wasn't exactly the grand confession she was expecting, but it was something. "You gave him the information about me coming here? Or going to Wyoming?"

"Here! Of course. You were totally safe in Wyoming," Stacy returned, and it was too hard to try and decide if she was an excellent liar or simply telling the truth.

"Truth be told, I don't understand why you came home when no one knew you were there."

"Because someone knew I was there, Stacy. I wasn't

safe there. Someone found me. Now, what exactly did you tell Jordan? This time and before."

"Nothing before! How can you think that of me?" Stacy muttered a curse. "Listen, listen, okay? I hadn't talked to Jordan in months, but he called me not long after the smoke bomb. He was fishing, I knew he was, but he knew all the right buttons to push. I didn't mean to tell him. I was… He was being irritating, and I was trying to one-up him. I said I'd seen you at my office and you were *fine*. It wasn't until long after I'd hung up that I realized he was goading me and I was just dumb enough to bite."

It sounded plausible enough. God knew Jordan could manipulate. But how had someone found her in Wyoming? And why had Stacy pulled her in the opposite direction of Zach at the office?

Stacy wasn't copping to any of that, so what on Earth was this 911 emergency all about?

"Were you the anonymous tip?" Stacy asked after some beats of silence.

Lucy's blood chilled. "Pretty sure if I had any tips they wouldn't be anonymous, and I would have handed them over when I found Tom dead in my dressing room."

"Jesus," Stacy said, sounding truly sickened by the thought.

"Someone knew I was in Wyoming. You were the only person I told."

"You really think I'm behind this," Stacy said, sounding so shocked and hurt Lucy's own heart twisted in pain. But she had to be strong. Because manipulations were apparently the name of the game, and she'd fallen for too many.

"You were the only one outside my immediate family who knew where I was going," Lucy said, doubling down.

"I didn't tell anyone. Not a soul. Not even Cory. Cory…" There was a long pause.

"Don't try to pin this on Cory. What possible reason would she have for being involved in this?"

"It wasn't me, Luce. Whatever you think. I haven't done anything. I swear to God. I made a mistake in talking to Jordan, but…nothing else. How is this getting so out of hand?"

"What exactly is getting out of hand, Stacy? Because I'm lost."

Stacy swore again. "I might know… I have a bad feeling I know who's behind all this. Jordan told me something a long time ago that I never told you. I know I should have, but you were head over heels for him. If it didn't connect to some things with Cory lately, I might not have even remembered, but…"

"But what? What is it?"

The line was quiet except for Stacy's breathing. "Someone's here," Stacy whispered. "Oh, God, someone's in my house."

Fear bolted through Lucy sharply, and she forgot all of her suspicions at the sheer terror trembling through Stacy's voice.

"Stacy. Hang up. Call 911. Okay? Stacy?" Still shallow breathing. "Stacy!" Lucy yelled. "Hang up and call 911."

"Help m—"

The line clicked off.

Chapter Sixteen

"Stacy's in trouble!"

Zach jumped to his feet, heart in his throat as Lucy ran into the living room.

"What?" he and Vaughn echoed in unison.

She waved her phone in both their faces. "I was talking to Stacy on the phone and—"

"Why the hell were you doing that?" Vaughn demanded. Which kept Zach from having to demand it.

"Zach," she said, turning to him, clearly thinking he'd be more reasonable than her brother. That wasn't the case, but he'd try to pretend. A sort of good-cop-bad-cop deal.

"She's at her house," Lucy said, panic in her voice and broad gestures. "She said someone was in her house and then the line went dead."

"Go back to the beginning," Zach said, trying to remain calm. "Explain everything."

She looked up at him helplessly. "There isn't time!"

"Lucy." He took her by the shoulders. "Just do it. Quickly, but from the beginning."

Lucy shook her head, still gripping the phone like it was a lifeline to Stacy. "She wanted me to call her. So I did, and she talked about Jordan being arrested, and said she accidentally told him about our meeting and me heading home."

Vaughn and Zach scoffed together.

"Look, I don't know. She seemed fishy and yet not and she was going to tell me something she thought I should know, then she said someone was in her house and her line went dead. She said *help*. Please." Blue eyes looked up at him, full of tears and fear. "Even if she's…part of this, she's in trouble."

Zach wasn't convinced that was true, but it was possible. It was also possible she was trying to lure Lucy to her house, and he'd use that if he could.

"Why didn't you tell us she was calling?" Zach asked, trying to be gentle.

"She wanted to talk privately," Lucy replied, sounding resigned. "But she was scared, Zach. That wasn't an act. I don't… It couldn't have been. I'm not saying it's on the up and up, but this is complicated and she's in *danger*."

Complicated was right.

"Call the cops," Zach instructed. He shook his head at Vaughn, who'd opened his mouth to speak. "Not you or me, her. She's the one who spoke with Stacy, so she's going to give them her account. You two stay put. But call the cops and tell them everything you remember about the phone call."

"You don't know that she's telling the truth," Vaughn said firmly.

"No, but I don't know that she's not," Zach returned, moving for his gun, his holster, keys, wallet. "If this is some sort of plot to get to Lucy, she'll be here, protected by you and out of harm's way. If it's not, then

I get close enough to see what she might be planning. I'll need her address."

"Wait, you're not...going," Lucy said incredulously.

"If she's in trouble, I'm going to help," Zach said, weapon already strapped to his body. "And if she's trying to lure you, I want to be there to figure out why."

"But the cops—"

"I want them to check it out, but I want to get there first in case something is off. The more information I can gather, the better chance we have of putting this away for good."

"But if it's a lure, it could be dangerous. You could be hurt."

"Not if you call the cops." He didn't like Lucy being out of his sight right now, but they were both going to have to deal with their worry. Vaughn would protect her. He was more than capable. "Make sure you tell the cops I'll be there and give my description and that I'll be happy to verify and ID who I am so they don't mix me up with anyone else."

He leaned forward to kiss her goodbye—just on the off chance this was dangerous and things went south—but the presence of her brother gave him pause.

Screw it. He kissed her. Hard. "Stay put. I mean it. Both of you." He didn't need to worry about Vaughn keeping an eye on her. There was no doubt in Zach's mind Vaughn would lay down his own life to save his sister's, just like Zach would do.

So Zach would go, no matter how much uncertainty plagued him. Because this didn't add up and if it was a lead, he'd darn well take it. "Text me the address."

By the time he was in the rental car, Stacy's address

was plugged into his navigation system and he was on his way.

He wished he had more time to plan, but if Lucy sincerely thought Stacy was in trouble there wasn't time for plans. He had to act. Stacy might be involved, like Jordan, and about to be hurt to protect a killer's true identity. Stacy could be luring Lucy to her, or trying to get her alone.

Endless possibilities. So he had to be ready for anything.

He beat the cops to her house, which wasn't too far from the farmhouse. That certainly gave him some pause, but he quickly got out of the car and began moving toward the house.

It was quiet. Stacy didn't have the same amount of property as the place they'd been staying, but it was still secluded from the neighbors by a pristine lawn and thick trees around the perimeter.

Zach glanced into the garage through the windows. There was a car parked inside the tidy building. If someone was here, there was no evidence of a vehicle besides Stacy's own.

He didn't want Stacy to be guilty for Lucy's sake, but believing things for Lucy's sake was bound to get people hurt. He'd already let his emotions get too involved here even after promising himself not to.

That was... Well, it had happened. He couldn't change it.

So he'd have to do better for Lucy than he'd done for Ethan. Neither Lucy nor her brother were getting hurt on his watch, so he'd follow this path wherever it led.

He moved to the front door, glanced around the quiet lawn. Nothing and no one, as far as he could tell.

Carefully, he tried the knob. Locked. He looked around again, hoping for police backup, but still no sign of cops or sounds of sirens.

He'd have to move around the house, looking in what windows he could. Then if there was still nothing—and no cops—he'd simply have to break in and hope for the best.

He moved stealthily around the house, peeking in windows and seeing nothing—no people, no signs of struggle, just a perfectly neat but lived-in-looking house.

Until he got to the back porch. There were two big French doors that led into a dining room and kitchen area.

The bolt of shock at what he saw stopped him in his tracks. Stacy was sitting in the middle of the kitchen—tied to a chair. She had duct tape around her mouth. He could see her profile, and her eyes were wide and terrified.

There didn't appear to be anyone around her—though he could only see part of the kitchen and dining room from his vantage point. He looked around the expansive backyard. No one.

It could be a trap—the way his heart beat hard against his chest warned him that this could all end very, very badly for him.

But a woman was tied up in a kitchen and he was armed. The least he could do was try to help her.

He could tell the doors weren't fully latched—likely where whoever was in there had gotten in—so he began to slowly move forward, watching every inch of the backyard for a flash of movement.

Every last hunch inside him screamed *trap*, but he

couldn't ignore the trickle of blood that started at Stacy's temple and slid down the side of her face and neck.

It was possible she'd done it to herself, possible she was *this* good of an actor, but he couldn't be sure.

Carefully, making as little noise as possible, Zach inched forward. He kept his gaze alert and his movements careful, gun at the ready. He moved up to the door and waited for some kind of movement.

When he reached forward and gave the door a slight nudge, Stacy's head whipped around. Her eyes went wide. Zach could only hope she recognized him as he stepped forward.

She didn't fidget or try to speak past the tape. She just watched him as she breathed heavily through her nose. Slowly, she moved her hand. Though her arms were tied to her sides and the chair, she lifted one finger and pointed upstairs.

At least, that was what he hoped she was pointing at. He moved closer and closer, studying the way she was tied. It would be best to free her arms and legs first, so she could run if need be, but he needed more information first. So the tape had to go.

"Brace yourself, okay?" he whispered, tapping the edge of the tape. "And try not to make a sound."

She nodded, tears trickling down her cheeks. Feeling awful, Zach pulled the tape from her mouth.

She gasped in pain, but she didn't make any extra noise.

"How many are there?" he asked, immediately crouching to untie the rope bonds.

"Just one. Just one. I don't know who he is. I don't know what's going on." She started crying in earnest, and Zach winced at the noise. "He's upstairs. He's looking for something, but I don't know what."

"That's fine. It's all going to be okay." He got the ropes off her and helped her to her feet. "Run outside. The police will be here soon. I'm going to stay right here and make sure he doesn't leave, so you just make sure to tell the police there are two of us in here—and one of us means them no harm." Hopefully, between Stacy's recount and Lucy's call giving his description, he'd avoid accidentally entangling with police.

"What are you going to do?" Stacy whispered, rubbing her arms where the rope had been.

"I'm going to find out what's going on once and for all. You run. Now."

She nodded tremulously, but then she eased out of the back door and left in a dead run.

Zach took a breath and then began to move. He wished he knew the layout of Stacy's house, but he could at least hear someone upstairs. As long as he did, he knew the perpetrator was up there and not on the same level as him.

Zach just needed to find him, get him to talk and then let the police do whatever they had to do.

Easy, right?

He eased closer to the staircase, weapon drawn and ready. Here he couldn't hear the footsteps as well as he'd been able to in the dining area.

Still, he moved slowly and as silently as possible. As he went up the stairs, some of his old FBI training took over—the way his body would cool, tense and let go of the wild fear. Focused on the job—on the end result, and the rest of the chips would fall where they fell.

Doing what he came to do was the most important thing.

When he crested the top, he leaned forward and looked around. There weren't any hallways, just a circle of an area—with four rooms around him.

All four doors were open, but only slightly ajar. If he started to move forward, he'd be able to get a glimpse into them, but he wouldn't be able to do anything else without drawing attention to himself.

Not ideal, but it could be worse, so he started forward. The first room didn't have anyone in it that he could see. Neither did the second room. As he approached the third, his foot landed on a floorboard that made a creak as loud as a bomb.

Immediately, the third door burst open and a gun went off. Zach felt the searing burn of metal hitting flesh, stumbled to his hands and knees and swore, then rolled forward to knock the shooter off his feet.

His arm throbbed, but not enough to be anything more than a flesh wound. The gunman let out a howl of pain as he crashed into the dresser. Violent cursing and threats spewed from the man, but it was drowned out by the thundering of feet and shouted orders to drop their weapons and stay down.

Zach winced at the searing ache in his arm, but praised the timing of the police. The man he'd knocked into wasn't taller than Zach, but he was built like a Mack truck. Zach could take on a bigger man, but in this tiny room he would have been beat to hell in the process, no doubt.

Once the cops verified who he was and cleared him to get up, he moved toward the man he didn't recognize being handcuffed.

"Who do you work for?" Zach demanded.

"We'll handle the questioning, Mr. Simmons."

Zach leveled the officer pushing him back with a scathing look. Zach kept trying to push forward, but the one cop kept pushing him back while two others arrested the thrashing man on the ground.

Zach cursed. Demanded answers. Got nothing but a brick wall of blank-faced cops as they hauled the assailant down the stairs.

The last cop eyed him, nodded toward his arm. "There's an ambulance outside."

Zach looked down. Blood was trickling down his arm and onto the white carpet. He blinked at the tiny pool of blood. For a second he felt a little light-headed, but then he shook it off.

"I'm fine." He had to find some answers before this escalated any further. "I need answers. I need—"

"Nasty gash on his head. He'll be transported to the hospital, and then we'll take him in for questioning. I'd suggest calling one of our detectives tomorrow to get an update on the situation."

Tomorrow. An *update*? He didn't have time to wait until tomorrow. "Where's the woman?" Zach asked.

"What woman?"

Zach's entire body went cold, his gut sinking with dread. "The one who ran out of here a good ten minutes ago."

The cop's eyebrows drew together, and he pulled his shoulder radio to his mouth and muttered a few things into it. After a few seconds of static and responses, the cop shrugged. "No one saw a woman."

Hell. "There was a woman here, tied up and mouth taped." He went through the whole event, gave Stacy's name and description, and then rushed back to the farm-house, trying to determine what on earth Stacy had been trying to pull. She'd been hurt, but now she was missing.

What was going on? He couldn't figure it out for the life of him, but one thing he knew for sure.

He had to get back to Lucy and make sure she was okay.

LUCY PACED IRRITABLY. "It's taking too long. Why hasn't he called? Or come back? What if he's hurt and we're just sitting here—"

"If the police are questioning him, it'll take a while," Vaughn replied calmly. "These things take time, and unfortunately going half-cocked is likely what Stacy wanted. We have to stay put and wait and trust the po-lice to do their jobs."

"Why would they question Zach?"

"Because they have to piece together what happened. If Zach sees anything over there, he'll need to explain. Maybe he's giving them more details on the case. You just don't know, and you can't read into the time that passes. Sit. Relax."

She snorted. "How can I relax when…when…" She plopped down on the couch next to Vaughn. She'd never told her brother anything about her personal life, and vice versa, but she didn't have anywhere else to put all this *stuff* roiling around inside her.

"I'm in love with him."

Vaughn leveled her with a bland gaze. "Gee. You don't say."

She frowned at him. She thought she'd get a lec-ture…one that would give her a reason to be mad and rage instead of be sad or worried.

Vaughn offered no such lecture and, in fact, seemed wholly unsurprised and unconcerned.

"You're okay with that?"

"Not *okay* exactly, but I know a thing or two about… falling in love under uncomfortable circumstances."

"He might not be in love with me," Lucy replied petulantly, because she wanted to be petulant about something if she couldn't be mad.

"Lucy, please. He's so head over heels even I can't be big-brother outraged over it. I might not be particularly comfortable with emotion, but I certainly recognize head-over-heels stupid love when I see it."

"It's just the pressure. He feels guilty. He had this thing go wrong when he was in the FBI, and… You don't fall in love over the course of a few days. It's adrenaline and stuff."

Vaughn didn't even have the decency to look away from the computer screen he was still doing research on. "I'll be sure to let Nat know the only reason I fell in love with her was *adrenaline and stuff.*"

"That's not the same."

This time he did look at her, but only to give her his patented condescending older-brother look. "How exactly?"

She didn't have a good answer, so she was more than happy that her phone trilling interrupted the question. She stood and answered without even looking at the caller ID. "Zach?"

"Lucy. No. No, it's me."

"Stacy?" She grabbed Vaughn's arm as he shot to his feet next to her. She was scared to death Stacy was calling to tell her Zach had been hurt or worse.

"What's happening? What is *happening*? I'm so scared. God."

"Stacy. Where are you? Where's Zach?" Lucy demanded through a tight throat.

Vaughn ripped the phone out of her hands. She thought he was going to talk to Stacy himself, demand answers, but he only put the call on speaker.

"He saved me," Stacy was saying over and over again. "He saved me, but… Lucy." Stacy was breathing hard, and the connection was spotty. "Listen to me."

The line cut in and out. "Stacy. Stacy. Stop…running? Or whatever you're doing. Stay in one place. I'm losing you."

"I'm so scared. Zach told me to run, so I ran and now… I don't know where I am. I ran into the trees and now… God, I'm so lost. I know I should have waited for the police, but I was so scared."

She started crying and Lucy's heart twisted, some awful mix of compassion and suspicion. What if this was another fake thing? "Stacy, tell me what's going on."

"I don't know. I don't understand it, but I think… Lucy, Jordan is Don Levinson's grand-nephew."

"What?" Daisy asked incredulously. The only reason she didn't lose her balance was because Vaughn held her up.

"Yes. God. He told me at some party eons ago. I didn't think much of it. You and I had already had a fight about Jordan and I didn't want to make you madder at me over Jordan. But then I mostly forgot about all that. He never brought it up again, and I never saw the old bastard. But I think Cory is involved, Lucy. I really do. I didn't tell anyone you'd been to Wyoming.

Not a *soul*. But Cory could have been listening. It's the only possibility."

Lucy shared a look with Vaughn. He didn't look convinced, but Jordan was related to *Don*? Why would Don want to hurt her after all this time? How did it all connect?

"Okay. Okay. You just stay put," Lucy instructed. They needed her safe and coherent to figure out if her story made any sense. "I'm going to come find you."

Before Vaughn could mount his argument, Stacy gave one. "No, Lucy. You can't. Whoever was in my house… I didn't recognize him or know him. Whoever wants to hurt you is still out there, pulling strings."

Which was when they heard a car squeal to a stop in front of the farmhouse.

Chapter Seventeen

Zach screeched to a stop in front of the farmhouse. He all but leaped out of the car and ran for the door. Stacy missing, the cops not having seen her at all, made every terrible scenario run through his head.

Stacy had already beaten him here. The whole thing had been a ruse to find out the location of the farmhouse. It was too late and Lucy was—

He stopped on the porch on a dime. What if he'd fallen for it, and led Stacy—or whoever—here right *now*? Stacy was a plant, but not the kind he'd expected. Not trying to lead Lucy to an ambush at her place, but a way to find Lucy at hers.

He turned, looked around the yard, but there was no sign of anyone that he could see. If someone had followed him, they were still far enough away that he could get to Lucy and keep her safe.

Unless they were already here. He jumped forward and shoved his key into the lock. He'd get to Lucy first. Move them out fast. Then they could figure it out, but first they had to be away from any place that could be dangerous and breeched.

The sound of an explosion shuddered through the air in perfect timing with a blast of pain in his thigh.

He staggered forward, the door opening as he did so. He crashed to the ground of the entryway, just barely recognizing the scream as Lucy's.

Lucy. Who he had to keep safe, no matter how his vision dimmed or the pain screamed through him. This wound was worse than his arm, but it wasn't fatal. Probably.

Even if it was, he'd do whatever it took to make sure nothing fatal touched Lucy.

Zach managed to scoot back and kick the door closed, but it wasn't fast enough. Before Vaughn could jump on the lock, it was being flung back open and Vaughn got knocked into the coffee table, which broke and splintered under his weight.

Two men stepped inside, one holding a gun, and one looking very, very smug. They shut the door behind them.

Zach didn't know why he was surprised. He'd known, hadn't he?

Emotion got people hurt and killed. He'd let his worry over Lucy cloud his thoughts, and now they'd all pay for it.

"WELL, LOOK AT YOU, Daisy girl. All grown."

Lucy's stomach pitched. The years had not been kind to Don Levinson, and yet that smarmy smile of his was exactly the same and still reminded her of things she'd tried long and hard to forget.

That smile made her remember all too clearly a young girl who'd thought her father would protect her and been wholly, utterly disillusioned.

But Dad was dead, and Don very much wasn't. Old, yes, but not dead, and certainly no less evil than he'd been all those years ago trying to take advantage of young women.

Vaughn sat in the wreckage of the coffee table. Zach lay on the ground, a concerning amount of blood pooling around his leg. Both were armed, but neither reached for their weapon. She supposed they wouldn't as long as Don's little buddy there had a very big and scary-looking gun pointed in her direction.

"I'm very disappointed in you, sweetheart. Your father always told me how smart you were, and yet you never once suspected your old pal Don. You didn't suspect that moron you married until it was too late."

Lucy didn't say anything. She barely let the words register, because she had to think. She had to survive this and get Zach and Vaughn out of this horrible mess.

"Don't worry. You're not half as disappointing as *him*," Don continued. "The time and effort I poured into that boy, and he's still dumb as a post. A bit of a coward, too. If I'd had my way, he would have killed you slowly and quietly when you were married, but *no*."

Killed her. Don and Jordan had plotted to kill her.

"He thought he'd use your fame instead of my know-how. Thought you being a wreck would sell him better than you being dead. Well, look where he is now. Like I said, dumb as a post."

"Yeah, I suppose we both were," Lucy replied, trying not to let the wave of nauseous regret fell her. Zach was bleeding. Vaughn would die to protect her and leave his family without a husband and father.

She couldn't—wouldn't—let that happen.

"What on earth do you have against me, Don?" Lucy asked, trying to sound bored and unaffected.

Don laughed. "Against *you*. Against *you*? As if you don't know. Your father told me what you did."

"Told him you were a dangerous pervert who couldn't keep his hands off teenage girls?"

"If you hadn't gone crying to him, pretending like you hadn't wanted my hands on you, do you know what I would have? He cut me out of his estate, and out of all I'd invested in *you*. So I had to bow and scrape and pay off my debts. The things I had to endure because I didn't get that money, all because you were a lying whore. Well, my hands'll be on you now."

Zach and Vaughn made almost identical sounds of outrage, and Don smiled down at them. "Don't worry," he said cheerfully. "It won't bother you any. You'll both be dead." His gaze went back to Daisy. "And boy, will the press eat this up. I'll have to figure out how I'm going to play it first. You'd think I'd know, with all the planning that's gone into it, but sometimes I do like to wing it. Murder-suicide? Or do I just frame you? So many options. But at least I finally realized I'd have to do it myself. The younger generation just doesn't have the chutzpa to get things done."

He turned to the other man. "Leave the one on the floor." He nudged Zach with his boot. Zach didn't so much as move or groan. Lucy tried not to panic that he'd lost consciousness. "He'll bleed out if he hasn't already." Don then studied Vaughn.

Lucy had to do something. Save her brother. Save Zach. But how? If someone was willing to kill like this, what kind of reasoning would work?

"You want money?" she demanded.

"I want *revenge*, little girl. I was supposed to have a piece of your pie, but your father held your lying story over me for years. Made me jump through all those hoops and then not even a *cent* of his estate? Which should have been rightfully left to me for all I'd done to make him a star, if you hadn't come along."

"I never lied. You grabbed me."

"You begged for it."

"You're delusional. And insane, I think, to have spent your life so obsessed with me—"

"Shoot her," Don ordered of the man with the gun. Then he held up a hand, before Vaughn could lunge to her rescue, and sighed dramatically. "No. That's rash. I want my fun with her first. And yours, as well," he said, nodding toward the man with the gun, who smiled.

Lucy hoped she didn't go gray, because it felt as though the very blood leaked out of her. But she needed to keep Don talking, not acting. She had to make him feel…superior. Anger would make him act, but condescension would keep his diatribes going.

"You were never supposed to have a piece of my career. My career was always separate from Dad's."

Don tipped his head back and laughed, all too heartily. Lucy noted Zach's lifeless body. Vaughn's hesitant, slow and deliberate move for his hand to get closer and closer to his weapon without drawing attention.

She needed a scene. Not just from Don, but from everyone to get the man with the gun's attention.

"You were always meant to be your daddy's pawn. Problem was you got too many ideas, and that uppity assistant of mine fed them. And if your father had listened to me, you both would have been taken down a peg. But he let you go instead. Costing me millions. *Millions.*"

The rage was starting to seep back in and Lucy racked her brain for a way to fix this. Save them. But

Don just kept going, eyes gleaming with vicious rage, spittle forming at the corners of his mouth.

And all the while the man with the gun had the barrel pointed right at Lucy's heart.

"Then he didn't even have the intelligence to be sorry. Every time, every single time I had a better idea for your father's career, one he didn't agree with, what did he say to me? *I guess Daisy going to the police wouldn't be such a good thing for* your *career, would it, Don?*"

"That sounds like a problem between you and my father," Lucy managed, though her throat was tight with fear and pain.

"A problem I solved." He grinned and Lucy's knees nearly gave out.

"You killed him?" she rasped.

Don shrugged, but his smile was sharp. "Not so much. Supply him enough drugs and he killed himself." But his smile turned into a sneer. "Then I started getting your notes."

"I never sent you any notes, Don. I'd forgotten you even existed. That's why I didn't suspect you were behind this, because you're so far beneath me and behind me I didn't give you a second thought." Notes. Notes. As if this wasn't complicated enough, someone had been sending him notes in her name?

"Sure, little girl. Sure."

"Maybe Jordan isn't as stupid as you thought," Lucy shot out. "He knew, you know. About what you did to me." It was a flat-out lie. The only person she'd ever told aside from Stacy was Zach.

Oh, God, it all circled back to Stacy, didn't it?

But she couldn't get caught up on that. She couldn't

let the tears that threatened, fall. She couldn't give in to panic or fear, because Zach was a lifeless, bleeding form on the floor and she had to save him.

Jordan was safe in jail. If she implicated him, if she got Don to believe it…well, he'd kill them all anyway, but maybe it would make him unbalanced for a few minutes.

Don narrowed his eyes at her. "I don't believe it."

"I didn't send you notes, Don. You would have been one of the top suspects if I had. It had to be Jordan. Unless you told someone else about it."

"Or your father did." He shook his head. "It doesn't matter. Result is still the same. This guy is dead." He pointed at Zach. Then he pointed at Vaughn. "That guy is going to be. And we're going to have our fun before you are, too."

No. That was not how this was going to go down, and the best way to get out of a sticky situation with a man who thought he was in charge was always, *always* act the overwrought female.

"Dead?" she moaned. "He's dead?" She made a choking, sobbing noise and flung herself on Zach's body.

She'd hoped it would be enough of an opening Vaughn would shoot, but Don just grumbled something about women. So Lucy sobbed as loudly as she could, moving her hand, discreetly trying to get to Zach's gun without anyone noticing.

It wasn't hard to keep crying when he didn't move. But he was breathing. Unless it was just the movement of her own body making his chest seem as though it was moving up and down. She was almost to his gun when she felt him twitch under her just a little.

She gave herself one second to just press her cheek

to his chest and breathe in some relief. He was alive but he desperately needed help. She'd give it. Get his gun and—

"Scream," Zach whispered through bloodless lips, but he was breathing and talking, so she didn't wait around for anything else. She did exactly what he said.

LUCY'S SCREAM SHATTERED through the air and though it hurt like hell, Zach whipped his gun out of his holster and shot the man with the gun—who'd been so intent on Vaughn's lunge he hadn't seen Zach move, and with Lucy sheltering his arm from Don, the old man hadn't been able to warn him.

Vaughn tackled Don to the floor amidst shouts and threats.

Zach tried to get to his feet, but leveling the gun had taken all his energy and focus. His vision wavered, and he wasn't all that certain he could feel his legs. There was only pain and a fog that he kept trying to fight.

It was starting to win.

"Get some pressure on the wound," he thought he heard Vaughn shout. Was Lucy hurt? No, she hadn't been—had she?

Zach had shot the right guy, and Vaughn had taken care of the rest. Lucy was safe. He relaxed a little into the fog, except there were still so many unanswered questions.

"Loose ends," Zach muttered.

Gentle hands were on his face. "Only a few. You just stay with me so we can figure them out, all right?"

"Lucy."

"That's right. That's right." There was a catch in her throat and even though he could only see black, he knew she was crying. But she was here and safe and that was what mattered.

He hissed out a breath, eyes opening as pain shot through his leg. Pressure, he supposed, but it hurt too much to hold on to consciousness. He tried not to slide away while Lucy whispered things in his ears.

"You're okay, baby. I promise."

Something floated around in his head, a feeling he had to tell her. But the words didn't form. Yet, it was imperative. He had to tell her so she knew, but every time he tried to speak it all floated away.

"Zach, stay with me. We need you here."

"I'm here." But he wasn't. He kept losing hold on himself, on her.

There was noise, and he was being jostled. Lucy faded away, and so did he, but words floated with him.

"I love you, Zach. I love you. So you just hold on to that or I'm going to be really pissed."

Those were the words he'd meant to find—*I love you, I love you*—if only he could manage to say them back.

Chapter Eighteen

Everyone insisted she go to the police station. Vaughn was with her, but no one was with Zach. No matter what Vaughn said about him being in surgery and her not being able to be with him anyway, she could only think about him being alone.

The detective who sat at the desk across from them looked frazzled, which wasn't exactly comforting. "It doesn't add up. Let's go over it again."

"She's gone over it enough," Vaughn said firmly. "You have to find Stacy Vine. She'll fill in some of these missing pieces."

"Yes, I know. We're searching for her. We've got a team combing the woods as Ms. Delaney described to us from their phone call, and we've got someone watching her office as well as her car." The detective sighed, and then tapped a few things on his computer. "We've got someone searching Don Levinson's place of residence for evidence of these letters allegedly from you. Also, obviously, any evidence pertaining to the murder of Tom Perelli, the break-in at Stacy Vine's house or any connection to the three hired men that have been involved in attacks on Ms. Delaney."

"That's all well and good, but it isn't answers."

"Answers take time, Ranger Cooper," the detective returned, losing some of his control as irritation snaked into his tone.

Lucy couldn't blame him. It seemed no matter how they dug, no one could find all the answers. And her being here wasn't changing that, so she had to go to the hospital.

Before she could thank him for his time, make her excuses to go to the hospital, a knock sounded at the door to the detective's office.

Lucy didn't know how long they'd been sitting here, but it felt interminable.

And then Cory, Stacy's assistant, was being walked in. Handcuffed.

"Cory?"

"I didn't do anything! I didn't do a *thing*." But Lucy's stomach sank as she noticed anger more than fear in the depths of Cory's eyes. The same kind of anger that had been in Don's.

"She was found in Ms. Vine's house. An officer found her placing these in Ms. Vine's belongings." The officer held out a ziplock bag and the detective studied them. Then he turned them to Lucy.

"Is this your handwriting, Ms. Delaney?"

Lucy studied the words. *You spineless lowlife, you owe me for what you did. I'm going to make you pay worse than my father did.*

"No. Not my handwriting and I didn't write those."

Cory started screaming, blaming Don and Lucy and Stacy at equal turns, not making much sense in the process. The officer who'd led her in led her back out.

Lucy closed her eyes against the roil of nausea. She felt…sorry for the girl, almost. It was too easy to be manipulated by powerful men who'd always trusted their own influence, when you always questioned your own.

Vaughn's arm came around her and she leaned into it.

Hours passed as she sat in the awful police station. They finally found Stacy, and Lucy didn't know how to repair the damage of the past few days. But the police seemed to believe Stacy was innocent—that Cory's connection to Don had led her to ferret out information and supply Don with it.

Cory, a woman Don had groomed from the time she'd moved to Nashville with a dream of becoming a country music star. He'd pushed her into getting a job for Stacy, pumped her for information about Daisy over the years. Don had used that information to supply bits and pieces to Jordan. Who had, in the end, not used it quite the way Don had wanted.

But Don also hadn't helped Cory the way she'd expected, so Cory had begun using the information *she* knew about Don against him—writing threatening letters supposedly from Daisy.

Which had finally forced Don to act, instead of just stew. Especially when Daisy had filed for divorce from Jordan.

Jordan, who hadn't been released from jail yet, but it was looking like he would be.

Vaughn was insisting the detectives look into the legality of him getting off scot-free when he'd known Don had wanted her dead, but Lucy didn't care about that.

"I just want to see Zach. And then I want…" She wanted to go home. Only she didn't have one.

"We'll take it one step at a time, and I'll be here for every step. Whether you want me to be or not. That's a promise for the rest of your life."

Lucy smiled, but she also cried. And Vaughn held her through the tears, no matter how uncomfortable he was. He always would have, but now she was promising herself to always let him.

Zach woke up, groggy and gray. Pain snaked through a void of numbness. He didn't know where he was or why he was here, except he was clearly hurt.

When he managed to open his eyes, blue ones stared right back at him. Something inside him eased. She was all right.

"Your mother will be so upset with me. I just convinced her to go back to her hotel and get some sleep and here you are waking up."

"Aw, hell. My mother?" Zach grumbled, his voice raw.

Lucy took his hand in hers. "She likes me, don't worry. Cam and Hilly wanted to come, too, but I think your mother told them to stay put so they could take shifts."

"Cam's probably pretty pissed I went dark."

"Cam will probably forgive the man who's been shot twice."

He looked at her, really looked, as he came back to himself. He didn't remember much of what had happened, and based on the itchy and uncomfortable scruff on his face, he'd been out for a while.

But he remembered her saying she loved him, like one bright, shining beacon in the middle of foggy dark.

"Supposed to be a Delaney that gets shot," he managed to say, earning one of her patented raised eyebrow looks that made the love sweep through him so hard, so fast, he'd never question anyone's view on meant-to-be again.

"You see, back in Bent, there's a feud," he said over the wave of pain.

"You've been holding another good story from me?"

A story she'd love. A story that didn't scare him anymore. Because when it came to love, there were lots of things to worry about, but none to be scared of. "Carsons and Delaneys. They don't like each other. My mother was a Carson. Your grandmother was a Delaney."

"Are we Romeo and Juliet, Zach?"

"No, because I'm willing to die for you, Lucy, but I'm not willing to kill myself over you. Besides, the past year or so it's been something of a...hate to love deal. Carsons and Delaneys kept pairing off. Until I was the only one left."

"So we're meant to be."

"I've never believed in meant-to-be," Zach replied, holding her hand in his. She was looking worse for the wear herself, worrying over him. So many loose ends, but she was here and okay, and he was here and okay, so the most important loose end was love. "But I believe we got thrown into each other's life for a chance at something I never really thought I'd have."

"A country duo?"

"You're on quite the comedic roll, aren't you?"

"If I don't laugh I might break down and cry, and I've cried myself dry. So, I'd rather laugh, if you don't mind."

"I don't mind. I don't mind anything, if you're here. I love you, Lucy."

She swallowed, eyes shining. "I want it to go down on the record I was brave enough to say it first."

"Or at least smart enough to realize it first. I needed to get shot. Twice."

"You're just more stubborn than me."

"Ha!" The scoffing laugh hurt and he winced.

"I need to call the nurse in."

"No, not just yet. Come here."

She scooted closer and brushed a gentle kiss across his cheekbone.

"Going to come visit me? A lot?"

"Nah."

The pain of getting shot had nothing on the simple slice of horror that cut through him, until he noted she was smiling and leaning forward.

"I'd rather come home with you instead. I've got some ideas for your little ghost town."

Relief coursed through him like a river. "Do you now?"

"I'll still make music, and tour, and you'll work with Cam and keep people safe even if it puts you in danger. Because my songs and your protection is who we are."

"Yes, it is."

"But I want to build a life with you where I can come home and be Lucy Cooper when Daisy Delaney wears me out."

"I want that, too." God. More than he could express.

"So you'll have to heal up quick. Nashville's got too many prying eyes, and one too many men named Jordan Jones."

"All right. I'm ready. Tell me the whole thing."

He fell asleep halfway through her explanation of Don's plans, Cory's role, Jordan's half guilt and Stacy's innocence. It took him another few days to make it through the whole story, and more time after that to get out of the hospital, and then back onto a plane to Wyoming.

With Lucy Cooper at his side. Just where she belonged.

Epilogue

Zach Simmons was not a sentimental man, or so he'd thought. The sight of his mother carefully assisting Hilly with her wedding dress outside the church that had been restored in Hope Town—the name Lucy had come up with for their little ghost town—shifted something inside him.

Hilly made a beautiful bride, and their mother's elegant form standing next to her, openly crying, made his heart swell—a mix of sweet and bitter. He knew Mom was missing Dad, but also happy for Hilly, who'd been through so much and deserved this pretty wedding.

"Mom, you're supposed to go take your seat."

She nodded, dabbing at her eyes. She gave him a quick hug, beaming at him.

"You're looking good," she offered before slipping out of the room.

Good was probably a tiny exaggeration. He still had a ways to go on his recovery for his leg, but even Lucy had gotten to a place where she didn't get irritated about his jokes over it. After all, only Delaneys got shot in their pursuit of happily-ever-after. He'd bucked tradition—being the best of the Carsons and all that.

"You look beautiful," he said to Hilly once Mom had gone.

Hilly shook her head. "Don't say nice things to me. I'm trying not to cry until I see Cam. Is he nervous?"

"Cool as a cucumber." Which had been true on the surface, but his obsessive attention to detail at the church had been a sure giveaway Cam wasn't as calm as he pretended.

Lucy had called it cute. Zach had scoffed at her.

Zach offered an arm and then walked out of the small room Hilly had gotten ready in. They moved into the lobby of the church. Hilly and Cam had foregone bridesmaids and groomsmen since they had so many family members they would want to stand up with them. They'd said a church full of people they loved was enough—and that was exactly what they were getting.

So Zach waited for the signal—a text from Jen—and when it came, he opened the door. He led Hilly down the aisle.

There were people missing from the wedding. Their father and brother. The man Hilly had considered a father growing up. But Hilly and Cam were surrounded by family—Carsons and Delaneys, and the offspring of such calamitous pairings—and Zach was going to walk his baby sister down the aisle.

So he did, bringing her to a man he loved like a brother anyway. And he watched two people pledge their love to each other with the woman he loved seated next to him.

When the wedding ended, and the interminable pictures that tested his leg's endurance were done, they all drove back over to Bent to have the reception at

Rightful Claim—filled to the brim with couples. Laurel and Vanessa made rounds with their girls in their arms before handing them off to Grady and Dylan respectively. Noah's adopted son ran around squealing as Addie looked tired with a little baby bump popping more each day. Jen had looked suspiciously nauseated for the past week—at least that was what Lucy had told him that Laurel had told her.

Lucy had jumped into Carson and Delaney life like she'd been born into it, and no one here called her Daisy Delaney, because she was Lucy Cooper here.

Except to Cam, on occasion.

Speaking of which, Grady and Lucy took the small makeshift stage shoved into the corner of the saloon's main room.

"All right, folks, we're going to have the first dance for Cam and Hilly, with our very, *very* special guest to serenade our couple. You all know her as Lucy Cooper, but let's give a warm round of applause for Daisy Delaney."

Everyone clapped, Zach cheered and whistled and Lucy took to the stage with her guitar. She grinned at the crowd and spoke into the microphone.

"When Hilly asked me if I'd sing Cam's favorite song at their wedding, I promised I would. But I also thought something as momentous as a first dance should be about two people, two families, coming together. A song about love and promises. So with Hilly's permission, I wrote a song not just for this moment, but for all of you, too. For love and family and hope. We'll save Cam's favorite song for later, and here's a tip. Get me drunk enough, I'll sing anything. But for now, this one's for all of you."

The crowd laughed, but it didn't take long for them to settle. For Daisy's amazing voice to fill the saloon. What's more, the words of the song Lucy had written, about love and forever and even a few lines about breaking curses, settled over a group made up of people who'd been brave enough to buck tradition and expectation and fall in love with the person they were never even supposed to tolerate.

Silence, tears, happy and hopeful smiles. Even the babies were quiet until Lucy finished her song.

She slid off the stage as Cam and Hilly still swayed to their own music while Grady hooked up the speakers to Hilly's curated playlist for the evening.

Though Lucy stopped and talked to anyone who called out her name, her eyes were on Zach's as she slowly made her way over.

When she finally reached him, she sized him up. "How's the leg, champ?"

"Good enough for a dance."

"So long as it's one and only one," she returned, letting him pull her into his arms. They swayed to the slow song, and Lucy rested her temple on his cheek.

"I wrote the song for Hilly and Cam, for all of them really, but I never would have had the words if I hadn't found you," she murmured into his ear.

He pulled her closer, overwhelmed by his love for her and the love in the air. "I never believed in curses. I still don't, but you convinced me to believe in meant-to-be."

And from that day forward in Bent, Wyoming, people didn't mention curses anymore. But they did talk about a love strong enough to stand the test of murder, loss, greed, terror and evil.

And a little bit about how some things are just meant to be.

* * * * *

KILLER
INVESTIGATION

AMANDA STEVENS

Chapter One

The house on Tradd Street hadn't changed much since Arden Mayfair had left home fourteen years ago. The beautiful grand piano still gathered dust at one end of the parlor while a long-dead ancestor remained on guard above the marble fireplace. Plantation shutters at all the long windows dimmed the late-afternoon sunlight that poured down through the live oaks, casting a pall over the once stately room. The echo of Arden's footfalls followed her through the double doors as the oppressive weight of memories and dark tragedy settled heavily upon her shoulders.

Her gaze went to the garden and then darted away. She wouldn't go out there just yet. If she left tomorrow, she could avoid the lush grounds altogether, but already the interior walls were closing in on her. She drew a breath and stared back at her ancestor, unfazed by the flared nostrils and pious expression. She'd never been afraid of the dead. It was the living that haunted her dreams.

She wrinkled her nose as she turned away from the portrait. The house smelled musty from time and neglect, and she would have liked nothing more than to throw open the windows to the breeze. The whole place needed a good airing, but the patio doors were kept closed for a reason.

Berdeaux Place hadn't always been a shuttered mausoleum. The gleaming Greek Revival with its elegant arches and shady piazzas had once been her grandmother's pride and joy, an ancestral treasure box filled with flowers and friends and delectable aromas wafting from the kitchen. When Arden thought back to her early childhood days, before the murder, she conjured up misty images of garden parties and elegant soirees. Of leisurely mornings in the playroom and long afternoons in the pool. Sometimes when it rained, her mother would devise elaborate scavenger hunts or endless games of hide-and-seek. Arden had once sequestered herself so well in the secret hidey-hole beneath the back staircase that the staff had spent hours frantically searching the house from top to bottom while she lay curled up asleep.

After a half-hearted scolding from her mother, Arden had been allowed to accompany her into the parlor for afternoon tea. The women gathered that day had chuckled affectionately at the incident as they spooned sugar cubes into their Earl Grey and nibbled on cucumber sandwiches. Basking in the limelight of their indulgence, Arden had gorged herself on shortbread cookies while stuffing her pockets with macaroons to later share with her best friend. When twilight fell, wrapping the city in shadows and sweet-scented mystery, she'd slipped out to the garden to watch the bats.

It was there in the garden that Arden had stumbled upon her mother's body. Camille Mayfair lay on her back, eyes lifted to the sky as if waiting for the moon to rise over the treetops. Something had been placed upon her lips—a crimson magnolia petal, Arden would later learn. But in that moment of breathless terror, she'd been aware of only one thing: the excited thumping of a human heart.

As Arden grew older, she told herself the sound had been her imagination or the throb of her own pulse. Yet, when she allowed herself to travel back to that twilight, the pulsation seemed to grow and swell until the cacophony filled the whole garden.

It was the sound of a beating heart that had lured her from her mother's prone body to the summerhouse, where a milky magnolia blossom had been left on the steps. The throbbing grew louder as Arden stood in the garden peering up into the ornate windows. Someone stared back at her. She was certain of it. She remained frozen—in fear and in fascination—until a bloodcurdling scream erupted from her throat.

As young as she was, Arden believed that bloom had been left for her to find. The killer had wanted her to know that he would one day come back for her.

Camille Mayfair had been the first known victim of Orson Lee Finch, the Twilight Killer. As the lives of other young, single mothers had been claimed that terrible summer, the offspring left behind had become known as Twilight's Children, a moniker that was still trotted out every year on the anniversary of Finch's arrest. New revelations about the case had recently propelled him back into the headlines, and Arden worried it was only a matter of time before some intrepid reporter came knocking on her door.

So why had she come back now? Why not wait until the publicity and curiosity had died down once again? She had business to attend to, but nothing urgent. After all, months had gone by since her grandmother's passing. She'd certainly been in no hurry to wrap up loose ends. She'd come in for the service, left the same day, and the hell of it was, no one had cared. No one had asked her to stay. Not her estranged grandfather, not her uncle, not the friends and distant relatives she'd left behind long ago.

Her invisibility had been a painful reminder that she didn't belong here anymore. Although Berdeaux Place was hers now, she had no intention of staying on in the city, much less in this house. Her grandmother's attorney was more than capable of settling the estate once Arden had signed all the necessary paperwork. The house would be privately listed, but, with all the inherent rules and regulations that bound historic properties, finding the right buyer could take some time.

So why *had* she come back?

Maybe a question best not answered, she decided.

As she turned back to the foyer to collect her bags, she caught a movement in the garden out of the corner of her eye. She swung around, pulse thudding as she searched the terrace. Someone was coming along one of the pathways. The setting sun was at his back, and the trees cast such long shadows across the flagstones that Arden could make out little more than a silhouette.

Reason told her he was just one of the yard crew hired by the attorney to take care of the grounds. No cause for panic. But being back in this house, wallowing in all those old memories had left her unnerved. She reached for the antique katana that her grandmother had kept at the ready atop her desk. Slipping off the sheath, Arden held the blade flat against the side of her leg as she turned back to the garden.

The man walked boldly up to one of the French doors and banged on the frame. Then he cupped his face as he peered in through one of the panes. "I see you in there," he called. "Open up!"

Arden's grip tightened around the gilded handle. "Who are you? What do you want?"

"Who am I? What the...?" He paused in his incredulity. "Cut it out, Arden. Would you just open the damn door?"

The familiarity of his voice raised goose bumps as she walked across the room to peer back out at him. Her heart tumbled in recognition. The eyes...the nose...that full, sensuous mouth... "Reid?"

His gaze dropped to the weapon in her hand. "Just who the hell were you expecting?"

She squared her shoulders, but her tone sounded more defensive than defiant. "I certainly wasn't expecting you."

"Are you going to let me in or should we just yell through the glass all night?"

She fumbled with the latch and then drew back the door. "What are you doing here anyway? You scared me half to death banging on the door like that."

He nodded toward the blade. "Were you really going to run me through with that thing?"

"I hadn't decided yet."

"In that case..." He took the sword from her hand and brushed past her into the parlor.

"By all means, come on in," she muttered as she followed him back into the room. She clenched her fists as if she could somehow control her racing pulse. He had startled her, was all. Gave her a bad fright leering in through the windows like a Peeping Tom. Her reaction had everything to do with the situation and nothing at all to do with the man. She was over Reid Sutton. He'd been nothing more than a memory ever since she'd left for college at eighteen, determined to put him and Charleston in her rearview mirror. They'd had a grand go of it. Given both families plenty of gray hairs and sleepless nights, and then the adventure had run its course. Arden had needed to get serious about her future and, at eighteen, Reid Sutton had been anything but serious. They'd both had a lot of growing up to do. At least Arden had been mature enough to realize she needed to break away before she made an irrevocable mistake.

She wondered if Reid had ever learned that lesson. She

took in his faded jeans, flip-flops and the wavy hair that needed a trim. He was still devastatingly handsome with a smile that could melt the polar ice caps, but she knew better than to succumb to his particular allure. He was still big-time trouble from everything she'd heard, and he still had too much of the rebel in him even at the age of thirty-two. Which was, she suspected, only one of many reasons he'd recently left his family's prestigious but stodgy law firm.

Arden watched him put away the weapon. She had to tear her gaze away from his backside, and that annoyed her to no end. "How did you get into the garden anyway? The side gate is always kept locked." Her grandmother had made certain of that ever since the murder.

He turned with a grin, flashing dimples and white teeth. "The same way you used to sneak out. I climbed up a tree and jumped down over the wall."

She sighed. "You couldn't just ring the doorbell like any normal person?"

"What fun would that be?" he teased. "Besides…" He glanced around. "I wasn't sure you'd be alone."

"So you decided to spy on me instead?"

"Arden, Arden." He shook his head sadly. "Since when did you become so pedestrian? You sound like an old lady. Though you certainly don't present as one." His gaze lingered, making Arden secretly relieved for the Pilates classes and the sleeveless white dress she'd worn to meet her grandmother's attorney. "Just look at you. Thirty-two and all grown-up."

"Which is more than I can say for you." She returned his perusal, taking in the faded jeans and flip-flops.

"It's after-hours, in case you hadn't noticed the time."

"Fair enough. But don't pretend this is our first meeting since I left Charleston. I saw you just six months ago at my grandmother's funeral."

"Yes, but that was from a distance and you were dressed all in black. The hat and veil were sexy as hell, but I barely caught a glimpse of you."

"You could have come by the house after the service."

"I did."

She lifted a brow. "When? I never saw you."

"I didn't come in," he admitted. "I sat out on the veranda for a while."

"Why?"

For a moment, he seemed uncharacteristically subdued. He tapped out a few notes on the piano as Arden waited for his response. The strains of an old love song swirled in her head, tugging loose an unwelcome nostalgia.

"Why didn't you come in?" she pressed.

He hit a sour note. "I guess I wasn't sure you'd want to see me after the way we ended things."

"That was a long time ago."

"I know. But it got pretty heated that last night. I always regretted some of the things I said before you drove off. I didn't even mean most of it."

"Sure you did, but your reaction was understandable. You were angry. We both were. I said some things, too." She shrugged, but inside she was far from cavalier about their current discussion. "I guess it made leaving easier."

"For you maybe."

She cut him a look. "Don't even try to put it all on me. You left, too, remember? That was the agreement. We'd both go off to separate colleges. Do our own thing for a while. Have our own friends. We needed some space. It was all for the best."

"But you never came back."

"That's not true. I came back on holidays and every summer break."

"You never came back to me," he said quietly.

Arden stared at him for a moment and then took a quick glance around. "Are we seriously having this conversation? I feel like I'm being pranked or something."

He didn't bat an eye as he continued to regard her. "You're not being pranked. We're just being honest for once. Airing our grievances, so to speak. Best way to move on."

Arden lifted her chin. "I don't have any grievances, and I moved on a long time ago."

"Everyone has grievances. Without them, there'd be no need for people like me."

"Lawyers, you mean." Her tone sounded more withering than she'd meant it.

He grinned, disarming her yet again. "Grievances are our lifeblood. But to get back on point… Yes, you're right, we did agree to separate colleges. We were supposed to go off and sow our wild oats and then come back to Charleston, settle down, marry and have a few kids, number negotiable."

She gave a quick shake of her head, unable to believe what she was hearing. "When did we ever talk about anything remotely like that?"

"I thought it was understood. In my mind, that was the way it was always supposed to end."

"Is this the part where you tell me you've been pining for me all these years? That I'm the reason you never married?"

"You never married, either," he said. "Have you been pining for me?"

"No, I have not." She planted a hand on one hip as she stared him down. "As fascinating as I'm finding this conversation, I really don't have time for a trip down memory lane. I have a lot of things to do and not much time to do

them. So if you'd like to tell me why you're really here…"
She tapped a toe impatiently.

"I was hoping we could have dinner some night and
catch up."

The suggestion hit her like a physical blow. Dinner?
With Reid Sutton? No, not a good idea, ever. The last thing
she needed was more drama in her life. All she wanted
these days was a little peace and quiet. A safe place where
she could reflect and regroup. Her life in Atlanta hadn't
turned out as she'd hoped. Not her career, not her personal relationships, not even her friendships. There had
been good times, of course, but not enough to overcome
the disappointment and humiliation of failure. Not enough
to ward off a dangerous discontent that had been gathering for months. None of that needed to be shared with
Reid Sutton.

She wandered over to the fireplace, running a finger
along the dusty mantel before turning back to him. "What
do you call this discussion if it's not catching up?"

"Airing grievances and catching up are two different
things." He followed her across the room. "The latter usually goes down better with a cocktail or two. The former
sometimes requires a whole bottle."

"The liquor has all been put away," she said. "And as
tempting as you make it sound, I'm leaving tomorrow so
there's no time for dinner."

He turned to glance back at the foyer where she'd
dropped her luggage. "That many suitcases for just one
night?"

She shrugged. "I like to be prepared. Besides, I may be
going somewhere else after I leave here."

"Where?"

"I haven't decided yet."

He cocked his head and narrowed his gaze. "Is that the

best you can do? Disappointing, Arden. You used to be a much better liar."

"I don't have as much practice these days without you egging me on."

His demeanor remained casual, but something dark flashed in his eyes. "As if I ever had to egg you on. About anything."

She felt the heat of an uncharacteristic blush and turned away. "Funny. I don't recall it that way."

"No? I could refresh your memory with any number of specifics, but suffice to say, you were always very good at deception and subterfuge. Better than me, in fact."

"No one was a better liar than you, Reid Sutton."

"It's good to excel at something, I guess. Seriously, though. How long are you really here for? The truth, this time."

She sighed. She could string him along until they both tired of the game, but what would be the point? "I haven't decided that, either." She brushed off her dusty fingers. "The house needs work before I can list it and I'm not sure I trust Grandmother's attorney to oversee even minor renovations. He's getting on in years and wants to retire." There. She'd owned up to Reid Sutton what she hadn't dared to admit to herself—that she'd come back to Charleston indefinitely.

"Ambrose Foucault still handling her affairs?"

"Yes."

"He's no spring chicken," Reid agreed. "First I'd heard of his retirement, though."

"It's not official. Please don't go chasing after his clients."

He smiled slyly. "Wouldn't dream of it. What about your job? Last I heard you were the director of some fancy art gallery in Atlanta."

"Not an art gallery, a private museum. And not the director, just a lowly archivist."

His eyes glinted. "I bet you ran things, though."

"I tried to, which is why I'm no longer employed there."

"You were fired?"

"Not fired," she said with a frown. "It was a mutual parting of the ways. And anyway, I was ready for a change. You should understand that. Didn't you just leave your father's law practice?"

"Yes, but I *was* fired. Disowned, too, in fact. I'm poor now in case you hadn't heard."

She was unmoved by his predicament. "By Sutton standards maybe. Seems as though I recall a fairly substantial trust fund from your grandfather. Or have you blown through that already?"

"Oh, I've had a good time and then some. But no worries. Provisions have been made for our old age. Nothing on this level, of course." He glanced around the gloomy room with the gilded portraits and priceless antiques. "But we'll have enough for a little place on the beach or a cabin in the mountains. Which do you prefer?"

Arden wasn't amused. The idea that they would grow old together was ludicrous and yet, if she were honest, somehow poignant. "Go away, Reid. I have things to do."

"I could help you unpack," he offered. "At least let me carry your bags upstairs."

"I can manage, thanks."

"Are you sure you want to be alone in this house tonight?"

His tone altered subtly, sending a prickle of alarm down Arden's spine. "Why? What aren't you telling me?" When he didn't answer immediately, she moved closer, peering into his eyes until he glanced away. "You didn't come over here to clear the air, did you? What's going on, Reid? For the last time, why are you really here?"

He peered past her shoulder into the garden. "You haven't heard, then."

"Heard what?"

His troubled gaze came back to her. "There's been a murder."

Chapter Two

"The victim was a young female Caucasian," Reid added as he studied Arden's expression.

She looked suddenly pale in the waning light from the garden, but her voice remained unnervingly calm. "A single mother?"

The question was only natural considering Orson Lee Finch's MO. He'd preyed on young single mothers from affluent families. It was assumed his predilection had been nurtured by contempt for his own unwed mother and resentment of the people he'd worked for. Some thought his killing spree had been triggered by the rejection of his daughter's mother. All psychobabble, as far as Reid was concerned, in a quest to understand the nightmarish urges of a serial killer.

"I don't know anything about the victim," he said. "But Orson Lee Finch will never see the outside of his prison walls again, so this can't have anything to do with him. At least not directly."

Arden's eyes pierced the distance between them. "Why are you here, then? You didn't just come about any old murder."

"A magnolia blossom was found at the scene."

Her eyes went wide before she quickly retreated back into the protection of her rigid composure.

This was the part where Reid would have once taken her in his arms, letting his strength and steady tone reassure her there was no need for panic. He wouldn't touch her now, of course. That wouldn't be appropriate and, anyway, he was probably overreacting. Homicides happened every day. But, irrational or not, he had a bad feeling about this one. He'd wanted Arden to hear about it from him rather than over the news.

She'd gone very still, her expression frozen so that Reid had a hard time reading her emotions. Her hazel eyes were greener than he remembered, her hair shorter than she'd worn it in her younger days, when the sun-bleached ends had brushed her waist. The tiny freckles across her nose, though. He recalled every single one of those.

If he looked closely, he could see the faintest of shadows beneath her eyes and the tug of what might have been unhappiness at the corners of her mouth. He didn't want to look that closely. He wanted to remember Arden Mayfair as that fearless golden girl—barefoot and tanned—who had captured his heart at the ripe old age of four. He wanted to remember those glorious days of swimming and crabbing and catching raindrops on their tongues. And then as they grew older and the hormones kicked in, all those moonlit nights on the beach. The soft sighs and intimate whispers and the music spilling from his open car doors.

The Arden that stood before him now was much too composed and untouchable in her pristine white dress and power high heels. This Arden was gorgeous and sexy, but too grown-up and far too put together. And here he was still tilting at windmills.

He canted his head as he studied her. "Arden? Did you hear what I said?"

"Yes, I heard you." Her hair shimmered about her shoulders as she tucked it behind her ears. "I'm just not sure what I'm supposed to do with the information."

"You don't have to do anything. I just thought it was something you'd want to know."

"Why?"

"*Why?* Are you really going to make me spell it out?"

"Murder happens all the time, unfortunately, and magnolia blossoms are as common as dirt in Charleston. You said yourself this has nothing to do with Orson Lee Finch."

"I did say that, yes."

"This city has always had a dark side. You know that as well as I do." She glanced toward the garden, her gaze distant and haunted. It wasn't hard to figure out what she was thinking, what she had to be remembering. She'd only been five when she found her mother's body. Reid was a few months older. Even then, he'd wanted to protect her, but they'd been hardly more than babies. Pampered and sheltered in their pretty little world South of Broad Street. The fairy tale had ended that night, but the magic between them had lasted until her car lights disappeared from his view on the night she left town.

No, that wasn't exactly true. If he was honest with himself, their relationship had soured long before that night. The magic had ended when they lost their baby.

But he didn't want to think about that. He'd long since relegated that sad time to the fringes of his memory. Best not to dredge up the fear and the blood and the look on Arden's face when she knew it was over. Best not to remember the panicked trip to the ER or the growing distance between them in the aftermath. The despair, the loneliness. The feeling inside him when he knew it was over.

Reid had learned a long time ago not to dwell on matters he couldn't control. Pick yourself up, dust yourself off and get on with life. Hadn't that been his motto for as long as he could remember? If you pretended long enough and hard enough, you might actually start to believe that you were happy.

In fairness, he hadn't been unhappy. He still knew how to have fun. He could still ferret out an adventure now and then. That was worth something, he reckoned.

With a jolt, he realized that Arden was watching him. She physically started when their gazes collided. Her hand went to her chest as if she could somehow calm her accelerated heartbeat. Or was he merely projecting?

He took a deep breath, but not so deep that she would notice. Instead, he let a note of impatience creep into his voice. "So that's it, then? You're just going to ignore the elephant in the room."

She smoothed a hand down the side of her dress as if to prove her nonchalance. "What would you have me do?"

"I would expect a little emotion. Some kind of reaction. Not this…" He trailed away before he said something he'd regret.

"Not this what?" she challenged.

He struggled to measure his tone. "You don't have to be so impassive, okay? It's me. You can drop the mask. I just told you that a magnolia blossom was found at the crime scene. Only a handful of people in this city would understand the significance. You and I are two of them."

"White or crimson?"

Finally, a spark. "White. A common variety. Nothing exotic or unusual as far as I've heard. It probably doesn't mean anything. It's not like the killer placed a crimson magnolia petal on the victim's lips. Still…" He paused. "I thought you'd want to know."

Arden's expression remained too calm. "Who was the victim?"

"I told you, I don't know anything about her. The name

hasn't been released to the public yet. Nor has the business about the magnolia blossom. We need to keep that to ourselves."

"How do you know about it?"

"I have a detective friend who drops by on occasion to shoot the breeze and drink my whiskey. He sometimes has one too many and let's something slip that he shouldn't."

"What does he think about the murder?" Arden asked. "Do they have any suspects yet?"

"He's not working the case. His information is secondhand. Police department gossip. The best I can tell, Charleston PD is treating it like any other homicide for now."

"For now." She walked over to the French doors and leaned a shoulder against the frame. Her back was to him. He couldn't help admiring the outline of her curves beneath the white dress or the way the high heels emphasized her toned calves. Arden had always been a looker. A real heartbreaker. No one knew that better than Reid.

She traced her reflection in the glass with her fingertip. "When did it happen?"

"The body was found early this morning in an alleyway off Logan." Only half a block from Reid's new place, but for some reason, he didn't see fit to mention that detail. There were a few other things he hadn't shared, either. He wasn't sure why. He told himself he wanted to keep the meeting simple, but when had his feelings for Arden Mayfair ever been simple?

She dropped her hand to her side as she stared out into the gathering dusk. Already, the garden beyond the French doors looked creepy as hell. The statues of angels and cherubs that her grandmother had collected had always been a little too funereal for Reid's tastes. The summerhouse, though. He could see the exotic dome peeking through the tree limbs. The Moroccan structure conjured images of starry nights and secret kisses. He and Arden had made that place their own despite the bad memories.

"Reid?"

He shook himself back to the present. "Sorry. You were saying?"

"The cabdriver had the radio on when I came in from the airport. There wasn't a word of this on the news. No mention of a homicide at all. Ambrose didn't say anything about it, either."

"No reason he would know. As I said, the details haven't yet been released. With all the Twilight Killer publicity recently, the police don't want to incite panic. Keeping certain facts out of the news is smart."

Arden turned away from the garden. "What do you think?"

"About the murder?"

"About the magnolia blossom."

Reid hesitated. "It's too early to speculate. The police are still gathering evidence. The best thing we can do is wait and see what they find out."

The hazel eyes darkened. "Since when have you ever waited for anything?"

I waited fourteen years for you to come back. "I have no choice in the matter. I don't have the connections or the clout I had when I was with Sutton & Associates. All I can do is keep my eyes and ears open. If my friend lets anything else slip, I'll let you know."

She regarded him suspiciously. "You're saying all the right things, but I don't believe you."

"You think I'm making this up?"

"No. I think you came over here for a reason, but it wasn't just to tell me about a murder or to suggest we wait and see what the cops uncover. You're right. Only a handful of people would remember that a white magnolia blossom was left on the summerhouse steps the night my mother was murdered. Everyone else, including the police, focused on the crimson petal placed on her lips—the kiss of death that became the Twilight Killer's signature. The creamy magnolia blossom was never repeated at any of the other murder scenes. Which means it was specific to my mother's death."

"That's speculation, too. We've never known that for certain."

"It's what we always believed," she insisted. "Just like we became convinced that the real killer remained free."

"We were just dumb kids," Reid said. "What were we—all of twelve—when we decided Orson Lee Finch must be innocent? No proof, no evidence, nothing driving our theory but boredom and imagination. We let ourselves get caught up in a mystery of our own making that summer."

"Maybe, but we learned a lot about my mother's case and about how far we were willing to push ourselves to uncover the truth. Don't you remember how dedicated we were? We sat in the summerhouse for hours combing through old newspaper accounts and scribbling in note-books. We even rode our bikes over to police headquarters and demanded to speak with one of the detectives who had worked the Twilight Killer case."

"For all the good that did us," Reid said dryly. "As I recall, we were not so politely shown the door."

"That didn't stop us though, did it?" For the first time, her eyes began to sparkle as she recalled their ardent pursuit of justice. The polished facade dropped and he glimpsed the girl she'd once been, that scrawny, suntanned dynamo who'd had the ability to wrap him around her little finger with nothing more than a smile.

"No, it didn't stop us," he agreed. "When did anything ever stop us?"

She let that one pass. "We decided the white magnolia blossom represented innocence, the opposite of the bloodred petal placed on my mother and the other victims' lips. Given the Twilight Killer's contempt for single mothers, he would have viewed all of them as tainted and unworthy, hence the crimson kiss of death."

In spite of himself, Reid warmed to the topic. "You were the innocent offspring. The first Child of Twilight."

She nodded. "The white blossom not only represented my virtue, but it was also meant as a warning not to follow in my mother's sullied footsteps."

They shared a moment and then both glanced quickly away. The memory of what they'd created and what they'd lost was as fleeting and bittersweet as the end of a long, hot summer.

"No one knew about the baby," he said softly.

Her gaze darted back to him. "Of course, someone knew. Someone always knows. Secrets rarely stay hidden."

"It never needed to be a secret. Not as far as I was concerned. But…" He closed his eyes briefly. "Water under the bridge. This murder has nothing to do with what happened to us. To you."

"If you believed that, you wouldn't be here."

"Arden—"

"I know why you're here, Reid. I know you. You won't come right out and say it, but you've been dancing around the obvious ever since you got here. Despite what you said earlier, this does involve Orson Lee Finch. The way I see it, there can only be two explanations for why a magnolia blossom was left at that murder scene. Either Finch really is innocent or we're dealing with someone who has been influenced by him. A copycat or a conduit. Maybe even someone with whom he's shared his secrets."

Reid stared at her in astonishment. "You got all that out of what I just told you? That's quite a leap, Arden."

"Is it? Can you honestly say the thought never crossed your mind?"

"You're forgetting one extremely important detail. No red magnolia petal found on the body. No crimson kiss of death placed on the lips. This isn't the work of a copycat and I seriously doubt that a dormant serial killer has suddenly been reawakened after all these years. A jury of Finch's peers found him guilty and none of his appeals has ever gone anywhere. This has to be something else."

Arden refused to back down. "Then I repeat, why are you here?"

He ran fingers through his hair as he tried to formulate the best answer. "Damned if I know at the moment."

She regarded him with another frown. "Just consider the possibility that you and I were right about Orson Lee Finch's innocence. The monster who killed all those women, including my mother, has remained free and well disguised all these years. Maybe I'm the reason he's suddenly reawakened. Maybe the white magnolia blossom left at the crime scene was meant as another warning."

"It's way too early to head down that road," Reid said. "If anything, we may be dealing with a killer who wants to throw the police off his scent."

"So you don't think my coming home has anything to do with this?"

"You just got in today. The murder occurred sometime last night or early this morning."

"A coincidence, then."

"What else could it be?"

She sighed in frustration. "I don't understand you, Reid

Sutton. You berate me when I don't show the proper reaction to your revelation about the magnolia blossom, and now you go out of your way to try and convince me—and yourself—that it has nothing to do with me. You came all the way over here just to tell me about a coincidence."

"I'm just trying to be sensible," Reid said.

"You were never any good at that."

"Maybe not, but someone needs to put on the brakes before we get too carried away."

"Now who's being pedestrian?" She brushed back her hair with a careless shrug. "Something's not right about all this. Something's not adding up. Why do I get the feeling you're still holding out on me?"

Reid glanced away. The proximity of the crime scene to his place niggled. Another coincidence, surely, but ever since he'd heard about the murder, he hadn't been able to shake a dark premonition. For days he'd had the feeling that his house was being watched. He'd caught sight of someone lurking in the shadows across the street. One night he'd heard the knob at the back door rattle.

The incidents had started at about the time Dave Brody had been released from prison. The ex-con had stopped by the office as soon as he'd hit town, strutting like a peacock with his smirks and leers and ominous tattoos. He blamed his incarceration on Sutton & Associates, claiming the attorneys that had represented him pro bono—in particular, Reid's father, Boone Sutton—had suppressed a witness that could have corroborated Brody's alibi.

Why he hadn't gone straight to the source of his resentment, Reid didn't know. He hadn't even been out of law school when Brody had been sent up, had only worked peripherally on the appeals. Yet he was apparently the attorney Dave Brody had decided to target for the simple reason that Reid was now the most vulnerable. Without the money and prestige of the firm backing him, he was the easiest to get to. Knock out the son in order to get to the father. But Brody would find out the hard way that Boone Sutton didn't cave so easily, even when family was involved.

Reid hadn't reported the incidents because police involvement would only provoke a guy like Brody. It wasn't the first time and it wouldn't be the last time an irate client had harassed him. Best just to ignore the creep, but still the location of that murder scene bothered him.

"Look, to be honest, I don't know what any of this means," Reid said. "I just knew that I wanted you to hear about that magnolia blossom from me."

He expected another argument; instead, she nodded. "Okay. Thank you. I mean it. I haven't been gracious about any of this. You caught me off guard. That's my only excuse."

"I understand."

"I'm not usually like this. It's just..." She seemed at a loss. "You and I have a complicated history."

"To put it mildly," he agreed.

She drew a breath. "Fourteen years is a long time and yet here we are, back where it all started."

He smiled. "History repeating."

"God, I hope not."

"I'll try not to take that personally."

"You know what I mean. Everything was so intense back then. So life and death. I don't think I could take all that drama these days."

"That's why we have booze. Adulthood has its perks."

"I don't want to numb myself," Arden said with a reproving glance. "But a little peace and quiet would be nice."

"You'll have that in spades here," he said as his gaze

traveled back into the foyer. "Are you sure I can't help you with those bags?"

"I can manage."

He lingered for a moment longer, letting his senses drink her up as memories flowed. Man, they'd had some good times together. He hadn't realized until that moment how much he'd missed her. Arden Mayfair wasn't just his ex-girlfriend. She'd been his best friend, his soul mate, and a true and enthusiastic partner in crime. He hadn't had anyone like her in his life since she'd left town. Oh, he had plenty of friends, some with benefits, some without. He never lacked for companionship, but there was no one like Arden. Maybe there never would be.

"I guess I'll say good-night then." He wondered if she noticed the hint of regret in his voice.

"Reid?" She crossed the room quickly and stood on tiptoe to kiss his cheek. She was like quicksilver in his arms, airy and elusive. Before he had time to catch his breath, she'd already retreated, leaving the scent of her honeysuckle shampoo to torment his senses.

He caught her arm and drew her back to him, brushing her lips and then deepening the kiss before she could protest. "Welcome home, Arden."

She looked stunned. "Good night, Reid."

Chapter Three

Arden finished unpacking and then took a quick shower, dressing in linen pants and a sleeveless top before going back downstairs to decide about dinner. There was no food in the house, of course. No one had been living in Berdeaux Place since her grandmother's passing. She would need to make a trip to the market, but for now she could walk over to East Bay and have a solitary meal at her favorite seafood place. Or she could unlock the liquor cabinet and skip dinner altogether. She was in no hurry to venture out now that twilight had fallen.

At loose ends and trying to avoid dwelling on Reid's visit, she wandered through the hallways, trailing her fingers along dusty tabletops and peering up into the faces of forgotten ancestors. Eventually she returned to the front parlor, where her grandmother had once held court. Arden had a vision of her now, sitting ramrod straight in her favorite chair, teacup in one hand and an ornate fan in the other as she surveyed her province with quiet satisfaction. No matter the season or temperature, Evelyn Mayfair always dressed in sophisticated black. Maybe that was the reason Arden's mother had been drawn to vivid hues, in particular the color red. Arden supposed there was irony—or was it symmetry?—in the killer's final act of placing a crimson petal upon her lips.

Enough reminiscing.

If she wasn't careful, she could drown in all those old memories.

Crossing over to the French doors, she took a peek out into the gardens. The subtle glow from the landscape lighting shimmered off the alabaster faces of the statues. She could hear the faint splash of the fountain and the lonely trill of a night bird high up in one of magnolia trees. Summer sounds that took her back to her early childhood days before tragedy and loss had cast a perpetual shroud over Berdeaux Place.

Checking the lock on the door, she turned away and then swung back. Another sound intruded. Rhythmic and distant.

The pound of a heartbeat was her first thought as her own pulse beat an uneasy tattoo against her throat.

No, not a heartbeat, she realized. Something far less sinister, but invasive nonetheless. *A loose shutter thumping in the breeze most likely. Nothing to worry about. No reason to panic.*

She took another glance into the garden as she reminded herself that her mother had been murdered more than twenty-five years ago. It was unreasonable and perhaps paranoid to think that the real killer had waited all these years to strike again. Reid was right. The magnolia blossom found at the murder scene couldn't be anything more than a coincidence.

Arden stood there for the longest time recounting his argument as she tried to reassure herself that everything was fine. A jury of Finch's peers had found him guilty beyond a reasonable doubt. He would never again be a free man. And even if another killer did prowl the streets, Arden was as safe here as she was anywhere. The property was sequestered behind brick walls and wrought-iron gates.

The house had good locks and, ever since the murder, a state-of-the-art security system that had been periodically updated for as long as she could remember. She was safe.

As if to prove to herself that she had nothing to fear, she turned the dead bolt and pushed open the French doors. The evening breeze swept in, fluttering the curtains and scenting the air with the perfume of the garden—jasmine, rose and magnolia from the tree that shaded the summerhouse. She'd smelled those same fragrances the night she'd found her mother's body.

She wouldn't think about that now. She wouldn't spoil her homecoming with old nightmares and lingering fears. If she played her cards right, this could be a new beginning for her. A bolder and more exciting chapter if she didn't let the past hold her back.

Bolstering her resolve, she walked down the flagstone path toward the summerhouse. The garden had been neglected since her grandmother was no longer around to browbeat the yard crew. In six months of Charleston heat and humidity the beds and hedges had exploded. Through the untrimmed canopy of the magnolias, the summerhouse dome rose majestically, and to the left Arden could see the slanted glass roof of the greenhouse.

The rhythmic thud was coming from that direction. The greenhouse door had undoubtedly been left unsecured and was bumping in the breeze.

Before Arden lost her nerve, she changed course, veering away from the summerhouse and heading straight into the heart of the jungle. It was a warm, lovely night and the garden lights guided her along the pathway. She detected a hint of brine in the breeze. The scent took her back to all those nights when she'd shimmied down the trellis outside her bedroom window to meet Reid. Back to the innocent kisses in the summerhouse and to those not so innocent nights spent together at the beach. Then hurrying home before sunup. Lying in bed and smiling to herself as the light turned golden on her ceiling.

Despite the dark shadow that had loomed over the house since her mother's murder, Arden had been happy at Berdeaux Place, thanks mostly to Reid. He'd given her a way out of the gloom, an escape from the despair that her grandmother had sunk more deeply into year after year. Evelyn Berdeaux Mayfair had never gotten over the death of her only daughter and sometimes Arden had wondered if her presence had been more of a curse than a blessing, a constant reminder of what she'd lost.

Her grandmother's desolation had worn on Arden, but Reid had always been there to lift her up. He'd been her best friend, her confidant, and for a time she'd thought him the love her life. Everything had changed that last summer.

Too soon, Arden. Don't go there.

There would be time enough later to reflect on what might have been.

But already wistfulness tugged. She paused on the flag-stones and inhaled sharply, letting the perfume of the night lull her. A moth flitted past her cheek as loneliness descended. It had been a long time since she'd felt so unmoored. She blamed her longing on Reid's unexpected visit. Seeing him again had stirred powerful memories.

Something darted through the trees and she whirled toward the movement. She'd been so lost in thought she hadn't kept track of her surroundings, of the danger that had entered the garden.

She stood frozen, her senses on full alert as she tried to pinpoint the source of her unease. The thumping had stopped, and now it wasn't so much a sound or a smell that alarmed her but a dreaded certainty that she was no longer alone.

Her heart started to pound in fear as she peered through the darkness. The reflection of the rising moon in the glass ceiling of the greenhouse cast a strange glow directly over the path where someone stood watching her.

In that moment of terror, Arden wanted nothing so much as to turn and run from the garden, to lock herself away in Berdeaux Place as her grandmother had done for decades. She could grow old in that house, withering away with each passing year, lonely and desolate yet safe from the outside world. Safe from the monster who had murdered her mother and would someday return for her.

She didn't run, though. She braced her shoulders and clenched her fists even as she conjured an image of her own prone body on the walkway, with blood on the flagstones and a crimson magnolia petal adorning her cold lips.

"Arden?"

The voice was at once familiar and strangely unsettling, the accent unmistakably Charleston. A thrill rippled along her backbone. She had lots of videos from her childhood. Her mother had pronounced her name in that same dreamy drawl. *Ah-den.*

He moved out of the shadows and started down the path toward her. Arden stood her ground even as her heart continued to flail. The man was almost upon her before recognition finally clicked. "Uncle Calvin?"

"I'm sorry. I didn't mean to frighten you," he said in his elegant drawl.

"No, it's okay. I just… I wasn't expecting anyone to be out here."

"Nor was I. You gave me quite the start, too, seeing you there in the moonlight. You look so much like your mother I thought for a moment I was seeing her ghost."

For some reason, his observation sent another shiver down Arden's spine.

As he continued toward her, she could pick out the familiar Mayfair features—the dimpled chin and piercing blue eyes melding seamlessly with the Berdeaux cheekbones and nose. Arden had the cheekbones and nose, but her hair wasn't quite so golden and her complexion was far from porcelain. Her hazel eyes had come from her father, she'd long ago decided. A frivolous charmer who'd skipped town the moment he'd learned she was on the way, according to her grandmother. Still, the resemblance was undeniable.

"Ambrose told me a few days ago that you were coming, but somehow it slipped my mind," her uncle said. "I'm so used to letting myself in through the garden gate I never even thought to stop by the house first." He came to a halt on the path, keeping distance between them as if he were worried he might startle her away. "I hope I didn't frighten you too badly."

"It's not you." She let out a breath as she cast a glance into the shadows. "It's this place. After all these years, the garden still unnerves me."

"I'm not surprised." His hair looked nearly white in the fragile light as he thrust it back from his forehead. He was tall, slender and somehow stylish even in his casual attire. In her younger years, Arden had thought her uncle quite dashing with his sophisticated demeanor and mysterious ways. She had always wanted to know him better, but his remoteness had helped foster his mystique. "Even after all these years, the ghosts linger," he murmured.

"You feel it, too," Arden said with a shudder.

"No matter the time of day or year." He paused with a wan smile. "You were so young when it happened. I'm surprised you still feel it so strongly."

"It's not something you ever get over."

"No, I suppose not. I was away at the time. Father and

I had had a falling out so I didn't find out until after the funeral. Maybe that's why the impact only hit me later. I'm sorry I wasn't around to at least offer some comfort."

"I had Grandmother."

"Yes. I remember hearing how she clung to you at the funeral. You were her strength."

"And she, mine, although I don't remember much about that day. It passed in a haze."

"Probably for the best." He gave her another sad smile. "So here you are. Back after all these years."

"Yes."

"It's been a long time. Everyone had begun to think that we'd lost you for good."

Arden wondered whom he included in that "everyone." Not her grandfather, surely. Clement Mayfair had never shown anything but a cursory concern for her welfare. "I've returned periodically for visits. I spent almost every Christmas with Grandmother."

"And now you've come home to any empty house and me looking like something the cat dragged in. I apologize for my appearance," he said as he held up his gloved hands. "I've been working in the greenhouse."

He looked nothing short of pristine. "At this hour?" Arden asked in surprise.

"Maybe you'd like to see what I've been up to. That is, if you don't mind the general disrepair. The greenhouse is in rather a dismal state so mind your step."

"What have you been working on?"

His eyes gleamed in the moonlight. "You'll see."

He turned and she fell into step behind him on the flag-stone pathway, following his graceful gait through borders of silvery artemisia and pale pink dianthus. She felt safe enough in the company of her uncle. She didn't know him well, but he'd always been kind. Still, she couldn't help glancing over her shoulder. She couldn't help remembering that her mother had been murdered on an evening such as this.

The greenhouse door opened with a squeal.

"The hinges have rusted and the latch doesn't catch like it should," he said. "Not that there's anything of value inside. The tools, what's left of them, are secured in the shed around back. The lock needs to be replaced, regardless. No one needs to be traipsing about inside. Could be a lawsuit waiting to happen."

"Ambrose should have had that taken care of," Arden said. "At any rate, I'll have someone come out as soon as possible."

Her uncle glanced over his shoulder. "You're here to stay then."

"I don't know. I haven't made any plans yet."

He looked as if he were on the verge of saying something else, but he shrugged. "You've plenty of time. There's no need to rush any decisions."

She stepped through the door and glanced around. The tables and racks were nearly empty except for a few chipped pots.

"Straight ahead," he said as he peeled off his gloves and tossed them aside.

"I'd nearly forgotten about this place." Arden glanced up in wonder through the glass panels where a few stars had begun to twinkle. "Grandmother never talked about it anymore and we didn't come out here on any of my visits. She gave up her orchids long ago. I'm surprised she didn't have the structure torn down."

"It served a purpose," Calvin said.

"You're being very mysterious," Arden observed.

"Just you wait."

Arden hugged her arms around her middle. "When I

was little, Grandmother used to let me come in here with her while she mixed her potions and boosters. Her orchids were the showstoppers at every exhibit, but secretly I always thought they were the strangest flowers with the spookiest names. Ghost orchid, fairy slipper, Dracula benedictii. They were too fussy for my taste. Required too much time and effort. I adored Mother's cacti and succulents. So hardy and yet so exotic. When they bloomed, the greenhouse was like a desert oasis."

"I can imagine."

Arden sighed. "The three of us spent hours in here together, but Grandmother lost interest after the—after Mother was gone. She hired someone to take care of the plants for a while… Eventually everything died."

"Not everything." Her uncle's blue eyes glinted in reflected moonlight. He stepped aside, leaning an arm on one of the tables as he waved her forward. "Take a look."

Arden moved around him and then glanced back. "Is that…it can't be Mother's cereus? It's nearly to the ceiling!" She trailed her gaze up the exotic cactus. "You kept it all this time?"

"Evelyn kept it," he said, referring to his mother and Arden's grandmother by her given name. "After you moved away, it was the only thing of Camille's she had left. She spent most of her time out here, trimming and propagating. As you said, mixing her potions and boosters. She may have lost interest in the orchids, but she never lost her touch."

Arden felt a twinge of guilt. She could too easily picture her grandmother bent to her work, a slight figure, wizened and withered in her solitude and grief. "I see lots of buds. How long until they open?"

"Another few nights. You're lucky. It's promising to be quite a show this year."

"That's why you're here," Arden said. "You've been coming by to take care of the cereus."

"I couldn't let it die. Not after Evelyn had nurtured it all those years. A Queen of the Night this size is rare in these parts and much too large to move. Besides, this is its home."

He spoke in a reverent tone as if concerned for the plant's sensibilities. That was nonsense, of course, nothing but Arden's overstimulated imagination; yet she couldn't help sneaking a glance at her uncle, marveling that she could look so much like him and know so little about him.

Arden's grandparents had divorced when their children were still young. Calvin had remained in the grand old mansion on East Bay Street with Clement Mayfair while his older sister, Camille—Arden's mother—had gone to live with Evelyn at Berdeaux Place. Outwardly, the divorce had been amicable; in reality, a simmering bitterness had kept the siblings apart.

Growing up, Arden could remember only a handful of visits from her uncle and she knew even less about her grandfather, a cold, taciturn man who disapproved of little girls with dirty fingernails and a sense of adventure. On the rare occasions when she'd been summoned to Mayfair House, she'd been expected to dress appropriately and mind her manners, which meant no fidgeting at the dinner table, no speaking unless spoken to.

Clement Mayfair was a tall, swarthy man who had inherited a fortune and doubled it by the time he was thirty. He was in shipping, although to this day, Arden had only a vague idea of what his enterprises entailed. His children had taken after their mother. In her heyday, Evelyn Berdeaux had been a blonde bombshell. Capricious and flirtatious, she must have driven a reclusive man like Clement mad at times. No wonder the marriage had ended so acrimoniously. Opposites might attract, but that didn't make for an easy relationship. On the other hand, Arden and Reid had been so much alike there'd been no one to restrain their impulses.

Her uncle watched her in the moonlight. He had the strangest expression on his face. "Is something wrong?" Arden asked.

Her voice seemed to startle him out of a deep reverie. "No, of course not. I just can't get over how much you look like your mother. Sometimes when you turn your head a certain way..." He trailed off on a note of wonder. "And it's not just your appearance. Your mannerisms, the way you pronounce certain words. It's really remarkable considering Camille died when you were so young."

"That's interesting to know."

He seemed not to hear her. "My sister was full of sunshine and life. She considered each day a new adventure. I was in awe of her when we were children. I sense that quality in you, too, although I think you view each day as something to be conquered," he said with a smile. "Evelyn always said you were a handful."

Arden trailed her finger across one of the scalloped leaves of the cereus. "I suppose I did give her a few gray hairs, although I'm sure she had her moments, too. She became almost a shut-in after Mother died, but I remember a time when she loved to entertain. She kept the house filled with fascinating people who'd traveled to all sorts of glamorous places. It was a bit like living in a fairy tale."

Her uncle remained silent, gazing down at her in the moonlight as if he were hanging on her every word.

"Did you know that she used to organize blooming socials for Mother's cereus? The buds would never open until well past my bedtime, but I was allowed to stay up on the first night to watch the first blossom. The unfurling was magical. And that heavenly scent." Arden closed her eyes and drew a deep breath. "I remember it so well. Not too sweet or cloying, more like a dark, lush jungle."

"I have cuttings at my place and I still do the same," Calvin said. "My friends and I sit out on the balcony with cameras and mint juleps. There's something to be said for Southern traditions. You should join us this year." His voice sounded strained and yet oddly excited.

"At Mayfair House?" Somehow Arden couldn't imagine her prim and proper grandfather being a party to such a frivolous gathering.

"I haven't lived at Mayfair House in years. I have a place near my studio."

"Your studio?"

His smile turned deprecating. "I paint and sculpt. I dabble a bit in pottery. I even manage to sell a piece now and then."

She put a hand to her forehead. "Of course. You're an artist. I don't know how I let that slip my mind. I'm afraid I haven't been very good at keeping in touch."

"None of us has. We're a very strange family in that regard. I suppose we all like our secrets too much."

Arden couldn't help wondering about his secrets. He was a handsome man, still young at forty-six and ever so charming in manner and speech. Yet now that she was older, the drawl seemed a little too affected and his elegance had a hint of decadence that hadn't aged well. Maybe she was being too critical. Looking for flaws to assuage her conscience. No one on either side of the family had been more distant or secretive than she. Her grandmother had given her a home and every advantage, and Arden had repaid that kindness with bimonthly phone calls and Christmas visits.

As unsatisfied as she'd been with her professional life

in Atlanta, she was even more discontent with her personal growth. She'd been selfish and entitled for as long as she could remember. Maybe that assessment was also too critical, but Arden had reached the stage of her life, a turning point, where hard truths needed to be faced. Maybe that was the real reason she'd come back to Charleston. Not to put old ghosts to rest, but to take stock and regroup.

Her uncle picked up a pair of clippers and busied himself cleaning the blades with a tattered rag and some rubbing alcohol. "You know the story of your grandparents' divorce," he said. "I stayed with Father and Camille came here with Evelyn. We lived only blocks apart, yet we became strangers. She blamed Father for the estrangement, but Evelyn could be just as contentious. She had her secrets, too," he added slyly as he tested the clippers by running his finger along the curved blades. Then he hung them on the wall and put away the alcohol.

Arden watched him work. His hands were graceful, his fingers long and tapered, but his movements were crisp and efficient. She marveled at the dichotomy. "No matter who was at fault, it was wrong to keep you and my mother apart. To force you to choose sides. She never wanted that. She used to tell me stories of how close the two of you were when you were little. I know she missed you."

"And yet she never reached out."

"Did you?"

He shrugged good-naturedly. "That's a fair point. Fear of rejection is a powerful deterrent. After the divorce, I'd sneak away from my father's house and come here every chance I got. Sometimes I would just sit in the garden and watch my mother and sister through the windows. Or I'd lie in the summerhouse and stare up at the clouds. Berdeaux Place was like a haven to me back then. A secret sanctuary. Even though Mayfair House has a multitude of sunlit piazzas with breathtaking views of the sea, it seemed a gloomy place after the divorce. It was like all the joy had been stolen and brought here to this house."

"You must have been lonely after they left." Arden knew loneliness, the kind of killing emptiness that was like a physical ache. She'd felt it often in this house and even more so in Atlanta. She felt it now thinking about Reid Sutton.

She brushed back her hair as she glanced up at the sky, trailing her gaze along the same twinkling stars that she and Reid had once counted together as children.

You see that falling star, Arden? You have to make a wish. It's a rule.

I already made a wish. But if I tell you, it won't come true.

That's dumb. Of course, it'll come true.

All right, then. I wish that you and I could be together forever.

That's a stupid thing to wish for because we will be. Promise?

Promise. Now hurry up and make another wish. Something important this time. Like a new bike or a pair of Rollerblades.

"Arden?"

She closed her eyes and drew another breath. "Yes?"

"Where did you go just now? You seemed a million miles away."

"Just lost in thought. This place takes me back."

"That's not a bad thing. Memories are how we keep those we've lost with us always. I made my peace with Evelyn before she passed. I'm thankful for that. And I'm thankful that you're back home where you belong. Perhaps I'm overstepping my bounds, but I can't help wondering…" He trailed away on a note of uncertainty.

"What is it?"

"You said you haven't made any definitive plans, but Ambrose tells me you're thinking of selling the house."

"When did he tell you that?" Arden asked with a frown. She didn't like the idea of her grandmother's attorney repeating a conversation that Arden had considered private.

"Don't blame Ambrose. He let it slip in passing. It's none of my business, of course, but I would hate to see you sell. This house has been in the Berdeaux family for generations."

Was that a hint of bitterness in her uncle's voice? He would have every right to resent her inheritance. He was Evelyn's only living offspring. Why she hadn't left the property to him, Arden could only guess. In the not-too-distant future, her uncle would be the soul beneficiary of Clement Mayfair's estate, which would dwarf the worth of Berdeaux Place.

She rested her hand on one of the wooden tables. "It's not like I want to sell. Though I can't see myself living here. The upkeep on a place like this is financially and emotionally draining. I don't want to be tied to a house for the rest of my life."

"I understand. Still, it would be nice to keep it in the family. Perhaps I could have a word with Father. He's always had an interest in historic properties and a keen eye for real estate. And I imagine the idea of Evelyn rolling over in her grave would have some appeal."

Hardly a convincing argument, Arden thought in distaste.

"A word of warning, though. Keep everything close to the vest. Father is a master at sniffing out weakness."

Arden detested the idea of her grandmother's beloved Berdeaux Place being used as a final weapon against her. She'd have Ambrose Foucault put out feelers in other directions, although she was no longer certain she could trust his discretion. Maybe it was time to look for a new attorney.

She glanced at her uncle. "Please don't say anything to anyone just yet. As I said, my plans are still up in the air."

"Mum's the word, then. I should get going. I'm sure you'd like to get settled."

"It's been a long day," she said.

"Don't forget about the blooming party. And do stop by the studio when you get a chance. I'll give you the grand tour."

"Thank you. I would like that."

"You should probably also know that the Mayor's Ball is coming up. It's being held at Mayfair House this year, all proceeds to go to the construction of a new arboretum. You know how political those things are. Everything revolves around optics. If Father gets wind that you're home, he'll expect an appearance."

"Balls are not really my thing," Arden said with a shrug. She could hardly imagine Clement Mayfair hosting an intimate dinner, much less a grand ball, but as her uncle said, those things were political. She doubted her grandfather had agreed to throw open his doors and his wallet without getting something very valuable in return.

"He can be relentless when he wants something," her uncle cautioned. "It's never a good idea to cross him."

Arden lifted her chin. "I'm pretty stubborn, too. I guess that's the Mayfair gene."

Calvin's expression froze for an instant before a smile flitted. "Yes, we are a hardheaded lot. Maybe Father will have finally met his match in you. At any rate, your presence at the ball would certainly make things more interesting."

They stepped out of the steamy greenhouse into the

cool evening air. He turned to her on the shadowy pathway. "Whether you come to the ball or not, Arden, I'm glad you're home. It's good to have someone in the house again."

"It's good to be here." *For now.*

"Good night, Niece."

"Good night, Uncle."

He strode down the flagstones toward the gate, pausing at the entrance to pluck a magnolia petal from a branch that draped over the wall. Lifting the blossom to his nose, he tilted his head to the moon as he closed his eyes and savored the fragrance.

Then he dropped the flower to the ground and walked through the gate without a backward glance.

Chapter Four

Reid pulled his car to the rear of the house and cut the engine. The bulb at the top of the back stairs was out. He'd been meaning to replace it, and now he decided that adding a couple of floodlights and cameras at the corners of the house might not be a bad idea. The neighborhood was normally a safe place, but a murder half a block from where he sat tended to make one reevaluate security. He scanned the shadows at the back of the house before he got out of the car. Then he stood for a moment listening to the night.

Somewhere down the block, two tomcats sized each other up, the guttural yowls unnerving in the dark. He was on edge tonight. He rubbed a hand over his tired eyes, feeling weary from too little sleep and too many conflicting emotions. Seeing Arden had affected him far more deeply than he cared to admit. Maybe that was why he'd remained on the veranda after Evelyn Mayfair's funeral rather than going inside to offer Arden his condolences. He'd sensed even then that a face-to-face would awaken all those old memories.

Too late now to put that genie back in the bottle. Already he could feel himself tumbling down the rabbit hole of their past.

He should have left well enough alone. There was no real reason she'd needed to hear about that magnolia blossom from him. She wasn't a little girl anymore. She could take care of herself. Truth be told, she'd never needed his protection, but there was a time when Reid had liked to think that she did.

Okay, so, big mistake. Miscalculated his feelings. Now he would have to make sure that he stayed on guard, stayed on his side of town, but why did she have to be one of those women who grew more attractive and interesting as she settled into her thirties? More desirable as the years went by with her sunlit hair and secretive smile?

A part of Reid wanted nothing more than to pick back up where they'd left off, while another part—the more distant and less-listened-to part—reminded him of the hurt she'd once inflicted. Maybe that assessment was overblown and unfair, but she'd turned her back on him when he needed her the most. When he'd been drowning in pain and confusion and desperately needed a lifeline. That she had been just as hurt and confused did little to soften the betrayal.

That was all water under the bridge. Reid had made peace with their estrangement years ago. He hadn't exactly been pining away. He'd sowed his wild oats and then some. No regrets. Still, no matter how much he wished otherwise, her homecoming wasn't something he could take in stride.

The back of his neck prickled as he scoured his surroundings. An indefinable worry blew a chill wind across his nerve endings, and he frowned as he tried to clear the cobwebs from his memory. Arden's return wasn't the only thing that had thrown him off his game tonight. The proximity of the murder disturbed him on a level that he didn't yet understand.

He'd come home last night, having called a cab from the bar where he'd spent the evening with friends. Vaguely he remembered paying the driver and watching the taillights disappear around the corner. As the sound of the engine faded, he'd heard the tomcats fighting. Or had the sound been something else entirely?

He told himself he'd been sober enough to discern cat-erwauling felines from a human scream. But he couldn't shake the feeling that he'd seen something, heard something that had gotten lost in his muddled dreams.

He thought about walking down to the alley where the body had been found to see if anything jarred loose. He discarded the notion at once. The entrance was still cor-doned off, and, for all he knew, the cops might have the street staked out in hopes the killer would return to the scene of the crime. Best not to get involved. He had enough on his plate at the moment. This was make-or-break time for the new firm, and he couldn't afford to get sidetracked by a murder or by Arden Mayfair or by an ex-con with an ax to grind against his family. *Keep your head down and stay focused.*

After locking the car door with the key fob, he climbed the back stairs and let himself into the apartment, flipping on lights as he walked through the rooms. The house was old and creaky, his living quarters in bad need of remodel-ing. But for now the space suited his needs. He didn't mind the peeling paint or the sagging doors or even the ceiling stains from a leaky roof. What he cared about were the long windows that let in plenty of natural light and the oak floors that had been worn to a beautiful patina. The house on Logan Street felt more like home to Reid than his sleek waterfront condo ever had. He'd never liked that place or the position at Sutton & Associates that had paid for it.

He poured himself a drink and then leaned against the counter to glance through the paper. The murder re-ceived only a scant mention. The victim's name was still being withheld, along with any details about the crime scene. Nothing about the magnolia blossom or any suspects. Nothing at all to explain that warning tingle at the back of Reid's neck.

He scanned the rest of the paper as he finished his whiskey and then poured another, telling himself he needed to relax, just needed to take the edge off that meeting with Arden. He still had a bit of a hangover from the night before so hair of the dog and all that. Booze had flowed freely at Sutton & Associates. The competitive nature of the firm had worn on the associates and junior partners, and Reid, like the others, had fallen into the habit of happy hour cocktails with clients and colleagues, wine with dinner, liqueur with coffee and then a nightcap to finish off the evening. Sometimes two or three nightcaps just so he could shut down and get to sleep.

Now that he was out of the pressure cooker environment of his father's firm, he needed to start taking better care of himself. Lay off the hooch. Hit the gym. Add a few miles to his morning run. Get back in shape mentally and physically. Turn over a new leaf, so to speak.

Resolved for at least the rest of the evening, he poured the remainder of his drink down the sink and then stuffed the newspaper in the trash can. Out of sight, out of mind.

It was too early to turn in so he went out to the balcony to enjoy the evening breeze. The house was built in the Charleston style—narrow and deep with the windows and balconies overlooking the side garden. If he turned his chair just so, he could glimpse the street through the lush vegetation. A ceiling fan whirled sluggishly overhead, stirring the scent of jasmine from his neighbor's fence. He propped his feet on the rail and clasped his hands behind his head.

This had become his favorite spot. Hidden from view, he could sit out in the cooling air and watch the comings and goings in the neighborhood while his mind wound down from the daily grind. Not that his schedule was all that packed these days, but he'd just taken on a couple of promising cases, and the stress of any new venture took a toll.

He'd been rocking gently as he let his mind drift, but now he stopped the motion and sat up straight as he listened to the night. The tomcats had long since called a truce and moved on. There was no traffic to speak of, no music or laughter from any of the nearby houses. Everything had gone deadly still. It was as if something dark had crept once more into the neighborhood. A shadowy menace that prowled the streets, luring young women into alleyways and leaving the kiss of death upon their lips.

Or white magnolia blossoms beside their dead bodies.

Reid chided himself for letting his imagination get the better of him. But the longer he stared into the darkness, the more certain he became that his house was being watched. Across the street, someone hunkered in the shadows.

It's nothing. Just a tree or a bush. No one is there.

But he was already up, leaning far over the balcony railing to peer through the oak leaves, zeroing in on a dark figure that didn't belong in the neighborhood.

The silhouette took on definition. Slumped shoulders. Tilted head. Reid could imagine the sneer.

Dave Brody.

Keeping to the shadows, Reid slipped back into the apartment, and then raced down the stairs and out the front door. But Brody had vanished by the time he crossed the street.

Probably not a good idea to go traipsing about his neighbor's yard, Reid decided. Good way to get shot. Instead, he circled the block, eyeing fences and garden gates until he found himself back on his street, standing at the alley-way where the young woman's body had been found early that morning. Police tape barricaded the entrance, but no one was about. No one that he could detect.

He lifted his gaze, searching along the buildings that walled in the alley. Apartment windows looked down on the narrow street. Someone must have seen something, *heard* something. Had the police done a thorough job can-vassing the area? Were they even now zeroing in on a suspect?

Reid turned to scour the street behind him, and he cocked his ear to the night sounds. The screech of a gate hinge. The scratch of a tree limb against glass. Somewhere at the back of the alley, a foot connected with an empty can. Or was that just the wind?

The sound jarred Reid and he told himself to go home. Leave the investigation to the police. He would be a fool to breach the police barricade and an even bigger idiot to pursue Dave Brody down a dark, deserted alley.

But when had he ever taken the prudent way out?

Ducking under the tape, he paused once more to glance over his shoulder. He could just make out his house through the lush foliage. He hadn't taken the time to lock up on his way out. If he was bound and determined to do this, he needed to be quick about it. For all he knew, Dave Brody could already be inside his house, hiding in a closet or un-derneath the bed.

Disturbing thought. Chilling image.

Almost as unnerving as exploring the scene of a vio-lent murder.

He shook off his disquiet as he entered the alley, hug-ging the side of the building to avoid the glow from the streetlights. He came upon the bloodstains. There were a lot of them. Whoever the young woman had been, she'd met with a violent end.

Crouching beside the stains, he lifted his gaze to the buildings. The night was very still except for the quick dart of a shadow on one the balconies. Reid's pulse quickened as he strained to make out a silhouette. No one was there. Just his imagination.

He rubbed the gooseflesh at the back of his neck as he scoured his surroundings. A dog barked from behind a garden gate, and a fluffy yellow cat eyed him from atop a brick wall before leaping headlong into darkness. Night creatures stirred. Bats circled overhead. And somewhere in the alley, a two-legged predator watched from the shadows.

"Evening, Counselor," a voice drawled.

It took everything Reid had not to react to that whiny twang. Instead, he rose slowly, peering back into the alley as he said in a matter-of-fact tone, "That you, Brody?" As Reid's eyes adjusted to the gloom, the man's form took shape. He lounged against the wall of the building, one foot propped against the brick facade as he regarded Reid in the filtered moonlight. Reid couldn't see his features clearly, but he had no trouble imagining the tattoos, the buzzed head, the perpetual smirk. He hardened his voice. "What the hell are you doing back there?"

"I could ask you the same thing. Me? I'm just enjoying the night air while I check out the neighborhood. I always liked this area. Quiet streets. Friendly people. Maybe I should start looking for a place around here. Put down some roots. What you think about that?"

Having Dave Brody for a neighbor was the last thing Reid wanted to contemplate. And the irony of waxing po- etically about the quiet streets while standing at the scene of a brutal murder seemed particularly creepy, but Reid knew better than to allow the man to goad him. "I saw you watching my house just now. You weren't out for a stroll. You were hiding in the bushes staring up at my balcony."

Brody turned his head and spit into the alley. "If I meant to hide, you wouldn't have seen me. I did tell you I aimed to keep an eye on you, didn't I?"

Reid clenched and unclenched his fists as he worked to keep his voice even. "We have more stringent stalker laws these days. You cross a line, I'll have your hide back in jail."

He could hear the amusement in Brody's voice. "I'm not too worried about that, Counselor. See, I had a lot of time on my hands in prison. Did a lot of reading. I know my rights and I know the law. I won't be crossing any lines. Just nudging up against them a little."

"You already crossed a police barricade. I could call the cops on you right now."

"But then you'd have to turn yourself in, and I don't think you want to get all jammed up with the Charleston PD right now."

Reid scowled. "What's that supposed to mean?"

Brody's gaze sliced through the darkness. "A good detective might start to wonder what *you're* doing in this alley, standing in the exact spot where a woman was stabbed last night. A good detective might start to dig a little deeper and find out you have a connection to the victim."

Reid's heart jumped in spite of himself. "Nothing about the victim has been released to the public. No name, no description, no cause of death. There's no way you could know anything about her unless you—"

"I didn't lay a hand on her. Didn't have to. I just happened to be at the right place at the right time." Brody pushed himself away from the wall and came toward Reid. Despite the heat, he wore steel-toed work boots and an

army jacket with crude lettering down the sleeves. It was
dark in the alley, but enough light filtered in to emphasize
the spiderweb tattoo on his neck and the three dots at the
corner of his right eye. Common enough prison ink, but
the images seemed even more ominous on Brody.

"Don't come any closer," Reid warned.

Brody laughed, displaying unnaturally white teeth in
the moonlight. "See, I was in a bar on Upper King Street
last night. Yeah, *that* bar. I saw you and your friends having
a grand old time, not a care in the world. You were attract-
ing plenty of female action, too, the way you were throwing
around all that money. One gal in particular seemed mighty
taken with you, Counselor. Kept trying to cozy up to you
at the bar, touching your arm, whispering sweet nothings
in your ear. She even passed you a note. Don't tell me you
don't remember her. About yay-high, bleached blond hair?"

Something niggled at the back of Reid's mind. Although
he tried to swat it away, a nebulous worry kept creeping
back into his consciousness. "There were a lot of people
in that bar last night. I didn't see you, though."

"Like I said, you won't see me unless I want to be seen.
I found myself a quiet corner just so I could take it all
in." Brody reached inside his jacket and Reid reflexively
stepped back. "Relax. I'm just trying to help jar your memory." He flung a photograph in the air and Reid flinched.
The snapshot hung on the breeze for a moment before fluttering to the ground at Reid's feet. "Pick it up."

Reluctantly, Reid retrieved the picture, positioning himself so that he could use the light on his phone while keeping Brody in his periphery. He could make out a few faces
in the photograph. His own, some of his friends. A woman
he'd never seen before stood gazing up at him at the bar.
Reid didn't recognize her, had only a hazy memory of
someone coming onto him as he waited for a drink.

"Now do you remember?" Brody pressed.

"Who is she?"

"Who *was* she, you mean."

Dread rolled around in Reid's stomach as he glanced up. "What did you do?"

"I told you, I didn't lay a hand on her. See, I was out for a walk this morning when a bunch of police cars go roaring by. A guy in my position tends to notice that sort of thing. So I walk down here to see if I can figure out what's what. Got a look at the body before they bagged her up. Imagine my surprise when I recognized the blonde from the bar, dead in an alley not even a block from your place. Pretty little thing, too, but nothing like that blonde you went to see earlier this evening. Now she's a real looker."

Reid's head came up. "You stay away from her. Whatever your beef is with me, she has nothing to do with it. You go near her place again, you even so much as glance down her street, I will personally see you back behind bars or in your own body bag."

"Mighty big words for a guy who's spent his whole life riding his daddy's coattails." Brody wiped his mouth with the back of his hand. "But no call to get all riled up, Counselor. I don't have any interest in your girlfriend so long as you help me get what I want."

"And what is it you want, Brody?"

"Justice."

"That's rich coming from you. What makes you think I'd ever want to help the likes of you? You haven't exactly been the poster child for rehabilitation since you hit town."

"Well, that's all in the past. Things have changed since last night. Now I'm in a position to help you out, too, Counselor. I'm hoping we can come to an understanding that will be mutually beneficial. See, that gal didn't just slip you a note last night. She put something in your drink."

Reid stared at him blankly. "What?"

"You wake up with a headache this morning? Have trouble remembering what you did and who you did it with?"

Reid's mind reeled back to the bar, to the cab ride home, to the cats fighting in the alley. When he'd finally tumbled into bed, he'd slept the sleep of the dead, awakening that morning to the sound of sirens outside his window. He'd had a dry mouth, a splitting headache and the sense that things had happened he couldn't remember.

All that flitted through his head in the blink of an eye.

Outwardly he remained calm as he casually glanced back at the street, telling himself to get the hell out of that alley. Whatever game Brody was playing, Reid wanted no part of it. Still, he lingered.

He turned back to Brody, dipping his head slightly as he peered into the shadows. "You just happened to be in a bar taking photographs when someone drugged my drink. That sounds totally believable."

"I didn't just *happen* to be anywhere," Brody said. "I followed you to that bar. I told you, I aim to keep an eye on you. As for the blonde, I never saw her before last night. She could have been working alone for all I know. Slipped you a roofie so she could roll you in the alley. You looked like an easy enough mark. My guess, though, is that someone paid her. Now you think about that for a minute. A woman comes on to you in a crowded bar and then she's later found dead half a block from your house. If the police start asking questions, someone will likely remember seeing the two of you leave together."

"I left the bar alone," Reid said. "I caught a cab and came straight home."

"Maybe you did, maybe you didn't. People tend to remember all sorts of things when an idea is put in their head.

It's called the power of suggestion. The point is, you were seen with a woman who later ended up dead. If I was a betting man, I'd say someone is setting you up, Counselor."

Reid was getting queasier by the minute. He told himself again to end the conversation. *Go home. Forget Brody. He's working a con on you.* "How do I know you're not making all this up? Or that you weren't the one who drugged me?"

"Plenty more photographs where that came from, and they tell a story. Two stories really. The blonde getting all touchy-feely—those photographs make you at the very least a person of interest if not an outright suspect. But the photographs of her slipping you a Mickey kind of make you look like a victim. Kind of proves someone is trying to set you up. See how that works? One set convicts, the other set clears. Now if the police were to get their hands on the wrong set, they might show up at your place of business, put you in cuffs, read you your rights and make a great big spectacle out of a Sutton arrest. Don't think they wouldn't get a charge out of that."

Oh, they would. Reid could see the headlines now. A famous defense attorney's son hauled in for questioning in a brutal homicide.

"Course, then your old man gets to swoop in and save the day," Brody continued. "But imagine his surprise when the one person who can clear his only son turns out to be yours truly." He gave a low, ugly laugh.

"You've given this a lot of thought," Reid said.

"Nah. The script practically wrote itself last night."

Dread was no longer tumbling around in Reid's stomach. It had settled like a red-hot coal in the pit. "You say you want justice, but what specifically do you want from me?"

"Now we're getting somewhere," Brody said with an

appreciative nod. "You worked for your old man's firm up until a couple of months ago. You know where they keep the files, the pass codes, where they bury the bodies, so to speak. I want you to find out what they did with a witness that could have corroborated my alibi. Her name was Ginger Vreeland, but I doubt she goes by that name anymore. She disappeared the night before she was to take the witness stand on my behalf."

"Maybe she got cold feet and left town," Reid said. "It happens more often than you think."

"Not Ginger. She was hard as nails, but she was loyal. We grew up together. She wouldn't have turned her back on me unless someone made her an offer she couldn't refuse. I've tried to find her over the years, but none of her kin is talking. I even hired a PI, someone I knew in the joint. He said it was like she fell off the face of the earth. Now, you don't vanish without a trace in this day and age unless deep pockets have funded your disappearance."

"You think someone paid her off," Reid said. "Why would they do that?"

"Not someone. Boone Sutton."

Reid stared at the man for a moment. "If you think my father would have intentionally thrown a case, you know nothing about him. Winning is everything in his book. Guilt or innocence is a distant second."

"Oh, I know him all right," Brody said. "I've studied up on all his cases. I know him inside and out and, yeah, you're right. He wouldn't have thrown a case unless he had a personal reason for doing so."

"And you think you know what that personal reason is?"

"I have a pretty good idea. Ginger was a working girl. The old-school type who kept track of her johns and their peculiarities in a little black book. If Boone Sutton's name was in that book, he might have been afraid of what she'd let slip on the witness stand. You say winning is every-thing to your daddy? I'd say reputation is right up there."

Reid wanted to deny the accusation, but he couldn't help thinking of all those nights his father never made it home. All the screaming matches between his parents that had eventually settled into contempt and then indifference. Their marriage had been one only in name for as long as Reid could remember. It was certainly possible his father had had a relationship with this Ginger Vreeland. If any-one could have helped her disappear without a trace it was Boone Sutton. He had contacts everywhere.

"There's no guarantee that Miss Vreeland's testimony would have cleared you," he said. "The evidence against you was overwhelming and the DA would have done ev-erything in his power to discredit her as a witness. The outcome would probably have been the same."

Brody was quiet for a moment, and then he said with barely controlled rage, "That's not the point, Counselor. The point is, I deserved a fair hearing. I deserved an at-torney who didn't sell me down the river. My rights should have been protected the same as anyone else's."

Reid steadied his voice. "In theory, I agree with you, but I don't know what you think I can do. How do you expect me to find someone who disappeared a decade ago when this person likely doesn't want to be found? I no longer work for my father. We barely even speak. The day I got fired, they took away my keys and changed the passwords and security codes after they escorted me out of the build-ing. Even if I could manage to finagle my way through the front door, I wouldn't get near a computer, much less the file room."

Brody shrugged. "You'll figure something out. I'd start with your old man's home office. He's careful, but he's old-school like Ginger. He likes records. A paper trail even if it incriminates. You've got a lot riding on this, Counselor, so don't you go trying to sell me down the river, too."

"This is insane," Reid muttered.

"It's a little crazy, but play your cards right and we can both get what we want. Don't tell me you wouldn't like to take your old man down a peg or two. Think about it. You have until morning to give me your answer. Best you keep that photograph for incentive."

Reid glanced down at the dead woman's face.

"If I were you," Brody drawled, "I'd get back on home and find that gal's note before someone else does."

Chapter Five

It was after nine by the time Reid dragged himself downstairs the next morning. He hated getting such a late start. Made him feel as if he'd already wasted half his day. His only excuse was that he'd had a rough night. He'd gone home from the confrontation with Dave Brody and torn his house apart searching for the note the dead woman had allegedly slipped him in the bar. Then he'd poured himself a drink and searched again.

One drink had turned into a double and the next thing he knew, he'd been sprawled across his bed with a pillow over his head to drown out the street noises. He got up at some point to check the doors, drank a bottle of water, showered and then dropped back into bed. Sunlight streaming across his face had awakened him the second time. He drank more water, went for a run and then, after another shower, some ibuprofen and two cups of black coffee, he was finally starting to feel human again.

He'd just finished cleaning up the kitchen when a sharp rap sounded at the front door. He hadn't opened up the office yet, so he took a quick glance through the blinds. A tall man with a detective shield clipped to his belt stood on the front porch. His slicked-back hair and hawkish nose gave him an ominous air as he rested his hands on his hips, parting his suit jacket so that Reid could glimpse the shoulder holster beneath.

He turned the dead bolt and drew back the door. "Can I help you?"

The detective pointed to the plaque attached to the wall, which read Sutton Law Group. Then he glanced at Reid. "You Sutton?"

"Yes, I'm Reid Sutton. How can I help you?"

"I'm Detective Graham with the Charleston PD." He flashed his credentials. "I'm investigating a homicide that occurred in the area night before last."

"I heard about that." Reid kept his tone one of mild concern while, on the inside, he braced himself. Had Brody turned over the photographs to the authorities already?

After searching every square inch of the house, Reid had convinced himself the man had made up the whole thing. Brody had no other photographs; nor had he witnessed anyone drugging Reid's drink. No one was setting him up unless it was Brody himself.

But what if he was wrong? Reid found himself in a tricky situation, and on the slim chance that Brody could do real harm, he had to watch his step. He was an officer of the court and he believed absolutely in the rule of law. He didn't want to mislead, much less outright lie to a police detective, but he also didn't want to volunteer unnecessary information. The less said, the better. Inviting scrutiny was never a good idea.

"Do you mind if I ask you a few questions?"

Reid nodded. "Whatever I can do to help, Detective."

"Can we talk inside? It's a real scorcher out here today."

"Sure. Come in." Reid pushed back the door to allow the detective to enter.

Graham stepped across the threshold and moved into the small foyer, glancing into what had once been the front parlor but now served as the reception area. On the other side of the entrance, the once formal dining room was now Reid's office, every inch of workable space piled high with file folders, contracts and briefs.

"Excuse the chaos," he said as he closed the front door. "I'm still getting settled."

"Just move in?"

"I've been here a couple of months."

The detective's gaze climbed the stairs. "What's up there?"

"My apartment."

"Just you here?"

"For the time being."

"Not much of a law group."

"Not yet, but I have big plans."

"I'm sure you do." Graham propped his hand on the banister as he scoured his surroundings. "Nice place."

"Thanks."

"An old house like this can be a real money pit, but the renovated buildings in the area are going for a mint. Good investment potential."

Reid could practically see dollar signs flashing in the detective's eyes. "Time will tell, I guess."

Graham dropped his hand to his side and turned with an apologetic smile. "Sorry. My wife's in real estate. I can't help noticing these things."

Reid brushed past him and stepped into his office. "Can I get you something to drink? Water, coffee…?"

"Water would be great if it's not too much trouble."

"No trouble." Reid walked back into the kitchen, where he grabbed a bottle of water from the fridge. When he returned to his office, Graham stood at one of the bookshelves perusing the contents. Reid placed the water bottle on the edge of his desk and then went around to take

his seat, purposely drawing the detective away from any
potential hiding spots he may have missed in his search
for that note.

Graham took a seat across from Reid and uncapped
the bottle. "I don't mean to stare, but you look familiar.
Have we met? I'm not so good with names, but I rarely
forget a face."

"It's possible," Reid said with a shrug. "Except for law
school and college, I've lived in Charleston my whole life.
I've practiced law here for the past five."

"You wouldn't be related to Boone Sutton, by any
chance?"

Something in the detective's voice put Reid on guard.
"He's my father."

Contempt flashed across the detective's face before he
could hide his true feelings.

"I take it you're familiar with his work," Reid said.

"He's a legal legend in these parts. Not too popular at
police headquarters, though."

"No, I don't imagine he would be. But you know what
they say. No one likes defense attorneys until they need
one."

"That is what they say." Graham glanced around the
room. He still seemed fixated on the house. "Long way
from Sutton & Associates on Broad Street. Talk about
your prime real estate. That building must be two hundred
years old if it's a day."

"It's a beautiful place," Reid agreed. "But I like it just
fine where I am."

Graham canted his head as he regarded Reid across the
desk. "Now I remember where we met."

"Oh?"

"I pulled you over once when I was still on patrol. You
were maybe eighteen, nineteen years old, hauling ass down

the I-26 in some fancy sports car. You failed the field so-briety test so I took you in. You're lucky you didn't kill someone that night."

"That was you?" Reid shifted uncomfortably. There were a lot of things in his past that he didn't much care to revisit. He'd gone through a reckless stage that could have ended badly for a lot of innocent people. Those days were long behind him, but some of his antics still haunted him.

"A kid like you needed a firm hand," Graham said. "But I guess your old man thought differently. He called in some favors and got you released without a mark on your record. And I was read the riot act for doing my job. Took me another five years to make detective because I pissed off some rich attorney with connections."

"I remember that night." Reid particularly recalled the part where he'd been used as a punching bag by a couple of thugs who'd joined him in the drunk tank. That experience had left a mark. "You had every right to take me in. I was a stupid kid back then and, yes, I am lucky I didn't kill someone. But if it makes you feel any better, I did learn my lesson. I don't get behind the wheel of a car if I've had so much as a glass of wine with dinner. I walk or I use a car service. So thank you. As for my father's inter-ference, I can't do much about that except apologize. Your actions that night likely saved my life or someone else's. I was on a bad path."

The detective seemed unimpressed. "Guys like you al-ways get second, third and fourth chances. Influence and money still go a long way in this town. Rules for me but not for thee, as they say. But if you really did turn over a new leaf, then more power to you." He sounded doubtful.

"I appreciate that." Reid sat back in his chair, discom-fited by the detective's hostility. "I don't want to take up any more of your time. I'm sure you have a lot of people you need to talk to."

Graham took out his phone and glanced at the screen, leisurely scrolling through a series of text messages. He seemed in no hurry to get on with the interview.

"There hasn't been much about the case in the news," Reid prompted. "I understand the victim was a young female Caucasian."

Graham glanced up. "Where did you hear that?"

"People in the neighborhood talk," Reid said. "Did she live around here?"

"I think it would be best if I ask the questions."

"Of course. Force of habit." Reid smiled.

"Where were you on Sunday night?"

Right to the chase. Reid took a quick breath. "I went out to a bar to meet some friends. We were there for most of the evening. We had a few drinks, played some darts. It must have been just past midnight when I got home."

"You're sure about the time?"

"As sure as I can be. I didn't look at my watch or phone. The others weren't ready to leave so I hailed a cab. You can probably check the dispatcher's logs if you need the exact time…"

Graham didn't take notes. Reid wasn't sure if that was a good thing or not.

"You didn't see or hear anything unusual on the street?"

Reid paused. "I heard two tomcats fighting, but that's not unusual. They've been going at it for weeks."

Graham extracted a photo from his inside jacket pocket and slid it across the desk. "Do you recognize this woman?"

Reid braced himself yet again. He didn't want to give anything away with his reaction, but on the other hand, he had nothing to hide and he only had Brody's word for what had gone down in the bar. Best to be as straightforward as he could while taking care to protect himself.

He picked up the photo, turning his chair slightly so that he could catch the morning light streaming through the blinds. He studied the dead woman's features. Blond hair, blue eyes. A wide smile. She was attractive, but not memorable. And yet there was something about her—

Was she the woman in Brody's photo? Hard to tell. His snapshot had caught her in profile in a dimly lit bar while this image was straight on.

Graham sat forward. "Do you recognize her?"

"I don't know her," Reid said definitively. "But there is something vaguely familiar about her. It's possible I've seen her before, especially if she lives in the neighborhood. Has her name been released yet?"

"Haley Cooper. Ring any bells?"

"No, I'm afraid not."

"She worked at one of the clothing shops on King Street. Roommate says she left their apartment around nine on Sunday night to meet up with a friend at a local bar. That's the last anyone heard of her until her body was found early Monday morning." The detective gave Reid a shrewd look. "You do any shopping on King Street recently? Maybe that's where you know her from."

"Or maybe she just has one of those faces," Reid said.

"That could be it." Graham tucked away the photograph. "I expect the chief will put out a full statement later today, but until her name is released to the public, I'd appreciate you keeping this conversation on the down low. If you think of anything…" He placed a business card on the desk.

"I'll call you," Reid said.

He got up to walk the detective out, trailing him onto the porch and then stopping short when he saw Arden lounging in one of the wicker chairs. She looked the embodiment of a Charleston summer morning in a yellow cotton dress and sandals. Her hair was pulled back in a loose bun and she wore only the barest hint of lipstick. The sprinkling of freckles across her nose gave her a youthful vibrancy that took Reid straight back to the old days. She looked at once wholesome and seductive, a suntanned temptation that smelled of raindrops and honeysuckle.

"What are you doing here?" he asked in surprise.

"Just dropping by to say hello. I hope I didn't come at a bad time." She rose and turned to the detective expectantly.

"Arden, this is Detective Graham. He's investigating a homicide in the neighborhood. Detective, this is Arden Mayfair, an old friend of mine."

She shot Reid a glance before turning back to Graham. "A homicide? That's alarming."

"Yes, ma'am, it is." The detective's attention lingered a shade too long on her slender form.

"Do you have any suspects?"

"That's not something I can discuss at the present."

"Of course. I should have realized that you're not allowed to talk about an ongoing investigation." She sounded contrite, but Reid detected a shrewd gleam at the back of her eyes. That was Arden. Wheels already turning ninety to nothing.

Graham continued to size her up. "Do you live in the area?"

"No, I live back that way." She gave a vague nod toward the tip of the peninsula. "I was just out for a stroll and decided to stop by and check out Reid's new place."

"You say your last name is Mayfair. As in Mayfair House on East Bay?"

"I don't live there, but Clement Mayfair is my grandfather. Do you know him?"

"Oh, sure. I was over there just last Sunday for dinner."

Arden blew off the detective's sarcasm with a smile and a shrug. "I find that hard to believe. I don't see any sign of frostbite."

"I beg your pardon?"

She exchanged another glance with Reid. "Mayfair House has a tendency to be bone cold even in the dead of summer."

"I see. Well, I'll have to take your word for that." Graham turned back to Reid. "You didn't mention the cab company you used."

"It was Green Taxi," Reid said. "I remember the driver's name. It was Louis."

"Shouldn't be too hard to track down. Maybe he saw something after he dropped you off."

"It's certainly possible."

Graham gave Arden a brisk nod. "Miss Mayfair."

"Detective."

She moved back beside Reid as they watched Graham depart. Once he was out of earshot, she said, "Not exactly the friendly sort, is he?"

"I get the distinct impression he doesn't like our kind."

"Our kind?"

"People who grew up South of Broad. Trust fund babies."

She wrinkled her nose. "Who does? Half the time, we can't even stand ourselves. Not that my trust fund is anything to write home about these days. Once work begins on Berdeaux Place, I'll be lucky to have two nickels to rub together."

"And I've been disowned so…"

They shared a knowing look before she turned back to the street. "What was he doing here anyway?"

"Graham? Just what I said. He's investigating a homicide in the area."

"*The* homicide?"

"Yes."

Her eyes widened. They looked very green in the morning light. "You never said anything last night about the murder being in your neighborhood."

"I didn't think it relevant."

She said incredulously, "Not relevant? Are you kidding me? After all our talk about the magnolia blossom found at the crime scene?"

Reid tried to downplay his omission. "I figured I'd already dropped enough bombshells on you for one night. I was going to tell you, just not right away."

Her gaze narrowed before she turned back to the street. "What did you tell the detective?"

"There wasn't much I could tell him. I don't know anything."

"Why did he come to see you?"

"He's talking to everyone on the street, apparently."

"Then why did he get in his car and drive off just now?"

"What is this, an inquisition? I don't know why he drove off. Maybe I was his last stop. I didn't ask for his schedule." Reid watched her for a moment as she watched the street. "Why are *you* here? Something tells me you didn't just drop by."

"No, I came for a reason," she admitted. "I have a proposition for you."

"A proposition? For me?" He ran fingers through his hair as he gave her a skeptical look. "The guy you couldn't get rid of fast enough last night?"

"That's not true. Things started out a bit rocky. You did catch me by surprise, after all. I wasn't expecting to see anyone in the garden, least of all you, and then you dropped your bombshells. Was I supposed to welcome you with open arms after that? I was a little preoccupied in case you didn't notice." She paused, slipping her hands into the pockets of her dress as she gave him a tentative smile. "The evening ended well enough, didn't it?"

He had been trying not to think about that kiss. The way she'd instantly parted her lips in response. The way, for just a split second, she'd melted into him. No one could melt like Arden. No one had ever made him feel as strong and protective and at the same time as vulnerable. "I guess that depends on one's perspective," he said.

Her smile faded and she grew tense. "I didn't come over here to pick a fight."

"Okay."

"I just…" She seemed at a loss as she closed her eyes and drew in a long breath. "Do you smell that?"

"You mean the jasmine? It's all over my neighbor's fence. Gets a little potent when the sun heats up."

"No, Reid. That's the scent of home."

Something in her voice—or maybe it was the dreamy look on her face—made it hard for him to keep up the pretense that her presence had no effect on him. He said almost sharply, "You didn't have jasmine in Atlanta?"

"Of course we did, but not like this. Not the kind of fragrance that sinks all the way down into your soul. There's no perfume in the world that can touch a Charleston summer morning." She hugged her arms around her middle as she drew in the scent. "I've missed this city. The gardens, the people, the history."

"Since when did you become so sentimental?"

"I get that way now and then. Comes with age, I guess. I even have my maudlin moments." She turned with her perfect Arden smile. "Would it be forward of me to admit that I missed you, too?"

Now it was Reid who had to take a deep breath. "Forward, no. Suspicious, yes. What are you up to, Arden?"

"Let's go inside and I'll tell you all about it."

He nodded and had started to turn back to the door when he spotted a familiar figure across the street. Dave Brody stood on the sidewalk, one shoulder propped against a signpost as he picked at his nails with a pocketknife. He dipped his head when he caught Reid's eye and gave him an unctuous grin.

"Go on in," Reid said. "I'll be right back."

Arden followed him to the edge of the porch. "Where are you going?"

"Wait for me inside. This won't take a minute."

He hurried down the steps and across the street. This time Brody didn't run away. He waited with that same oily smile as Reid approached.

"Morning, Counselor. Mighty fine company you've got waiting for you over there on your front porch." He nodded in the direction of Reid's house and then lifted the hand with the knife to wave at Arden.

Reid glanced over his shoulder. Instead of going inside, she lingered on the porch, watching them from the shade. He could almost hear the wheels spinning inside her head. He turned back to Brody. "I told you last night, she's off-limits. That means don't wave at her. Don't talk about her. Don't so much as glance in her direction."

"Touchy, aren't we?" Brody pushed himself away from the post. "And I told you I have no interest in your girlfriend so long as you help me get what I want. I gave you the night to make your decision so here I am." He spread his arms wide as he moved toward Reid, displaying his ominous tattoos. "What's it going to be, Counselor?"

Reid frowned. "Not so fast. Did you have anything to do with a police detective showing up at my door this morning?"

"No, I did not, but I'm flattered you think I have that kind of sway, considering my background and all. I couldn't help noticing the good detective—Graham, was it?—didn't look too happy when he drove away just now."

"How do you know his name?"

Brody gestured with the knife. The action seemed innocent enough, but Reid had no doubt it was meant as subtle intimidation. "He's been hanging around the neighborhood ever since the body was found. Surprised you didn't know that. Been preoccupied, have you?"

Reid wasn't buying any of it. "Are you sure you didn't say something to him? Maybe put a bug in his ear that caused him to come sniffing around my place?"

"Now that sounds downright paranoid. You're the lawyer. Don't it stand to reason he'd be talking to everyone in the neighborhood? Of course, it could be that word has already gotten out about your activities on the night in question. Or…" Brody shaded his eyes as he peered across the street. "Maybe someone else put that bug in the detective's ear. The same someone who's trying to set you up. Seems to me like you've made a powerful enemy in this town."

"And just who is this enemy?" Reid demanded. "Does he or she have a name?"

Brody dropped his hand to his side and shrugged. "How would I know? I'm just a guy who happened to be in the right place at the right time."

Reid thought about that for a moment. "Okay, let's say I do have an enemy. If this person is already talking to the police, then how does it benefit me to help you?"

"A fair question, but you're forgetting something, aren't you? I have photographs that prove someone drugged you. I believe that's called exculpatory evidence? And then there's the matter of some video footage that happened to come my way."

Reid's pulse quickened even though he wasn't about to let Brody prod him into a reaction. "What footage?"

"I'll be happy to email you a copy for your edification, but for now a little preview will have to do." Brody took out his phone. "Amazing what they can do these days. Sure is a lot fancier than the one I had when I got sent up." He scrolled until he found what he wanted. Then he moved into the shade and held up the phone so that Reid could view the screen.

The video was grainy and greenish, like the feed from an outdoor security camera. Reid appeared in the frame and stood silhouetted at the entrance of the alley. Then he ducked under the crime scene tape and walked quickly to the spot where the body had been found, crouching beside the bloodstains as he glanced up to scour the windows and balconies that overlooked the alley. In actuality, he had been wondering if anyone had heard the victim's screams, but to the police, it might appear that he had come back to the scene of the crime to determine whether or not he'd been seen.

"I'm not a cop, but that looks mighty incriminating to me," Brody said.

Reid glanced up. "Where did you get this?"

"Like I said, it just happened to come my way and I'm not one to look a gift horse in the mouth."

"That video doesn't prove anything."

"Maybe, maybe not, but people get convicted on circumstantial evidence every day of the week. No one knows that better than me."

"Your situation was completely different," Reid said. "The evidence against you was overwhelming."

Brody looked as if he wanted to dispute that fact, but he let it pass with a shrug. "You're right. The video and those photographs won't send a guy like you to prison, but at the very least they can instigate an uncomfortable conversation with the cops. A perp walk is all it would take to scare off a sizable portion of your clientele. But there's no need for it to come to that. You help me find Ginger Vreeland and nobody sees any of this but us."

Reid glanced over his shoulder. Arden was still on the front porch waiting for him. He could imagine the questions going through her head. He nodded and gave a brief wave to let her know he'd be right there. "Even if I could find Ginger Vreeland after all these years, do you think I'd give you her name and address so that you can terrorize the poor woman?"

"You've got me all wrong, Counselor. I've got no beef with Ginger. She had to claw and scratch for everything she got just like I did. If somebody made her an offer she couldn't refuse, I can't fault her for taking it. I would have done the same thing in her place. All I want to know is who paid her to leave town and why. If it was Boone Sutton, then I want to know what she wrote in that little black book of hers every time he came calling. I bet, deep down, you'd like to know that, too."

"You'll never touch him," Reid warned.

"We'll have to see about that, won't we? Like I said last night, the best place to go looking is in his personal papers. A little birdie tells me that your mama spends a whole lot of time all by her lonesome in that fancy house on Water Street. I bet she'd dearly love a visit from her one and only son."

"Leave my mother out of this."

"That's up to you. If you can't or won't finish the job, then I'll have no recourse but to have a little chat with Mrs. Sutton. Find out what she knows about her husband's affairs. No pun intended." He went back to work on his nails with the pocketknife.

"All right, you win," Reid said. "I'll do what I can to find Ginger Vreeland, but she's been gone for ten years. The trail is ice-cold by now. I'll need some time."

"I'll give you till Friday. If you haven't made what I deem as sufficient headway, we'll have to reevaluate our arrangement. But fair warning, Counselor."

Reid waited.

Brody's gaze hardened as he moved out of the shade and stood peering across the street at Arden, running his thumb along the sharp edge of the knife blade. "I wouldn't go getting any ideas about trying to double-cross me. I have friends in low places. You know the kind I mean. Hardscrabble guys that would slit a man's throat—or a woman's—for not much more than the loose change in your pocket."

Chapter Six

"Who is that man?" Arden asked as Reid came up the porch steps.

"No one." He pushed past her and opened the front door.

"Didn't seem like no one to me. From where I stood, it appeared the two of you were in a pretty heated exchange."

"He's an ex-client," Reid said. "No one you need to worry about."

She gave him a long scrutiny. "Really? Because *you* sure look worried."

"Didn't you say you have a proposition for me?" He stepped back and motioned for her to enter, catching a whiff of her fragrance as she glided by him. The top note was honeysuckle, but he'd never been able to place the softer notes. He thought again of raindrops. And sunshine. Darkness and light. That was Arden. She'd always been a walking contradiction. An irresistible riddle with a killer smile.

Her timing was lousy, though. He considered making some excuse to send her on her way, but he didn't like the idea of her being out on the street even in broad daylight with Dave Brody lurking nearby. Smarter to keep her inside until Brody had had time to move on.

She hovered in the foyer, suspended in a sunbeam as her

gaze traveled from the front parlor into his office and then up the stairs, just as Detective Graham had done before her.

"So this is your new place."

He checked across the street and glanced both ways before he closed the door. Despite Brody being nowhere in sight, Reid had a feeling he hadn't gone far. "What do you think?"

Arden shot him a look over her shoulder. "You want my honest opinion?"

"I would expect nothing less from you."

"You've got your work cut out for you. I would advise a gut job, but at the very least, the floors will need to be refinished and the windows replaced. The electrical and plumbing will undoubtedly cost a small fortune to bring up to code, and then you still have the less costly but time-consuming tasks of scraping wallpaper and painting drywall. But…" She turned with gleaming eyes. "I love it, Reid. I really do. The millwork is beautiful and the location is perfect. And all this natural light." She stepped into his office and went straight for one of the long windows that opened into the side garden. "This is my favorite style of architecture. I used to dream of owning a house like this. Do you remember? Berdeaux Place always seemed so oppressive to me."

"I remember."

Her gaze turned playful. "You always wanted something sleek and glamorous on the waterfront."

"I had that for a while. I discovered it didn't suit me at all."

She gave him an inquisitive look before turning back to the window. The yellow dress left her tanned back and shoulders bare. Reid had to tear his gaze from her slender form. Too many memories floated between them and his mind had a tendency to linger in dark places when he thought too much about the past. He needed a clear head to deal with Dave Brody. Needed to remain focused if he wanted to stay a step ahead of the police. And to think his life had been relatively uncomplicated just two short days ago.

"Do you want something to drink?" he asked. "I have some iced tea in the fridge."

"That sounds divine. The walk over was longer than I anticipated."

"You're not likely to cool off in here," he warned. "I've been meaning to get someone in to check the AC, but I'm spread a little thin these days." He picked up the detective's water bottle and carried it into the kitchen. Then he got down two tall glasses and poured the tea, taking his time until he had his mask back in place. "I have a couple of cases that have been consuming most of my time," he said in a conversational tone as he came back into his office and placed the drinks on his desk. Arden had already taken a seat, looking as comfortable as could be with her legs crossed and hands folded in her lap. One of the straps of her sundress had fallen down her arm. Reid had the urge to slide it back into place with his fingertip. Or to tug it all the way down with his teeth.

Yes, way to stay focused.

Arden seemed oblivious of his attention. Swiveling her chair around, she gestured to the file boxes strewn across the floor. "All that for just two cases?"

"One of them could be a class action."

"That's exciting." She leaned in to claim her glass and the strap slipped lower, revealing more than a hint of cleavage. Reid tried not to stare, but *damn*.

"What is it?"

"Nothing."

"You seem distracted."

"No, I'm all yours."

She looked doubtful. "I suppose we should get down to it then. I don't want to take up too much of your time."

He nodded. "Whenever you're ready."

She settled back against her chair. "My uncle Calvin was at Berdeaux Place last night. I ran into him in the garden. He said he'd been working in the greenhouse."

Reid frowned. "At night?"

"That's what I said, too. It just seemed odd. But considering his strained relationship with Grandmother, I would have been surprised to see him there at any hour."

"How did he get in?"

"He said he'd been letting himself in through the side gate so someone must have given him a key. Maybe Grandmother made arrangements before she died. I don't know. But, evidently, he's been coming by every evening to take care of Mother's cereus."

"Her what?"

Arden made a dismissive gesture with her hand. "It's a night-blooming cactus. Some call it a Queen of the Night. When it blooms, the scent is out of this world."

"You people and your flowers," Reid muttered.

"I know. We were all thwarted horticulturists, I think. Anyway, Calvin told me that Ambrose Foucault had mentioned my plans to sell Berdeaux Place. As you can imagine, I was pretty upset to learn that a conversation with my grandmother's attorney, one that I considered confidential, had been shared with my uncle."

Reid folded his arms on his desk. "Have you talked to Ambrose about it?"

"Not yet, but I intend to. As you can also imagine, Calvin wasn't too happy with the idea of my selling the house. He reminded me that Berdeaux Place has been in Grandmother's family for generations. I understand his position.

Even though he never lived there, the house is his legacy, too. I don't want to be insensitive to his feelings, and at the same time—"

"Your grandmother left the property to you. You have the final decision."

"Exactly. And I don't take that responsibility lightly. Berdeaux Place was her pride and joy. Whatever I do, I want to make certain that the house and her memory are honored. But I have to be realistic about my prospects. Historic properties of that age and size come with a ton of legalities, so the pool of prospective buyers is limited. Grandmother left a contingency account and I still have money in the trust fund, but neither will last forever. I don't want to rush a decision, but I also can't afford to wait until I'm desperate and out of options."

"So put the place on the market as is," Reid suggested. "Get the ball rolling. You may be pleasantly surprised by the amount of interest the listing generates."

She idly twirled a loose strand of hair around her fingertip. "I've considered that, but now may not be the best time. I've reason to believe vultures are circling."

That got Reid's attention. He lifted a brow. "Are you worried about anyone in particular?"

"Yes." A shadow flitted through her eyes. She turned to stare out the front window as she gathered her thoughts. When she glanced back at Reid, the shadow had resettled into the hard gleam of determination. "Calvin told me that Grandfather might be interested in acquiring the house. He's always had an appreciation for historic properties."

"Well, there you go," Reid said. "Wouldn't that solve all your problems? The house stays in the family, and the burden is lifted from your shoulders."

"You're presuming his intentions are honorable, but I've never known Clement Mayfair to have an altruistic bone in his body. He's up to something. I just know it. His own son made the offhand comment that he might be interested in buying the house for no other reason than to imagine my grandmother rolling over in her grave."

"I'm sure Calvin was joking," Reid said.

"A joke based on an ugly truth," Arden insisted.

Reid canted his head as he studied her. "What are you really worried about?"

She took her time answering. "You'll think I'm paranoid, but I have a bad feeling that Grandfather is planning to take Berdeaux Place away from me somehow. He may even try to convince Calvin to challenge Grandmother's will. All I know for certain is that he has no sentimental interest in that house. He wants it out of pure spite."

"You really think he'd go to that much trouble and expense just to get back at a dead woman?"

"You have no idea the animosity that festered between them," Arden said. "They despised each other so much that they raised their children as strangers. Grandmother took my mother when she left and my uncle stayed behind with Grandfather. They barely ever saw each other even though they lived only blocks apart. I ask you, who does that kind of thing?"

"Relationships can be complicated, but that does seem a bit extreme." Reid thought about his mother spending so much time alone in the stately old mansion on Water Street. He felt a pang of guilt that he hadn't gone to see her in weeks, but they'd never been close. Her emotional distance had kept the two of them almost strangers. Why she stayed with Reid's father after so many years of contempt and neglect, he could only guess; undoubtedly, money played a role. She was a woman who appreciated her creature comforts. Now that Dave Brody had brought her into his machinations, Reid resolved to keep a closer eye on her.

He put that thought away for the time being and refocused on Arden. "You don't know what happened between them?"

Arden lifted a shoulder. "Grandmother would never talk about it, but I think it was something really bad. If Grandfather manages to get his hands on Berdeaux Place, I can only imagine the pleasure he would take in destroying it."

"You said yourself, there are rules and regulations that protect historic properties."

"He could burn it to the ground before anyone could stop him."

She'd worked herself into a state. Color tinged her cheeks and anger flared in her eyes, reminding Reid that Arden Mayfair had always been a woman of passion. In love, in anger, in hate. She gave it her all. Watching that fire burn out had pained him more than he wanted to remember.

"What can I do to help?" he asked quietly.

She glanced up gratefully. "If Ambrose can so easily be manipulated into revealing the details of our private conversation, then I can no longer trust him to have my best interests at heart. I'd like to hire you as my attorney."

That took him aback. "You want me to represent you?"

"Why not? Unless you don't want my business."

"It's not that. I think you'd be better served with someone who has expertise in probate and real estate law."

She waved off his argument with another dismissive gesture. "How do I know another attorney couldn't be bought off by my grandfather? You're the only one I trust, Reid. I know you can't be bribed or intimidated. Not by Clement Mayfair, not by anyone. Quite the contrary, in fact."

She was just full of surprises today. He was the only one she trusted? A man she'd barely clapped eyes on in over a decade? A man whose heart she'd once broken and scattered to the wind without a hint of remorse?

Anger niggled and he gave it free rein for a moment even though he knew the emotion was irrational and unproductive. He sat in silence, observing her through his passive mask until he trusted himself to speak.

"I have to say, that's a pretty bold statement, Arden."

"It's true. I do trust you. I always have." She leaned in. "Will you do this for me? Will you take my case?"

"We don't know yet that there is a case. First things first, okay? I'll need to see a copy of your grandmother's will."

"I can get you one. Does this mean—"

"It means I'll take a look at the will. But the minute you start requesting documents from Ambrose, he'll know something is up."

"I know. I plan to talk to him as soon as I can arrange a meeting. I doubt he'll be upset. If anything, he'll probably be relieved not to be caught in the middle of a Mayfair war."

"If you're right about your grandfather's intentions, the dispute could get ugly," Reid warned. "He has the resources to drag this out for years. Are you sure you don't want to sell him the house and be done with it?"

"Oh, I'm sure." She had that look on her face, the one that signaled to Reid she'd already dug in her heels. "Clement Mayfair needs to know that I'm not afraid of him."

Reid nodded. "Okay. I'll make some discreet calls and see if I can get wind of his plans."

"Thank you, Reid."

"Don't thank me yet. Let's just wait and see what happens." When she made no move to end the conversation, he shuffled a few papers on his desk. He would have liked to check the street, but she was already suspicious. The last thing he wanted was to put Dave Brody on her radar. "If that's all, I have a meeting to get to soon…"

She settled more deeply into her chair.

He sighed. "Something else on your mind, Arden?"

"I couldn't help noticing all the clutter here and in the other room. Books and files stacked every which way. It's the first thing you notice when you walk in the door and it hardly inspires confidence."

"That's blunt, but you're right. I haven't had a chance to put everything away yet. As I said, I'm spread a little thin these days."

She swiveled her chair back around to face him. "I could do it for you."

He stared at her blankly. "Why would you want to do that?"

"You need help and I need work."

He said in astonishment, "Are you asking me for a job?"

Her own mask slipped, revealing a rare vulnerability, but she tugged it back into place and lifted her chin. "Don't look so shocked. I'm not exactly a slacker, you know. I've been gainfully employed since college."

"My surprise has nothing to do with your work ethic."

She continued on as if he hadn't spoken. "What do you think I did at the museum all those years? I researched, appraised, processed and cataloged. Seems to me that is the kind of experience you need around here. I may not have a law degree, but I'm a fast learner and a hard worker. And you know you can trust me."

Did he know that? Fourteen years was a long time. People changed. Reid knew very little about her life in Atlanta or why she'd decided to come back to Charleston at this particular time. He had a feeling there was more to her story than settling her grandmother's estate.

But then, he was hardly in a position to cast stones. He hadn't been altogether forthcoming with her, either.

"Even if I thought this was a good idea, which I don't," he stressed "take a look around. Do you see a receptionist? A paralegal? Any associates? I haven't staffed up because I can't afford to. I used most of my cash to buy this house, and I promised myself I wouldn't dig any deeper until I was certain I could make a go of it on my own."

She tucked back the loose strand of hair as she gave him her most earnest, Arden appeal. "But wouldn't that be a lot easier with help? Just think about it, okay? I could file briefs, track down witnesses, do all the research and legwork that eats up so much your time. You don't even have to pay me at first. Maybe we can work something out with your legal fees. Give me a month, and I know I can prove myself."

"A month is a long time," he said.

"Two weeks, then, but you have to give me a fighting chance."

"I don't have to do anything."

The edge in his voice stopped her cold. Now she was the one who looked stunned. Rejection wasn't something Arden Mayfair would have ever gotten used to, he reckoned. The more things changed, the more they stayed the same.

"We were a good team once," she said. "Always a step ahead of everyone else, always in sync with each other. Together, we were formidable."

"That was a long time ago."

The furrows deepened as she gave him a long scrutiny. "Be honest, Reid. Are you letting our past color your decision?"

"I don't know what you mean."

"I'll be frank then. Are you still holding a grudge for

the way I left town? What was all that business last night about airing our grievances? Were you just paying lip service to moving on?"

"We can move on without being in each other's face ten to twelve hours a day." He regretted the sharpness of his words the moment they left his mouth. He regretted even more the hurt that flashed in her eyes before she dropped her gaze to her hands.

"Point taken."

"Arden—"

"No, that's fine. It was a crazy idea. I mean, how could we ever work together after everything that happened between us, right?"

"Arden—"

"Don't say anything else. Please. Just let me walk out of here with as much dignity as I can muster." She rose. "I'll send over a copy of Grandmother's will as soon as I can make the arrangements. Unless you've changed your mind."

"No. I said I'd take a look and I will."

She turned toward the door.

"Wait." He winced inwardly, berating himself for succumbing to her emotional manipulation. He didn't think she was maliciously playing him, but she'd always known how to push his buttons.

She sat back down.

"We'll probably both live to regret this, but I may have something for you." He paused, deciding how far he wanted to take this. He could give her an errand or two, something that would occupy her time while he figured things out with Brody. Or he could just send her home where she would be protected behind the high walls of Berdeaux Place. Still, she was alone there and Reid had no way of knowing if the security system had been sufficiently updated. She might be safer here, with a police presence on the street and neighbors who were on guard for anyone suspicious.

"Reid?"

"Sorry. I was just thinking. I have outside meetings for the rest of the day. I won't be back here until late this afternoon, so you'll have the place to yourself. Take a look around, get acquainted with the house and help me figure out how I can best utilize the space. Long term, we can talk about tearing down walls and a possible expansion. For now, we work with what we've got. Upstairs is off-limits. That's my personal space and I don't want to be surrounded by work."

She nodded. "I can do that."

"You say you're good at research? See what you can do with this." He scribbled a name on a piece of paper and slid it across the desk to her.

She scanned the note. "Who is Ginger Vreeland?"

"Ten years ago my father represented a man named Dave Brody on a second-degree murder charge. The evidence against him was overwhelming, but Ginger Vreeland claimed she could corroborate Brody's alibi. She disappeared the night before she was to take the witness stand on his behalf. Brody was found guilty and sent to the state penitentiary."

Arden glanced up. "You suspected foul play?"

"No, more than likely someone bought her off."

"I don't understand. If this was your father's case, why are you getting involved?"

"Let's just say, Dave Brody has become my problem. He's out of prison and looking for answers."

"And you've agreed to represent him?"

"It's a complicated matter," Reid hedged as he opened a desk drawer and extracted a file folder. "There's more where this came from, but the information inside is a good place to start. It includes notes from the attorney that interviewed and prepped Ginger Vreeland for her testimony. Read through the whole thing and see if you can pick up any threads. It won't be easy," he said. "Ten years is a long time and she's likely changed her name at least once. She was a call girl back then so there's no trail of W-2s to follow. I'm not expecting miracles, but at the very least, you can go through all the public databases in case something may have slipped through the cracks."

Arden looked intrigued. "I'll need my laptop."

"You can use mine. I'll log you on as a guest." He pushed back his chair and stood. "One more thing. As soon as I leave here, make sure you lock the door behind me. Don't let anyone in that you don't know. In fact, don't let anyone in but me."

She rose, too. "What about clients?"

"No one," he said firmly. "If anyone needs to get in touch with me, they can leave a voice mail."

She followed him into the foyer. "What's going on, Reid?"

He resisted the urge to put a hand on her arm. The less physical contact the better for his sanity. "We can't lose sight of what's happened, Arden. A woman's body was found down the street from my house and a magnolia blossom was left at the crime scene. That connects us both to the murder. Until the police make an arrest, you need to be careful. We both do."

Something flashed in her eyes. A touch of fear, Reid thought, but she looked no less dauntless or determined. Her chin came up in that way he remembered so well. "I'll be careful. I'll lock the door behind you and I won't let anyone in until you get back. But you need to understand something, too." Her hazel eyes shimmered in golden sunlight. "No matter what happens, I'm not running away this time."

He drew a long breath and nodded. "That's what worries me the most."

Chapter Seven

Reid noticed the Mercedes as soon as he came out of the courthouse. Given the location, he might have assumed his father had tracked him down. The historical building that housed Sutton & Associates was just down the street from the intersection known as the Four Corners of Law at Broad and Meeting. But the long, sleek car was no longer Boone Sutton's style. He'd given up his limo and driver for a shiny red sports car on his sixtieth birthday. The way he tooled around town in his six-figure convertible was an embarrassing cliché, but that was his business. Reid had enough problems without worrying about his father's perpetual pursuit of his youth.

As he headed down the sidewalk, the driver got out and waited by the rear door.

"Mr. Sutton?"

"Yes." He tried to peer around the driver into the car, but the windows were too darkly tinted.

"Mr. Mayfair would like a word."

"Which Mr. Mayfair?"

"Mr. Clement Mayfair." The driver opened the back door. "Would you mind getting inside the car?"

Reid had never spoken more than a dozen words to Arden's grandfather. Truth be told, Clement Mayfair had intimidated Reid when he was younger, but he was a grown man now and his curiosity had been piqued. He nodded to the driver and climbed in.

The interior of the car smelled of new leather and a scent Reid couldn't pin down. Although the fragrance wasn't unpleasant, the mystery of it bothered him, like a memory that niggled. He drew in a subtle breath as he placed his briefcase at his feet and sank down into the buttery seat.

Clement Mayfair sat stone-faced and ramrod straight. Reid tried to recall the older man's age. He must surely be in his seventies, but time had worn easily on his trim frame. He had the same regal bearing, the same aristocratic profile that Reid remembered so well. His hair was naturally sparse and he wore it slicked back from a wide forehead. His face was suntanned, and his eyes behind wire-rimmed glasses were the same piercing blue that had once stupefied Reid into long, sullen silences.

Reid sat quietly now, only a bit apprehensive as he wondered what business the older man had with him.

"Mr. Mayfair," he finally said. "You wanted to see me, sir?"

"Do you mind if we drive? This is a very busy intersection and I don't like tying up traffic." His rich baritone had thinned only slightly with age.

Reid nodded. "I don't mind. But I have a meeting in half an hour. I'll need to be back at the courthouse by then."

Clement Mayfair responded with a sharp rap on the glass partition. The driver pulled away from the curb and glided into traffic.

Reid watched the elegant neoclassical courthouse recede from his view with a strange, sinking sensation. He couldn't shake the notion that he had just made a serious mistake. Willingly entered the lion's den, so to speak.

He kept his voice neutral as he returned Mayfair's scrutiny. "How did you know where to find me?"

"You're an attorney. Call it an educated guess."

"That was some guess," Reid said.

The older man sat perfectly still, one hand on the armrest, the other on the seat between them. He wore a gold signet ring on his pinkie, which surprised Reid. Bespoke suit notwithstanding, Clement Mayfair didn't seem the type to appreciate embellishments.

He smiled, as if he had intuited Reid's assessment. "It might surprise you to know that I've kept track of you over the years."

"Why?" Reid asked bluntly.

"You were once important to my granddaughter. Therefore, you were of some consequence to me. Enough that I took an interest in your career. You were top of your class at Tulane Law. Passed the bar on your first try."

"I'm flattered you took the trouble," Reid said, though *flattered* was hardly the right word. Intrigued, yes, and certainly suspicious, especially after his conversation with Arden. He thought about her insistence that her grandfather was up to something. Reid was now inclined to agree and he braced himself for whatever attack or trickery might be forthcoming.

"You could have had your pick of any number of top-tier law firms in the country," Mayfair said. "But you came back to Charleston to work for your father's firm. I've had dealings with Boone Sutton in the past. I never liked or trusted the man."

"That makes two of us."

The blue eyes pinned him. "And yet you're very much like him. Overconfident and self-indulgent."

"One man's opinion," Reid said with a careless shrug.

Mayfair's gaze turned withering. "I suppose some might find your glibness charming—I've always considered it a sign of a weak mind. You're educated and reasonably intelligent, but you've never been a deep thinker. You were never a match for my granddaughter."

Reid shrugged again. "On that we can agree."

"Then why did you go see her the moment she got back into town?"

A warning bell sounded in Reid's head, reminding him to watch his step. A lion's den was no place to let down one's guard. "Are you keeping track of her...or me?"

"Charleston is still a small town in all ways that matter. Word gets around."

"Let me guess," Reid said. "Calvin told you I'd been by."

"I haven't spoken to my son in days. This isn't about him. This is about my granddaughter." Clement Mayfair leaned in slightly. "You ruined her life once. Why not leave her alone?"

"That's an interesting perspective considering Arden is the one who left me."

"You got her pregnant when she was barely eighteen years old."

"*I* was barely eighteen years old."

"You were old enough to know that precautions should have been taken."

"We were not the first careless teenagers," Reid said.

"Still so cavalier."

Reid was silent for a moment. "How did you even know about the pregnancy? We didn't tell anyone."

"Did you really think I wouldn't find out?" His expression turned contemptuous. "I doubt my granddaughter would have agreed with me back then, but losing that baby was the best thing that could have happened to her."

Reid's fingers curled into tight fists as images flashed at the back of his mind. Arden's pale face against the hospital bed. Her hand clutching his as tears rolled down her cheeks.

"I can't speak for Arden, but I wouldn't have agreed with you then or now. And frankly, that's a pretty callous way of putting things."

"Doesn't make it any less true." Mayfair took off his glasses and methodically polished them with a handkerchief he had removed from his inner jacket pocket. His fingernails were cut very short and buffed to a subtle sheen. "Where do you think either of you would be if things had turned out differently? Would you have married her? Moved her with you to New Orleans and stuck her in some dismal campus apartment while you completed your degree? What about *her* education? *Her* ambitions?"

"This is the twenty-first century, in case you hadn't noticed. Women can do whatever they want."

"Don't fool yourself, young man. A teenager with a baby has limited options, even one with Arden's advantages. The marriage would never have lasted. You may not even have finished law school. I've little doubt that my granddaughter would have ended up raising the child alone."

"Well, we'll never know for certain, will we?" Reid turned to glance out the window as he pushed old memories back into their dark hiding places. In the close confines of the car, he caught yet another whiff of the mysterious fragrance, elusive and cloying. "I have to say, I'm curious about your sudden interest in Arden's well-being." He decided to go on the offensive. "You barely gave her the time of day when she was younger. Even when you invited her to dinner, she sometimes ended up eating alone."

"Arden told you this?"

"She told me everything."

The hand on the seat twitched as if Reid had struck a nerve. "I sometimes had to attend business even at the dinner hour. That was hardly my fault. A man in my position

has obligations. But I'm not surprised Arden's recollec-
tion would cast me in a bad light. Her grandmother did
everything in her power to poison the girl's mind against
me just as she kept my own daughter from me years ago.
Now that Evelyn is gone, I finally have the chance for a
relationship with my granddaughter and I won't have you
getting in the way."

Reid gave a humorless chuckle. "That you think I have
influence over Arden shows how little you really know
about her."

Clement Mayfair gave a grudging nod. "You have more
fire than I remembered. Is that why you left your father's
firm? The two of you butted heads? Well, I give you credit
for that. It takes guts to strike out on your own, especially
after being under Boone Sutton's thumb for so long. But I
don't have to tell you the streets of Charleston are littered
with failed attorneys."

Reid didn't trust the man's change in tactics. "I'm well
aware of the risks."

"Then you must also know that in Charleston, it's more
about whom you know than what you know. As for me,
I never had much use for the elite, the so-called movers
and shakers. I preferred building an empire on my own
terms and, for the most part, I've been left alone. But you
were raised in that environment. You know how the game
is played. One word from the right person can make or
break a career."

Reid said impatiently, "Is there a point to all this?"

Clement Mayfair put back on his glasses and tucked
away the handkerchief. He blinked a few times as if bringing Reid back into focus. "I'm a quiet man who leads a
quiet life. I prefer shadows to limelight. But don't mistake
my low profile for impotence. A well-placed word from me
will bring you more clients than you ever dared to imagine.

Possibly even some of your father's accounts. A desirable feather in any son's cap. Or…" He leaned toward Reid, eyes gleaming behind the polished lenses. "I can see to it that your doors are permanently closed within six months."

Reid fought back another rush of anger. An emotional rejoinder would play right into Mayfair's hands. The older man was obviously trying to get a rise out of him. Trying to prove that he had all the power.

Reid smiled. "For all the interest you've apparently shown in me over the years, you seem to have missed the fact that I don't respond well to threats or ultimatums."

"I assure you, I've missed nothing, young man."

The car glided to a stop in front of the courthouse.

Reid reached for the door handle. "Thank you for the conversation. It's been illuminating."

Before he could exit the car, Clement Mayfair's hand clamped around his wrist. The man's grip was strong for his age. His fingers were long and bony, and Reid could have sworn he felt a chill where they made contact. He thought about Arden's claim that Mayfair House was bone-deep cold even in the dead of summer.

He resisted the urge to shake off Mayfair's hand. Instead, he lifted his gaze, refusing to back down. "Was there something else?"

"Stay away from my granddaughter."

Reid glanced at the man's hand on his arm and then looked up, straight into Clement Mayfair's glacial stare. "That's up to Arden."

The grip tightened a split second before he released Reid. "Trust me when I tell you that you do not want me for an enemy."

There was a quality in his voice that sent a chill down Reid's backbone. "Seems as if I don't have much choice in the matter."

"I'm giving you fair warning. You've no idea the pain I can cause you." The older man's gaze deepened, and for a moment Reid saw something unpleasant in those icy pools, something that echoed the dark promise of his words.

Images swirled in Reid's head as he recalled Dave Brody's insistence that he had a powerful enemy in this city. He thought about the young woman from the bar who had ended up dead in the alley, her body riddled with stab wounds. Then he thought about Camille Mayfair, who had met the same fate, and Arden, only five years old and frozen in fear as her gaze locked onto the killer's through the summerhouse window.

It came to Reid in a flash, as his gaze locked onto Clement Mayfair's, that the elusive fragrance inside the car was magnolia. The scent seemed to emanate from the older man's clothing. Or did it come from the deep, dark depths of his soul?

That smell was surely a fantasy, Reid told himself. The sense of evil that suddenly permeated the car was nothing more than his imagination. Clement Mayfair was just a blustery old man. Powerful, yes, but not malevolent.

Even so, when the driver opened the door, Reid climbed out more shaken than he would have ever dared to admit.

ARDEN SPENT THE rest of the morning sketching floor plans as she went from room to room. She would bring a measuring tape the next day so that she could work to scale, but for now the exploration kept her highly entertained.

Curious about Reid's apartment, she took a peek upstairs. He'd been adamant that his private domain should remain off-limits, but only in so far as using it for an expanded work space. At least that's how Arden interpreted his instructions. Surely, he wouldn't mind if she had a look around. And, anyway, he wasn't here, so…

She climbed the stairs slowly, pausing at the top to glance around. The living area was sparsely furnished with a sleek sofa and an iconic leather lounger that had undoubtedly been transported from his modern apartment. A short hallway led back to the bedroom, a spacious and airy space with a high-coved ceiling and French doors that opened onto a balcony. A pair of old-fashioned rockers faced the street. Holdovers from the previous owner, Arden decided. She pictured Reid out there in the evenings, breeze in the trees, crickets serenading from the garden. She could see herself rocking beside him, head back, eyes closed as the night deepened around them.

Thinking about Reid in such an intimate setting evoked too many memories. He'd once been the most important person in her life. Her soul mate and lifeline. Sad to contemplate how far they'd drifted apart. Sadder still that pride and willfulness had kept her away for so long. She wondered what his reaction would be if he discovered the real reason she'd come back to Charleston, tail between her legs, looking to start anew from the unpleasantness she'd left behind in Atlanta. No use dwelling on bad memories. No sense conjuring up the pain and humiliation that had hung like a bad smell over her abrupt departure. She had a mission now. A purpose. No more spinning her wheels.

She closed the French doors and went back downstairs. Taking a seat behind Reid's desk, she set to work, scribbling notes on a yellow legal pad she'd found in one of the boxes before turning her attention to the name she'd been tasked to research. Ginger Vreeland.

Taking his suggestion, she read through the file, quickly the first time and then more slowly the second, making more notes on the same legal pad. The hours flew by, and before she knew it her stomach reminded her that she'd worked through lunchtime. She went into the kitchen to check the refrigerator, helping herself to the last container of blueberry yogurt before returning to her assignment.

Research could be tedious, and she knew enough to pause now and then to stretch her legs and work out the kinks in her neck and shoulders. She'd just settled back down from a brief respite when she heard someone at the back door. She assumed Reid had returned and barely gave the intrusion a second thought until she remembered he was supposed to be away until late that afternoon.

Rising slowly, she walked across the room to peer into the kitchen. She could see someone moving about on the porch through the glass panel in the door. The man was about the same height and size as Reid, but she knew instinctively it wasn't him even though she never got a look at his face.

Pressing against the wall, she had started to take another peek when she heard the scrape of a key in the lock. Then the door handle jiggled. Alarmed, Arden glanced around the office, wondering what she should do. Wait and confront the interloper? Let him know she was there before he got inside?

She did neither, opting to heed the little voice in her head that commanded her to hide. She had no idea who else would have a key to Reid's house, but she wasn't about to wait around and find out. Hadn't Reid warned her not to let anyone inside? Hadn't he reminded her that the proximity of his office and the magnolia blossom left at the crime scene connected them both to the murder? And to the murderer?

Hurrying across the office, Arden stepped into the foyer, taking another quick glance around. Slipping off her sandals, she hooked them over her finger as she ran quietly up the stairs, pausing on the landing to peer over the banister. She heard the back door close a split second before she retreated into Reid's apartment. She made for the bedroom, wincing as a floorboard creaked beneath her bare feet. After tiptoeing across the hardwood floor, she opened the closet door and dropped to her knees, pulling the door closed behind her. Then she scrambled into the corner, concealing herself as best she could with Reid's clothing.

The closet wasn't large. If the intruder wanted to find her he could do so without much effort, but Arden had been nearly silent in her escape. He hadn't heard her. He didn't know she was there. She kept telling herself that as she drew her knees to her chest, trying to make herself as small a target as possible. There could be any number of legitimate reasons someone would have a key to Reid's house. Maybe he'd given a spare to a repairman or a neighbor. Maybe he had a cleaning service that he'd neglected to tell her about. Maybe Reid himself had returned and she'd allowed panic to spur her imagination.

She kept telling herself all those things right up until the moment she heard slow, heavy footsteps on the stairs. The intruder approached the second floor with purpose. He knew she was there. Knew there was no escape.

Why hadn't she gone out the front door or even onto the balcony? Maybe she could have shimmied down a tree or a trellis. She wasn't afraid of heights. She could have even climbed up to the roof and waited him out.

She scooted toward the door, thinking she might still have time. She reached for the knob and then dropped her hand to her side. He was in the bedroom already. How had she missed the sound of his footsteps in the other room?

Holding her breath, she flattened her hands on the floor and pushed herself back into the corner, taking care not to disturb the hangers. She pulled her knees back up and waited in the dark.

He walked around the room, taking his time as he opened and closed drawers, checked the balcony and then moved back into the room. Arden clamped a hand over her mouth to silence her breathing. She couldn't see anything in the closet. Could barely detect his footsteps. Had he left already? Did she dare take a peek?

The closet door opened and a stream of light edged up against her. She shrank back, unable to see the intruder. She didn't dare part the clothes to get a look at his face, but she sensed him in the doorway. Waiting. Listening.

An image came to her of a woman's body in a dark alleyway, and of a figure—gloved and hooded—bending over her as he placed a magnolia blossom on the ground beside her. She could almost smell that scent. The headiness took her back to that summer twilight when she'd discovered her mother's lifeless body in the garden with the crimson kiss of death upon her lips. Arden thought of the killer watching her from the summerhouse window, leaving a pristine blossom on the steps as a warning that he would someday return for her.

Adrenaline pumped hard and fast through her veins. She smothered a scream as the wooden hangers clacked together. In another moment, he would part Reid's clothing and discover her cowering in the corner.

He rifled through a few items and then stepped back. A folded paper square fell to the floor. Arden could see it in a patch of sunlight. She didn't know if the note had come from one of Reid's pockets or if the intruder had dropped it. If he bent to pick it up, he would surely see her. He didn't pick it up. Instead, he kicked the note back into the closet, as if he didn't want it to be found. At least not right away.

The closet door closed. The footsteps receded across the bedroom floor, into the living room and then down the stairs. Arden lifted her head, turning her ear to the sound

She was almost certain she heard the back door close, but she waited for what seemed an eternity before she ventured from her hiding place.

She grabbed the note as she scrambled to her feet and all but lunged from the closet, drawing long breaths as she tried to calm her pounding heart. Then she slipped through the rooms, pausing at the top of the stairs to listen once more before slowly descending. She went through every room checking doors and windows, and only when she was satisfied that she was alone did she go back into Reid's office and open the folded note.

A woman's name and phone number were scrawled in flowery cursive across the paper and sealed with a vivid red lipstick print.

The crimson kiss of death.

Chapter Eight

Arden jumped when she heard footsteps on the front porch. She was seated at Reid's desk trying to concentrate on work, but now she leaped to her feet and hurried over to the window to glance out. She could see Reid through the sidelight. Before he had a chance to insert his key in the lock, she drew back the door, grabbed his arm and all but yanked him inside. She'd never been so relieved to see anyone.

"Hello to you, too," he quipped, and then he saw her face as she closed the door and turned the dead bolt. He tossed his jacket on the banister and removed his sunglasses. "Arden? What's going on?"

"Someone broke into your house after you left."

"What?" He took her arm. "Are you okay? Were you hurt?"

Even as shaken as she was, his concern still gratified her. "I'm fine. I wasn't touched. He never even saw me. When I realized it wasn't you, I went upstairs and hid."

"How did he get in?"

"He came in through the back door."

His hand tightened on her arm as he glanced past her into the kitchen. Then his gaze shot back to her. "Are you sure you're okay?"

"I was scared and I'm still a little wobbly, but I'm fine."

He laid his sunglasses on the entrance table without ever releasing her. "When did all this happen?"

"A little while ago."

"Did you call the police?"

Arden hesitated. She hadn't called the police. She hadn't called anyone. The reason didn't matter at the moment. They would get to that later. "There wasn't time. It happened so quickly…"

He took both her arms and studied her intently as if he needed to prove to himself she wasn't injured. She inhaled sharply. She'd forgotten how dark his eyes were. A deep, rich brown with gold flecks that looked like tiny flares in the sunlight streaming in through the windows. He'd removed his tie and rolled up his shirtsleeves. He was very tanned, Arden noticed. She wondered if he still went to the beach on weekends. She wondered a lot of things about Reid's life, but now was not the appropriate time to ask questions or wallow in memories. An hour ago, she'd been certain an old killer had come to track her down. She could still picture his shadow across the closet floor, could still hear the sound of his breath as he stood in the doorway searching through Reid's clothes. Had he known she was there all along? Had he left her alone in order to prolong his sick game?

"Arden?"

She jumped. "I'm sorry. What did you say?"

Reid canted his head as if trying to figure something out. "Can you tell me what happened?"

She nodded. "I said someone broke in, but that's not entirely accurate. He had a key. He let himself in the back door, and he didn't seem at all worried about being caught. He must have seen you leave and thought the house was empty." She moved away from Reid's touch and turned to glance back out at the street. Everything looked normal, but she could imagine someone out there watching the house, perhaps plucking a magnolia blossom from a nearby tree as he vectored in on the window where she stood.

"Did you get a look at him?" Reid asked. "Can you describe him?"

"Not really. I only glimpsed him through the window. He seemed to be about your general height and build." She scoured a neighbor's yard before turning back to Reid. "Have you given a key to anyone lately? A repairman or a neighbor maybe?"

"I don't give out my keys." He spoke adamantly.

"Did you get the locks changed after you moved in?"

He winced. "I've been meaning to."

"*Reid.* That's the first thing you're supposed to do when you move into a new place."

"I know that, but I've been a little busy lately." Now he was the one who turned to glance out the window. He looked tense as he studied the street. They were both on edge. "This is my fault," he said. "I should never have left you here alone."

She scoffed at his reasoning. "Don't be ridiculous. You couldn't have known something like this would happen. And you did caution me not to let anyone in. That's why I hid. I kept thinking about what you said earlier. We're both connected to that murder. If your warning hadn't been fresh on my mind, I might have confronted him. Who knows what would have happened then?"

"You've always been quick on your feet," Reid said. "So you went upstairs to hide. Could you tell if anything was missing when you came back down?"

"I don't think he took anything. But he may have left something."

Reid frowned at her obliqueness. "What do you mean?"

"He went up to your apartment. By that time, I was hiding in your closet and I couldn't see anything. I heard him walking around in the bedroom, opening dresser drawers and looking out on the balcony. When he came over to the closet, I was certain he knew I was in there. You can't imagine the things that went through my head. I even thought I smelled magnolia…" She rubbed a hand up and down the chill bumps on her arm. "You must think I'm crazy."

He gave her a strange look. "Because you smelled magnolia? No, I don't think you're crazy. Far from it. What happened then?"

"He dropped a note on the floor. Or else it fell out of one of your pockets. He kicked it to the back of the closet as if he didn't want you to find it right away."

Reid had gone very still. Something flickered in his eyes. "Do you have the note?"

She took it from her dress pocket and handed it to him. He unfolded the paper and scanned the contents. Arden watched his expression. The look that came over his face frightened her more than the intruder.

"That's the dead woman's name, isn't it?" she asked quietly.

He glanced up from the note. "How did you know?"

"The police chief had a press conference earlier. I streamed it while I worked."

"Did he say anything about suspects? Or the magnolia blossom?"

"He was pretty vague. They're pursuing several leads, leaving no stone unturned and all that, but he didn't say a word about the magnolia blossom."

"They're still keeping that close to the vest," Reid said.

"Or else they have no idea of the significance."

"I think they know. They don't want to panic the public with premature talk of a copycat killer."

"Maybe," Arden said pensively. "I keep going back to my mother's murder. The magnolia blossom left on the summerhouse steps was all but forgotten because the crimson kiss of death soon became Finch's signature. You said yourself only a handful of people would understand the implication of a *white* magnolia blossom. You and I are two of them. My mother's killer is a third."

"I don't want to get sidetracked with a long conversation about Orson Lee Finch's guilt or innocence," Reid said. "Right now, we need to focus on our immediate situation."

"I agree. First things first. Why would someone break into your home and leave that note? Did you know this woman?" Arden had expected an instant denial; instead, he dropped his gaze to the note, pausing for so long that her heart skipped a beat. "Reid?"

He glanced up. "I didn't know her, but it's possible I may have seen her on the night she was murdered."

Arden caught her breath. "When? Where? Why didn't you say anything?"

"Because I didn't know until last night. I'm still not certain it was her."

"Reid—"

He headed her off. "I'll tell you everything I know, but I need a drink first. It's been a long day."

Arden followed him into the kitchen. When he got a bottle of whiskey from one of the cabinets, she took it from him and poured the contents down the sink.

He didn't try to stop her, though his look was one of annoyance. "Why did you do that?"

"Because a drink is the last thing you need," she said firmly. "Until we figure out what's going on, we both need to keep a clear head."

He looked as if he wanted to argue, and then he shrugged. "Water, then."

She handed him a chilled bottle from the refrigerator. He took a long swig before recapping and setting it aside. "Let's go sit in my office. This could take a while."

Arden led the way this time, taking the position behind his desk where she had been working earlier. Reid didn't seem to notice or care. He plopped down in a chair across from her, his long legs sprawled in front of him as he braced his elbows on the armrests.

"Where should we start?" Arden asked.

"I'm still trying to figure out why you didn't call the police," he said.

"I told you. There wasn't time."

"I mean afterward. Why didn't you at least call me?"

"You said you had meetings all afternoon. I didn't want to leave a voice mail. I thought it better that I tell you in person. As for the police…" She paused. "How long have we known each other? Since we were four years old, right? Has there ever been a time when I couldn't read you like a book?"

He lifted a brow but kept silent.

"I knew the moment you came to Berdeaux Place last evening that you were keeping something from me. I felt it even stronger this morning. I didn't want to involve the police until I could figure out what you might be mixed up in."

Reid looked taken aback by her revelation. "You were trying to protect me?"

"Why does that surprise you? We've always had each other's back."

"Fourteen years, Arden."

"So?"

"That's a long time."

"Some things don't change, Reid." She tried not to think about the loneliness of those fourteen years. "My turn to ask the questions," she said briskly. "Who was that man on the street you talked to this morning?"

He answered without hesitation, as if he'd decided it was pointless to keep things from her any longer. "Dave Brody."

"Your father's ex-client? What did he want?"

Reid sighed. "It's a long story—in a nutshell, he has a bone to pick about his defense. Ever since he got out of prison, he's been coming around making veiled threats. He watches the house, follows me when I leave. That sort of thing."

"But you weren't his attorney. Why is he harassing you?"

"He wants me to help prove that my father was responsible for Ginger Vreeland's disappearance."

Arden stared at him in shock. "Responsible...how? He doesn't think—"

"No, nothing like that. He thinks she was paid to leave town."

"That's still insane. Boone Sutton is one of the best defense attorneys in the state. Why would he get rid of his own witness?"

"Apparently, Ginger kept a little black book with all her clients' names and their preferences. Kinks. Whatever you want to call them. Brody is convinced my father was one of her clients. He was afraid of what might come out during her testimony so he arranged for her to disappear."

"But she was prepped for her testimony. Wouldn't he have known what she would say before he called her to the witness stand?"

"Witnesses have been known to fall apart under cross-examination," Reid said. "Plus, we don't know what went down between them before she left town. Maybe she blackmailed him. Offered to keep quiet in exchange for money."

"Wow." Arden sat back against the chair. "I have to say, this is getting really interesting."

"I'm glad you're entertained."

"Don't tell me you're not. Boone Sutton and a prostitute? Wouldn't that set tongues to wagging!" A dozen questions bubbled, but Arden batted them away so that she could remain focused on the situation at hand. "What happens if we find Ginger Vreeland and her little black book? What does Brody plan to do with the contents?"

"My guess is, he's looking for a big payday. Barring that, he'll settle for my father's public humiliation."

"And you're helping him," Arden said. "So what does he have on you?"

"Are you sure you want to hear this?"

"Yes, I think I'd better."

He told her about the confrontation in the alley and Brody's claim that he had photographs from the bar. He told her about the note, the laced drink and the possibility that someone with a lot of power was setting him up for murder. Arden leaned forward, watching his expression as she hung on his every word.

By the time he finished, she was aghast. "This is unreal. Who would do such a thing?"

"I don't know."

"Are you sure Brody's not the one setting you up? Or maybe he's just making it all up to get you to help him."

"He showed me a photograph from the bar, so he's not making everything up. As to the rest…" Reid shrugged. "I don't put anything past him."

"What are you going to do?"

"For the time being, try to keep a low profile." He massaged his temples with his fingertips.

"What did you tell the detective who came by here this morning?"

"Nothing of what I just told you."

"Why not? If someone is setting you up, the police need to know about it. At the very least, you should tell them about Brody's threats."

Reid dropped his hands back to the armrests. "You saw the way Detective Graham looked at us this morning. He didn't even bother to hide his contempt."

"He did have an attitude," Arden agreed.

"More than an attitude. He came to my front door with a chip on his shoulder. Turns out, our paths have crossed before. He arrested me several years back. Apparently, my father pulled strings to arrange for my release and have my record expunged. Then he made sure Graham wasn't promoted to detective for another five years."

Arden digested that for a moment. "Does your father have that kind of clout with the police department?"

"Yes. But if he interfered with anyone's career, it likely had more to do with my black eye and cracked ribs than it did with the initial arrest."

"Graham beat you up?"

"Not personally, no. Two thugs jumped me in the holding cell, and I'd be willing to bet Graham was behind the attack. I think he wanted to teach me a lesson. Maybe he still does. The point is, if he gets a look at those photographs, he'll zero in on me to the exclusion of any other leads or suspects. If he goes to the bar and asks the right questions, someone may remember that they saw me leave with the victim. I didn't," he added quickly. "But Brody is right. The power of suggestion is a real thing. That's why eye-witness testimony can be so unreliable."

Arden shook her head. "I had no idea all this was going on. No wonder you looked like death warmed over when I got here this morning."

"Felt like it, too."

She said hesitantly, "This is a long shot, but you don't think your father could be behind this, do you? You said you were fired from Sutton & Associates. It must have been a serious falling-out if he also disowned you. Maybe this is *his* way of teaching you a lesson."

"Boone Sutton is a lot of things, but he's no murderer," Reid said.

"Maybe that girl wasn't supposed to die. Maybe Brody was just supposed to harass you so that you would be forced to return to the firm. But he took matters into his own hands because he has his own agenda."

"It's possible, of course, but I don't see my father getting into bed with a guy like Dave Brody. Not with their history."

"Their history is precisely why he would have thought of Brody in the first place. But leaving that aside, is there anyone else who would want to frame you? Do you have any other enemies that you know of?"

He scowled at the window as if he were deep in thought. "There may be someone," he said slowly. "You're not going to like hearing about it, though."

"I take it you don't mean Detective Graham."

Reid's gaze came back to hers. "Your grandfather was waiting for me when I came out of the courthouse earlier. He asked me to take a ride."

"What?" Arden could hardly comprehend such a thing. "Clement Mayfair asked you to take a ride? Why? What did he want?"

"He warned me to stay away from you."

"What?"

Reid nodded. "He thinks now that your grandmother is gone he can have a relationship with you. He doesn't want me standing in the way."

"He said that? I'm...speechless," Arden sputtered.

"I was pretty surprised myself," Reid said.

"Surprised doesn't even begin to cover it. That man...that *insufferable man*...has never once shown the slightest bit of interest in me, and now he's warning you to stay away from me?" She got up and paced to the window. "This just proves I'm right. He's up to something."

"I think so, too," Reid said. "Until we can figure out his agenda, you should stay away from him."

She marched back to the desk and plopped down. "Oh, no. I'm going over there tonight to give him a piece of my mind."

"Arden, don't do that."

"Who does he think he is? He can't bully my friends and get away with it. He can't bully me. I won't let him."

"Calm down, okay? I understand how you feel but listen to me for a minute. Arden? Are you listening?"

She folded her arms. "What?"

"Clement Mayfair is a powerful man with unlimited resources. We have to be careful how we take him on. We have to keep our cool. He said I didn't want him for an enemy and I believe him."

She glanced at Reid in alarm. "Does this mean you don't want to take my case? Maybe you don't want me working here, either. I understand if you don't. I could walk out the door right now, no hard feelings."

"I didn't say any of that."

"I know, but I came here this morning and more or less forced myself on you."

A smile flitted. "I'm not sure I would put it quite that way."

"You know what I mean. I made it nearly impossible for you to say no to me. I'm giving you that chance now. Say the word, Reid."

He gave her an exasperated look. "Did you even hear

what I said? We need to be careful how we take him on. *We.* Us. You and me."

"You don't have to do this."

He entwined his fingers beneath his chin as he gazed at her across the desk. "Weren't you the one who said we make a formidable pair?"

"Yes, but that was before I knew my grandfather had threatened you. You're trying to start your own firm. The last thing you need is Clement Mayfair making trouble for you. And you don't need to protect me. I can take care of myself."

The gold flecks in his eyes suddenly seemed on fire as his gaze intensified. "I told you before, old habits die hard."

"Fourteen years, Reid."

"Some things don't change."

ARDEN HAD A difficult time forgetting that look in Reid's eyes. She thought about it all the way home. She thought about it during an early, solitary dinner, and she was still thinking about those golden flecks when she drifted out to the garden. The sun had dipped below the treetops, but the air had not yet cooled. The breeze that blew through the palmettos was hot and sticky, making her wonder if a storm might be brewing somewhere off the coast.

She started down the walkway, taking note of what needed to be done to the gardens. She wouldn't linger long outside. Once the light started to fade, she would hurry back inside, lock the doors, set the alarm and curl up with a mindless TV program until she grew drowsy. For now, though, she still had plenty of light, and the exotic dome of the summerhouse beckoned.

As tempted as she was by memories, she couldn't bring herself to climb the steps and explore the shadowy interior. She diverted course just as she had last evening, finding herself once again at the greenhouse. She peered through the glass walls, letting her gaze travel along the empty tables and aisles. No one was about. She wondered if her uncle had already been by before she got home. He had been cordial and pleasant, but Arden still didn't feel comfortable with his having the run of the place. Did she dare risk offending him by asking for the key back? Or should she take the advice she'd given to Reid and have all the locks changed?

That wouldn't be a bad idea in any case, she decided. For all she knew, there could be any number of keys floating around. The notion that her grandfather might have gotten his hands on one was distinctly unnerving.

As she stood gazing into the greenhouse, her mind drifted back to her conversation with her uncle and how as a child he'd snuck out of his father's house every chance he got so that he could come here to Berdeaux Place. Arden could imagine him in the garden, peering through the glass walls of the greenhouse to watch his mother and sister as they happily worked among the plants. How lonely he must have been back then. How abandoned he must have felt. What could have happened in her grandparents' marriage to drive Evelyn away, taking her daughter and leaving her son behind to be raised by a cold, loveless man? How could any mother make that choice?

The answer was simple. She hadn't been given a choice.

And now Clement Mayfair wanted a relationship with Arden, his only granddaughter. After all these years, why the sudden interest in her welfare? The answer again was simple. She had something he wanted.

Maybe it was her imagination, but the breeze suddenly grew chilly as the shadows in the garden lengthened. She turned away from the greenhouse, trusting that her mother's cereus wouldn't bloom for another few nights.

She paused again on her way back to the house, her gaze going once more to the summerhouse dome. Did she dare take a closer look? Once the sun went down, the light would fade quickly and she didn't want to be caught out in the garden at twilight. Orson Lee Finch was in prison and would likely remain there for the rest of his natural life, but another killer was out there somewhere. One who knew about the magnolia blossom that had been left on the summerhouse steps.

Arden approached those steps now with a curious blend of excitement and dread. She stood at the bottom, letting her gaze roam over the domed roof and the intricate latticework walls, peering up at the window from which her mother's killer had once stared back at her. Then she drew an unsteady breath as her mind went back to that twilight. She had stood then exactly where she stood now, her heart hammering against her chest. Her mother had lain motionless on the grass, her skin as pale as moonlight.

Even without the bloodstains on her mother's dress, Arden would have known that something truly horrible had happened. She hadn't fully understood that her mother was gone, not at first, but she knew she wanted nothing so much as to turn and run back to the safety of the house and into her grandmother's comforting embrace. A scent, a sound…a strange *knowing*…had held her in thrall until a scream finally bubbled up from her paralyzed throat. Then she hadn't been able to stop screaming even when help arrived, even when she'd been led back inside, away from the body, away from those disembodied eyes in the summerhouse window. She hadn't calmed down until her grandmother had sent for her best friend, Reid.

His father had brought him right over. Back then, he had always come when she needed him. *Some things don't change.*

The breeze was still warm, but Arden felt the deepest of chills. She hugged her arms to herself as she placed a foot on the bottom step. A rustling sound from inside the summerhouse froze her. Was someone in there?

More likely a squirrel or a bird, she told herself.

Still, she retreated back to the garden, rushing along the flagstone path, tripping as she glanced over her shoulder. No one was there, of course. That didn't stop her. She hurried inside and locked the door against the encroaching shadows. Then she unlocked the liquor cabinet and poured herself a shot of her grandmother's best whiskey.

Arden downed the fiery drink and poured another, carrying the glass with her upstairs to her bedroom. She turned on all the lights and searched through her closet until she found her secret stash—the reams of notes she and Reid had compiled during their summer investigation. They had only been children playing at detective, but even then they'd been resourceful and inquisitive. *Formidable.* It wasn't inconceivable that they may have stumbled across something important without realizing it.

Carrying everything back down to the front parlor, she dropped to the floor and spread the notebooks around her on the rug. Imagining her grandmother's irritation at such a mess, she muttered a quick apology before digging in.

Thumbing through the pages, she marveled at how much time and attention a couple of twelve-year-olds had devoted to their endeavor. She finished her drink and poured another. She wasn't used to hard liquor and the whiskey soon went to her head. It was dark out by this time and she turned on a lamp before curling up on the sofa, leaving notebooks and markers strewn across the floor. It was too early to sleep. She would be up at the crack of dawn if she went to bed now. She would rest her eyes just for a few minutes. She would simply lie there very still as the room spun around her.

Sometime later, her eyes flew open, and for a moment she couldn't remember where she was. Then she wondered what had awakened her so abruptly. A sound…a smell… an instinct?

Just a dream, she told herself as she settled back against the couch. Nothing to worry about.

But she could hear something overhead…upstairs. Where exactly was the scrabbling sound coming from?

Bolting upright, she sat in the lamplight listening to the house. Berdeaux Place was over a hundred and fifty years old. Creaks and groans were to be expected. Nothing to worry about.

The sound came again, bringing her to her feet. Squirrels, she told herself. Just squirrels. *Nothing to worry about.*

A family of squirrels had once invaded the attic, wreaking havoc on wiring and insulation until her grandmother had hired an exterminator. He'd trapped mother and babies and transported them to White Point Garden. At least that was the story Arden had been told.

She wasn't afraid of squirrels or mice, but she knew she wouldn't be able to sleep until she made sure nothing had found its way inside the house. Grabbing her grandmother's sword, she followed the sound out into the foyer. She wasn't sure what she hoped to accomplish with the blade. She certainly wouldn't run a poor squirrel through, but she liked to think she had enough grit to protect herself from an intruder. If nothing else, the feel of the curved hilt in her hand brought out her inner warrior woman. She went up the stairs without hesitation, pausing only at the top to listen.

Her grandmother's bedroom was at the front of the

house, a large, airy room with an ancient, opulent en suite. Arden's room was at the back, with long windows that overlooked the garden. Her mother's room was across the hall.

Arden following the rummaging sound down the hallway, pausing only long enough to glance in her room. Everything was as she'd left it that morning. Bed neatly made up, suitcases unpacked, clothing all stored away.

She crossed to her mother's room, hovering in the hallway with her hand on the knob. After the murder, Arden's grandmother had locked the room, allowing only the housekeeper inside once a week to dust and vacuum. The room had become a mausoleum, abandoned and forbidden until Arden had gone to her grandmother and told her how much she hated the locked door. It was as if they were trying to lock their memories away, trying to forget her mother ever existed.

After that, the door had been opened, and Arden had been free to visit her mother's room whenever she desired. She used to spend hours inside, sitting by the windows or playing dress up in front of the long, gilded mirror. Sometimes she would just lie on the bed and stare at the ceiling as she drank in the lingering scent of her mother's candles.

Arden wasn't sure why she hesitated to go inside now. She wasn't afraid of ghosts. She wasn't afraid to remember her mother, whom she had loved with all her heart. She had a strange sense of guilt and displacement. Like she had been gone for so long she had no business violating this sacred place. Her emotions made little sense and felt irrational.

Taking a breath, she opened the door and stepped across the threshold. Moonlight flooded the room, glinting so brilliantly off the mirror that Arden was startled back into the hallway. Then she laughed at herself and reached for the light switch, her gaze roaming the room as she waited for her pulse to settle.

Her mother's domain was just as she'd left it all those years ago. The room was pretty and eclectic, bordering on Bohemian with the silk bed throw and thick floor pillows at all the windows. A suitable space for the mysterious young woman her mother had been. Arden could still smell the scented candles, but how was that possible? Surely the scent would have faded by now. Unless her grandmother had periodically replaced them. She may have even lit them from time to time.

Arden walked over to the dresser and lifted one of the candles to her nose. Sandalwood. The second was patchouli. The third…*magnolia.*

She was so shocked by the scent, she almost dropped the glass holder. Her fingers trembled, her heart pounded. She quickly set the candle aside. It's just a *scent*, she told herself. Nothing to worry about.

Hadn't she been the one who had talked her grandmother out of chopping down the magnificent old magnolia tree that shaded the summerhouse?

It's just a tree, Grandmother.

"It's just a scent," she whispered.

But the notion that someone other than her grandmother had been in her mother's room, burning a magnolia candle…

It *was* just a scent. Just a dream. Just squirrels…

Arden backtracked out of the room and closed the door. She hurried across the hall to her room, locking the door behind her and then shoving a chair up under the knob. She was safe enough at Berdeaux Place. The doors were all locked and the security system activated. No one could get in without her knowing.

She went over to the window to glance down into the

garden. She could see the top of the summerhouse peeking through the trees and the glint of moonlight on the green-house. The night was still and calm, and yet she couldn't shake the scary notion that someone was down there hidden among the shadows. She'd once been expert at climbing down the trellis to escape her room. What if someone else had the notion to climb up? Was she really safe here?

She couldn't stand guard at the window all night. Neither could she close her eyes and fall back asleep. She was too keyed up now. Too wary of every night sound, no matter how slight.

Scouring the grounds one last time, she finally left the window and lay down on the bed, her grandmother's sword beside her. She thought again of Orson Lee Finch in prison, but the image of an aging killer behind bars gave her no comfort because another killer had already struck once. If someone wanted to set Reid up for murder, who better than her as his next victim?

She pulled the covers up over her and snuggled her head against the pillow, but she didn't fall asleep until dawn broke over the city and the light in her room turned golden.

Chapter Nine

Reid was already on his second cup of coffee by the time Arden arrived the next morning. The locksmith had come and gone and he was seated at his desk glancing through the paper as he chowed down on a breakfast burrito he'd bought at the corner store. He'd finally gotten a good night's sleep and felt better than he had in days. Arden, on the other hand, looked as if she hadn't slept a wink. The dark circles under her eyes had deepened and her response to his greeting had been lukewarm at best.

He gave her a lingering appraisal as she stood in his office doorway. "What's wrong?" he asked in concern. "You look like something the cat dragged in."

She gave him a pained smile. Then she glanced away as if she didn't want him to stare too deeply into her eyes. "I didn't get much sleep last night."

"I can tell." He took a quick sip of his coffee. "Anything I should know about?"

"Squirrels in the attic," she muttered.

Reid carefully set aside his cup. "Are you sure that's all it was? Not residual nerves from what happened here yesterday?"

"I don't think so." Her gaze darted back to him and she shrugged. "Honestly, I think it's that house. I never imagined it would be so disconcerting to be there alone. Every time I go out into the garden, I remember what happened. I close my eyes and I picture my mother's body, so cold and still, on the ground. I imagine someone staring back at me from the summerhouse windows."

"You lived in that house for years after your mother died," Reid said. "You never seemed to dwell on it back then."

She brushed back her hair with a careless gesture. "I was a kid. I thought I was invincible. Plus, I had you."

His heart gave a funny little jump. "No one is invincible."

"I've never been more aware of that fact since you came to my house the other evening and told me about the latest murder. And speaking of invincible..." She glanced over her shoulder toward the entrance. "I noticed you had the locks changed. That was fast."

"I have a friend in the business. He sent someone out first thing this morning. I don't want a repeat of what happened yesterday."

"That's smart," she said with a nod. "I've been thinking it would be a good idea to change the locks at Berdeaux Place, as well. If my uncle has a key to the side gate, then he may also have one to the house. And if he has a key to the house—"

"Your grandfather could gain access," Reid finished. "I'll set you up with my friend. You can trust him. I've known him for years. In fact, he was one of my first clients. You should also have him check out your security system, make sure everything is up-to-date. At the very least, you need to change your code."

"I've already done that." She had remained hovering in the doorway of his office all this time; now she came in and dumped the contents of her tote bag on his desk.

He took in the black-and-white notebooks and then glanced up. "What's all this?"

"Don't you recognize them?" Arden sat down in a chair across from his desk. She wore white jeans and a summery top that left her toned arms bare. Her hair was down today and tucked behind her ears. He caught the glitter of tiny diamonds in her lobes, could smell the barest hint of honeysuckle as she settled into her chair. "They're the notebooks from our investigation," she explained.

He picked one out of the pile and opened the cover. "I can't believe you kept these things."

"Why wouldn't I? We worked really hard that summer. I know it's mostly kid stuff, but we actually uncovered some interesting details. For instance, do you remember that Orson Lee Finch once worked down the street from Berdeaux Place?"

"As I recall, he worked for a number of families that resided in the Historic District. He was a well-regarded gardener at one time."

"Yes, but I somehow let all that slip my mind. Deliberately so, perhaps. Grandmother even hired him a few times to do some of the heavy chores that her aging gardener couldn't manage. I vaguely remember Finch. He was a short, thin man with kind eyes and a sweet smile. He once gave me a stick of gum."

"Ted Bundy was a real charmer, too," Reid said as he rifled through a few pages of the notebook. "What's your point?"

"I'm just pointing out that he had ample opportunity to acquaint himself with my mother's circumstances and habits. He had ample opportunity to watch me, too. But then so did a lot of other people. And who's to say the real killer didn't have occasion to observe Finch's circumstances and habits and determine he'd make a good patsy?"

"'The real killer'? 'A patsy'?" Reid gave her a skeptical look.

"If we're working from our old theory that Finch was framed." She reached over and plucked one of the notebooks from Reid's desk. "I went through some of the pages last night and highlighted the entries that caught my eye. When you have time, you might want to take a closer look, too."

"Why?" Reid closed the notebook and set it aside. He had also been doing a lot of thinking since last night. She wasn't going to like what he had to say.

"Why?" She stared him down. "Because a young woman was murdered down the block from where we sit. You said yourself the location of your office and the magnolia blossom left at the crime scene link us to the murder."

"Link *us*. But that doesn't mean there's a connection to your mother's murder. That's a long shot in my opinion."

Arden's expression turned suspicious. "What's going on with you? Why do you keep saying one thing and then five minutes later say the opposite? My head is spinning trying to keep up with you."

He'd be frustrated, too, if he were in her position, but she'd thrown him off his game. He'd said things he shouldn't have and made rash decisions that weren't in either of their best interests. Time to rectify his mistakes. "Unlike you, I got plenty of rest last night. My head is clearer than it's been in days. I'm trying to look at the situation rationally instead of emotionally."

"Okay. But what would be the harm in at least glancing through our notes?" Arden asked. "Who knows? We might find something that would help us with your current predicament."

"By current predicament, I assume you mean Dave Brody. I don't see how."

"If Finch really was framed, maybe the same person is now trying to frame you."

"Arden."

"Don't Arden me. We'll never get to the bottom of anything unless you keep an open mind. But forget about the notebooks for a moment." She sat forward, eyes gleaming. "I think I've figured how we can find Ginger Vreeland."

Reid wrapped up his half-eaten burrito carefully and set it aside.

"Don't you at least want to hear my idea?"

"I don't think so." He folded his arms on the desk and tried to remain resolved. "I've done some thinking, too, and I've decided it's a bad idea to involve you in my problems. We have to be smart about this. If someone is trying to set me up, they wouldn't hesitate to come after you if they thought you were in the way."

"I can take care of myself," she insisted. "Besides that, has it not occurred to you that the killer may come after me whether I'm helping you or not? What better way to frame you for murder than to take out an old girlfriend? Think about that, Reid. There's safety in numbers. We need to stick together. And you need someone you can trust watching your back."

She had a point, but that someone didn't need to be her. *If anything happened to Arden—*

He banished the thought before it could take root.

"I appreciate your enthusiasm. I do. But you need to keep your distance. At least for now."

She rolled her eyes in frustration. "There you go again. Changing your mind on a dime. I don't get you, Reid Sutton. We had all of this resolved yesterday afternoon. What's changed?"

"I'm trying to do what's best for both of us." *Don't back down. And don't get distracted by her I'm-so-disappointed-*

in-you look. The disapproval in her eyes meant nothing to him. This was his house, his business. He had a right to make whatever decisions he deemed necessary. "Why do you want to work here anyway? Don't you have better things to do with your time?"

"Such as?"

"You said you wanted to oversee the renovations to Berdeaux Place because you don't trust anyone else. You even mentioned your plan to take on some of the work yourself. Do you have any idea how time-consuming a project like that can be?"

"Of course I do. I also know I'll go out of my mind if I have to stay in that house twenty-four hours a day."

He picked up a pen and examined the barrel. "Then why not get a job in your field? There are any number of museums and art galleries in this city that would jump at the chance to have someone with your expertise."

"Not a one of them will touch me," she said.

He glanced up. "What?"

She met his gaze boldly. "You heard me. The places you mentioned won't hire me."

"Why not?"

She hesitated, her defiance wilting under cross-examination. "I wasn't altogether truthful with you the other night about the reason I left my job."

"You were fired?"

She sighed. "Try not to gloat? This is hard enough without that smirk."

He didn't think he was gloating or smirking, but he apologized anyway. "Sorry. Go on."

"I wasn't fired. I resigned before it came to that. But just barely," she admitted.

"What happened?"

She entwined her fingers in her lap. "The museum was

sold several months ago. The new owners brought in some of their own staff, including a new director. He was funny, handsome, charismatic. We found we had a lot in common. We liked the same music, read the same books. We became friends. Close friends."

"Is that what they're calling it these days?" Reid had a sudden, inexplicable pain in his chest. He sat up straighter, as if good posture could make the ache go away.

"Call it whatever you like. A friendship. A relationship." She dropped her gaze. "An intense flirtation."

The knife twisted as Reid remained silent.

She fixated on her tangled fingers. "Turns out he was married."

Stab me again, why don't you? "You had an affair with a married man?" He hadn't meant to sound so aghast or judgmental. He hardly had the moral ground here, but still. This was Arden.

She looked up at his tone. "It wasn't an affair. It was never physical. Not *that* physical and I had no idea he was married. Maybe I didn't want to know. But looking back, there were no obvious clues or signs. Nothing that would give him away. He was that good. Or maybe I was just that stupid." Color tinged her cheeks. "Anyway, I later learned that he and his wife had been separated for a time. She followed him to Atlanta and they reconciled. When she got wind of our…"

"Intense flirtation."

Arden's blush deepened. "She stormed into the museum one day and made a scene. She was very upset. Over-wrought. You can't even imagine the things she said to me."

"Oh, I bet I can."

"She was under the impression that I was the one who

had come on to her husband. When he rejected my advances, I became aggressive. He told her I *stalked* him."

"Wow."

Arden nodded. "Her accusations blindsided me. I don't consider myself naive, but I was completely fooled."

"Sounds like a real catch, this guy."

She frowned. "It's not funny, Reid."

No, but if he didn't make light of the situation, he might get on the first flight to Atlanta, track this guy down and do something really stupid. "No one who knows you would ever believe such a ridiculous claim."

She gave a weak shrug. "My friends stuck by me, but I was humiliated in front of my coworkers and damaged in the eyes of the new owners. I had no choice but to leave."

"So you came back home to lick your wounds," Reid said.

"Something like that. You see now why I can't apply for a job in my field? The moment anyone calls for a reference, all that ugliness follows me here."

Reid flexed his fingers and tried to relax. "Why didn't you tell me any of this yesterday?"

"It's a hard thing to talk about. It goes against the image I've always had of myself. Strong. Independent. Fearless. The truth of the matter is, I'm none of those things." She glanced out the window before she turned back to Reid. "Do you want to hear something else about me? Another dark truth about Arden Mayfair?"

"Always."

"I'd been spinning my wheels in the same position forever. I only ever became friends with him because I thought he could help advance my career. Turns out, I'm not such a great catch, either."

"I don't know about that," Reid said. "I can name about

a dozen guys right here in Charleston who would disagree with you."

Her gaze burned into his, begging the question: *Are you one of them?*

Reid refused to speak on the grounds he might incriminate himself.

She gave him a tentative smile. The same smile that had held him enthralled since they were four years old. The same smile that had once made him believe he could climb mountains and slay dragons on her behalf.

She broke the silence with another question. "How is it that you always know the right thing to say?" she asked softly.

"It seems to me I've been saying the wrong thing ever since you came back. The one thing I do know is that everyone makes mistakes. Even you. You pick yourself up and you move on. That's all you can do."

"Is that what you did after we split up?"

"Yes, after a while. But we're talking about you right now."

She nodded. "It wasn't my intent to come here yesterday and ask you for a job. I wanted your legal advice. That's all. Then I saw this house…" She glanced around the messy office, lifting her gaze to the stained ceiling before returning her focus to Reid. "I understand your vision for this place. I got it the minute I walked through the door. An unpretentious but respectable neighborhood law firm where ordinary, everyday people in need can come in without fear of rejection or intimidation. In other words, the antithesis of Sutton & Associates."

"And here I thought my vision was just to keep this place afloat."

"You can play it off that way, but I know you have big plans for this firm. Whether you want to admit it or not, I can help you. I'm smart—at least most of the time—and you won't find a harder worker. But you have to get over the antiquated notion that I need to be protected. I'm a big girl, Reid."

"Oh, I know."

"Then what's it to be? Should I leave now, never again to darken your door? Or should I sit right here and tell you how we can smoke Ginger Vreeland out of her hiding place?"

He had already lost the battle and they both knew it. The trick now was to salvage as much of the war as he could. "If we're going to do this, we need to set some ground rules."

"Okay."

He looked her right in the eyes. "This is my house, my firm. I have the final say. If I don't want to take on a particular client, we don't take on that client. If I say something is too dangerous to pursue, that's the end of it."

"Of course."

His gaze narrowed. "That was too easy."

"Maybe," she agreed with a conciliatory smile. "I want this to work, but we have to be realistic. We're both stubborn, impulsive, passionate people. We're bound to clash now and then. But I do agree that when it comes to this firm, you have the final say."

"Then why do I feel like I've just been snookered," he muttered.

"This will work out for both of us. You'll see." She scooted to the edge of her seat. "*Now* do you want to hear about my plan?"

"I'm pretty sure I don't have a choice."

She gave him a brilliant smile, one without arrogance or guile. "It may sound a little convoluted at first, so just hear me out. I studied the file you gave me yesterday, in particular the transcript of Ginger Vreeland's interview. She was once married. Did you know that? She married right out of high school and her husband joined the service a month later. They divorced when he came back from overseas. He died some years back in a motorcycle accident. Her closest living relative is an uncle who lives just outside of town. He practically raised her when her mother would be off on a bender. If anyone knows where she is now, it would be this uncle."

Reid stared at her for a moment. "You got all that from the file I gave you?"

"Yes, didn't you read through it?"

"Not as closely as you did, apparently, but let me see if I can contribute to the conversation. Brody said he'd hired a private detective while he was in prison, someone he'd known in the joint. According to this guy, Ginger's family still wouldn't talk. I'm assuming that includes the uncle."

Arden wasn't the least bit thwarted. If anything, she became more animated. "Then we have to give him an incentive. I thought of something last night when I couldn't sleep."

"Of course you did." Reid couldn't believe this was the same aloof woman he'd confronted on Sunday night. His accusation that she'd become pedestrian over the years suddenly rang hollow. She hadn't changed. Maybe, deep down, he hadn't either. He wasn't sure if that was a good thing or not. But her excitement was infectious and he found himself leaning forward, anticipating her every word.

"A few years ago, I was part of a class action suit against a bank that had opened unauthorized accounts in some of their customers' names. Something like that has been in the news recently with a much larger bank on a much larger scale, but the premise was the same. I was barely even aware of the suit until I was notified that money from the settlement had been deposited into my account. It was only a few hundred dollars, but that's beside the point." She paused to tuck back her hair. "What if we contact Ginger's uncle and tell him that Ginger is still listed as her dead ex-husband's beneficiary? His bank account is considered inactive and unless she acts quickly, she won't be able to claim the money from the settlement. The amount would have to be large enough to tempt her out of hiding, yet not so large as to arouse her suspicions. We'll say our firm specializes in helping people collect forgotten money. For a finder's fee, we'll file all the necessary paperwork to have the funds released to her, but we need to speak with her in person to verify her identity."

"In other words, we lie," Reid said.

"Yes, but would you rather Dave Brody find her first?" Arden asked. "We may be lying but we know we won't hurt her. We can't say the same about him. We'll leave the uncle a business card and tell him time is of the essence."

Reid ran fingers through his hair. "You're right about one thing. This scheme is plenty convoluted."

"It can work, though."

"Maybe, but I see at least one glaring problem. She's bound to recognize my name."

"Then I'll be the contact person. I'll have some business cards printed up with a burner phone number. The name Mayfair might even carry a little weight. I can put up a website, too. Simple but classy. Should only take a couple of days to get everything set up."

"If Ginger suspects a con, it could drive her even deeper underground," he said.

"That's just a chance we'll have to take. And it's still preferable to Brody finding her first."

Reid was silent for a moment as he ran the scenario

through his head. "You say you can get this all set up in just two days' time?"

"Yes, if I put in some overtime, but I'll need a place to work." She glanced in the other room. "I can't sit on the floor all day."

"I'll get you a desk," Reid said. "In the meantime, you can use mine. I'll be out for most of the day anyway. That is, if you're sure you'll be okay here alone."

"I feel safer here than I do at Berdeaux Place. You've had the locks changed and I won't let anyone in while you're gone. I'll be fine."

"You'll need this." He handed her a key.

She looked surprised. "I thought you said you didn't give out keys to anyone."

"Just take it, Arden."

Chapter Ten

Reid had been gone for a few hours when Arden decided to take a lunch break. Since the fridge was pretty much empty, she walked down to a little café on Queen Street that offered a delicious array of wraps and salads. She made her selection and then perused her notes as she ate. She didn't dawdle once she finished and, instead, stuffed everything back into her bag and quickly paid the check. She was just stepping outside when someone across the street caught her attention. Arden recognized him immediately as the man Reid had spoken to the day before. Dave Brody.

Her heart skipped a beat and she started to retreat back into the eatery while she waited for him to pass. But he seemed oblivious to her presence. He had his phone to his ear and appeared agitated by the conversation. He gestured with his free arm and then rubbed a hand across his buzzed head in apparent frustration. Even after he returned the phone to his pocket, he continued to rail at the air and then gestured menacingly at a passerby before he stomped off down the street.

Arden decided he must be heading to Reid's office, and she told herself just to wait inside the café until he'd put plenty of distance between them. Why take a chance on being seen? Hadn't she promised Reid she would be careful?

Still, an opportunity had presented itself. Brody had spent hours watching Reid's place and tailing him around town. Why not turn the tables? She could follow at a discreet distance and observe his behavior and interactions. If he tried to break into the house, she would call the police.

Fishing her sunglasses out of her bag, she slipped them on as she waited underneath the awning to make sure he didn't turn around. But she didn't want him to get too far ahead, so she fell in behind a family of five strolling by. The two adults and tallest child would provide enough cover so that if Brody happened to glance back, he wouldn't be able to see her. That worked for about two blocks and then the family turned a corner, leaving Arden exposed. She hugged the inside edge of the sidewalk, hoping the shade of the buildings would somewhat protect her.

What are you doing, Arden? What on earth are you thinking?

She shoved the voice aside as she hooked her bag over her shoulder and kept walking. Somewhere in the back of her mind, a plan took shape. What if Brody really was working for someone powerful who wanted to frame Reid for murder? What if he was on his way to meet that person right now? It was a long shot and not without risk, but wouldn't it be something if she could solve this whole mystery simply by tailing Brody to his final destination? The trick was to stay out of his periphery. It was broad daylight and traffic was fairly brisk. *Just don't let him get so far ahead of you that he can double back without your knowing.*

They were headed west on Queen Street. If his final destination had been Reid's office, he would have turned right on Logan, but instead he kept going all the way to Rutledge, finally turning left on Wentworth. Then came a series of quick turns onto side streets that left Arden completely disoriented. She didn't know the area well and might have thought Brody was deliberately trying to lose her, but from everything Reid had told her, evasion was hardly Brody's style. He was more likely to turn around and confront her openly.

Still, she widened the distance between them, trying to blend into the scenery as best she could. He made another turn and she finally recognized where they were. The houses along the street had seen better days, but the yards were shady, and every now and then, the breeze carried the scent of jasmine over garden fences.

Traffic dwindled and Arden crossed the street to trail behind a pair of college students, who undoubtedly lived in one of the nearby apartment complexes. Up ahead, Brody stopped in front of a two-story house with a wrought-iron fence encasing the front walkway and garden. Arden broke away from the students and darted into an alley, where she could watch Brody from a safe distance. As he opened the gate and stepped into the garden, a middle-aged woman wearing shorts and a baggy T-shirt came down the porch steps to confront him.

Their raised voices carried across to the alley, but Arden could make out only a word now and then of the argument, something about late rent. The woman, presumably Brody's landlady, gestured toward the outside staircase that led up to a second-story apartment. Brody became so agitated that Arden worried he might actually assault the poor woman.

Although she braced herself to intervene, the disagreement never became physical. Brody headed up the stairs and disappeared inside the door at the top of the landing. He came back out a few minutes later and flung money at the woman. She screamed an oath and then scrambled to grab the bills before the breeze carried them away. Brody watched her for a moment, then turned on his heel and exited the gate, heading back up the street the way he'd come.

Arden pressed herself against the wall, trying to disappear into the shadows until he was safely past the alley. Then she glanced up the street. She could still see him in the distance. She would have left the alley to follow except for the woman across the street, who had once again caught her attention. She plucked the last of the bills from the ground, folded the wad and tucked it into her shorts pocket. Then she came through the gate and stood on the sidewalk, hand shading her eyes as she watched Brody's receding form. Once he rounded a corner, she went back inside the fence and marched up the stairs, pausing on the landing to glance over her shoulder. Satisfied that she was alone, she retrieved a key from a flowerpot and let herself into the apartment.

By this time, Brody was long gone. As much as Arden wanted to try to catch up with him, she was intrigued by the woman's behavior. She waited in the shadows, her gaze fixated on the door at the top of the stairs. The woman reappeared a few minutes later, glanced around once more to make sure no one had seen her and returned the key to the flowerpot. She came down the stairs and rounded the house to the porch. A moment later Arden heard a door slam.

Leaning back against the building, she placed a hand over her pounding heart. The adrenaline pulsating through her veins was a rush she hadn't experienced in years. She was reminded of the time she and Reid had taken his father's boat out for a midnight sail. They'd stayed on the water all night, drunk with freedom and adventure as they contemplated how far they dared go before turning back.

Now, a little voice goaded her. *Now is the time to turn back.*

Arden once again ignored that voice.

Leaving the alley, she glanced both ways before cross-ing the street. Without hesitation, she made for the garden gate, rehearsing in her mind what she would say if she were caught. She wasn't so worried about the landlady. Arden had always been able to think on her feet. She'd make up an excuse about having the wrong address or look-ing for an old friend. Brody was a different story. She'd glimpsed his temper and had no doubt he was dangerous. Now, though, she was more convinced than ever that he had to be working for someone. The area was seedy, but apartments this close to downtown didn't come cheap no matter the neighborhood.

How could she pass up this chance? Someone was try-ing to set Reid up for murder. What if she could determine the identity of the real killer by searching Brody's posses-sions? What if she could prove Reid's innocence once and for all? Wasn't he worth taking that risk?

On and on, the devil on her shoulder goaded her.

Arden knew what Reid would say. He'd tell her to go back to the office and lock the doors. Hunker down until he returned later that afternoon. But cowering inside locked doors wouldn't help him out of his current predicament. There'd been a time when he would have applauded her efforts.

In a way, she was doing this as much for herself as for him, Arden decided. She wanted to be that girl again. The one who threw caution to the wind and followed her heart.

Let's not get carried away.

She found the key in the flowerpot, unlocked the door and then returned the key, using her foot to hold open the door. She slipped inside and took off her sunglasses. The apartment was dim and overly warm. Or maybe she was just overly excited. A scene from one of her favorite mov-ies came to mind. A determined young woman risking life and limb to get the goods on a murderer so she could prove to her adventurous lover she was more than his match.

Focus, Arden. You are not Grace Kelly. And this is not a movie.

She stood with her back against the closed door and drew in air as she tried to quiet her thundering heart. Then her gaze darted about the small space, taking it all in before she began to explore. To the left of the entrance was a tiny bathroom; to the right, a bedroom. The narrow foyer opened directly into a living area and the kitchen was just through an archway. The space was tight but efficient.

Her gaze lit on a wooden table beneath the only window in the living room. An expensive laptop and printer were set up, along with a flat-screen TV. How did someone fresh out of prison afford such expensive devices?

She moved across the room as silently as she could manage on aging floorboards. After taking a quick peek through a stack of papers on the table, she turned her attention to the laptop. It opened to the desktop and she navigated to the Pictures folder, scanning dozens of thumbnails before she found the incriminating photos of Reid. Brody must have been following him for days. He'd captured Reid through his office window, at the courthouse on Broad Street, on the sidewalk in front of Berdeaux Place. When she reached the images from the bar, Arden grew even more agitated. The angle of some of the shots made it look as though Reid and the victim were interacting.

Arden could have spent hours examining every nuance of those photographs, but she'd already spent too much time in Brody's apartment. She'd pressed her luck long enough. Panic had set in so she did the only thing she could think of in the moment. She attached the images to an email and sent them to her account. Then she deleted the message from the Sent folder. *What else? What else?* Grabbing a tissue from her bag, she wiped down the computer and anything else in the vicinity she might have touched.

She was just finishing up when she heard footsteps on the wooden stairs outside the apartment. Quickly she gathered up her bag and took one last look at the table, then hurried to peek out the front widow.

Brody was coming up the stairs. He was almost at the landing.

Arden cast a frantic glance around and then darted inside the tiny bathroom. She flattened herself in the tub and pulled the shower curtain closed.

The door opened and Brody came inside the apartment. She listened as he clomped through the rooms, praying he wouldn't need to use the bathroom or, even worse, decide to take a shower.

A ringtone sounded and he answered with an impatient grunt.

"Yeah, yeah, I know I'm late. Unforeseen circumstances."

Arden heard a drawer slide open. She hadn't left anything on the table, had she? She hadn't moved his laptop enough so that he would notice? She squeezed her eyes closed and waited. Into the silence came the metallic click of what she imagined to be a switchblade. She pictured him testing the vicious blade with his thumb as he glanced toward the bathroom…

"Relax, dude. I'm on my way now. You just make sure you have the money."

He left the apartment and slammed the door behind him. Arden waited to make sure he wasn't coming back, and then she climbed shuddering out of the tub. She went back over to the table to make sure nothing was amiss and quickly exited the apartment.

By the time she got to the street, Brody was well ahead

of her. She accelerated her pace, trying to shorten the distance between them without calling attention to herself. He strode along, a man on a mission, turning here, turning there until they finally reached King Street and she lost him.

Arden came to a stop, glancing up and down the street. The sidewalks were crowded for a weekday, but his appearance would make him stand out among the tourists and shoppers. Maybe he'd gone inside one of the boutiques. That hardly seemed likely, but he couldn't have just vanished.

As she stood there contemplating where he might have gone, a hand fell on her shoulder.

She jumped and turned with a gasp. Her arm went back in self-defense. Instead of swinging her bag at Brody's head, she said incredulously, "Uncle Calvin! What are you doing here?"

A smile flashed, disarming her instantly. "I was just about to ask you the same thing, but then I assumed you'd come for a tour of the studio."

She tried to act natural as she dropped the bag to her side and smoothed back her hair. "Actually, I was just out doing a little shopping. Although if I'd known the address of your studio, I would have stopped by."

He motioned to a building across the street. "I'm on the second floor. Lots of beautiful light. Come up. I'll fix you something cold to drink and give you the grand tour."

"That sounds lovely." Arden shot a glance over her shoulder before she followed her uncle across the street and up to his studio. Despite the heat, he looked cool and collected in khaki chinos and a cotton shirt that complemented his eyes and the white-gold hair that curled at his collar.

Arden marveled at how young he looked for his age. A

stranger would never have guessed that he was well into his forties. It was only when he turned at the top of the stairs and gave her a little smile that she noticed the crinkles at the corners of his eyes and the deeper crevices in his brow. "It's a working studio," he said. "Nothing too fancy and it's a bit of a mess right now. I've been inspired lately and painting like a madman."

"I'm eager to see it."

He stepped back for her to enter, and she stood gazing around. The space was wide open, with an industrial flavor from the original plank flooring, brick walls and long windows that reached to the beamed ceiling. Canvases were stacked at least three deep along the walls and an easel had been set up to take advantage of the morning sunlight.

"It's a wonderful space," Arden said as she moved into the center of the room. "Bigger than I imagined, and the light really is beautiful. So soft and golden. I can see how you'd be inspired here."

"It's not the studio that inspires me, though I do consider myself lucky for having found this place," Calvin said. "It's one of a kind."

"How long have you been here?"

"A while."

"You mentioned that you live nearby?"

"Only a few blocks away. It's very convenient."

Arden walked over to one of the windows that looked down on the street. "If I had this studio, I don't think I'd ever want to leave."

"You haven't seen my apartment," he said with another smile.

"That's true."

"Minuscule compared to Mayfair House, but it suits my needs perfectly."

"I've decided big homes are overrated," Arden said. "Not to mention overwhelming."

"Yes. We tend to take those grand old places and all the accompanying creature comforts for granted when someone else is footing the bill. But there is something to be said for freedom." His gaze darkened before he reclaimed his good humor. "Anyway, you'll have to come to dinner soon. I'm not a bad cook."

"That would be nice. Just let me get settled first."

"Of course. In the meantime, what will you have to drink? I have iced tea, lemonade…"

"Iced tea is perfect."

He disappeared into another room. "Make yourself at home," he called out. "I'll be right back."

"Is it okay if I look at your paintings?"

"Certainly. Nothing in the studio is off-limits."

She wandered around the perimeter of the room, examining the canvases and admiring the iconic landmarks that he had painted. The church towers, the cemeteries, the pastel homes on Rainbow Row. Even Berdeaux Place. The paintings were colorful, the subject matter dear to Arden's heart, and yet an inexplicable melancholy descended. She was home now. She could visit any of these places whenever she liked. But studying her uncle's art was like observing her beloved city through a mist. There was an unsettling disconnection. Was that how Calvin had felt as a child visiting Berdeaux Place? A lonely little boy observing from a distance a happier life that should have been his?

She shrugged, dismissing the thought, deciding it was best to leave the psychoanalysis to the experts.

Circling the room, she finally came to a stop in front of the easel. The unfinished painting jolted her. She blinked and then blinked again. It was like her previous thoughts had suddenly materialized.

"You've painted Mother's cereus." *Through a greenhouse window. From the outside peering in.*

"I've attempted to. It's a rather complicated plant. The texture of the leaves is tricky."

"Are you kidding me? The detail is amazing," Arden said in wonder.

"Thank you for that." He came back into the room and handed her a frosty glass. "I'll paint a companion piece once the blooms have opened. That is, if you have no objection."

"Of course not. Your work is very beautiful and you seem to be quite prolific. I had no idea." She glanced around the room at all the canvases. "Do you paint everything from memory?"

"Not always. I sketch and sometimes I work from photographs."

"This painting almost looks like a photograph. I feel as if I'm gazing through the greenhouse window." She took a sip of tea as she gave him a sidelong glance. "I went out to the garden last night, but I didn't see you working."

"I didn't want to disturb you again. Besides, there's little point in coming every night until the blooms are further along."

"I can't get over the colors," Arden murmured, her attention still on the cereus. "It's almost as if…" She trailed away, shy about her thoughts all of a sudden.

"As if…what?"

"You'll think I'm crazy."

Her uncle smiled. "Artists are by nature crazy. Who am I to judge?"

Still, Arden hesitated. "It's like Grandmother is there in

the greenhouse. Mother, too. You didn't paint them. You can't see them. But I can feel them."

He drew a sharp breath.

"I'm sorry," Arden said. "Did I say something wrong?"

"No, quite the opposite, in fact. It's just so rare to find someone who feels about your work the way you do. You couldn't have known what was in my heart or in my head when I painted that scene and yet…" Now he was the one who broke off. "Forgive me. I'm just… I'm blown away by your insight." He walked over to the easel and picked up the canvas. "I think you must have this."

"Oh, I couldn't. As beautiful as it is, I can't take your work."

"Why not? I'm offering it to you as a gift. Although…" He returned the canvas to the easel. "I have one that you might appreciate more." He set his drink aside and disappeared through another doorway. He returned carrying a small canvas, which he offered to Arden. "My welcome-home gift to you. I hope you like this one as much as I do. And before you say anything, I won't take no for an answer."

Arden went very still as he turned the painting and she got her first glimpse of the subject. Uneasiness crept over her as she took the canvas from his hands and turned toward the light. He had painted her mother in the moonlit garden at Berdeaux Place with the summerhouse dome in the background. Camille Mayfair looked just as Arden remembered her. The mysterious glint in her eyes. The dazzling smile. But there was a feeling of distance again. The perception of admiring her from afar.

The red chiffon gown she wore appeared so soft and airy that Arden could almost imagine the frothy layers floating up from the canvas. Camille's bare arms and shoulders gleamed softly in the moonlight and her blond hair was pulled back and fastened with a creamy magnolia blossom.

A magnolia blossom.

Arden was speechless.

"Do you like it?" her uncle asked softly. "I tried to catch her whimsy and drama, but I'm not that talented."

"No, you are. It's wonderful. I can't stop looking at her." Arden tried to swallow past the sudden knot in her throat.

Calvin seemed overcome, as well. "Now you know why I was so taken aback when I saw you standing in the moonlight the other night."

Arden couldn't tear her gaze from the canvas. "When did you paint this?"

"A few years ago from a photograph that was taken on the night of the Mayor's Ball. It was held at Berdeaux Place that year. I was away at school, but I remember reading about it in the paper."

"I remember it, too," Arden said. "She came into my room before she went downstairs. She looked like a princess in that red dress. I can still remember the way the magnolia blossom smelled in her hair when she leaned over the bed to kiss me good-night. A few days later, she was gone."

Calvin gently took the canvas from her fingers. "I'll wrap this up and have it delivered to the house."

Arden glanced up. "Are you sure?"

"I couldn't bear for anyone but you to have it," he said.

"I don't know what to say. Thank you, Uncle."

"You're welcome, Niece. I have something else for you, too." He placed the canvas on his worktable and took a key from a peg on the wall. "This is the key to the side gate. It was one thing for me to come and go as I pleased when no one was in the house, but the last thing I want to do is intrude on your privacy."

He offered her the key and she took it without argument. "That's very thoughtful of you. Actually, I've been thinking about having all the locks changed. The house has been empty for so long. Who knows how many keys may be floating around?"

Something flashed in his eyes, an emotion that unnerved Arden even more than the painting had. "Probably a good idea," he murmured. "Your safety is paramount."

His mood had changed, though. Arden couldn't figure out what had happened. Maybe he had expected her to refuse the key or to at least offer a token resistance. In any case, it was time for her to leave.

"I should be going. I've taken up enough of your time. Thank you for showing me your studio. As for the painting…" She trailed away. "You have no idea what it means to me."

"I'm glad that it makes you happy." He walked her to the top of the stairs.

"I can see myself down," she said. "Thank you again."

"Come back soon. I've a lot more to show you."

"I'll do that." She went down the stairs without looking back, but when she crossed the street, she couldn't help glancing up at the studio. He stood at one of the long windows staring down at her.

Chapter Eleven

Reid approached the house on Water Street on foot. He'd parked a block over so that his car wouldn't be spotted entering or leaving the driveway. He opened the wrought-iron gate and strode up the walkway to the front door, glancing over his shoulder as he rang the bell. His mother played bridge on Wednesdays and the housekeeper had the day off. He expected the house to be empty, but he still had a key and the security code unless either or both had been changed since his last visit.

He waited a few minutes and then let himself in, disarming the system as he called out to his mother. Then he called out the housekeeper's name. "Anyone home?" He folded his sunglasses and slipped them in his pocket as his gaze traveled up the curving staircase. Nothing stirred. The house was empty except for the ghosts.

Still, he felt uneasy being in his childhood home un-invited. He tried to shake off his disquiet as he headed to the back of the house where his father's office was located, a rich, masculine room that looked out on the pool. The drapes were open and Reid could see the dance of sunlight on blue water as he stepped through the pocket doors. He had no idea what he was looking for. His father's equivalent of a little black book, he supposed. The heavy oak desk was kept locked, but Reid had known since he was a kid that the key rested on a ledge underneath the smooth top.

Plopping down in his father's chair, he felt underneath the desk until he located the key. He was just about to open the top drawer when he heard a car pull up outside. He returned the key to the ledge and got up from the desk, slipping silently into the hallway. He heard the back door close and then someone moving about in the kitchen. Maybe Tess had changed her day off, Reid thought, and he quickly came up with an excuse for his presence as he eased down the corridor.

The kitchen was spacious with gleaming stainless steel appliances and a marble island large enough to accommodate six people. His father stood behind the counter splashing whiskey into a tumbler. Watching him from the doorway, Reid wondered if he was catching a glimpse of his future. The notion was hardly comforting. His father had never been an easy man to know or love. He was brilliant and wildly successful, but he'd never struck Reid as particularly happy, which had not made for a particularly happy household. Yet, despite Boone's failings as a parent and husband, he'd always taken as his due the devotion and respect of those around him.

But credit where credit was due, the man seemed committed to keeping the years at bay. He was as sharp and ruthless as ever, and he kept himself in excellent physical shape. Reid would give him that. He worked out, played tennis twice a week and watched his diet. A cocktail in the middle of the day seemed out of character, but how well did Reid really know his father?

He cleared his throat and Boone looked up in surprise. "What the hell are you doing here?" he demanded.

"I came to see Mother."

"Your mother has had a standing bridge date every

Wednesday for the past thirty years. You know that as well as I do."

"I guess it slipped my mind," Reid said.

His father frowned at him over the rim of his glass. "How did you get in here anyway?"

Reid sauntered into the kitchen. "I still have a key. You disowned me. Mother didn't."

Boone scoffed as he downed his drink. "Disowned is a little dramatic."

"Is it? Let's recap. You had Security escort me from the building after you fired me, and then you stood on the sidewalk and told me that I was no son of yours, that I would never see a penny of inheritance and that I shouldn't even think about trying to capitalize on the Sutton name. I'd say that's pretty much the dictionary definition of *disowned*, but we can agree to disagree." Reid hadn't realized until that moment how much his father's words still rankled. He'd convinced himself the estrangement was for the best. Time away from the old man suited him just fine. But no son, no matter his age, wanted to be ostracized by his father. A tiny part of Reid still craved a word of encouragement, no matter how fleeting.

"I was angry," Boone said. "And you were insubordinate and disrespectful. I treated you as I would have any other associate."

"I was trying to protect my client. The client you ordered me to drop because one of your cronies had a problem with my representing a man he considered an upstart competitor. Whatever happened to loyalty?"

"Some might say I'm loyal to a fault," his father countered. "That crony, as you call him, has thrown more work my way than you'll ever see in a lifetime. So I made a judgment call. My firm, my decision."

Had he sounded like that much of a pompous ass with

Arden that morning? Reid wondered. The term *like father, like son* had never grated more.

His father glanced up from his drink. "You know what your problem is?"

"No, but I'm sure you're dying to tell me."

"You're too much like your mother. You personalize everything and then you cling to your grudges. Me? I let off steam and then I move on."

"You've moved on?"

"Water under the bridge." His father got down a second glass. "Come have a drink with me."

"It's a little early for me," Reid said as he straddled one of the bar stools.

"What's the saying…? It has to be five o'clock somewhere." Boone poured a whiskey and slid the glass across the island.

Reid cradled the tumbler in both hands, but he didn't drink. "What are you doing home at this time of day anyway?"

Boone shrugged. "I needed a quiet place to work. You know how it gets around the office. So much going on you can't hear yourself think."

"Why not go to the apartment?"

His father had been in the process of lifting his drink, but his hand froze for a split second before he took a sip.

"Yeah," Reid said. "I know about the apartment. So does everyone else in the office. I'm sure Mother knows about it, too."

Something hard glittered in Boone's eyes as he polished off his drink and poured himself another. "I hear you sold your condo. Bought one of those old properties on Logan Street and opened an office. How's that working out for you?"

"It's early days, but I'm staying busy."

"I also hear you had a meeting with Clement Mayfair yesterday. Trying to land yourself a big one, are you?"

Reid frowned. "Where did you hear that?"

"You know how things work in this town. Small circles, big mouths." His father observed him for a moment. "A word of advice?"

"Why not?"

"Think twice before you get into bed with a guy like Clement Mayfair. He's as vicious and vindictive as they come. You cross a line with him, you make an enemy for life."

Reid thought about Clement Mayfair's earlier warning. "He told me he had dealings with you in the past. He called you overconfident and self-indulgent. To be fair, he said the same about me."

Boone smirked. "It's not overconfidence if you can deliver."

"No, I suppose not," Reid said. "You were his attorney?"

"About a hundred years ago."

"What happened?"

Boone made a dismissive gesture with his hand. "Nothing seismic. Your mother and I were good friends with Evelyn. When they separated, it created a conflict of interest."

"So you chose Evelyn."

"It really wasn't much of a choice. I was glad to see the last of Clement Mayfair."

Reid toyed with his glass. "Do you know why they split?"

His father gave him a curious look. "It didn't have anything to do with me if that's what you're implying. I thought the world of Evelyn. She was something back in her day, but I've never gone for older women."

Reid said drily, "Not everything is about you, you know."

"Just most things." Boone grinned.

Reid wasn't amused. "From what Arden has told me, the separation was anything but amicable. Evelyn took the daughter and Clement kept the son. Sounds like a pretty screwed-up arrangement if you ask me."

"The Mayfairs are a pretty screwed-up lot," Boone said. "I don't say that to malign your girlfriend. I've always been fond of Arden."

"She's not my girlfriend."

The denial didn't seem to register. His father leaned an elbow on the marble countertop as he nursed his third drink. "Has Arden ever showed you the family photograph albums?"

"I guess. A long time ago."

"Have her show you again. Take a close look at the faces, the eyes. Arden is the spitting image of her mother, just as Camille was the mirror image of Evelyn. Calvin takes after the old man but with enough Berdeaux blood to soften the hard edges. Ask yourself why Calvin favors both his mother and father, but there is nothing of Clement Mayfair in either of the girls."

Reid stared at him across the counter. "Are you suggesting—"

"I'm not suggesting anything. It's merely an observation." Although Boone sounded sober enough, Reid wondered if his father had been drinking before he ever reached the kitchen door. There was a strange glitter in his eyes, as if he might be enjoying his disparagement of Clement Mayfair a little too much.

Reid thought about the implications of his father's observation. If Clement had found out that Camille wasn't his biological daughter, that would explain the acrimonious separation and the lingering bitterness. That would also explain why Evelyn was allowed to take Camille and forced to leave Calvin behind.

"Why are you so interested in Mayfair ancient history anyway?" his father asked.

"Arden thinks Clement may try to take Berdeaux Place away from her."

His father lifted a brow. "Is that so? Well, I can't say I'm surprised. He's always had a thing about that house. It represents everything he ever desired and could never attain. Legacy. Respectability. Acceptance."

"What are you talking about? Mayfair House is twice the size of Berdeaux Place, and it's been a part of the iconic imagery of Battery Row for generations."

"His grandfather..." Boone frowned. "Or was it his great-grandfather? No matter. Some dead Mayfair lost the house and most of the family money in a series of shady business deals. Another family lived in Mayfair House until Clement made his own fortune. He bought back the property and had money left to burn, but he still wasn't welcome in certain circles. Only his marriage to Evelyn opened those doors and he always resented her for it. After the divorce, he withdrew from society. Sent Calvin away to boarding school, and became reclusive and hostile. Lately, though, I've heard rumbles about efforts to rehabilitate his image. Maybe that has something to do with Arden. He is getting on in years. In any case, she's smart to be on guard."

Reid declined to point out that Clement Mayfair wasn't so much older than Boone. "You haven't heard anything brewing in regards to Berdeaux Place?"

"No, but I'll keep my ear to the ground. If I hear anything I'll let you know."

"Thanks. I appreciate that. Arden will, too."

His father tilted his head, regarding Reid through bloodshot eyes. "This thing with you and Arden. It's just business these days?"

Reid lifted the glass and took his first sip, buying himself a moment. "I told her I'd ask around about her grandfather and, in turn, she's helping me on another case. One of your old clients, as a matter of fact. Dave Brody."

Boone paused just a fraction too long. "Who?"

"Dave Brody. He hasn't tried to contact you?"

"I'm a hard man to reach unless you have my cell number, and I don't give that out to just anybody."

"Brody was sent up on a second-degree murder conviction ten years ago. He got out of prison a few weeks ago and he's been following me around, watching my house. Making a general nuisance of himself."

Boone's face had grown tense and wary. "What does he want with you?"

"He wants me to find Ginger Vreeland." Reid saw the dart of a shadow across his father's expression. "I take it that name rings a bell?"

Boone lifted his drink. "What did he tell you?"

"He thinks you're the reason she left town the night before she was to take the witness stand on his behalf."

"What?"

Reid nodded. "He claims Ginger kept a little black book with all her clients' numbers and—shall we say—preferences? You were afraid of what she might reveal on the witness stand so you paid her to disappear."

"That's ludicrous." Boone slammed his glass to the marble counter so aggressively Reid wondered that the crystal didn't shatter. "Brody was a real piece of work even back then. Guilty as hell, but always wanting to blame his misfortune on someone else. I suggest you keep your distance. Take out a restraining order if you have to."

"I can't do that," Reid said. "He claims someone is trying to set me up for murder and he's the only one who can help clear me."

"Murder?" His father looked stunned. "What are you talking about?"

"You heard about the body that was found Monday morning in an alley down the street from my place? Turns out, the victim and I were in the same bar on the night she was killed. I don't remember her. I don't remember much of anything about that night, but Brody claims he has photographs of the two of us together. He'll take them to the police if I don't help him find Ginger Vreeland. A restraining order wouldn't stop him. It would only egg him on."

"Then just back off. Let me take care of Brody."

That was like him, Reid thought. Always thinking he knew best. Reid couldn't help but remember Brody's taunt about Boone Sutton swooping in to save the day. Or Arden's tentative speculation that his father could be behind everything.

"It's not that simple," Reid said. "One of the detectives on the case is a man named John Graham. He arrested me years ago for driving under the influence. He thinks you not only called in favors to get my record expunged, but you also meddled in his career. So you getting involved will only make things worse all the way around."

"I remember that cop," Boone said. "Bad temper. God complex. Guys like him give all the other police officers a bad name. If he had career setbacks, it was because of his incompetence and attitude. He'd already been suspended once for unreasonable force, by the way. Then he had those two inmates work you over. He should have been fired on the spot. No second chances."

"Why wasn't he?"

"My guess is someone with enough money and clout decided he could be useful. That's how this town works, too."

Was it you? Reid wondered. *Are you the reason John Graham still has a badge?*

"I'll talk to some people," Boone said.

"No, don't do that. All I want from you is Ginger Vreeland's address. Or at least her last known whereabouts."

"So you can try to bargain with Brody?" His father leaned in so close that Reid could follow the roadmap of those tiny red veins in his eyes. "Has it ever occurred to you that Ginger would have had more than one name in her book? More than one name, more than one secret. Her disappearance had nothing to do with me. Maybe she left town because she was afraid."

That stopped Reid cold. "Someone threatened her?"

Boone straightened. "I've said all I can say. You need to let this one go, Reid. Forget you ever heard the name Ginger Vreeland. You have no idea the can of worms you're trying to open."

Chapter Twelve

Arden was seated behind Reid's desk working on her laptop when he got back to the office that afternoon. Despite yesterday's experience, she barely glanced up when he came in the back door, she was that engrossed in the photographs.

"What a day I've had." He glanced in from the kitchen doorway. "You want a drink?"

She answered without looking up. "Thought you'd stopped drinking for now."

"I meant water or a Coke."

"No, I'm fine. I've had a day, too," she said, letting excitement creep into her voice. "You'll never believe what I have to show you."

She heard him close the fridge and then pop the tab on a soda. "So what are you working on?" he asked. "The website?"

"No, not yet. Right now, I'm going through some photographs." She finally glanced up. He stood in the archway leaning a shoulder against the door frame. He'd removed his coat and tie and rolled up his shirtsleeves, revealing his tanned forearms. He looked tall and lean and handsome, the grown-up version of the boy she'd once loved beyond all reason. A thrill raced up her spine in spite of her best efforts. And with those tingles came a memory.

Don't be like that, Reid. Just say it.

Why do I need to say it? You know how I feel.

Because I need to hear it, that's why.

All right, then. I love you, Arden Mayfair. I've loved you from the moment I first laid eyes on you, and I'll love you until the moment I leave this earth. How's that?

"What photographs?" Reid asked.

"What?"

He nodded to the laptop. "You said you were going through some photographs."

"Oh. Right. The photos." She cleared her throat and glanced away. She was letting herself think too much about the past today, falling into the trap of all those old memories. She and Reid had known each other forever, and, yes, she'd once felt closer to him than anyone else on earth. But that was a long time ago. They were adults now with career setbacks and bills and a plethora of other problems that had to be dealt with before she could even think about the future.

"Arden?"

She cleared her throat again. "I want to show you something, but you have to promise you won't get upset."

"I already don't like the sound of that, so no." He pushed away from the door frame and ambled over to the desk, leaning against the edge as he gazed down at her. "I'm not making you any promises."

"Okay. Just keep in mind that I'm perfectly safe. Nothing happened."

"Arden." He drawled out her name. "What have you done?"

The intensity of his gaze…the way he tilted his head as he stared down at her…

She sighed. Even suspicious Reid was suddenly irresistible to her. Maybe it was that death thing she'd read about.

Someone dies and suddenly all you want to do is have sex so that you can feel alive. She'd never personally experienced such a reaction. Maybe it wasn't even a real thing. Maybe she was just—

"What is going on with you?" Reid asked. "I've never seen you so distracted."

"I have a lot on my mind, as I'm sure you do." She brushed back her hair. "Maybe I should just show you the images and then we'll talk. Talk not yell," she added.

"We'll see."

He turned to lean in, placing a hand on the desk and another on the back of her chair. Too close. She couldn't breathe, so she rolled away slightly, hoping he wouldn't notice.

"What? Did my deodorant fail me or something?"

"You smell fine," she said with an inward cringe.

"You're acting really weird today."

"I know. Let's concentrate on the photographs." She clicked on the thumbnails to enlarge the images. "Brody didn't lie. He really did take photos of you and the victim in that bar."

Reid leaned in even closer. "Where did you get these?"

"Someone emailed them to me."

He reached over and clicked another image. "Who?"

"I did," she admitted. "I emailed them to myself."

He turned with a frown. "Where did you get them?"

"They were on Dave Brody's laptop, which I found in his apartment after I broke in." She said it all in a rush.

"You *what*?"

"I didn't actually break in," she clarified. "I used a key that I found in a flowerpot."

He gave a quick shake of his head as if he couldn't keep up with her explanation. "Hold on. What key, what flowerpot?"

She gave him a mostly abbreviated version of events,

but there was no way to sugarcoat her hiding in Brody's bathtub to avoid him.

Reid swiveled her chair around so that she couldn't avoid his gaze. "What were you thinking? Did you even consider what would happen if he caught you in his apartment?"

"But he didn't catch me. I'm perfectly fine. And I kept my head enough to wipe my fingerprints off the laptop before I left. He'll never know I was there."

"Did you wipe down the doorknobs? What about the key? Are you certain the landlady didn't see you enter or leave?" Reid looked to be hanging on to his cool by a thread. "Damn it, Arden. That could have gone wrong in so many ways. I don't even know what to say to you right now."

"How about, good job, Arden. How about, let's take a closer look at these photographs."

He wasn't amused. "How about, you put yourself needlessly at risk and proved that I can't trust you."

Arden was starting to get a little irritated. "You're making too big a deal of this."

"I've barely gotten started. We had an agreement, remember? My office, my firm, my rules."

"I wasn't in the office. I was on my lunch break. I would assume my free time is my own."

"Now you're just being deliberately willful."

"And you're being—what was the word you used the other night—pedestrian," she shot back. "When has either of us ever played by the rules? You actually followed Brody into a dark alley where a woman had been killed the night before. So don't tell me you wouldn't have done the same thing in my place."

"That's different."

"Oh, because you're a man and I'm a woman?"

"No, because this is my problem. I don't want you taking that kind of risk on my behalf."

"It's not just your problem and, for your information, I didn't do it just for you. I want to find out who killed Haley Cooper as much as you do. For all we know, I could be the next victim."

That seemed to take the wind out of his sails. "I won't let that happen."

"Unless we find out what's really going on, you may not be able to stop it. That's why I went up to Brody's apartment. I hoped I could find evidence of the real killer's identity or, at the very least, whether or not someone is paying him to frame you. If you'd settle down for a minute and look at the photographs, I mean, *really look* at the photographs, you might find something interesting."

"Arden…"

"I don't want to fight about this anymore," she said.

"I don't want to fight, either. I was just about to say I'm sorry."

"For what?" she asked suspiciously.

His eyes glinted and a smile flickered. "For being too much like Boone Sutton."

"You're nothing like Boone Sutton. You never were."

His hands were still on the chair arms as he gazed into her eyes. Lips slightly parted. Heart starting to race. Or was that hers?

He leaned in, brushing his lips against hers and Arden's pulse jumped. It was a brief kiss, barely any contact at all, and yet she felt a tremor go straight through her, making her crave a deeper connection. She wanted to feel his tongue in her mouth and his hands on her breasts. She wanted him to whisk her upstairs and undress her slowly with the balcony doors open and the scent of jasmine drifting in on the breeze. She wanted time to melt away, but those fourteen years of estrangement were right there between them, creating obstacles and barriers that she didn't dare breach.

He moved his head away, just a few inches, and smiled down at her. "Sorry again."

"For what?"

"For being too much like the old Reid Sutton."

"Don't ever apologize for that. The old Reid Sutton was pretty wonderful."

"As opposed to the current Reid Sutton?"

"Time will tell," she teased.

For a moment, she thought he might accept the challenge and kiss her again, but he turned back to the laptop and the moment was gone.

Arden scooted back up to the desk and sorted through the photographs until she found the one she wanted, and then she magnified the image.

"What am I looking for?" Reid asked.

"Just study the picture and tell me what you see."

"It's pretty dark, but I recognize a couple of my friends in the background. There I am standing at the bar. The woman next to me is the victim, Haley Cooper. I know because Detective Graham showed me a picture of her. At least I think she's the same woman. It's hard to know for certain."

"Even in the dim lighting, certain faces stand out," Arden said. "Keep looking."

Reid frowned. "Why don't you just tell me who or what I'm looking for?"

"Check out the man at the end of the bar. His head is turned toward you, and he appears to be staring at either you or the victim or both."

Reid concentrated for a moment and slowly turned his head toward Arden. "Is that who I think it is?"

"Sure looks like him to me. What are the chances that Detective Graham would be in that particular bar on that particular night?"

Reid focused on the photograph. "Are you sure it's him?"

"Not one hundred percent. As you said, the photograph is dark, but look at the hair, the way he holds his drink. The expression on his face. You can almost feel the contempt. I don't think his being there was a coincidence. My question is this. Why didn't he tell you that he'd seen you on the night Haley Cooper was murdered?"

"Maybe he wanted to catch me in a lie. Or see if I'd incriminate myself."

"Did you? Lie to him, I mean?"

"I told him she looked vaguely familiar. There was a chance I might have seen her around the neighborhood."

"And he didn't say or do anything to give himself away?"

"No, but I was concentrating pretty hard on not giving myself away. I might not have noticed."

"I did some digging while you were out," Arden said. "There's a lot of information on the internet about cops if you know where to look. Detective Graham has a pretty checkered history with the Charleston PD. Suspensions. Internal Affairs investigations. And that's not all. His personal life is a mess, too. He's going through a second bad divorce. Lots of debt. That kind of guy could be bought off."

Reid gave her an admiring look. "Where did you find all this stuff?"

"Blogs, message boards, news sites. A person's whole life is online." She paused. "Do you think he could be the one who came into your house yesterday?"

"You tell me. You saw him on the porch. Could he have been the intruder?"

She thought about that for a moment. "He's the right size and height, but I never got a look at the man's face. I figured Dave Brody. Regardless, how did the intruder get a key?"

"Maybe he found it in a flowerpot," Reid deadpanned.

She made a face. "Or maybe he got it from the real estate agent who sold you this house. He could have spun any kind of story to get the agent to cooperate. What about motive, though? I get that he doesn't like rich people, but it's hard to believe he'd nurse a grudge against you personally. All because your father got you out of jail?"

"He also thinks Boone meddled in his career. Don't forget that part. And speaking of the devil…" Reid went around the desk and sat down in one of the client chairs. "I saw him today."

"Your father? You went to his office?"

"No, I went by the house. I thought Mother and the housekeeper would be out and I could search his office. See if I could find anything that connects him to Ginger Vreeland."

"Did you?"

"He came home before I had a chance to look around. I told him I was there to see Mother, but I don't think he believed me. Luckily, he was too preoccupied—and possibly inebriated—to press me. Anyway, I brought up Brody's name. He pretended he didn't know who he was until I mentioned Ginger Vreeland. Then he became visibly distressed and implied that she'd left town because one of her clients had threatened her."

"Did he say who?"

"No, but he was pretty adamant that I leave Ginger

alone. He told me in no uncertain terms that I should walk away."

"You're not going to, are you?"

Reid's gaze hardened. "How can I as long as Brody has leverage over me?"

"Then should I move forward with the website and business cards? The sooner we contact her uncle, the closer we are to finding Ginger."

"Yes, go ahead, and make sure you run everything by me before you do anything else. In other words, don't go off on your own trying to track this guy down."

"You have my word." Arden closed the laptop and began gathering up her things. "It's been a long day. I'm heading home now. I've been so distracted by everything that's happened here, I'm behind on the things I need to do at Berdeaux Place."

"Whenever you're ready, I'll drive you," Reid said.

Arden stood and hooked her bag over her shoulder. "That's not necessary. I enjoy the walk. Gives me a chance to get reacquainted with the city."

Reid rose, too. "You'll have plenty of time for that later. It's a long walk and it'll be twilight soon. I don't want you out on the street with Brody lurking around. Before you argue—it has nothing to do with your gender," he said. "It's just common sense."

Hard to disagree with that. Arden nodded. "You're right. We both need to take precautions these days. A ride would be great."

They walked out the back door, pausing on the porch for Reid to lock up. Then they went down the steps together and crossed the yard to the driveway. Arden took a moment to admire the sleek lines of his car before she climbed inside and settled comfortably onto the seat. She ran a hand over the padded leather as Reid started the engine.

"Nice ride. But it kind of stands out in this neighborhood, don't you think?"

He grinned. "Why do you think I park around back? I thought about selling it when I got rid of the condo. I could have used the extra cash, but I'm a Southern boy born and bred. When it comes right down to it, I'd sooner cut off my right arm than get rid of my wheels."

"I sold my car before I left Atlanta," Arden said. "I sold or gave away everything except whatever I could pack in my bags."

Reid shot her a glance. "Clean break."

"Yeah."

They were out on the street now heading toward the tip of the peninsula. Reid checked the rearview mirror and then checked it again.

"What is it?" she asked anxiously.

"Probably nothing. A beige sedan has been behind us for a few blocks. No, don't turn around," he said.

Arden looked in the outside mirror. "Two cars back? Do you think it could be Graham? Looks like an unmarked cop car."

"Let's find out." Reid gave her a warning glance. "You better hold on!"

Chapter Thirteen

Reid jerked the wheel, executing a sharp right turn at the last minute. Then he goosed the accelerator for half a block, threw on the brakes and reversed into an alley.

Through all the maneuvers, Arden clung to the armrest and the edge of her seat. When he finally came to a full stop, she released her held breath. "Are you insane? You nearly gave me a heart attack back there."

"I did warn you to hold on." He focused his gaze on the street in front of them. "Anyway, that's just adrenaline. Don't pretend you didn't like it."

"Maybe I did," she conceded. "That doesn't make you any less crazy."

"No, but it does give me back my partner in crime."

"I don't know if I would go that far." Arden tried not to react to his words. She told herself they meant nothing. It was a slip of the tongue in the heat of the moment. But adrenaline buzzed through her veins. "Where did you learn to drive like that anyway?"

Another grin flashed. "Just a God-given talent. I'm surprised you didn't remember that about me."

"Maybe I tried to forget." Arden faced forward, watching the street. "Do you think we lost him? That is, if anyone was following us in the first place."

"We'll sit here for a minute or two and make sure." Reid

seemed to relax as time ticked away. He rolled down his windows so they could hear the sounds from the street. The smell of barbecue and fresh bread drifted in. "You hungry? We could stop somewhere for a bite to eat."

Arden was starving, as a matter of fact, and it would be so easy to take Reid up on his offer. Drift right back into the comfortable relationship of their youth. Have some wine, some food, some good conversation. She couldn't think of a more pleasant way to spend the evening, but rushing things was a very bad idea. They were still building a work rapport and for now a little personal distance was necessary. *Just wait and see how things play out.* She didn't have the stamina for a broken heart. "I appreciate the offer, but I'm beat. Another time?"

He nodded. "Yeah, no problem. I could use an early night myself." He eased out of the alley and melded into the late-afternoon traffic. Keeping an eye on the rearview mirror, he maneuvered effortlessly through the clogged streets, pulling to the curb in front of Berdeaux Place within a matter of minutes.

Arden reached for the door handle. "You don't need to get out," she said when he killed the engine. "I changed the security code so that even if anyone used a key to get in, they'd set off the alarm. I would have been notified if there'd been a breach." Brave words, but the truth of the matter was that Arden dreaded going inside the empty house. Feared another long night of sounds and shadows and dark memories.

"I'll come in and take a quick look around. For my own peace of mind." He reached across her and removed a small pistol from the glove box.

Arden gasped. "Reid. What are you doing with a gun?"

"I have a license, don't worry."

"That doesn't answer my question."

"Lawyers make enemies," he said as he tucked the gun into the back of his belt.

"You mean like Brody?"

"He or someone else came into my house while you were there alone. I don't intend to be caught off guard again."

Arden started to protest—guns scared her—but who was she to cast stones? Hadn't she slept with her grandmother's katana the night before?

They got out of the car and walked up the veranda steps together. She unlocked the door, turned off the alarm and trailed Reid through the house as he went from room to room. Then she led the way upstairs. She refused to go inside her mother's room. She leaned a shoulder against the wall and waved toward the door. "I'll wait out here for you."

While he was inside, she hollered through the doorway. "See anything?"

"Nope, all clear in here."

"Smell anything?"

There was a significant pause. "Like what?"

"Nothing. I just wondered."

He came out into the hallway and gave her a puzzled look. "What was that about?"

"I heard something last night. I went into my mother's room to check things out and I noticed a magnolia-scented candle on her dresser. For a split second, I had the crazy notion that someone had been inside her room burning that candle."

Reid frowned down at her. "You told me you were kept awake by squirrels."

"A scrabbling sound brought me upstairs, and yes, it probably was just squirrels. Or worse, rats." She shuddered. "I told you this morning. Being in this house is a lot more unnerving than I thought it would be."

"Then move into a hotel for the time being. It would certainly make me feel better."

"I can't afford that right now and, besides, I don't want to. I don't want to become that person who's afraid of her own shadow. I'll take the necessary precautions, but I'm not going to be forced out of my own home. I'm sure that's just what my grandfather would like to happen."

"Stubborn as always."

"I prefer to think of myself as determined."

Reid checked the second-floor bedrooms and took a peek in the attic. Satisfied that everything was as it should be, they went back downstairs. He paused in the doorway of the parlor to glance out into the garden. "You think your uncle is working in the greenhouse?"

"I doubt it. I saw him earlier today. He gave me back the key to the side gate. He'd have to crawl over the wall like you did to get inside."

"Assuming he didn't make himself a spare key," Reid said.

"Why would he do that? Why not just keep the original key? I never asked for it back."

"Maybe he thought you would eventually. I'm just thinking out loud." Reid went over and opened one of the doors, letting in the late-afternoon breeze. He moved out into the garden and Arden followed reluctantly. If the house unnerved her, the garden put her even more on edge, especially when the sun went down and the bats came out.

She folded her arms around her middle. "I saw him today. My uncle Calvin. He gave me a portrait he'd painted of my mother. He said he worked from a picture of her that was taken here in the garden on the night of the Mayor's Ball. I remember the dress she wore that night. Red chiffon. It floated like a dream around her when she walked. And she'd tucked a magnolia blossom in her hair." Arden paused, suddenly drowning in memories. "You can't imagine how beautiful she looked."

"I think I have some idea," Reid murmured. "Some people think you're the spitting image of Camille."

"A pale copy, maybe." His gaze on her was a little too intense so Arden made a production of plucking a sprig of jasmine and holding it to her nose. "Should we check the greenhouse while we're out here? I don't think my uncle came by, but I'd like to make sure the door is secure. The latch sometimes doesn't catch and I'd rather not have the wind bumping it at all hours…" She trailed off, letting the jasmine drop to her feet as she stared up into the trees. The light shimmering down through the leaves was already starting to wane. Twilight would soon fall and then darkness. She pictured the shadowy sidewalks outside the walls of Berdeaux Place and shivered. "Do you remember how it was that summer?" she asked.

"The summer your mother died?"

"Yes, I mean afterward, when we started hearing about the other victims. No one ever talked about the Twilight Killer in front of me, of course, but I overheard just enough to be terrified. I used to wake up in the middle of the night and think that I could hear his heartbeat in my room. I imagined him underneath my bed or hiding in my closet. Sometimes I would get up and go over to the window just to make sure he wasn't down in the garden staring up at my window."

"It was a very dark time in this city."

"Reid, what if we were right all those years ago?" Arden turned to him in the failing light. He stood in shadows, his features dark and mysterious and yet becoming once again as familiar to her as her own reflection. "What if the person who murdered all those women, including my mother, is still out there somewhere? The real Twilight Killer. Maybe he's taken more lives over the years, even before Haley Cooper. He could have broadened his hunting ground and spread out his kills so that the police never connected his victims. An animal with those kinds of cravings can't remain dormant forever. If he is still out there, then he framed an innocent man once. Maybe his impulses are growing stronger and he feels another spree coming on so he needs another scapegoat. He started seeding the ground with Haley."

"By scapegoat, you mean me?"

"That's what worries me," she said.

Reid didn't chide her for letting her imagination get the better of her as she thought he might. Instead, he let his gaze travel over the grounds, settling his focus on the summerhouse dome. "Assuming Orson Lee Finch really is innocent, he made the perfect patsy. Nearly invisible and moving at will in and out of the gardens South of Broad Street. Plenty of opportunities to observe and follow his victims. And once arrested, he had to rely on a public defender. No money, no friends, no family to speak of." He turned back to Arden. "I'm not Finch. I have access to the finest defense team in the city, not to mention a plethora of private detectives. I'm hardly powerless, so you have to ask yourself why a spree killer would want to try and frame someone with my resources. That doesn't make sense."

"Unless you're not even the real target. Maybe I am." Arden shivered. With the setting sun, a stronger breeze blew in from the harbor, carrying the faintest trace of pluff mud through the trees. Her grandmother used to call that particular aroma the perfume of rumors and old scandal. The fecund smell was there one moment, gone the next, replaced by the ubiquitous scent of jasmine.

"Maybe we're overthinking this," Reid said. "Trying to connect everything back to the Twilight Killer is making us overlook the revenge angle. Maybe this is nothing more than a simple frame job. A way to get to my father because Brody can't touch him."

"So Detective Graham being in the bar the night of the murder was just a coincidence?"

"I don't know what to think about Graham." The breeze ruffled Reid's hair, making Arden long to run her fingers through the mussed strands. "I need to tell you something else about my conversation with Boone today."

His tone made her breath catch. "What?"

"He suggested that we should take a look at your family photo albums."

"Why?" she asked in surprise.

"He thinks Clement Mayfair might not have been your mother's biological father."

Arden whirled. "What?"

"You've never considered the possibility?" Reid asked. "You never heard any talk to that effect?"

"Not a word. But…" She trailed off as her mind went back through those photo albums. So many portraits and candid shots of Arden and her mother and grandmother, fewer of Calvin, and none at all of her grandfather. Hardly surprising considering the lingering animosity. "If I'm honest, I can't say that would surprise me. It makes a sick kind of sense, doesn't it? Why Grandmother took my mother and left Calvin behind with my grandfather? He probably threatened to take both her children away from her."

"Has he made contact?"

"No. But I'm more certain than ever that his real interest is in acquiring this house. He doesn't care anything about me. He never did."

"His loss," Reid said.

Arden shrugged. "I'm sure he doesn't see it that way. I think I should go see him. I know you advised against it, but I want to make it clear that I'm not afraid of him and that he is never going to get his hands on Grandmother's house."

"Just hold off for a bit," Reid said. "Everything we've talked about is pure speculation. There's no point in antagonizing him until he makes a move. It's possible that he really does want to make amends."

"I'll wait. But not forever." Arden turned to make her way to the greenhouse. Reid had stopped on the path and was staring in the opposite direction. "What's wrong?"

"Let's check out the summerhouse first." He nodded toward the ornate dome. "We're right here and I'd like to see how it's held up over the years."

"I'd rather not. I don't like going inside," Arden admitted.

"Since when? You used to love the summerhouse. It was our place."

"It was his place first," she said.

He gave her a bemused look. "Are you talking about your mother's killer? There was never any evidence that he hid inside."

"The magnolia blossom on the steps would suggest otherwise."

"Okay, but that was a long time ago, and you and I made this place our headquarters for years. Why so reticent now?"

"I can't explain it," Arden said. "It just feels...wrong. Evil."

"It's just a place. A beautiful old summerhouse. You've been away too long. You've forgotten the good things that happened inside. Maybe a quick look around is all you need to put the ghosts to rest. You may find the good memories outweigh the bad."

Maybe that's what I'm really afraid of.

Nevertheless, she followed him up the steps and into the summerhouse. The latticework windows cast mysterious shadows on the floor while twilight edged toward the domed ceiling. Arden turned in a slow circle. The pillows that had cushioned their heads as they'd lain on their backs staring up at the stars were gone, along with all their treasures. The place smelled of dust and decay. But some things remained. Somewhere on the wall were their carved initials; Arden didn't want to look too closely. She didn't want to remember how much she'd given up when she left Charleston fourteen years ago.

"It's a little the worse for wear," Reid said as he moved around the space. "But it does bring back memories."

"Our first grown-up kiss was here," she murmured. "Do you remember?"

"Of course, I remember."

She turned at the tenderness in his voice. Tenderness… and something more. Something darker and headier. Desire. Throbbing just below the surface. Not so strange, she supposed, that they would both feel strong emotions in this place.

"I kissed you and then you ran away," he said. "It was quite a blow to my ego."

"I was afraid."

"Of me?"

"Of what it meant. I knew after that kiss that nothing would ever be the same. I was afraid of losing my best friend."

His voice lowered intimately. "You didn't lose me."

"Easy to say. Not so easy to believe after fourteen years."

"I've always been right here, Arden." He slid his fingers into her hair, tilting her head so that he could stare down at her. "See?" he said. "There's nothing to be afraid of in here."

Arden wasn't so sure. She parted her lips, waiting to see what he would do.

Into the quivering silence came a distant sound, a rhythmic thumping that she could have easily believed was her own heartbeat.

Reid glanced toward the door as his hand fell to his side. "Did you hear that?"

She turned to peer out into the garden. "It's coming from the greenhouse. The wind is rising. It must have caught the door."

Reid was all business now. "We'd better go have a look."

They hurried down the steps together and Arden was overly conscious of Reid beside her, of the memories that still swirled in the ether as they approached the greenhouse. Enough daylight remained so that they could see inside the glass walls. Arden was once again reminded of her uncle's paintings and the feeling his art had evoked of being on the outside looking in.

She gazed down the empty aisles toward the back of the greenhouse, where she could see the silhouette of her mother's cereus. "I should check the progress while we're here. I don't want to risk missing the blooms and that luscious scent." *Like moonlight and romance and deep, dark secrets*, her mother would say.

"Arden, wait," Reid said as she stepped through the door.

"It's fine. There's no one here. Come have a closer look."

She was well down the aisle when she heard a loud crack above her and glanced up a split second before Reid grabbed her from behind. They dropped to the ground and

instinctively rolled beneath one of the worktables. Arden
tucked her legs and wrapped her arms around her head
as Reid covered her body with his. She heard a series of
pops as one of the heavy panels gave way and crashed to
the stone floor beside them. The tempered glass exploded
into harmless chips, but the weight of the panel would have
crushed anyone standing in the aisle.

Chapter Fourteen

A structural issue—that was the consensus of the inspectors Arden hired to check out the greenhouse. Over the years, some of the clips that held the glass panels in place had come loose or fallen off altogether and the elements had eroded the silicone sealant. Add in a rusted frame, and the roof panels had been one stray breeze away from disaster for years. Everything pointed to coincidence, and Arden told herself she should just be thankful no one had been hurt. Still, she couldn't stop the little voice in her head that whispered of sabotage.

Before the greenhouse was disassembled and carted away, she had workers move her mother's cereus to the terrace. She liked that location better anyway. Now she could watch the blooms open from the safety of a locked door if she so chose.

Her return to Charleston had been harrowing, to say the least. Luckily, she knew how to tuck and roll and keep her head down. She spent a lot of time at work, burying herself in research and planning. Reid had outside meetings almost every day so she spent hours alone in his house. The solitude never bothered her, which was strange since she could barely spend one night alone in Berdeaux Place without succumbing to her dark imagination. She hadn't experienced any more strange sounds or scents, but every now and then her gaze would stray to her mother's bedroom door and she would wonder again if someone had been inside burning that magnolia-scented candle.

By Friday, the website had gone live, the business cards were printed, and everything was in place to approach Ginger Vreeland's uncle—a retired welder named Tate Smith—about her whereabouts.

She and Reid made the trek down south into marsh country together. The drive was pleasant, the day crystal clear, but the results of their search proved frustrating. Although Arden had searched public records for the last known address, the house appeared abandoned, as if no one had lived there in months, if not years. No one answered the door and none of the neighbors claimed to know Tate Smith or his niece. Arden wondered if Mr. Smith had been that reclusive or if the neighbors were simply protecting his privacy. She clipped a business card to a hastily scribbled message and slipped it underneath his door. Then she and Reid headed back to the city.

The weekend passed without further incident, but Arden couldn't relax. She worked in the office for a little while on Saturday morning and then went home to finish the list of everything that needed to be done to Berdeaux Place. Obviously, with the greenhouse failure, things were direr than she'd anticipated. As she explored the premises and grounds, she kept an eye out for her uncle so that she could explain what had happened. He never turned up. Dave Brody had vanished, as well. The deadline he'd set for Reid had come and gone, but for the moment, he seemed intent on keeping a low profile. Or else he'd gotten a message from Boone Sutton. No Dave Brody, no Detective Graham. No word from her grandfather, either.

Still, Arden knew better than to let down her guard, and as the days wore on, a pall seemed to settle over the city.

An encroaching gloom that portended dark days ahead. She wanted to believe that Haley Cooper's murder had been random, a victim caught in the wrong place at the wrong time, but she had a feeling nothing about the woman's death or the killer's agenda was random. She now had an inkling of what Charleston had experienced during the Twilight Killer's reign of terror. The waiting. The imagined sounds. The impulse to hurry home before sundown and sequester oneself behind locked doors as shadows lengthened and dogs howled behind neighbors' fences.

She feared this quiet time might be the calm before the storm.

Another worry began to niggle. Reid had said nothing about extending her assignment, much less making the arrangement permanent. She hated to think of their time coming to an end. They'd settled into an amiable working relationship and Arden loved having a place to go to every morning. She admired his long-term plans for the firm, and, more than anything, she wanted to contribute to the success of those plans. But she refused to press him for an answer. His firm, his call.

Since the greenhouse incident, he'd kept things casual and that was a very good thing, Arden decided. The easy camaraderie had given them a chance to become friends again. Perhaps not the best buddies of their childhood—not yet—but the tension lessened with each passing day.

Or so she'd thought.

One afternoon she looked up from her work to find Reid standing in the doorway watching her with a puzzled expression, as if he couldn't quite figure her out. The intensity of his gaze caught her by surprise and her heart thudded, though she tried to keep her tone light.

"Everything okay?"

He folded his arms and leaned a shoulder against the

door frame. He didn't have outside meetings that day and was dressed casually in jeans and a dark gray shirt open at the neck. "Do you ever wonder what our lives would be like now if things had worked out differently fourteen years ago?"

The question took Arden by surprise. She pretended to write herself a note while she pondered an answer. "I think about it sometimes, but I try not to dwell. We can't change the past." She shrugged. "Why bring it up now? I thought we'd moved past all that. We're working well together, aren't we?"

"We are," he agreed. "But don't you ever get the feeling we have unfinished business between us?"

Her heart knocked even harder against her rib cage. "What do you mean?"

He shifted his gaze to the window, frowning into the sunlight that streamed through the glass. "I've always wondered why you left the way you did. Why you barely even took the time to say goodbye. We were so close and after everything we'd been through, ending things the way we did felt…wrong."

"I thought it was better to get it over with quickly. Rip the bandage off and all that." She paused thoughtfully. "You always make it sound as if my leaving came out of the blue, but you know that's not the way it happened. We agreed that time apart would be good for us. Separate colleges gave us a chance to be independent. We were so young, and we had so much growing up to do. Maybe things worked out for the best. What's the point in looking back?"

He came into the office and sat down in a chair facing her desk. "It's not healthy to leave issues to fester."

"What issues?"

"All those times you were in Charleston for holidays

and summer break. You *visited*, but you never really came back. You were here physically, but your mind and your heart were a million miles away. It was like you couldn't even stand the sight of me anymore. Like you hated me for what happened."

How would you know? Arden wanted to lash out. *You all but ignored me when I came home. You made me think there was nothing left for me here.*

Instead, she said, "That's what you thought? I didn't hate you. I never could. It was just hard for me to be here after everything that had happened. I felt so guilty. If only I'd taken better care of myself. If only I'd gone to the doctor sooner, if only I'd gotten more rest. And I felt even guiltier because a part of me was relieved when it happened. I know how awful that sounds, but it's the truth. That guilt is why I couldn't look at you."

"What happened wasn't your fault," he said.

"I know that. I probably knew it then, too, but my emotions were so fragile and everything between us seemed to be falling apart. We wanted different things, and that was never more apparent than in the way we each coped with our pain. You took comfort in the familiar. You wanted to cling to what we had. I wanted to run away. Maybe I should have tried harder to explain my feelings to you, but I probably didn't even understand them myself back then. I just knew I needed to get away from my grandmother's house."

"And from me."

"Yes, if I'm honest. We'd been inseparable since childhood. I needed a fresh start. I wanted to meet new people, have new adventures."

"I always thought we would have those adventures together," he said. "I didn't see why a baby had to stop us. I was young and stupid, and I had some crazy, romantic notion of how it could be, the three of us taking on the world. I never took into account what you would be giving up for my dream."

"As long as we're getting everything out in the open, I've always wondered why you never came to find me," she said. "In all those years, not a single phone call, email or text."

"You wanted your space."

"I thought I did." She shrugged. "Things don't always work out the way we want them to."

"And sometimes they work out in the way we least expect." He held her gaze for the longest moment before he rose to leave.

"Reid?"

He glanced over his shoulder.

"Thank you for what you said just now. That it wasn't my fault."

"It wasn't. I should have told you a long time ago."

"You did. You told me over and over. I just wasn't ready to listen. Anyway…it's good to clear the air."

"Yeah."

He went back to his office without further comment.

Arden sat quietly for a few minutes and then got up to follow him. She said from his doorway, "Can I ask you something else? It's not about the past. Actually, it's more of a favor than a question."

He set aside his phone. "Should I be worried?"

"No, it's not like that." She pulled a creamy envelope from her dress pocket and walked over to slide it across his desk.

He picked up the envelope and glanced at the address. "What's this?"

"An invitation to the Mayor's Ball. It was delivered to Berdeaux Place earlier this week."

He glanced up. "That's cutting it a little close. Isn't the ball tomorrow night?"

"I was obviously a late addition to the guest list," she said. "I assume you got your invitation weeks ago."

He didn't seem the least bit interested. "I remember seeing one in the mail. Probably still around here somewhere."

"You weren't planning on going?"

He leaned back in his chair with a broad smile, the seriousness of their earlier conversation forgotten. "That's one of the perks of having my own firm. I no longer have to climb into a monkey suit to please my old man."

Arden sat down in the chair across from his desk, reversing their roles. "Did you happen to notice that it's being held at Mayfair House this year?"

He gave her a curious look. "How do you feel about that?"

"It's very strange. I never remember my grandfather having so much as a dinner party. He hated anyone, including me, intruding on his privacy, and now, suddenly, he's throwing open his doors to half of Charleston."

"My father said he'd heard rumblings about the old man trying to rehabilitate his image. He thought it might be for your benefit."

Arden shrugged. "I don't see how it could be. This had to be in the planning for months. Still, if I didn't suspect he was up to something before, I certainly do now."

"You really don't trust him, do you? Are you sure you aren't letting your grandmother's animosity cloud your judgment?"

She gave him an incredulous look. "You're asking me that after the conversation you had with him last week? Aren't you the one who told me to stay away from him?"

He leaned forward, his expression suspicious. "Yes, I

did. Which is why I'm hoping you aren't planning to go to this thing tomorrow night."

She plucked at an invisible thread on her dress. "Of course, I'm going. It's the perfect place to interact with him for the first time. If I'm lucky, I may get some insight into what he's up to."

"Assuming he does have an agenda, he won't give himself away that easily," Reid warned. "Mayfair Place will be packed. Lots of press, lots of cameras. He'll be on his best behavior."

"Unless he's caught off guard."

"Arden." He drawled her name in that way he had. "What are you up to?"

"Nothing," she said innocently. "I just want to talk to him. And if you're really concerned about my safety, you'll go with me."

His eyes glinted, reminding her of the old Reid Sutton. "As your date?"

She hesitated. "As my friend or my boss. Whatever makes you feel most comfortable."

"Nothing about the Mayor's Ball makes me comfortable."

"Because you're looking at it all wrong," Arden insisted. "This is no longer about your father. This is about you and the future of your firm. Think about the guest list. Word will already have gotten around about Ambrose Foucault's imminent retirement. His clients will be there, ripe for the picking."

"I thought I wasn't allowed to go after his clients until his retirement is official," Reid said.

Arden tucked back her hair. "That was before he shared a private conversation with my uncle and possibly my grandfather. All bets are off now. As far as I'm concerned, anyone who comes to that ball is fair game. Think of it as a scouting expedition. I may be a little rusty, but I daresay I can still work a room. And we both know you can charm birds out of a tree when you set your mind to it."

"Listen to you being all cutthroat."

She met his gaze straight on. "No, I'm being practical. A few of those old-money clients could help subsidize the other cases we want to take on." *You. The other cases* you *want to take on.* She started to correct herself, then decided changing the pronoun would call too much attention to her slip. Instead, she rushed to add, "If I haven't convinced you yet, then imagine all those wagging tongues when we walk into Mayfair House together."

He tapped the corner of the envelope on his desk. "I'll think about it."

She pounced. "What's there to think about? You know I'm right. I assume you still have a tux?"

"Buried in the back of my closet, where I like it."

"Dig it out for just this one night. And I'll wear something appropriately provocative."

"I'm almost afraid to ask what that means."

She merely smiled. "The invitation says eight. We'll arrive no earlier than nine thirty. Parking will be a nightmare, so leave your car at my house and we'll walk over together. It'll be so much easier than dealing with the valet service."

"You've got this all planned out, I see."

"Yes. All you have to do is show up on time." She stood to leave.

"Arden?"

She paused at the door.

"This surprise you're planning for your grandfather... You're not going to catch me off guard, too, are you?"

"You worry too much. It'll be a fun night. You'll see."

"Famous last words," he muttered.

ARDEN SPENT SATURDAY morning running errands. She picked up her dress at the dry cleaners and then dropped off her favorite necklace at a jewelry shop to have the clasp replaced. While she waited for the repair, she window-shopped along King Street, browsing some of the high-end boutiques to kill time. A crystal-studded belt in a window caught her eye, and she wandered in to check the price. A candle flickered on the counter next to the photograph of a young blonde woman whom Arden recognized as Haley Cooper.

The smiling countenance of the murder victim shocked her. She couldn't seem to get away from the horror. Then she remembered reading somewhere that Haley Cooper had worked in a shop on King Street.

She found the belt and decided the accessory would go so well with her gown that the splurge would be worth it. Plus, the purchase gave her the opportunity to speak with the woman behind the counter. As she rang up the item, Arden nodded to the photograph. "That's Haley, isn't it?"

The woman glanced up in surprise. "Did you know her?"

"No. I just recognize her photo from the news."

The woman gave her a grim smile. "At least you called her by name. Most of the people who comment on the photo ask if she's the dead woman. It's so impersonal to them. Just a news item or a crime statistic. They forget that Haley was a human being with friends and family who still miss her terribly." She bit her lip. "I'm so sorry. I don't know why I dumped all that on you. The last two weeks have been difficult."

"No apology necessary. Sometimes it's easier to talk to a stranger," Arden said with genuine sympathy. "Were the two of you close?"

"We became good friends after she started working

here last year. She had a great personality. Funny. Smart. She was good with the customers, too." The woman hesitated, as if she wanted to resist but needed to get it all out. She busied her hands with tissue paper. "I know it must seem macabre that I have her photograph on display, but it's my shop. I can do what I want."

"Of course. And I don't think it's macabre at all," Arden said. "You're paying tribute to your friend."

"Yes, that. And I also promised myself I'd keep that candle burning until her killer is brought to justice. But, after two weeks, I'm starting to lose hope."

"I understand better than you think," Arden said. "My mother was murdered. Months went by before an arrest was made. I was young, but I remember the toll it took on my grandmother."

The woman's voice softened. "I'm so sorry. What a terrible thing to have happen to you."

Arden nodded. "It was a long time ago. But you don't forget." She paused. "Do you know if the police have any suspects?"

The woman carefully folded the tissue paper around the belt and secured it with a gold-embossed sticker. "They have *a* suspect. Who knows if anything will come of it?"

Arden tried to keep her tone soothingly neutral. "Do you know who it is?"

The woman took a quick perusal of the shop. A sales associate was busy with another customer at the clearance rack, too far away to overhear. The owner dropped her voice anyway. "You know what they say. It's always the spouse or boyfriend."

Arden lifted a brow. "Haley was seeing someone?"

"Yes. I never met him and she wouldn't say much about him. I had the impression he was an older man with money. That would have impressed Haley. She liked nice things."

"She never mentioned a name?"

"She was always careful not to let anything slip. She said he would be very upset if he knew she had mentioned him at all. He guarded his privacy. That didn't always sit well with Haley. She was young and she liked to go out. She wanted to be wined and dined."

"I heard on the news that she'd gone out to meet someone on the night of the murder. Do you think she met this man?"

The woman shrugged. "It's possible. But I know they had a falling-out a few days before it happened. Haley was seeing someone on the side, but I never got the impression it was romantic. If anything, I think she was trying to spite the older guy."

"Then that would make two suspects," Arden said.

The owner looked as if she wanted to comment further, but three young women came into the shop talking and laughing and drawing her attention. She placed the belt and receipt in a glossy black bag and handed Arden the purchase.

"Enjoy the belt. I'm sure it will look lovely on you."

"Thank you."

Arden walked out of the boutique and glanced around. Her uncle's studio was just up the block. She wondered if she should stop by and warn him about the greenhouse. No, he was probably busy and she'd be seeing him later that night anyway. She realized she was avoiding him and she wasn't sure why. He'd been nothing but cordial and welcoming, and yet she sensed that he, too, had an ulterior motive for his interest in her.

Her phone rang as she walked back toward the jewelry store. She fished it out of her bag and then realized the ringtone belonged to the burner phone she'd purchased for contacting Ginger Vreeland. She didn't recognize the incoming number. Lifting the phone to her ear, she said crisply, "Arden Mayfair."

Silence.

"Hello? Anyone there?"

A female voice said anxiously, "I hear you've been looking for me."

Arden's pulse jumped. "Is this Ginger?"

"Don't say that name."

"Sorry." Arden backed up against the building so that she didn't block pedestrian traffic. "You got my message?"

"What do you want?" The woman's Low Country drawl was deep and hardened by suspicion and hostility.

"As I tried to explain in my note, we need to see you in person so that—"

"You think I don't recognize a con when I hear one? There's no bank, there's no money and I seriously doubt you're an attorney. You have five seconds to tell me what you really want."

"I just want to talk."

"What about?"

"Did you know Dave Brody is out of prison?"

A brief pause. "So? What's that to do with you?"

"I work for an attorney named Reid Sutton. I'm sure you recognize his name. Brody is threatening to make life unpleasant for a lot of people if we don't get him what he wants."

"Which is?"

"He thinks someone paid you to leave town before you could testify on his behalf, and he wants to know who and why. Personally, I think you were threatened. I think you left town because you were afraid."

A longer pause. "You don't know anything about me. If you're smart, you'll keep it that way."

Arden's pulse quickened. She'd hit a nerve. "We can

help you. Just name a time and place and we'll come meet you."

"That's not going to happen."

"Why not?"

"Did you really think he'd stop at one?"

The hair prickled at the back of Arden's neck. Phone still to her ear, she turned to glance over her shoulder, scouring the street behind her. "What do you mean?"

"The body that was found in the alley," Ginger said. "She wasn't his first victim. If you're not careful, she won't be his last."

"If you know who he is—"

"Just leave me alone, okay? I can take care of myself. And whatever you do, don't contact my uncle again. If anything happens to him, his blood will be on your hands."

Arden could hear traffic noises over the phone before the connection dropped. She positioned her body so that she could watch the sidewalk in both directions. No one looked suspicious. No one stared at her for an unseemly amount of time. That made no difference. Her every instinct warned of danger.

Somewhere close by, a coiled snake lay in wait.

Chapter Fifteen

Reid found himself surprisingly nervous when he arrived at Berdeaux Place that night. He told himself he was being ridiculous. Arden had gone out of her way to clarify that she didn't consider this a date. He was escorting her to the Mayor's Ball as a friend or her boss. *Whatever makes you feel more comfortable.*

He tugged at his bow tie as she buzzed him in through the gate. He parked, locked his car and then headed across the side lawn to the garden doors. She whisked them open and stepped out onto the patio, backlit by the lamplight spilling out from the parlor.

Reid froze, his breath escaping in a long, slow whistle as he took her in.

She spun so that the airy fabric of her gown caught the breeze. The scent of jasmine deepened in the dark, and the moon rising over the treetops cast the garden in a misty glow. The night suddenly seemed surreal to Reid, as though he were remembering a dream.

He shook his head slightly as if to clear his senses. "That dress…"

She lifted the frothy fabric. "Do you like it?"

"You look… Well, I suspect you already know how you look." Her hair fell in gleaming waves about her bare shoulders, and when she moved, moonlight sparked off the diamond studs in her earlobes and the crystal belt she wore around her waist.

"It was my mother's," she said. "I found it in my grandmother's closet. I didn't have time to shop for a new one, and since I got rid of most of my wardrobe before leaving Atlanta, it was either this or nothing." She turned slowly this time so that he could appreciate the full effect of the flowing fabric. "The fit isn't perfect, but I don't think anyone will notice."

The dress fit her like a damn glove. Reid shook his head again, this time to try to get her out of his head. Not that it had ever worked for him before. "Is this the surprise you have planned for your grandfather? Turning up at the ball looking the spitting image of your murdered mother? You said you wanted to provoke a reaction. This should do it."

"Yes, but it's not just for his benefit. I want to see if anyone else is provoked."

Reid frowned. "You mean the killer? Is that what this is all about? You're trying to draw him out? I'm surprised you don't have a magnolia blossom in your hair."

"I have one inside."

"I hope you're kidding."

She picked a spray of jasmine and tucked it behind her ear. "Better?"

"Not really."

She removed the spray and lifted the tiny blossoms to her nose. "Okay, maybe I am trying to stir the pot. Listen, there's something you don't know. I talked to Ginger Vreeland today. She called on the burner phone."

Reid stared down at her in the moonlight. "Why didn't you tell me earlier?"

"Because I knew I'd be seeing you tonight. And because I didn't want you to try and talk me out of going to the ball. Reid, she knows who killed Haley Cooper."

"She said that? Who?"

"She wouldn't give me a name. She wouldn't agree to meet me, either. She's still afraid. She said Haley wasn't his first victim and if he's not caught, she won't be his last."

"So you decided to bait him?" Reid moved in closer. He wanted to take her by the arms and shake some sense into her. Not literally, of course, but what in the hell was she thinking?

"Someone has to do something. He's eluded the police for weeks, maybe even for years. If this dress or my appearance catches him by surprise, maybe he'll give himself away."

"Or maybe he'll come after you." Reid turned to scan the dark garden. The ornate dome stood silhouetted against the night sky, reminding him all too vividly of Arden's certainty that the killer had watched her from inside the summerhouse, still with her mother's blood on his hands. He turned back to Arden. "You know this is a terrible idea."

"What else are we going to do? Sit around and wait for him to kill again? If this is the same person who murdered my mother, you think he won't come after me anyway? Why do you think he left a white magnolia blossom on the summerhouse steps? He was warning me even then that he'd someday come back for me."

"You don't know that."

"Do you have a better explanation?" When he didn't reply, she shrugged. "Maybe I am off-base. Maybe Orson Lee Finch really did kill my mother. In which case, we have nothing to worry about. Let's just go tonight. Maybe we can even have a little fun. Nothing is going to happen with so many people around."

"You sound so sure of yourself," Reid said. "But it's afterwards that I'm worried about."

"I've taken precautions. Changed the locks, updated the

security system. I'm safe here. Try to relax, okay? Maybe we should have a drink before we go. Just a little something to calm the nerves."

"Calm my nerves, you mean. You're as cool as a cucumber."

She gave an excited little laugh. "Not really. I feel buzzed even without anything to drink."

"You're enjoying this," he accused.

"So are you. You just don't want to admit it."

She turned and moved back inside. Reid followed, closing and locking the French doors as he stepped into the parlor. Evidently, Arden had found the key to the liquor cabinet. A crystal decanter, an ice bucket and two glasses had been arranged on a drink cart. Arden went over and picked up the tongs.

Reid watched her move in that dress. The bodice was strapless, the skirt so gossamer that when the light struck her from a certain angle, he could glimpse the silhouette of her long legs beneath.

"Sure I can't tempt you?" she asked.

He swallowed. "Maybe just a small one."

She put ice and whiskey into the glasses and held one out to him. "To partners in crime," she said.

He clinked his glass to hers. "To surviving the night." He downed the contents in one swallow. "It's getting late. Should we go?"

"In a minute." She set her glass aside untouched. "Do you mind helping me with my dress first?"

His gaze dropped appreciatively. "What's wrong with it?"

She turned her back to him. "I managed the zipper, but I couldn't reach the hook. Do you mind?"

He felt clumsy all of a sudden, but it wasn't the alcohol

that made him fumble with the hook. It was the situation, the woman. All those memories.

"Do you see it?"

"Yeah." He dealt with the fastener, but his hand lingered. Her skin felt like warm satin. Reid had never touched anything so sexy.

His hands drifted to her shoulders as he bent to drop a kiss at her nape. He felt a shudder go through her, but she didn't turn, she didn't move away.

She said in a tremulous voice, "Reid?"

"Arden."

HER HEART WAS suddenly beating so hard she couldn't breathe. She took a moment to try to collect her poise before she turned to stare up at him. A mistake. How well she remembered that smoldering intensity. The tilt of his head. The knowing half smile.

She drew a shaky breath as she held his gaze. "Is this really a good idea?"

He caught her hand and pulled her to him. "Nothing about this night is a good idea. But you can't open the door looking like that and expect me not to react."

Her hands fluttered to his lapels. "We'll be late."

"When has that ever stopped us?"

Never. Not any event, not any curfew. Nothing had ever stopped them when they wanted to be together.

"We're not kids anymore," she said. "Our actions have consequences. If we do this, our working relationship will never be the same."

He slid his hands down her arms, drawing a shiver. "You said it yourself. Nothing has ever been the same since the first time we kissed in the summerhouse."

She closed her eyes briefly. "Fourteen years is a long time. What if the magic is gone?"

His arms were around her waist now, holding her close. "What if it isn't?"

She reached up to touch his cheek. He caught her hand and turned his lips into her palm. Such a soft kiss. Such an innocent touch. Arden whispered his name.

His kissed the inside of her wrist, a more sensuous seduction she could hardly imagine. She turned silently in his arms, allowing him to undo the hook he'd fastened mere seconds ago. Then he slid down the zipper and Arden took care of the rest, stepping out of the red chiffon dress and then her high heels.

She untied his bow tie, unbuttoned his collar and slid his jacket off his shoulders. He shrugged out of the sleeves and inhaled sharply when her fingers brushed across his zipper as she tugged loose his shirt. She took his hand, leading him out of the parlor, across the foyer and up the stairs. He paused on the landing, pressing her against the banister as they kissed.

"I didn't come here expecting this," he said.

She threaded her fingers through his hair. "Are you trying to tell me you're unprepared?"

"I'm always prepared. Isn't that the Scout Motto?"

"You were never a Scout, Reid Sutton. Not even close."

He shed his shirt as they kissed their way down the hallway to her room. Moonlight filtered in from the long windows, throwing long shadows across the ceiling.

"Nothing's changed," Reid said as he glanced around the room. "I wonder if you can still shimmy down the trellis."

"I wonder if you can still climb up." She lay down on the bed and propped herself on her elbows, spreading her legs slightly as she watched him undress.

He didn't seem to mind her stare. He'd never been the least bit shy about intimacy. Nor had she, for that matter.

But fourteen years was a long time. Thirty-two was not the same as eighteen.

He placed a knee on the bed and she lay back as he moved over her. Arden found herself thinking about those fourteen years, the loneliness and disappointments. The guilt and then the pride that had kept her away. She thought about their first kiss in the summerhouse, the first time they'd made love at the beach, the first time he'd told her he loved her. She could drown in those memories, good and bad, but she didn't want to lose herself to the past. Not with Reid's tongue in her mouth and his hand between her thighs. Not when that delicious pressure just kept building and building.

Slipping her hand between them, she guided him into her, then wrapped her arms and legs around him. He was leaner than she remembered. Older and more experienced. And yet he still knew her. Knew where to touch her, when to kiss her, how tightly to hold her when her body began to shudder.

And when it was over, he remembered to clasp her hand as they lay on their backs and stared up at the ceiling.

Chapter Sixteen

Reid couldn't take his eyes off Arden. He could barely keep his hands off her.

He tugged at his bow tie as he leaned a shoulder against the wall and watched her move about the room. He told himself he should be on the lookout for anyone suspicious or anything out of the ordinary. Arden's dress was bound to provoke strong reactions, but his gaze lingered as his mind drifted back to earlier in the evening.

If he'd had his way, he'd still be comfortably stretched out in her bed, but Arden had insisted they make an appearance at Mayfair House. So they'd climbed out of bed, hit the shower, and one thing had led to another. He closed his eyes briefly, imagining her hands flattened against the tile wall as she pressed her glistening body against his.

Afterward, she'd dried her damp hair, foregoing the magnolia blossom at his insistence, and touched up her makeup. Then they'd redressed like an old married couple. He'd zipped her gown and she'd straightened his bow tie. Now here they were, clothing looking the worse for wear, but totally worth it.

He brushed an invisible speck of dust from his sleeve as he forced himself to survey his surroundings.

He tried to remember the last time he'd been in Mayfair House. He and Arden had been kids, and she'd talked him into going with her because she hadn't wanted to spend the evening alone with her grandfather. Clement hadn't been pleased to see him. All through dinner, he'd stared at Reid in moody silence and as soon as the dishes had been cleared, he'd had his driver take them home.

"This place is something, isn't it? Flowers, champagne, live band. Must have set the old man back a pretty penny. And would you look at those chandeliers."

Reid turned to acknowledge his father, and lifted his gaze to the ornate ceiling. "Imported from Italy," he said.

"What?"

"The chandeliers."

"Is that so? I thought for a moment you were talking about Arden's dress. She's something, too. A real head-turner. Though I have to say, I'm a little surprised to see the two of you here together."

"Why's that?"

Boone gestured with his champagne flute. "You made a point of telling me she's not your girlfriend, remember?"

"She's not. We work together."

Boone smirked. "Do you look at all your employees that way?"

"I only have the one. And I don't think you're in any position to cast stones."

"Oh, I'm not casting stones. I'm just here to enjoy the show."

"Is Mother with you?" Reid asked pointedly.

Boone sipped his champagne. "She isn't feeling well tonight. I'm flying solo."

"Just the way you like it."

"Let's make a deal. You stay out of my private life and I'll stay out of yours."

Reid shrugged. "Whatever you say."

Boone set his glass on a passing waiter's tray. "Since

you and Arden have only a working relationship, you won't mind if I ask her to dance."

"Knock yourself out," Reid said. "But don't be surprised if she wants to lead."

"I think I can handle Arden Mayfair."

"Yeah. That's what I used to think, too."

ARDEN HAD FORGOTTEN how charming Boone Sutton could be. Handsome and debonair, and always just a little too smooth in her book. She was surprised when he had asked her to dance. She used the opportunity to glance around the room as they moved over the floor. Curious eyes met hers. She nodded to acquaintances and smiled at her uncle, who stood watching from one of the arched doorways.

"Strange guy," Boone muttered.

"My uncle? I would say he comes by it honestly, wouldn't you? My grandfather is nothing if not eccentric." Her gaze strayed again to the edge of the dance floor where she'd last seen Reid. He'd disappeared, but she couldn't imagine he'd gone far. She turned her attention back to Boone. "Reid told me about your theory. You think my mother wasn't Clement Mayfair's biological child. That would explain a lot, actually."

"Well, it is just a theory." He spun her unexpectedly. Arden had to concentrate to keep up.

"You knew my grandmother well," she said. "She never confided in you?"

"Evelyn kept things close to the vest. She wasn't the type to air dirty laundry even among friends. I don't pretend to know what went on in this house before she divorced Clement, but I can say with utter confidence that she would have done anything to protect her family. You and your mother were everything to her."

"What about her son?"

"As I said, Calvin is a strange fellow. Always has been." A frown flickered as if he'd thought of something unpleasant. "I was surprised to hear that you'd moved back to Charleston. I thought you were done with this city for good. Maybe that would have been for the best."

"For Reid's sake?"

He hesitated. "For your own. These are troubling times. Reid has gotten himself into something of a bind, it seems. It would be a shame if you became entangled in that mess, too."

"You surely don't think he had anything to do with Haley Cooper's murder."

A shadow flitted across his expression. "Of course, I don't. But he put himself into a position of being blackmailed by the likes of Dave Brody. A man in Reid's position has to be more careful. Someone like Brody is always looking to take advantage."

"Maybe Brody isn't the real problem," Arden said. "He claims someone powerful is trying to frame Reid. Maybe that same person paid Haley to spike Reid's drink."

Boone froze for half a beat. "What are you talking about?"

"Reid didn't tell you? She slipped something into his drink that night at the bar. Why would she do that to a perfect stranger unless someone paid her? From what I understand, she liked the finer things in life."

"She wasn't—"

"She wasn't what?"

"Nothing."

No sooner had the conversation fizzled than something the shop owner had revealed came back to Arden. Haley had been seeing someone older, someone wealthy. Someone who guarded his privacy. Because he was married?

She told herself she was being ridiculous. Any number

of men in the city fit that description, many of them here at the ball. Boone Sutton was a lot of things, but he was no murderer.

How do you know?

Her gaze met her uncle's again, moved on and then came back. He couldn't seem to take his eyes off her, and no wonder—he'd painted her mother in this very dress.

Suddenly the walls started to close in and Arden wished she'd heeded Reid's warning. Coming here tonight had been a very bad idea.

The music ended, but Boone's arm seemed to tighten around her waist. "Something wrong?"

"No, of course, not." Arden backed away. "Thank you for the dance, but I think I'll go find Reid now."

She wandered through the house, avoiding anyone who looked familiar while she searched for Reid. The terrace doors in the library were open and she stepped through, scanning the silhouettes that lingered in the garden. A cool breeze blew in from the harbor, stirring her hair and fanning her dress. She turned to go back inside, but someone blocked her path.

Her heart beat a startled tattoo as she stared up at her grandfather. He had always intimidated and unsettled her; however, she was a grown woman now. No reason to fear him.

"Grandfather," she said on a breath. "I didn't hear you come up."

He said nothing for the longest moment, just stood there in the dark staring down at her.

"I'm looking for Reid," she said. "Have you seen him?"

"I have not."

His voice was like a cold wind down her back, devoid of warmth or affection. Hard to believe that he had actually warned Reid away from her. Why would he even care?

"This is quite an event." She waved a hand toward the terrace doors. "You've outdone yourself."

"As have you."

She suspected he was talking about the dress, and she pretended not to understand. "I was surprised to hear that you were hosting the Mayor's Ball this year. Somehow it doesn't seem your kind of thing."

Moonlight reflected off his glasses as he tilted his head slightly. "And just what is my kind of thing?"

"You never used to like company, much less a crowd. But then, I've been away for a long time. People change, I suppose."

"You haven't. This is exactly the kind of stunt you would have pulled as a child. You're an adult now. I had high hopes that you would outgrow your unseemly tendencies. But you're too much like your mother. Evelyn always had to be the center of the universe. You apparently have her morals, too."

A chill shot down Arden's backbone. "Evelyn was my grandmother. I'm Arden."

"Go home, girl. Don't come back until you've learned how to dress and behave like a lady."

"Grandfather—"

A commotion from inside the house drew their attention. Arden trailed her grandfather inside as he headed toward the raised voices. The music had stopped and everyone seemed suspended in shock. Arden followed their gazes. Detective Graham and two uniformed cops had surrounded Reid.

Arden rushed toward them. "What's going on?"

One of the officers put up his hand. "Stand back, miss."

"Reid?"

"There's nothing to worry about," he said in a calm

voice. "Detective Graham has a few questions that apparently can only be answered at police headquarters."

"This couldn't have waited until the morning?" Clement demanded.

The two men exchanged glances.

The detective said in a conciliatory tone, "My apologies for the disturbance. We felt this a matter of some urgency."

"Oh, I'm sure you did." Boone materialized at Arden's side. "I'm sure the urgency had nothing at all to do with the press being here tonight or the fact that your picture will likely be on the front page of the newspaper tomorrow."

The detective's expression had grown cold with contempt. "I'm just doing my job."

"Is he under arrest?"

"We just have a few questions."

Boone turned to Reid. "Don't say a word. Not one word. You hear me?"

"I know what I'm doing," Reid said. "Let's just get this over with. No need to ruin everyone else's evening."

They all traipsed outside to a waiting squad car. After another few minutes of discussion, Reid willingly climbed into the back and the car pulled away. Boone waited for the valet service to fetch his car while Arden called a cab.

"I hope you called that cab to take you home," Boone said.

"Of course not. I'm going to police headquarters."

"That's not a good idea. You heard the detective. Reid isn't under arrest. Let's make sure we keep it that way."

"Someone is trying to set him up," Arden said. "We can't let that happen."

"Which is why I need you to do something for me." He pulled her away from the crowd that had assembled on the steps and lowered his voice. "Go to Reid's place right now and make sure everything is clean."

Arden frowned up at him. "What are you talking about?"

"Use your head. You think a dirty cop like Graham is above planting evidence?"

"But—" Arden started to protest being sidelined. If nothing else, she wanted to offer Reid her moral support. Then she thought of the note that had been left in his closet by the intruder. What if Graham had somehow managed to plant the murder weapon inside Reid's house?

She swallowed back her panic and nodded. "Okay. But you take care of this. You get him out of there, you hear me?"

ARDEN HAD THE DRIVER drop her off at the end of the block, and she hurried along the shadowy street to Reid's house. Glancing over her shoulder, she let herself in and locked the door behind her. She moved quickly from room to room, drawing the blinds at all the front windows before she turned on the lights.

She started the task in his office and worked her way through the house, combing the obvious places and then looking for more obscure hiding places. When a third search turned up nothing, she had the unsettling notion that maybe evidence had been planted elsewhere. Some-place less likely yet still incriminating, like the summer-house at Berdeaux Place.

She called another cab and paced the front porch until the car arrived. Five minutes later she was home. She let herself in, locked the door behind her and turned off the security system. Then she headed through the parlor to the French doors.

Her hand froze on the latch. Her mother's cereus had bloomed during the evening. Someone had cut off every last flower and chopped the petals to bits with her grand-mother's antique katana.

Shredded them in a rage, Arden thought.

The katana had been tossed aside in the grass. The sword had been in its usual place when Arden and Reid had left for the ball. Someone had been inside the house. How was that possible? The alarm had been set, the front door locked tight...

She whirled, her focus moving across the room to the foyer. Someone was coming down the stairs, slowly, deliberately, taking his time as he anticipated the encounter...

Arden reacted on instinct. She went out the French doors and grabbed the katana. The lush, heady fragrance of the destroyed blooms filled her nostrils. The moon was up, flooding the terrace and garden with hazy light. She dove for the shadows, concealing herself as best she could as she rushed toward the side entrance. The wrought-iron gate had been padlocked from the other side and the low-hanging limb that she had once used to propel herself over the wall had long since been cut away.

She was trapped in the garden. No way out except to go back through the house.

Whirling, she moved down the path toward the summerhouse. She couldn't hide there, of course. He would surely look for her inside. She broke off a sprig of jasmine and tossed it to the ground and then another. Deliberate breadcrumbs. Then she plunged deep into the shadowy jungle of her grandmother's garden and hunkered down out of sight.

He came along the path, calling out to her. "Come out, come out wherever you are!"

Arden pressed herself back into the bushes, clapping a hand over her mouth to silence her breath. She knew who he was now. Knew why the Twilight Killer had come back for her.

"Did you really think you could keep me out of

Berdeaux Place by changing the locks?" he called. "Did you really think I wouldn't have my own way in without tripping the alarm? I know every square inch of that house. Every nook and cranny. Every single one of your little hiding places."

Her uncle was at the summerhouse steps now. He climbed the stairs slowly, a kitchen knife glinting in his hand. He turned at the top and surveyed the garden before ducking inside. Arden shifted her weight, positioning herself to make a dash for the house, but he came back out too quickly, pausing again on the steps as his gaze seemed to zero in on her hiding place.

"I used to come here all the time after Mother left me. I'd sneak inside and stand at Camille's bedside while she slept. Mother caught me once. She told Father, and the next day he sent me away to boarding school. Military school came next and then university. They did what they could to keep us separated. Did you know that's why Mother took Camille away from Mayfair House? She was afraid for her. Afraid of me. Her own son."

Arden was trembling now, picturing him creeping through the house. Watching her mother sleep. Watching *her*.

"That night when I saw her in the garden wearing the red dress, I knew it had to be her. She would be my first. The waiting became unbearable so I came back a few days later and did what I had to do. You saw me that night, here in the summerhouse. I left a magnolia blossom just for you. Do you remember?"

Arden clutched the handle of her grandmother's sword. She'd put her bag down with her phone when she first came in. She couldn't call Reid or the police for help. She was on her own. She had to somehow get inside the house. Lock the doors. Find her phone…

But what good would that do when he had a secret way in?

"I have something else for you tonight," he said. "I know you can see me. I know you're close. I can hear your heartbeat. Can you hear mine?"

Yes, yes, there it was, a throbbing that filled her senses until she wanted to press her hands to her ears and scream. She knew on some level that it was her own heartbeat thudding in her ears, and yet she could have sworn the cacophony filled the garden just as it had on the night of her mother's death.

"Look what I have for you, Arden."

She peered through the bushes, wanting to glance away but mesmerized by the red magnolia petals he scattered across the summerhouse steps. The breeze lifted one and carried it toward her. The crimson kiss of death.

"That night was magical," he said. "So thrilling I can hardly believe it actually happened. The others that came afterward were just pale imitations. I thought I'd never again experience such ecstasy until you walked into Mayfair House tonight wearing that red dress." He came down the steps and stood in the moonlight, staring through the bushes straight at her. "Come out, Arden. Come see what else I have for you."

She stood, hiding the katana in the folds of her gown. "You killed my mother. You killed all those other women, leaving their children motherless, and then you let an innocent man rot in prison for your crimes."

"I'm a Mayfair," he said, as if that were the only explanation needed.

He moved toward her slowly, a cat closing in on his prey. Arden stood her ground, gripping the handle of the hidden weapon until he was almost upon her. He pounced, more quickly than she had anticipated. She swung the katana, slicing him across the lower rib cage, wounding but not felling him. He staggered back, eyes wild, expression contorted as he gripped his side and took several deep breaths.

Arden sprinted away from him, nearly tripping as the bushes caught the gossamer layers of her dress. She kicked off her shoes and ran barefoot toward the house, spurred on by fear and pure adrenaline. She had almost made it to the terrace when he tackled her from behind and she landed face-first on the stone pathway.

Dazed and breathless, she tried to fight him off. The blood from his wound soaked her dress and dripped onto the grass as he pulled her deeper into the garden, to the exact spot where he had taken her mother's life.

She'd lost the katana, Arden realized. She dug her fingernails into the ground, trying to stop his momentum, while on and on he dragged her. She kicked and writhed, but he seemed to have supernatural strength. Bloodlust drove him. Years and years of pent up rage and resentment.

Pinning her arms with his knees, he rose over her, backlit by the moon. He gazed down at her as he must have stared down at her mother. He lifted the knife overhead, preparing for a thrust that would take her life just as he had taken her mother's.

She heard voices. Someone called out her name. A shadow appeared in the garden and then another.

One of the shadows tackled her uncle, knocking him back into the bushes. The two men fought viciously. The knife struck home, slashing Reid's arm. He grunted in pain and grabbed Calvin's wrist, holding the weapon at bay. Arden looked around desperately for the katana. She grabbed it, stumbled forward. Before she could strike, a shot rang out. Her uncle froze for a split second and then he toppled backward to the ground, his eyes open as he stared blindly at the moon.

Arden rushed to Reid's side, checking his wound and holding him close. They both gazed up at Boone Sutton, who still clutched his weapon. He said to no one in particular, "Sometimes the mad dog has to be put down."

Then he turned and walked away, giving them a moment of privacy before the police descended once again on Berdeaux Place.

Chapter Seventeen

"Orson Lee Finch will soon be a free man," Reid said the next day as he reclined back in his chair. His feet were propped on his desk, his arm in a sling. Everything considered, he looked cool and collected.

Arden was seated in the chair opposite his desk. She was still strung out from the night's events and from the hours she'd spent at police headquarters. It would take a long time before she felt normal again, but at least something good had come from tragedy. "I read that his daughter and grown grandchildren will be there to greet him when he walks through the gate. I can hardly imagine what they all must be feeling right now. If only I'd recognized my uncle that night. If only I'd been able to stop him."

"None of this is your fault," Reid said.

"I know. I was just a child when Mother died. Whatever I saw that night… I couldn't make sense of it."

"Boone knew. Or at least he suspected. That's why he helped Ginger Vreeland leave town. Calvin had roughed her up, and she was afraid he'd come back and kill her. He says he told the police, but Clement Mayfair is a powerful man. You don't go after his son unless you have irrefutable proof."

"Grandmother knew, too," Arden said. "That's why she

took my mother away from that house. Why she left her son behind. She knew even then what he was."

"What a terrible thing to have to live with," Reid said.

"She was never the same after my mother's death. None of us were." Arden fell silent. "Why do you think he killed Haley Cooper? She wasn't a single mother. She didn't fit his usual profile. Why her?"

Reid shrugged. "We can only speculate. She'd had a brief relationship with Boone. Calvin probably used her and Dave Brody to set me up. It was never about a conviction. He wanted to cast doubt on my father's character so that if he came forward with his suspicions, it would seem as though he was casting aspersions to clear his own son."

"My uncle must have started planning this as soon as he heard I was coming back."

"That's why your grandfather wanted Berdeaux Place so badly. He thought if he took that house away from you, you'd have no reason to stay in Charleston."

"And that's why he warned you away from me," Arden said.

"For all the good it did."

She got up and rounded the desk, leaning against the side as she gazed down at Reid. "In all the commotion, we haven't had time to discuss us."

"What's there to discuss?" He took her arm and pulled her down to his lap. "I let you go once without a fight. I'm not about to do that again."

"You don't see me running, do you?"

"Partners in crime?"

"Partners in crime." She settled in, taking care not to jostle his wounded arm as she reached up and touched his cheek. "But you still have to say it."

He smiled. "Why do I have to say it? You already know how I feel."

"Because a girl needs to hear it."

"All right then." He held her close. "I love you, Arden Mayfair. I've loved you from the moment I first laid eyes on you, and I'll love you until my last day on this earth. How's that?"

"That'll do just fine," she said with a sigh.

* * * * *

COMING SOON!

We really hope you enjoyed reading this book. If you're looking for more romance, be sure to head to the shops when new books are available on

Thursday 11th July

To see which titles are coming soon, please visit

millsandboon.co.uk/nextmonth

LET'S TALK
Romance

For exclusive extracts, competitions
and special offers, find us online: